Praise for Sarah Castille's
Legal Heat

"The title of the book *Legal Heat* certainly fits...it is hot. This fast paced, gritty mystery with its number of twists and turns will leave the reader breathless."

~ *Fresh Fiction*

"*Legal Heat* has everything you could possibly want in a good Romantic Suspense. Intrigue, sex, death threats, lust, sex, a hot attorney, sex. Yea, loved this story! Oh, and the sex wasn't bad either."

~ *Guilty Pleasures Book reviews*

"Sarah Castille did a great job of encompassing mystery, suspense and hot sexy scenes! [...] The adrenaline rush I felt once I started reading didn't stop until I read the last page. Highly recommend this book to those who love to read romantic suspense with some hot scorching scenes on top!"

~ *Romance Junkies*

Look for these titles by
Sarah Castille

Now Available:

Legal Heat
Legal Heat
Barely Undercover

Legal Heat

Sarah Castille

SAMHAIN
PUBLISHING

Samhain Publishing, Ltd.
11821 Mason Montgomery Road, 4B
Cincinnati, OH 45249
www.samhainpublishing.com

Legal Heat
Copyright © 2014 by Sarah Castille
Print ISBN: 978-1-61921-710-2
Digital ISBN: 978-1-61921-573-3

Editing by Christa Desir
Cover by Angela Waters

First Samhain Publishing, Ltd. electronic publication: April 2013
First Samhain Publishing, Ltd. print publication: April 2014

Dedication

To John, who believes in dreams.

Chapter One

"Are you lost, sugar?"

Katy Sinclair gasped and spun around. There was nothing alarming in the appearance of the man behind her. He was dressed in jeans and a black T-shirt, carrying nothing more threatening than a duffel bag. But there was only one reason for anyone to be in the dead-end alley on the disreputable side of Vancouver's historic Gastown. Now that she had been spotted, she lost her nerve.

"Yes, I must have taken a wrong turn." She crushed the brochure she held in her hand, but the sound echoed in the small space, drawing his attention. His gaze locked on the name still visible at the top of the crush of paper.

"You have the right place. Carpe Noctem is through the red door behind you." He smiled, a flash of white in a lean, tanned face.

How did he know about the club? Who was he? Suddenly she wanted out of the dimly-lit alley. This was a mistake. Respectable young lawyers did not visit underground fetish clubs. Especially single moms. And a misunderstanding could tarnish her reputation.

"I have to get going." She looked past him toward the bright lights of Water Street.

He didn't move from her path. "You're afraid to go in." It wasn't a question, but a challenge.

"I am not."

He raised an eyebrow and amusement flickered across his face, softening the strong, fierce features just visible under the orange glow of the street light. His sable hair, more black than brown, was short and neatly cut, and his eyes were deep brown, richly hued and totally unreadable.

"Well, let's go then." His tall, muscular body quickly closed the distance between them, tight, hard abs rippling under his snug T-shirt.

Only then did she notice the thin, white scar circling his neck, the only blemish in his otherwise flawless, tanned skin. She caught the scent of sandalwood and a hint of leather. Exotic and dangerous.

Katy gazed at him in fascination until she realized her moment of appraisal had given him control of the situation. A mistake she would never make in court.

He pulled open the door and reached out his hand. "Come with me."

Music and laughter drifted into the alley, followed by the scents of dry ice and stale beer. Katy looked again toward the street. If she didn't go in she could kiss her partnership dreams goodbye. And what was waiting for her at home? Steven, her ex, had the kids for the weekend. Her friends were busy with their own families, and she hadn't had time since the divorce to even go on a date. Not that she was here to meet anyone. Business, not pleasure, awaited her through the red door.

She hesitated only a moment longer, then took the man's hand, drawn by his self-assurance and authority. With a firm but gentle touch, he let her know there would be no changing her mind.

Her heart pounded as she followed him down the long, steep staircase. Carpe Noctem wasn't the social venue of choice for Vancouver's young professionals, but she had always been curious about what went on at the infamous and very exclusive sex club.

She stepped out into a brightly lit foyer decorated with black and white tiles, a red leather couch and potted palms. Disappointingly normal.

"Welcome to Carpe Noctem. I'm Trixie."

Katy's eyes widened as she stared at the woman in front of her. Definitely not normal, at least in her world.

Generous, creamy breasts strained against the top of the tight corset dress encasing the woman's voluptuous body, threatening to spill over the line of public decency. Golden tassels fringed the top and bottom of the dress, swinging from side to side as she walked over to greet them on shiny, gold stilettos. The cuffs buckled to her wrists matched the red leather of the couch, making her as much a part of the decor as the glossy black and white burlesque photos dotting the walls.

Good manners told her not to stare, but she couldn't help letting her gaze travel upward to the multiple facial piercings, spiked platinum hair and sparkling, warm, green eyes.

Katy looked down at her own clothes—black wool pencil skirt, white button-up blouse, black suit jacket and sensible black pumps. Definitely overdressed. But even if she had known where to buy a corset, she would never have worn one. She already felt daring with the top two buttons of her shirt undone.

"You'll be fine, sugar." The deep wine-rich voice reassured her, just as she lost her nerve.

She had almost forgotten about her mystery man, but when he let her hand go, a sense of loss washed over her.

"It's Katy, not Sugar."

He chuckled. "I'll see you inside...Katy. Come to the bar and I'll buy you a drink."

After giving the corset-clad woman a wink, he disappeared through another red door, his ass so perfectly tight in his snug, low-cut jeans, her mouth watered.

"Can I help you?" Trixie's eyes made a slow sweep of Katy's outfit and then fixed on the briefcase Katy clutched in her hand.

"I'm here to interview one of your waitresses, Valerie Wood. I called earlier."

Trixie beckoned Katy forward and pushed open the second red door. "She's inside. I'd better escort you. The way you're dressed, you might need some back-up."

Anticipation ratcheted through Katy as she followed the clatter of Trixie's four-inch heels down a long, brightly-lit corridor. Her mind conjured up images of dimly-lit rooms filled with leather-clad Goths and silk-suited drug dealers whipping naked women bound in chains. She pulled her briefcase against her chest and tightened her grip as they rounded the corner and emerged into...a huge, airy, open lounge.

Red dominated the room. From the curtains hiding private alcoves hugging the curve of the wall, to the cushions on the contemporary, tan leather couches and the plush carpet on the floor. At the back of the club, a huge, leather-clad bouncer guarded a set of ornately carved wooden doors marked *Private*.

"For some reason I thought everything would be black, dark and ominous," she murmured, slightly disappointed at the upscale, modern décor.

Trixie laughed. "Not at this club. The owners, Tony and Mark, have expensive taste and an eclectic sense of style."

Katy stiffened as the crowd closed in around them. Swallowing hard, she forced herself to follow Trixie across the room. *Just a bar, like any other.* Rock music competed with the sounds of laughter and the clink of glassware. Heavy perfume won the olfactory battle against the scents of...leather and latex?

Well, maybe not quite the same.

"If your eyes get any bigger, you'll have men swarming all over you," Trixie said. "They love the wide-eyed innocent look here." She patted Katy's arm. "Try to relax. We might dress differently at the club, but we're all pretty normal."

Differently? Give the girl an award for understatement of the year. Fetish wear surrounded her. Everything from pink PVC to black leather straps, from rubber to chains. Katy swallowed hard as she looked over the sea of beautiful, scantily-clad club members. None of the women appeared to be over twenty-five. Had she looked that young five years ago?

"There's Valerie." Trixie pointed to a curvy, leather-clad woman stalking toward them.

Katy followed Trixie's gesture. Although partially hidden by a swinging black bob, Valerie's face commanded attention. Perfectly heart-shaped with smooth, unblemished skin and high cheekbones. She looked like a very sexy porcelain doll.

The doll stopped in front of her and stared.

Big blue eyes looked her up and down. Perfect cherry red lips curled into a smirk.

Katy twisted her skirt in her fist. Why hadn't she asked Valerie to just come to her office? Was she that desperate for a little excitement in her life?

"You Jimmy's ambulance chaser?"

The stench of *Poison*, Steven's favorite perfume, assailed Katy's nose. She narrowed her eyes as she fought back a sneeze. "I prefer lawyer."

"Who do we have here?" The loud, booming voice drew Katy's attention away from Valerie's hostile glare.

Tall and broad, the dark-haired man who stood before her wore a leather vest over his broad chest and tight, black leather trousers over thick, muscular legs. Very tight. She forced her eyes up.

He peered at her under dark eyebrows and held out his hand. "I'm Tony. You don't belong here."

No kidding, Sherlock. "I came to interview Valerie." She shook his hand, wincing when he squeezed overly hard. Fortunately, she dealt with squeezers every day. She returned the pressure twofold, biting her lip to repress a smile when he grunted and pulled his hand away.

Beside him, Valerie gave a very unlady-like snort. "Jimmy decided to lawyer up with little Miss Twiggy here. He wasn't happy with the duty counsel and he didn't want no legal aid lawyer neither. He had to get some over-priced, big city girl to handle his case."

Twiggy? Not with these thighs. Katy gritted her teeth. "Look, if you don't want to keep Jimmy out of jail, let me know and I'll be more than happy to leave. I'm really not interested in listening to any more professional pejoratives."

"What the hell did she just say?" Valerie snapped.

Tony frowned. "I don't think this is an appropriate place for your discussion." He looked around and then pointed toward the far wall. "Valerie, why don't you ask James to find you a spare room? He's over there."

Katy followed his gaze to the man partially hidden in the shadow of a large pillar. With his sharply angled jaw, fierce scowl, close-cropped blond hair and ropey muscles, he exuded pure danger.

Ice blue eyes caught her own.

Katy shivered. She sensed something dark in him. Forbidden. Hungry. A man who would not accept disobedience. Or failure. Definitely not someone she would want to meet in a dark alley. So unlike the gorgeous guy she had met earlier. Now there was a man she

13

would want to see again. Any place. Any time.

Trixie leaned over to mouth in her ear. "James moonlights as head of security at the club when he's between cases. He's a homicide cop, and pretty damned intense. I'd keep my distance if I were you. I've never seen him smile. Not once."

Katy shuddered and glanced behind her at the door. "I really have no interest in staying after I talk to Valerie."

Tony raised an eyebrow. "Are you sure? I think you might find the club...enlightening." He reached for the black leather whip attached to his belt.

"Whoa, cowboy." Katy's eyes widened and she took a step back. "I'm not into any of this...stuff...that goes on here. I'd better be on my way."

She pulled a card from her purse and handed it to Valerie. "If you want to help Jimmy, you can come to my office first thing on Monday morning."

Tony smiled and replaced the whip on his belt. "Such a shame. But, you're welcome to stay if you change your mind." His voice mellowed as if he hadn't just threatened to whip her in the middle of the bar, and he gave her a wink. "I don't think you'll have trouble making friends. You've already caught Mark's attention."

Katy glanced around for the mysterious Mark but she couldn't see through the crowd.

"Don't mind him." Trixie patted Katy's arm after Tony left them to join a group of tall, willowy, PVC-clad blondes in the corner. "He's just a big tease."

"The whip sort of spoiled the joke for me." Katy sighed. Her exciting evening had just gone down the tubes. She had a few hours of work, a bad sitcom and a bubble bath waiting for her at home.

She moved toward the door only to pull up short when Valerie stepped in front of her. "Wait, please. I do want to help Jimmy."

Katy barely managed to suppress a frown. The bubble bath held more appeal than spending an hour with Jimmy's surly girlfriend. But she had a job to do and a client depending on her.

An hour later, Katy emailed Valerie's draft witness statement to her office and packed up her laptop. Valerie promised to stop by her office to sign the statement before Jimmy's court date and waved goodbye as she melted into the crowd.

Katy took one last look around the club and headed toward the door. Once upon a time before Steven, she would have jumped at the chance to explore a club like this. Dangerous. Decadent. But a long, unfulfilling marriage had sucked her curiosity and her sense of adventure away.

Trixie caught up to her before she made it to the safety of the hallway.

"Why don't you stay for a drink? It's Friday night, and you look like you need to unwind."

Katy hesitated. She couldn't even remember the last time she had been in a bar for purely social reasons. Work and life as a single mom kept her too busy to waste time on leisure activities. But a fetish club...?

"This place isn't really me," she said. "Plus, I'm a bit overdressed...and I don't know anyone...unless...maybe...you could have a drink with me?"

Trixie shook her head. "I'm on duty at reception tonight."

"I'm sorry." Katy rushed her words. "You're working. I totally forgot."

"But..." Trixie gave her a wink, "...I could get someone to cover for me if we had a new *member* who needed me to introduce her around."

Katy took another look around the club, taking in the sea of fetish wear, whips, chains and assorted torture devices. "Actually, maybe not."

Trixie gave her shoulder a reassuring squeeze. "Not everyone here has a kink. Some people just like to hang out at the club or are friends of members. We have a private area in the back for people who are into serious play. So, how about it? Should I go get the application form and ask someone to cover my shift while you find us a table?"

Trixie's warm smile and the temptation to do something for herself—something outside her narrow world of contracts, kids and conservatives—were impossible to resist. "Okay. I'll stay."

Katy found a quiet table in the corner and Trixie joined her a few minutes later with a handful of papers and two glasses of white wine. Katy filled in the forms and they chatted about Trixie's work at the club until they were joined by a few curious members and then a few more. Their table soon became a revolving door for Trixie's friends and acquaintances, all eager to welcome a new face to the club.

Several glasses of wine later, Katy slipped off her jacket and pulled the ponytail holder out of her hair. She hadn't enjoyed herself as much in years. Good company. Great music. Interesting people. Awful wine. But it was her turn to buy the next round.

Katy looked over at the huge bar curving out from one corner of the wall. With its black granite counters, tan leather bar stools and huge, mirrored bottle display, it would not have been out of place in a fancy hotel.

And behind the counter, cleaning glasses, stood her mystery man.

He winked, a casual gesture, but beneath his hooded lids, she caught a glimpse of power. Her cheeks bloomed. He had to be well over six feet of sexy, mouth-watering muscle.

"What's the story with the hot bartender?" Katy caught another glimpse of him from beneath her lashes. The bartender gave her a curious smile, partly amused, partly intrigued, definitely interested. Katy lowered her eyes and her cheeks flamed.

"Trixie!" The deep, booming voice drew her attention away from the bar.

"Uh oh." Trixie grimaced as Tony bore down on them, his face taut with anger, his whip slapping against his thigh.

"I need you at reception. Now. Rick had to deal with a security issue and there's no one at the front desk. I don't know why you asked him, of all people, to cover for you."

Trixie gave him a contrite smile. "Sorry. I was trying to be sociable. Keep the clients happy and all that."

"Go." He pointed toward the door. "You'll be getting a formal warning notice at the end of your shift, if you're lucky. Fired, if you're not."

Katy swallowed. "It's my fault. I asked Trixie to stay and keep me company."

"This has nothing to do with you," Tony snapped. "We're busy tonight and Trixie knows shift changes have to be pre-approved."

"Sorry, Katy." Trixie pushed herself away from the table. "Next time I'll make sure I have all the necessary forms and approvals before we have a drink. Is that okay with you, sir?"

Tony's nostrils flared. "Don't take that tone with me, Trixie. You know how I deal with disrespectful behavior."

"Which is why I'm using that tone." She muttered so quietly only Katy could hear. "Seriously. What does a girl have to do to get a little discipline around here?"

Katy pushed herself out of her chair and stood toe to toe with Tony, her hands clenched by her sides. "You can't reprimand her for something that isn't her fault. I was going to leave. She encouraged me to stay. You benefited because I spent money in the club."

Tony's face tightened. "I told you not to interfere."

"It wasn't her fault." Resolve gave her the courage to face him down. "I won't let her take the blame for something I instigated."

Red flushed Tony's cheeks and he narrowed his eyes. Pulling himself up to his full leather-clad height, he leaned over Katy. "Last chance to make a graceful escape."

Katy trembled but damned if she was going to back down. "Not without your assurance she won't suffer the consequences of my actions."

Tony grabbed her wrist and his voice dropped to a low growl. "Time for you to go, sweetheart."

"I don't think so." A deep voice intruded on the conversation, washing over her like smooth bourbon.

Katy caught the familiar, heady scent of sandalwood. She turned to look over her shoulder.

Oh, God.

Her mystery man stood only a foot behind her. Devastatingly handsome, sinfully erotic and very, very amused.

Katy flamed. She had been wrong about him. He wasn't just hot. He was sex personified.

"I'll deal with her, Tony," he said, his voice calm and even. "She's right about Trixie. I overheard their conversation. Katy is the troublemaker here."

Heart racing, Katy shook off Tony's hand. "I'll...get going."

"Stay," her mystery man whispered.

Her body froze in place before her mind had even processed it was not a request.

Mark put his hands on Katy's shoulders. Electricity jolted his body at the simple touch.

What would Tony do now? He didn't like a challenge, and he clearly hadn't expected Mark to get in his way. And why should he? Except for the occasional one-night fling, Mark didn't get involved with women. No relationships. No entanglements. No dating. It had worked for him for ten years. Ever since Claire. Ever since he had discovered the one disadvantage of his upbringing he could not overcome. The one need he could not fill.

But ten years of resolve had crumbled in a heartbeat when the feisty brunette from the alley had so fiercely challenged one of the most formidable litigators in the city. Not even Tony's imposing bulk or the whip in his hand had deterred her.

Although she didn't move, her shudder betrayed her anxiety. An intriguing mix of self-assurance and vulnerability.

Sexy as hell.

Impossible to resist.

His gaze locked on Tony, his message clear.

Tony snorted a laugh. "She's all yours. Make sure she stays out of trouble."

Mark watched his friend weave his way through the crowd. He knew Tony would bring up the incident at the office on Monday and the ribbing would go on for days. But with their law firm's financial stability now totally dependent on Mark's relationship with their biggest client, Tony needed to keep him happy. And right now, happiness shivered beneath his hands.

Katy glanced back again over her shoulder, her eyes wide and wary. Beautiful eyes, sky blue, fringed in thick, dark lashes.

"Your hands are on my shoulders."

Mark caught the undercurrent of tension in her voice, but chose not to take the hint. "So they are."

"Are you planning to take them off any time soon?"

Encouraged by the glimmer of amusement in her eyes, he leaned over to whisper in her ear, "I like where they are."

"Do you like having a briefcase slammed between your legs? Because that's what's going to happen if you don't move them."

He turned her toward him and studied the perfect oval of her face, taking in her high cheekbones and full, sensuous lips. He tucked a stray curl behind her ear before allowing his gaze to drift down to the sumptuous breasts he had admired from his vantage point at the bar. He imagined capturing their warm, heavy weight in his palms as he kneaded and stroked the sweetly curved swells.

She drew in a long, ragged breath. "Um. Hello. I'm up here."

Mark removed his hands from her shoulders and tore his eyes away, embarrassed only at his uncharacteristic lack of control.

An azure storm chased through her eyes as she tried to hold his gaze. Long, dark lashes dusted her cheeks when she failed. "I...I'd better get going." Her words came out in a throaty whisper and his body stiffened in response.

"I believe I deserve a reward. It wasn't easy to take my hands away." He ran his thumb gently over her bottom lip, feeling the faintest quiver. Soft lips. Sensuously elegant. Lips that were made to be kissed.

As if she could read his mind, a faint, soft whimper escaped her throat.

God, what a beautiful sound. Desire ripped through his body, shocking him after so many years of passionless nights.

"Is that a yes?" He shouldn't have started this. He should never have touched her. Now, he burned with the need to get her alone.

Katy sucked in a breath and stepped back. "It's a no. You don't get a reward for doing the right thing."

Excitement drummed through him. He enjoyed verbal sparring in court, but here in the club, with this sensual creature, it had an erotic

19

edge that fired his blood.

"What do I have to do to get a reward?" The husky rasp of his voice betrayed his desire.

Her lips curved upward before she quickly looked down and away, the sweep of her long lashes hiding the true emotion in her eyes.

Teasing? Maybe. Tantalizing? Definitely. He didn't know how much more he could take.

"You could buy me a drink," she murmured. "Isn't that the way things normally work?"

"Come." He held out his hand.

She raised an eyebrow and put her warm palm in his. "Just one drink, then I have to go."

Mark led her over to the bar and took his place behind the counter. He enjoyed working the bar when the club was short-staffed. It gave him a much-needed break from his all-consuming legal practice and a chance to meet people who weren't in law. The irony of his attraction to one of the few lawyers in the bar did not escape him.

He fought the urge to pour himself a shot of whiskey while she settled herself at the counter. Nothing short of total inebriation would quench the fire raging inside him tonight. Never in his life had a woman affected him this way and he burned to understand why.

"What can I get for you?"

"Trixie and I were drinking white wine. I guess I should stick with that." Her gaze flickered over the vast display on the wall behind him.

"Anything in particular?" He picked up a glass from the rack and polished it to a crystal shine.

Sinfully plump lips curved into a smile. "I don't suppose you have any Meursault?"

He knew exactly where he wanted those lips.

The thin, delicate stem of the wine glass snapped in his hand.

He frowned. The glass must have been flawed. He would have to check the rest of the shipment downstairs.

Suddenly he knew how to get her alone without taking her away from the ostensible safety of the bar. "We may have a few bottles down in the wine cellar."

He opened a door beside the mirrored display. "Come and take a look."

Chapter Two

"You have a wine cellar? In a fetish club?" Curiosity warred with Katy's natural instinct to stay out of dark places and away from devastatingly handsome men who could stoke her arousal with one scorching look.

Did she dare go down another rabbit hole? With him?

As if sensing her trepidation, he slipped a wedge under the door. "I'll leave the door open, although it'll play havoc with the climate controls."

Katy's mouth watered in anticipation. She rarely indulged her passion for wine. A cardiac surgeon, and almost always on call, Steven rarely drank and she didn't like to drink alone. Since the divorce, work and the kids had taken precedence over nights out with the girls and she had learned her lesson about drinking at client functions as a law student.

One quick look and she would come back upstairs.

She followed him through the door and down a well-lit, stone stairway into the cellar of her dreams. No expense had been spared. Floor-to-ceiling redwood racking housed a vast collection of what she suspected were vintage bottles. Cooling units, flagstone floors and incandescent lighting modernized the room. She breathed in the rich, heady scent of wine and cedar. "This is amazing. Can I look around?"

He nodded and settled himself in a high-backed, red leather chair. "Take your time."

Katy roamed the wine cellar, randomly pulling out bottles. Shivers ran through her body, but they were not solely from her delight at finding rare and exclusive labels. She could feel his eyes on her, following her every movement, watching her every breath, boring into her soul.

"So what do you think of the club?" His deep rumble filled the silence.

"It's very intimidating." *But not as intimidating as you.*

He chuckled. "You've only seen the public space. The private playrooms are in the back."

Katy shivered, suddenly regretting her decision to leave the safety of the crowd. "I'm not really interested in that side of things. I don't usually come to places like this."

She paused and gave him a sidelong glance. "Do you come here often? I mean, other than working the bar?"

Mark laughed. "Are you using a line on me?"

Katy bit her lip and turned away to hide her heated cheeks. "No. Of course not. I was wondering if you were..."

"You want to know if I'm in the scene."

His gentle tone gave her the courage to turn around. "Are you?"

"It's not something I need, but it can be enjoyable with the right person."

Katy breathed out a soft *oh* and then froze. Had he heard her? Could he tell her response was one of curiosity and not condemnation?

"What about you?" He folded his arms and cocked an eyebrow. "Did you come here with a secret agenda?"

"No secret agenda. When Valerie told me she worked at the club, I was curious so I agreed to meet her here instead of at my office."

"Brave girl," he murmured.

Katy cocked an eyebrow and put her hands on her hips. She hadn't been called a girl since she turned eighteen. "That was slightly condescending."

His eyes crinkled and a smile played at the corners of his broad, sensuous mouth. "The correct response to a compliment is thank you."

She walked over to another part of the collection and pulled out a dusty bottle. "I hardly think that was—"

"I'm waiting."

Surprised by his warning tone, she turned to face him.

He sat back in his chair, long, muscular legs spread, corded forearms crossed, dark eyes calm and focused. But despite his casual

23

Sarah Castille

manner, she sensed power and tension coiled in his lean body, like a cobra ready to spring.

A thrill of fear raced through her, followed by a sharp spike of arousal. She tempered it quickly. No way would she be pushed around even if secretly his commanding tone turned her on. She replaced the bottle in the rack. "I think we'd better get back upstairs."

His voice softened. "Why are you running away?"

She spun around to face him. "I'm not running away. I...I've seen the wine cellar so I thought—"

"You're afraid."

Katy folded her arms. "Not at all."

"Your body says otherwise."

She froze and then sucked in a breath. "What do you mean by that?"

"Body language. You're flushed, trembling. Your breathing rate has increased. Your eyes are wide. Your hands are clenched into fists. Your tongue..." He paused and his voice lowered to a husky growl. "Your tongue keeps darting out to lick your lips. If that isn't fear, sugar, what could it be?"

Arousal, fierce and unfamiliar, shot through her like an electric current, flaming her body, burning a path to her core. Sweat broke out on her heated skin. Her mouth opened and closed but no sound came out.

Mark's lips curled into a slow, sensual smile. "Come here, Katy-who-isn't-afraid." The sound of his voice, hard and low, sent a chill down her spine.

No, not a chill. A heat wave. A fever. Maybe she was ill. Maybe that's why her cheeks burned and sweat trickled between her breasts.

But that didn't explain the deep yearning that had risen up within her. Oh, she wanted to go to him, tear his clothes off, climb onto his lap, run her hands over his broad chest and then lower. It was as if she had been starving for years and he was a banquet waiting to be tasted.

Maybe that was the truth of it.

Giving herself a mental shake, she willed the sensation to go

24

away. What the hell was going on? Was she seriously contemplating having sex with a stranger in the basement of a fetish club?

She swallowed past the lump in her throat. "Why?"

"Didn't you want the Meursault?"

Katy nodded and her pulse kicked up a notch.

"Third row down, second bottle from the left." He pointed above his head.

Katy raised an eyebrow. "A gentleman would get it for me."

"I'm not feeling like a gentleman right now. Especially after your stirring performance upstairs and the way you're looking at me now— like you want to devour me." The heat in his eyes matched his voice, dark and sinful, like a rich Amarone. How long had it been since a man gazed at her with such desire? After Justin's birth, Steven had never once looked at her with anything more than mild interest.

Katy lowered her eyes. "I wasn't... I didn't mean..."

He cut her off. "Katy."

She looked up into amused brown eyes and then drank in the sight of his hard, muscular body sprawled across the chair; his long legs open and inviting.

Craving, deep and delicious, flooded her veins.

"Come here, sugar. I won't bite."

"It's not the biting I'm worried about." Nor was it him. Her gut told her he wouldn't hurt her. If he had wanted to try anything, he wouldn't have waited this long. No, it was her. She had lost control of herself and she had no idea what this new, lust-driven Katy Sinclair was about to do.

Still, his soft, cajoling voice drew her forward. Although she wanted the wine, she wanted him more. But after ten years on the bench, she didn't remember how to play the game.

Her heels clicked on the flagstone floor as she closed the distance between them, stopping only a foot away. Even seated, he intimidated her. But God was he sexy. Her pulse raced and her throat turned dry.

He studied her for a long moment, his gaze intense and unwavering. "I'm beginning to wonder if we haven't met before."

Katy shook her head. "We haven't. I'm sure of it. You're not

25

someone I would ever forget." *Or ever will.* She stepped closer, her body now only inches from his. She caught the scent of his spicy aftershave and something raw and purely masculine. A quiver of fear ran through her followed again by the fierce rush of arousal.

"Good girl."

"I'm hardly a girl."

He reached out and put his hands on her hips, drawing her close, until she could feel the heat of his breath on her breasts through the thin cotton of her shirt. She bit her lip to stifle a moan.

"Most definitely not," he murmured.

Inexplicable desires wracked Katy's body. She wanted to thread her fingers through his hair, straddle his body and press her breasts against his full, sensuous lips.

Her briefcase dropped, unbidden, to the floor. She ran a tentative finger along the square line of his jaw, rough with stubble, but pulled away at his sharp intake of breath.

"Put it back." He lifted her hand and pressed it against his cheek, trapping it with his own. His skin was warm, firm. So sexy. She felt the slip of arousal between her thighs and drew in a ragged breath.

Get a grip, Katy. This isn't you.

She eased herself out of his grasp. "You're going to have to move. I'm not reaching over you."

"Shame." He stood with easy grace and pulled the chair out of her way.

Katy reached for the bottle. Too high. She looked over her shoulder. Mark's gaze was fixed firmly on her...ass. She snorted a laugh. "When you're done, maybe you could give me a hand."

Mark grinned and walked toward her, stopping so close she could feel the heat radiating from his body across every inch of her back. He put one arm around her waist and pulled her into his broad chest.

"Where do you want it, sugar?" he whispered, his breath warm and moist in her ear.

Red, hot flames of need licked through her body. "Want what?"

"My hand."

She could think of several places she wanted his hand. Places

Steven had rarely touched. Emboldened by his obvious interest, and her own simmering arousal, she let her head fall back on his shoulder and looked up at him. "I'm not that kind of girl."

His body shook with laughter. "What kind of girl?"

"The kind of girl who tells a man where she wants his hand."

He stroked the curve of her waist and brushed his lips over her ear. "You don't have to tell me, sugar. I know."

Ardor overwhelmed her and she scrambled to justify her actions. Sex club. Too much alcohol. Sinfully hot guy. Romantic wine cellar. Ten years of cold, loveless marriage, loneliness and unfulfilled need.

Good enough. She put her hand over his, sliding them both across her stomach. Mark grunted his approval and pulled her tight against his body. His soft lips blazed a trail of gentle kisses down her neck.

"You are so beautiful," he growled. "So fucking hot."

Katy hissed out a breath. She had steeled herself for a little flirting, not for the raw hunger of desire or the burning need for the touch of a stranger. Embarrassed and shocked by her body's response, she made a half-hearted attempt to pull away.

His arm tightened around her, pressing her so closely against his chest she could feel the steady beat of his heart against her back. He traced his fingers along her shoulder, over her collarbone and down the V of her shirt to the swell of her breasts.

Katy shuddered. His touch electrified her, sending shivers of sparks along every nerve in her body. How long had she dreamed of such an erotic, sensual caress? So different from Steven's ham-fisted pawing in the dark.

Ever so gently, he traced a finger along the lace edge of her bra, burning a slow trail over each soft crescent. A shiver of need chased down her spine and her betraying body arched toward his touch.

Emboldened by her response, he slowly undid the first few buttons of her shirt and slid his hand beneath the cotton barrier to cup her breast in his heated palm. With firm, but gentle strokes of his thumb, he teased her nipple into a tight peak through the thin lace of her bra, stoking her arousal hot enough to make her whimper with need.

"Shh, sugar. Tony won't be too happy if I lose control in his prized wine cellar."

Her sex clenched at his words and delicious anticipation ratcheted through her body. *Please. Lose. Control.*

The tips of his fingers drifted lower, exploring her, gliding over every curve and into every hollow of her body.

Desire became a raging inferno, incinerating reality in a tidal wave of emotion. Within minutes this stranger had aroused a passion in her she didn't even know she had.

"Why did you really come to the club, sugar? Is there something here that called to you?" He inched up her skirt and skimmed his fingers along the inside of her thigh, closer and closer to the tender folds hidden by her very wet, red lace panties.

Dark, erotic sensations pulsed through her body. Yes, something called to her, but she couldn't put it in words. She couldn't muster the effort to think instead of feel, speak instead of whimper. So she didn't even try.

"I'm waiting." The hint of warning pulled at something low in her belly.

She hissed in a breath and forced the words out. "It's different. Dangerous. I thought it might be...exciting."

"Are you excited, sugar?" He cupped her breast and kissed the sensitive hollow at the base of her neck.

Her head fell back against his shoulder and her strangled groan pierced the quiet of the cellar. Lust electrified her skin and sizzled away the last of her doubts.

Mark eased his hand away and smoothed down her skirt. "We'd better slow down."

"No." Katy shocked herself at the vehemence in her response. She should be happy. He was, in a perverse way, being a gentleman. But in her wild state of arousal, she had no desire to be a lady.

She spun around to face him. At the sight of his handsome face, now taut with need, something loosened in her core. She pressed her body against his and cupped his face in her hands. "Don't stop."

"Christ," he murmured. "You are tempting beyond belief." His hands splayed across the curve of her buttocks and he crushed her pelvis against his, pressing his hot, hard erection into her belly.

The evidence of his desire only served to further inflame her arousal. She wrapped her arms around his neck and pulled him down toward her aching lips.

But Mark wouldn't play the game. He kissed her throat, her breasts, her neck—everywhere but where she wanted his hot, wet mouth. His fingers dug into her flesh so hard the pleasure pain ripped a moan from her throat. She tilted her head back, desperately seeking the kiss he was so mercilessly withholding.

Suddenly Mark released her and pushed her away. "I can't...I want you, sugar. But not like this."

Reeling, confused, Katy looked away. She didn't want him to see the bloom in her cheeks. She had never been forward or sexually aggressive in her life. Was it really the combination of alcohol and the highly erotic, sensual environment? Or was it desperation for the intimacy she had craved so long? Maybe it was chemistry, pure and simple. All she knew was that she wanted him so badly, she would do almost anything to have him. Despite his rejection.

"Sugar?" His handsome face rumpled with consternation.

Katy swallowed past the lump in her throat. She was never going to see him again. If she was going to spend the next year getting off on this fantasy, she wanted at least one taste to remember him by.

Heart pounding, she closed the distance between them and leaned up to brush her lips over his. Warm. Firm. He tasted of the richest wine and the darkest coffee. Lush and sensual. She had never known it until now, but sex had a taste. And he was it.

He stiffened and then groaned—a low, guttural, entirely thrilling sound. His mouth moved over hers, softly, gently, sweetly, but only for heartbeat, and then his lips slid away. Cool air rushed into the heated space between them.

Case closed.

She spun away, quickly buttoning her shirt before she grabbed her briefcase. "Time to rejoin the party."

"Katy."

She steeled herself to keep her face impassive as she turned around to face him, feigning calm, even as her bottom lip trembled and her body shook at the sudden drop in her arousal.

"Don't think I don't want you. I do. More than you could possibly imagine. But maybe...we should have that drink."

She shrugged and then nodded. For the first time in her life, she had nothing to say.

What the hell was wrong with him?

He couldn't believe he had stopped himself. Everything had been perfect: the intimate space, the dim lighting, the rich, heady scents of cedar and wine, and the lush beauty in his arms.

But a part of him knew if he took their encounter even a step further, he would never see her again. He sensed she truly was, as she had said, not that kind of girl, and he didn't want to be the one to make her think otherwise.

He grabbed the Meursault and motioned for her to go up the stairs, enjoying the sway of her hips beneath the thin wool of her pencil skirt. He couldn't let her just walk away. He wanted to unravel her secrets, bare her soul and discover the real reason behind his intense attraction.

They emerged from the quiet intimacy of the cellar into a maelstrom of light and sound, dancers and drinkers. Catching Katy's desperate glance at the door, Mark grasped her arm. "Stay for a glass of the Meursault. You won't find a better vintage in Vancouver, I promise you."

He held up the bottle and smiled at her careful appraisal of the label. He didn't often meet a woman who shared his appreciation of wine.

She bit her lip and studied him for a long moment. He steeled his mouth into a neutral expression while his heart thundered in his chest, ripe with anxiety.

Finally she gave him a non-committal shrug and rounded the bar.

Mark nodded toward a vacant seat while he fished around for a corkscrew. He pulled two glasses from the rack and turned to place them on the counter. Only then did he realize he was alone.

He made a quick visual sweep of the club, but it was once again a sea of PVC and leather. A trip to reception told him what his gut already knew.

Katy was gone.

And he was damn sure she wouldn't be back.

"The body is this way, Detective Hunter."

James shuffled through the living room of the run-down apartment, his crime suit rustling as he walked. The thrill of attending a new crime scene never faded, even after twelve years with Homicide, six in the drug unit and a couple of years on patrol. His colleagues called him a lifer. He called it love.

Mike, the newest member of his investigation team, shifted his weight from foot to foot as he waited on the other side of the room. New rules meant Mike had made it through to the homicide team with only three years under his belt instead of the usual seven. His youth and inexperience were evident in his lack of patience. As primary investigator, James had responsibility for the overall investigation and he needed time to take a good look around.

He nodded to the forensics squad scattered around the small space. With the blaze of floodlights setting their white suits aglow, the scene had a surreal, alien feel. He had never been interested in the painstaking and detailed procedures involved in forensic science. He enjoyed putting the pieces together. A big-picture kinda guy.

He skirted the empty pizza boxes and beer cans strewn across the threadbare carpet in the main living space. Peeling wallpaper hung in strands off the water-stained walls, and the scent of stale cigarette smoke filtered through his mask. Typical East Side apartment. Cheap. Run down. Rented by the week, sometimes by the day.

His feet thumped on the scratched linoleum tiles and he followed Mike down a narrow hallway to the bedroom. Mike pulled away the police tape and stood to the side to let James through. The coroner, always the first person allowed in the crime scene, had already come and gone, as had James's supervisor, Sergeant Donaldson. Something in the room had rattled the two most imperturbable men he knew, and he steeled himself as he stepped across the threshold.

"We've unofficially identified him as Manuel Garcia, but the forensics department and the coroner's service will have to confirm the identity because of the state of the body." Mike swallowed hard and stiffened his spine. "No passport or immigration papers and nothing showing up on the database except a fake driver's license. We believe he's illegal. Wallet shows he works as a taxi driver for Speedaway Taxi Service. His girlfriend found him and called it in. She talked to him just a few hours ago."

They skirted past a wooden dresser, broken armchair and small table. Garcia's personal effects had already been tagged and bagged. No obvious signs of a struggle or break-in, but then people in this neighborhood didn't have anything worth stealing.

Mike sucked in a sharp breath when they reached the bed. Garcia lay curled in a fetal position, covers drawn up to his shoulder and clutched between his hands. A silver bowl lay on the floor beside him. The pungent, acrid smell of bile permeated James's protective mask and he gagged as he crouched down beside the victim to get a closer look.

"What the fuck?"

For a split second he thought his first assessment of aliens might be true. Barely recognizable as human, Garcia's swollen, misshapen head dwarfed the small pillow on which it lay. He had seen pictures of John Merrick, the Elephant Man. The similarities were remarkable.

"Forensics has only just started processing the bed, and I'm not planning to be around when they lift the sheet," Mike said.

James stood and took a step back. He thought he had seen everything after his years in the homicide unit, but there had been nothing like this. "Is it congenital?"

Mike shook his head. "We interviewed the landlord. He described Garcia as a regular guy. Nothing out of the ordinary. Hard-working. Honest."

"Looks like some kind of allergic reaction. I have a friend who's allergic to bees. He swells up whenever he gets stung, although I've never seen him as bad as that."

"Maybe...we should tell Sergeant Donaldson it might not be homicide-related. He breezed in and out of here pretty fast."

James snorted a laugh. "You don't tell Donaldson anything. He tells you. He's decided we should be involved, so we're involved. You'll benefit from the experience. Sometimes years go by with nothing more than gang murders and domestic violence to keep us busy."

His cell buzzed against his hip. "I've seen all I need to see. I'm going to head back to the office. Let me know which pathologist the coroner's office puts on the autopsy. We'll definitely need a toxicology report on this one."

James left the apartment and quickly shed his crime suit. Flipping open the phone he checked the caller ID. *Mark.* He hit Call Back and walked down the street, dodging pop bottles and condom wrappers as he headed toward his standard-issue dull gray Crown Victoria.

Mark didn't mince words. "There was a woman at the bar on Friday. A lawyer. I want you to find out who she is."

"I remember her." James tried to suppress a smile. Mark must have it bad. In the twenty-three years they'd been friends, he had only rarely asked for a favor.

"I've searched the Law Society website but there are dozens of female lawyers named Katy. I can't call them all. Valerie knows where she works but I can't get in touch with her."

"You could wait." James stifled a laugh. "Valerie will be at the club next weekend."

"I can't wait," Mark snapped. "Trixie walked her to her car. A black GM Acadia. First two letters of the plate are TX."

"Trust Trixie to remember a detail like that." James stopped to pick up a shard of broken glass and deposit it in a nearby garbage can.

"Trixie said the license plate reminded her of her name."

James couldn't help pushing his agitated friend. "Has she committed a crime? Because I'm finishing up at a crime scene and wasn't really looking to waste an afternoon breaking into the police database because you're desperate and can't control your dick."

Mark was immediately contrite. "Sorry. Bad time?"

"Same old, same old. So, did your mystery woman commit a crime or not?"

"She was probably illegally parked." Mark huffed into the phone. "We arrived at the same time and I couldn't find a parking space within five blocks."

James chuckled. "Maybe I'll go with theft. She seems to have stolen your sanity. Has it occurred to you, if she wanted to see you again, she would have given you her number?"

"I knew you weren't going to make this easy for me," Mark sighed. "Maybe I'll have to start a civil suit for negligence and intentional infliction of mental distress."

James turned the corner and looked for his vehicle. "I have a friend who's a private investigator. I'll give him a call. Not worth losing my career over a girl. What are you going to do when you find her? You can't just show up at her door."

Mark's long silence told James everything he didn't want to know.

"Don't do anything stupid," James warned. "They don't pay me enough to bail your ass out of jail."

"I won't have to," Mark said quickly. "She's a lawyer. I can think of a dozen places I might accidentally bump into her."

James exhaled the breath he hadn't realized he was holding. "Don't bump too hard."

Lana Parker, private investigator, hung her shiny new license on her wall. The frame had been an extravagance, considering she barely had enough money to fuel her beloved Jetta, much less eat, but she couldn't resist. She had completed the private investigator course and realized her dream. She wanted everyone to know that a badass, high school dropout could turn her life around. Not that any of her friends or family would ever visit her cheap East Side apartment, but when they did, they would see the evidence of her tremendous accomplishment.

Now, she just needed some clients.

She picked up the stack of brochures she had printed with the last of her savings. She hated windshield flyers, but she couldn't think of a better, or cheaper, way to advertise her services. She had already scouted out the parking lots she planned to hit in her first advertising blitz. Then, she could sit back and wait for the calls to roll in.

She stuffed the flyers in her worn backpack and headed out the door, taking care to lock the three deadbolts. Security was essential if she intended to run her business from home. She would be dealing with highly confidential information and she had to ensure her clients' privacy would be well protected.

After jogging down the stairs to burn off a few extra calories, she slowed to a walk and headed up the street. Emergency vehicles lined the sidewalk and police tape cordoned off a nearby apartment building. She didn't stop to look. Typical day in East Van. She turned the corner and spotted a gray Crown Victoria parked just ahead of her. Ghost car. So mundane it stood out like a sore thumb. She walked over and pressed her face against the window. A siren glinted on the dashboard.

No. But her hand had already reached into her bag. "Self-destructive impulsiveness" her high school principal had called it. Her mum just thought she was cheeky.

She pulled out a brochure and slid it under the windshield wipers. Her instructor had hinted at friction between private investigators and the police in Vancouver. She couldn't resist letting the cops know there was a new PI in town.

"Hey. Get away from the vehicle."

Lana spun around. *Damn.* She should have checked the street. The cop stalking toward her was no one she wanted to meet. Hard, angular face, lean tight body, severe buzz cut. Cute, but menacing scowl. She hauled ass around the corner and raced down the road. Her breath came out in short pants as she pushed her usually sedentary body into action. At least she'd had a warm up.

After a block of torture, she glanced over her shoulder and collapsed against a wall. The cop wasn't coming after her. She wheezed out a giggle until she realized with horror he didn't need to.

If he wanted to find her, all he had to do was call.

Chapter Three

"Mom, where's my lunch?" Melissa's voice echoed down the hallway.

"It's on the counter, darling." Katy flipped through the file on her desk and sighed. Her five minutes of peace were over. She had been lucky to get even that on a Monday morning.

"Mom, where's my soccer uniform?"

"It's on your bed, Justin. I washed it on the weekend."

"Mom, Justin pulled my hair."

"Did not."

"Did too."

Katy closed her file. She shouldn't have tried to prep at home for the examination for discovery this morning, but nervous anticipation about her first high-profile, solo case had awakened her early. Ted, her managing partner, had given her the file last night and a promise of partnership if she rose to the challenge.

She pulled out her briefing note and took one last look at the key points she had jotted down last night. The case was simple enough. Martha Saunders, a laboratory technician, had started an action for wrongful dismissal against her former employer, pharmaceutical giant, Hi-Tech. Martha's previous lawyer had unexpectedly dropped the case and Ted had picked it up at the last minute. Usually a case involving a high-profile party would be handled by one of the partners, but Ted had given it to her. A test.

Like Friday night.

What had she been thinking? What if someone had recognized her? She shouldn't have taken the risk of being seen in a fetish club as she now headed toward the culmination of years of work. Lawyers loved to gossip and anyone who saw her would have been delighted to spread a rumor, even if they knew it wasn't the truth.

Still, Mark had haunted her dreams. The warmth of his hand on her body, the burn of desire in his eyes and the sensual brush of his lips over her skin in the wine cellar.

Oh, God. The wine cellar.

She twirled her desk chair in a slow circle, remembering the soft rumble of his velvet-smooth voice. Her fantasy come to life. The man she imagined when she lost herself in romance novels or sensual films. Someone who would love the unlovable control freak that was Katy Sinclair.

"Good morning, Kate."

A control freak with one fatal weakness. The inability to get her philandering ex-husband out of her life.

Katy grimaced as Steven's voice shattered the organized chaos of the morning. He always insisted on calling her Kate even though she hated the name. Friends and family called her Katy. Clients called her Katherine. She had thought the divorce would be enough to get rid of "Kate". Wrong again.

"Steven, I've told you before to knock or ring the bell," she shouted from her study.

His shadow darkened the doorway. "It's still half my house, even though the judge gave you possession. I shouldn't have to knock if I want to see my own kids."

He leaned against the doorframe and folded his arms. He had aged in the year since the divorce. His salt-and-pepper hair now sported streaks of gray, and his once-lean muscles had softened. Still handsome, but the steel blue eyes and chiseled jaw, captivating to the young, impressionable, eighteen-year-old girl she had once been, no longer held any appeal. Now, after meeting Mark, he looked...average.

She slammed the file into her briefcase. "He gave me the house because the kids live with me. If you recall, the judge thought the constant stream of young interns in your bed created an unsuitable lifestyle for raising children."

Steven held up his hands in a gesture of mock surrender. "We've been through this already. I offered to go for counseling, but you're the one who decided to rip the family apart."

"I ripped the family apart?" Katy clenched her teeth and drew in a ragged breath. "I endured your affairs so our kids could have the stable family I never had and you left me anyway...for an intern." She closed her briefcase with a bang. "Now you blame me because I'm the one who filed for the divorce. Unbelievable."

"Sally left." He said the two words without emotion or remorse.

"Oh, God." Katy looked away to hide her horror. "So now you want to come back, is that it?"

He walked across the room and put his hands on her shoulders. "Kate, it was just a blip. A minor diversion. I needed to release some stress and Sally was there for me when you were busy working. It never changed how I felt about our family. I want us back together. For the kids."

Katy shuddered and wriggled out of his grasp. "I've heard this all before. You apologize. You promise it won't happen again. Then you're in bed with the next young intern who catches your eye. I won't go through it again. That was supposed to be your takeaway message when I filed the divorce petition."

"The message I got was that you were stressed because of that big corporate espionage trial and you took it out on me by filing the petition. But I understand and I'm willing to forgive you. We all get stressed sometimes."

Katy closed her eyes and took a long, deep breath. *Stay cool. Stay calm. He's baiting you. Don't give him the satisfaction of a response.*

"I have an important hearing at ten o'clock and I have to go." She picked up her briefcase and squeezed the handle so tight her knuckles turned white. "If you don't take the kids now, they'll be late."

He shrugged.

"You are here to take the kids to school, aren't you? It's your day to take them." She closed her eyes, dreading his response.

Steven shook his head. "I'm in surgery this morning. I just came by to let you know that since Sally is gone—she left last night—I'll be visiting more often to see the kids...and you."

Katy's eyes widened. "She only left last night and you're already trying to come back? You've sunk to a new low." Bile rose in her stomach as she contemplated the upcoming weeks of trying to fend off Steven's attempts to insinuate himself into her life.

She pushed past him, calling for Melissa and Justin. She had just enough time to get them to school, but it would be touch and go with the examination for discovery.

Steven gave her ponytail a quick, casual tug as she stalked away, winking when she glared over her shoulder.

"Later, Kate."

Katy shuddered. His assault had only begun.

Martha Saunders, divorced and now unemployed, smiled when Katy introduced herself. In her faded black suit, white blouse, sensible pumps and tidy, bleached blonde bob, Martha resembled a middle-aged accountant and not a thirty-three year old laboratory technician. But being with Steven had taught Katy never to judge by appearance alone. Who would have known her mature, handsome, attentive surgeon would turn out to be a distant, pathologically self-absorbed, financially irresponsible philanderer?

"I'm sorry our meeting has to be so brief, but I only got your file yesterday and this morning I had an unexpected delay." Katy motioned for her new client to sit down. She hated the stuffy, windowless counsel rooms in the Vancouver Law Courts, but they were private and Steven's untimely visit meant they didn't have time for the comprehensive meeting she had originally planned to have at her office.

Katy took her seat and pulled out her file, skimming through the papers Martha's previous solicitor had provided. "This looks like a pretty clear case of wrongful dismissal. I've read all your outstanding performance reviews, employee awards and the statements from your colleagues about your dedication to the company. As I understand it, the CEO, Darkon Steele, just called you into his office one day, fired you and had a security guard march you out with your box of belongings. Is that right?"

Martha pulled a tissue from her purse and dabbed behind her gold-rimmed glasses. "Not quite. He fired me after I tried to report the

39

company to the regulators."

Katy raised an eyebrow. "Whistle-blowing? What did you allege they were doing?"

"Falsifying data and reports about a new drug."

"Those are pretty serious allegations. Did you have any proof?"

Martha stared down at her hands and twisted her watch around her wrist. "I gave the regulators a sample of the drug and a few documents I had found, but the really incriminating evidence was hidden away."

She sniffed and a tear trickled down her cheek. Katy looked up at the clock. Her pulse sped up and she silently willed Martha to hurry.

"It's okay, Martha, go on."

"The regulators didn't believe me." Martha swallowed and wiped away another tear. "Or maybe they did but Mr. Steele bought them all off. The drug will probably be the biggest thing to come out of North America in the last few years."

Katy jotted a few notes on her paper and motioned for Martha to keep talking.

Martha shrugged. "There isn't much more to say. I filed a report, and then the regulators sent a few people to interview me. They promised it would all be confidential and my name would never be released. A few weeks later, Mr. Steele called me into his office and fired me. He said I had been in the building after hours, which isn't true."

"You were never in the building after hours?"

"Well, once I went in because I had forgotten my purse, but I had to go through security before I went to my office so it wasn't like I was sneaking around."

Katy studied Martha's face but didn't see any hint of deception. "Did you talk to the regulators again to let them know you had been fired shortly after you reported the company?"

Martha nodded. "They said they had investigated and couldn't substantiate my complaints. They also said they never released my name to Hi-Tech. I didn't believe them."

Katy checked her watch. She hadn't recognized the name of the partner listed on the pleadings as defense counsel and couldn't assume he would be amenable to a late start. Usually she researched her opposition and strategized accordingly, but in this instance she just hadn't had the time.

"So you think you were dismissed because Steele found out about the whistle-blowing?"

Martha nodded. "Mr. Steele also accused me of being a corporate spy when he dismissed me, but I think he was just fishing for an excuse. I was a good employee. He had no reason to let me go."

Her impassioned words left Katy in no doubt Martha would be a convincing witness. She came across as open, honest and without guile. Sometimes a good witness made it worth the risk to up the stakes in a strong case. "I think we might be able to establish an ulterior motive for your dismissal and make a substantial punitive damage claim."

Martha leaned forward. "It's not about the money. It's about getting enough evidence to make the regulators believe me. Hi-Tech has to be shut down. The drug has very serious side effects. I don't want anyone to get hurt."

Not about the money? Given the high cost of litigation and the time and effort required to run a case through to trial, it was always about the money. She had seen Martha's tax returns and her client was far from wealthy. Either Martha was the most altruistic person she had ever met, or there was more to the case than she had revealed.

"We have a fairly wide scope for requesting documents and interviewing witnesses," Katy said. "I'll go on a little fishing expedition to see what we can turn up."

Martha smiled and dried her eyes. "It's nice to finally have someone in my corner—someone who believes me."

Maybe. Maybe not. Katy knew better than to take her client's story at face value. But given her uncertainty about opposing counsel, a more detailed examination of Martha's story would have to wait.

"We'll have to finish up later. I've got enough to make Mr. Steele squirm for a few hours, and we can always drag him in again if something unexpected turns up in the discovery today."

"There's something else you should know," Martha blurted out.

"I'm sorry," Katy said, genuinely contrite. "We're out of time."

Seven minutes to ten.

Mark tapped his pen on the table, matching the rhythm of the ticking clock.

His client, Darkon Steele, frowned. "I hope we aren't kept waiting much longer. This discovery is already a waste of my valuable time."

"I'll make sure plaintiff's counsel is aware we intend to finish on time even if we start late," Mark said. Anything to ensure the CEO of his firm's biggest client, Hi-Tech Pharmaceuticals, continued to send work his way. He needed a win on this case to secure Hi-Tech's business and his firm's future.

Steele leaned back in his chair and folded his arms. "I'll just tell the plaintiff's lawyer his client is a corporate spy and belongs in jail, not running around launching frivolous civil suits. We'll be done in five minutes."

Mark sighed. With Steele already defensive and angry, he could imagine how the discovery would go. "You'll do no such thing. You'll speak only to answer the questions opposing counsel asks, and your answers will be as brief and as succinct as possible. If you say anything inappropriate, it will affect your credibility and could damage our defense at trial. You'll be under oath and the court reporter will transcribe everything. Isn't that right, Tim? "

Tim Daniels, one of Vancouver's most sought-after court reporters, turned on his computer and gave Mark a nod.

"That's right. Everything is recorded, even coughs and pauses." Tim rubbed his hand through his thatch of red hair and flashed a smile. "Bible okay, Mr. Steele, or do you wish to affirm?"

"No Bible."

Tim nodded. "I'll get the affirmation sheet ready."

Steele spun his pen across his thumb without taking his eyes off Mark. "So what do you do while I'm answering the barrage of questions?"

"My job is to object to questions that aren't relevant, or are in any way inappropriate, privileged or prejudicial. There's a lot more to it in terms of tactics, but I won't bore you."

"Good. That's what I pay you for." Steele slicked down his neatly cut black hair. With his cold, dark eyes, heavy features and shiny, black Italian suit, he had the look of a gangster. Not far from the truth. The savvy, ruthless, hard-edged businessman didn't hesitate to take risks or bend the rules to get ahead. But he relied on Mark to keep things legal.

Tim excused himself to find an affirmation sheet. Cool air rushed into the stuffy, windowless boardroom as he hurried out the door.

"Speaking of money, how's the firm doing?" Steele leaned back in his chair and folded his arms.

A loaded question. Steele knew how the firm was doing. The recession had hit litigation boutiques hard, and law firms all over the city were scrambling over the few clients with the capital to run the long and expensive courtroom battles that were a litigator's bread and butter.

"Fine." Mark had no interest in getting involved in a discussion about the firm's financial struggles. Steele knew he was the sole reason Richards & Moretti had not folded like so many other firms. He just wanted to rub it in.

Just like Tony.

The barrage of questions he had had to endure from Tony both in the club following Katy's departure and on Monday morning at the office had made him rethink his decision to run a second business with his fellow partner.

Mark flipped open his file and tried to shut out any thoughts about Carpe Noctem. Too late. His betraying mind had already conjured up images of Katy. He could still feel her soft curves under his palm and her warm skin under his lips. If he breathed in deeply, he could even smell the faintest trace of her perfume. Had he pushed too hard? If he had shown some restraint, would she have run away?

Tim returned with the affirmation sheet. "I didn't see opposing counsel, but I'm sure she'll be here on time. The Wildcat is never late."

"Opposing counsel is a woman?" Steele smirked. "And she's called the Wildcat?"

Mark frowned. Although common for members of the Vancouver litigation community to give each other nicknames, only the best and brightest were singled out for the dubious accolade. He thought he knew every nicknamed litigation partner in the city, but he had never heard of the Wildcat.

"Katherine Sinclair," Tim said in response to Mark's quizzical look. "She's an associate lawyer at Knight and Frank, which is why you wouldn't have heard of her. They've only just started pitting her against partners."

Steele laughed. "An associate? With Mark on the other side? He'll have this case wrapped up before lunch."

"Why would her firm put an associate on such a high-profile case?" Mark's frown deepened. Any lawsuit involving Hi-Tech, no matter how small, would be big news and big news meant big business. The kind of business usually handled by a partner.

Tim leaned back in his chair and folded his arms. "Not my place to tell."

The door behind Mark opened with a bang. A rush of cool air ruffled his papers, carrying with it the scent of lilies.

Two sets of heels tapped across the tiled floor.

The game had begun.

Mark scribbled nonsense on his notepad, resisting the urge to turn around. The first few minutes of any legal hearing were critical for establishing control of the room. And he specialized in control.

He waited until he heard a chair slide and then looked up; ready to feast his eyes on the Wildcat associate and put her in her place.

Katy.

His pen dropped to the table with a soft thud. Shock gripped him and wouldn't let go. Blood pounded through his veins as he fought a losing battle to keep his face impassive and his body still.

He drank in the sight of her, his hungry gaze missing nothing. Her stiff wool suit did little to hide the sweet curves underneath. Firm, full breasts, gently molded by her fine, white silk blouse. Rounded hips hugged by a pencil skirt, nipping her trim waist. Long, slim fingers clutching a file folder, knuckles white.

Their gazes met and locked, sweeping him back to the crushing disappointment of discovering her gone, and a weekend of unfulfilled fantasies.

He had a sudden desire to wrench her hair free and let the silken waterfall cascade down her back. Tear off her jacket. Shred the thin white blouse. Push that tight skirt up to her waist...

Maybe not such a good idea.

He would ask her out for coffee.

Better.

Then he would take her to his bed, draw those plump lips into his mouth and kiss her until she writhed under his body and begged him for...

No.

Although their brief encounter was unlikely to give rise to a conflict of interest, it was as far as they could go while they opposed each other on the same case.

Mark shook his head, trying to chase away the onslaught of erotic images and focus on the legal proceeding and the room full of people waiting for him to engage in the proper social conventions. But his brain and body had a disconnect.

He could almost see her pulse throbbing in the sweet spot at the base of her neck.

How would she taste if he licked her now?

No, no, no. Not him.

Katy dropped her books on the table with a bang. Beside her, Martha jumped. Hundreds of lawyers in the city, and the man who seduced her had to be opposing counsel on the most important case of her career.

Or had she seduced him?

Get a grip, Katy. But her throat had seized up and she couldn't speak. His gaze drew her in and the world fell away.

She flushed as his gaze traveled the length of her body with a slow, arrogant sweep, baring her just as surely as he had done in the club, roaming where his hands had touched. Heat seared through her

45

at the memory of every caress.

Masculine approval flashed in his eyes.

She frowned at his continued scrutiny. Did he expect some kind of emotional response? A gasp of horror, perhaps, or a quiver of fear?

Well, get used to disappointment. She locked away her emotional turmoil, forced her lips into a smile and held out her hand. "Katherine Sinclair, for the plaintiff."

He rose from his chair and rounded the table. Strong, muscular legs carried him toward her until he stood only inches away. Confident. Calm. He showed no hint of disquiet or surprise at her presence.

She couldn't take her eyes off him. In his impeccable wool suit and blue silk tie, he embodied the man of her fantasies. Tall and devastatingly handsome. Powerful and in control. She caught the familiar scent of soap and sandalwood.

Hot. Sexy. Her mouth watered.

Stop it.

She gritted her teeth and stared at her...opponent. All that stood between her and the partnership dream. If she didn't keep that clearly in her mind, she would lose everything she had worked so hard to achieve.

"Mark Richards, for the defendant." He shook her hand; his thumb brushed over the sensitive underside of her wrist drawing a sharp breath from her lips. His slow, deliberate stroke sent her senses into overdrive.

Richards. Now she could search him to her heart's content on the Internet. She jerked her hand back and away. If he thought he could seduce her here, he was sorely mistaken.

"Pleasure," she murmured.

"You're late, Ms. Sinclair." His deep voice held a hint of amusement.

Katy looked up at the clock and frowned. "Perhaps you need glasses. According to that clock, we still have two minutes."

"By the time you set up, it'll be past ten and my client is not prepared to stay late to make up your lost time."

She narrowed her eyes at his condescending tone. "I suggest you seat yourself quickly, Mr. Richards. You may require set-up time, but I don't. I'm ready to begin." She paused for effect. "Now."

Mark raised an eyebrow then gave her a curt nod and returned to his seat.

Don't look at him.

How could she not? Longing gripped her fiercely, crushing her lungs. She took a deep breath and forced her pulse to slow. If she couldn't handle five minutes in a hearing with him, how would she manage for the next few years until the case ran its course?

Or was it even an issue? Maybe they had a professional conflict. She mentally sifted through the professional conduct rules she had studied in law school. A quick wine cellar seduction was unlikely to affect her ability to represent her client, much less amount to a conflict. Plus, Mark hadn't said anything. He was a partner and the senior lawyer in the room. He would have had experience dealing with conflicts like this. With those looks, that voice and the alpha attitude, he probably seduced young female lawyers every week—maybe every day.

Katy took her seat and focused on his client, the famous Darkon Steele. How did it feel to head one of the most powerful pharmaceutical companies in North America? She had seen his picture splashed across newspapers and magazines, always with some Barbie-doll blonde in tow. In the press, he had appeared handsome, with his inky black hair, dark eyes and muscular body. But in person, the sharply hewn cheekbones and thin, red lips contrasted with the rough features, giving him a more sinister look.

Katy stiffened her spine. She'd faced down intimidating witnesses before. Hell, she'd even sued the partners in the firm where she had trained as a lawyer after they terminated her employment contract when they discovered she was pregnant. After the settlement, no one would hire her. Then Ted came knocking at her door. He could smell an opportunity for profit a mile away. An infamous associate drew attention. Attention meant publicity. Publicity meant clients. Clients meant profit. Her litigation skills had just been the icing on the cake.

The sinfully rich rumble of Mark's voice broke the spell. "Ms. Sinclair, this is Darkon Steele. I believe our clients are already acquainted."

She nodded at Steele instead of offering her hand. A deliberate power play. Amusement glimmered in Steele's eyes.

Katy glanced up at the clock. Ten o'clock. She smiled at Tim to let him know they could start and he gave her a wink. Tension ebbed from her body. She liked Tim, not just as a reporter, but also as a friend. Recently he had hinted he wanted more than friendship, but she had neither the time nor the energy to pursue any kind of relationship and after Steven, she didn't want another man messing up her life.

She took a deep breath to steady herself. "Mr. Steele, as you are aware, my client worked as a laboratory technician at Hi-Tech for approximately two years. She has filed a claim against your company in which she alleges Hi-Tech wrongfully dismissed her from her job. I understand she ultimately reported to you, is that correct?"

"It is." Steele's deep voice reverberated around the stark, windowless room.

"You were the one who made the decision to terminate her employment?"

"Yes." Steele leaned back, crossed his arms behind his head and yawned.

Katy raised an eyebrow to let him know his disrespectful behavior had not gone unnoticed. "Is that the reason the company selected you as its representative for the case?"

"Objection."

Katy tried not to smile as the corners of Mark's mouth lifted slightly. He knew she was testing him. Hi-Tech's Board of Directors had to select someone to represent the company for the duration of the legal hearing. Their reason for selecting Steele was not directly relevant to the case, but she did want to know why a CEO was involved in what should have been a simple human resource matter.

Mark raised a questioning eyebrow and Katy shook her head. No point wasting time arguing the objection. If she really wanted an answer, she could apply to the court. Instead, she launched into a series of questions about Martha's performance. Nothing in Martha's work history indicated anything but a dedicated, competent, hard-working employee. Surprisingly, Steele agreed.

She flipped through her file as she considered her next line of questioning. "In the Statement of Defense, the stated reason for my client's dismissal is a violation of company policy, is that correct?"

"Yes." The quick glance Steele gave Mark suggested the official reason for dismissal might be a legal fabrication.

Interesting.

"What policy was that?"

"A prohibition on entering the premises after hours without authorization."

"I want to see that policy."

Mark smiled, his eyes crinkling at the corners. "And you shall."

She tore her gaze away from his full, sensuous lips. "Do you, Mr. Steele, believe the policy violation was sufficient grounds for dismissing an employee with a stellar work record, and without any recourse to proper statutory or company disciplinary procedures?"

Mark sucked in a sharp breath. "Objection. Stick to the facts, Ms. Sinclair, and let the judge make the conclusions."

She clenched her teeth and attacked again. "Mr. Steele, weren't your actions unusually heavy-handed?"

"Ms. Sinclair."

She flinched at the sharp warning in Mark's voice, but she didn't take her eyes off Steele and she didn't back down. "Is dismissal the usual consequence for breach of that particular policy?"

Steele narrowed his eyes. "We have a zero-tolerance policy for corporate spies."

Katy raised her eyebrows and shifted her gaze to Mark. "Mr. Richards, perhaps you might remind your client to refrain from making unfounded accusations on the record, unless he has evidence to substantiate his claims."

Steele leaned across the table. "I don't need evidence. I've been in this business a long time. I know a spy when I see one."

Katy folded her arms. "I've warned you once already. I want this to stop."

"I know what you want, kitty," Steele growled, his eyes raking a path across her body.

"Leash your dog, Mr. Richards!" Katy's shout echoed off the walls in the confined space.

Oh. My. God. Did I just say that?

Steele pushed back his chair and rose from his seat, his massive frame blocking her only escape route. Mark sighed, seemingly unconcerned his client had pulled himself up to his full height and was about to pounce on Katy and rip out her throat.

"Perhaps we should take a break." Mark's voice was calm and even.

Katy flipped through her file as she fought back the tidal wave of emotion still spilling through her veins. She had never lost control in a legal hearing and it wouldn't—couldn't—happen again. Especially here. Especially now. "I apologize for the outburst. It was...unprofessional. I'm happy to break if Mr. Steele needs a moment, although I'm quite prepared to continue."

Steele dropped back into his seat. "I don't need a break, kitty. Your little claws didn't even scratch the surface."

Before Katy could retort, Martha shoved a note along the table with a hastily scrawled drawing of a happy face. Katy gave her a reluctant smile. At least her client approved. She crumpled the note in her hand and met Steele's cold, hard gaze with her own.

Bastard. She could hardly wait to get him on the stand at trial. She would rip him to shreds. He would be begging for mercy by the time she was done with him.

She took a deep, fortifying breath and picked up her questions where she had left off. "Did my client not explain to you she had simply forgotten her purse?"

Steele snorted. "I didn't care why she was in the building. I fired her. You're clearly too young to understand the pharmaceutical industry, but it is a highly secretive and competitive business. A new drug can be worth billions of dollars, and spying is endemic. When we have someone sneaking around the building after hours, we can't take any risks."

Katy raised an eyebrow. "You don't strike me as a man averse to taking risks, Mr. Steele."

Steele stared at her with frank, obvious interest. Uncomfortable with the assessment, Katy looked down and picked up her file. When she looked up again, his lips quirked into a smile.

"Do you really think you can take me on, kitty?" Steele's low, seductive voice did not disguise the clear threat underlying his words.

"Steele." Mark's sharp rebuke went unnoticed by his client.

Katy's knees trembled, but she had a client depending on her and a career at stake. She exhaled loudly and forced her gaze to meet his. "Mr. Steele, in this forum, I ask the questions."

Chapter Four

Crap.

He should have known Steele, the quintessential misogynist, wouldn't respond well to being challenged by a woman. The situation was about to go from bad to disastrous.

Mark gritted his teeth. Ethically his hands were tied. He had to act in his client's best interests, even if they conflicted with his own, and his client clearly wanted to break opposing counsel.

"If everyone doesn't mind, I need a quick break to rest my hands. Fifteen minutes should be enough." Tim's voice cut through the tension in the room. He turned off the recorder with a firm click. In a legal proceeding where one word could cost a company billions of dollars, the accuracy of a transcript overrode all other concerns. If the reporter needed a break, no one would protest.

Mark breathed in a sigh of relief. Time for some damage control. With his usual tact, Tim had just given him a chance to diffuse Steele's explosive temper and Katy the opportunity to cool down.

Katy collected her files from the table and headed for the door with her client and Tim in tow. Mark stared after her. Damned fine lawyer. And what a show. No wonder they called her the Wildcat. He wouldn't want to be on the wrong end of those claws.

While Steele checked his phone messages, Mark sent a quick text to James, letting him know he had found his mystery woman. The slew of exclamation marks after James's responding message told Mark he would be spending the evening being interrogated at the bar—Hunter style.

"That little kitty needs to be tamed." Steele tucked his phone into his pocket. "What do you know about her?"

Mark shrugged, feigning disinterest. If Steele found out she had been at Carpe Noctem, he wouldn't hesitate to use that information against her, even if her visit had been perfectly innocent. Or, at least, had started out that way.

"She's new to the case."

"Find out everything you can about her. Hire an investigator. I want to know all her secrets. Then run the case into the ground. I want it off my desk by the end of the month."

Mark frowned. Although his firm needed the business, he wasn't prepared to sacrifice his career to get it. "I can't do it. Investigating opposing counsel would be considered professional misconduct."

Steele snorted his disgust. "Sometimes you have to take a risk. Break the rules. That's how you get what you really want."

"That's not why you hired me." Mark tried and failed to hide his disdain. "If you want to break the rules, you have Gordon."

Steele needed Mark's by-the-book approach to legal practice to keep Hi-Tech clear of the regulators. For everything else, he had Gordon Stanton, Hi-Tech's in-house counsel and resident bully who had no qualms about straying from the right side of the law.

"You're too uptight," Steele scoffed. "You need to relax. Let go. Get your head out of the law books and spice up your life. You haven't been to one of my parties in years."

Mark gritted his teeth and bit back his resentment in the name of client relations. "Thanks for the advice."

As usual, Steele didn't take the hint. "You need a woman, Mark. It's been years since your girlfriend died. You need to move on. Find someone new."

Mark bristled at the oblique reference to Claire. Steele had some nerve mentioning her. He knew Claire only from the few occasions Mark had let her accompany him to Steele's extravagant parties. Not well enough to even begin to understand the depth of Mark's guilt over her death.

Steele pulled out his cell phone and flipped to a picture of a doe-eyed blonde. "Melody. We've been together for over a year now."

Mark nodded at the picture. "Pretty."

"She reminds me of her...Claire."

Mark couldn't stifle his grunt of irritation. He tapped his pen on the table and willed the break to end.

"Melody's my longest relationship," Steele said. "Too long, actually. Men aren't designed to be monogamous. That's why kitty caught my eye. I couldn't hold out the way you do."

"I don't have time to even look after myself, much less put in the time to build a relationship." Nor did he have the inclination to open himself up again. His heart had been rubbed raw once before and he had no intention of repeating the experience.

Steele's gaze drifted across the table to Katy's jacket hanging on her seat. "She's a pretty little kitty, probably a wildcat in bed, but she needs to be tamed by someone with the "steel" to handle her." He laughed at his own joke.

Mine.

A wave of possessiveness surged through Mark's body. Unexpected. Unwanted. Undeniable. He balled his hands into fists and concentrated on keeping them down by his sides.

Although Steele didn't know it yet, for the first time ever, he wasn't going to get what he wanted.

And unless Mark could resolve the potential conflict, neither would he.

"You were amazing." Martha hugged herself as they walked down the hallway. "I've never heard anyone speak to him like that. He's Darkon Steele. He has ministers and regulators eating out of his hand and women falling at his feet. Boy was Jimmy right when he recommended your firm."

Katy cringed. She just wanted to erase the last stressful hour from her memory. How could Fate be so cruel? If she'd had any thoughts about seeing Mark again, she could just lay them to rest. No way would she risk her career on a legal conflict. Especially with a man who had so easily broken down her defenses.

"What did you want to tell me earlier?" She stopped beside a glass barrier overlooking the open atrium. Sunshine sparkled in the windows overhead and danced off the leaves on the trees scattered in the foyer below.

"I wanted to tell you about this note." Martha reached into her purse and pulled out a crumpled piece of paper.

Katy smoothed the page and skimmed over a list of names and phone numbers, none of which were familiar.

"It's from Martin Kowalski. He was a senior researcher at Hi-Tech. He was like a mentor to me, although we didn't work in the same lab. He didn't agree with some things they were doing so he quit. When I told him I had gone to the regulators, he gave me this list and said it would help prove my allegations. He asked me not to tell them where I got it."

Katy turned the paper over. "Did you show this to your previous lawyer?"

Martha shook her head. "He was too busy to even meet with me and I didn't really trust him. I got the feeling he saw this as another routine dismissal case. But you seem more interested and...aggressive."

Katy gave her a wry smile. "Assertive maybe, but not usually aggressive."

She knew when to pull back. Except today. What the hell had happened in there? She had faced down the best and brightest of the corporate world but something about Steele turned her knees to jelly. She sensed in him the same streak of cruelty Steven hid so well beneath his cloak of respectability.

Unlike Mark. She barely knew him, but he had already shown her he had limits...and compassion. "What did the regulators say?"

Martha sighed. "The regulators weren't interested in the list. They had already decided my claim had no merit."

Katy tucked the paper into her folder. "Who are the men on the list?"

Martha shrugged her shoulders. "I didn't recognize their names. I had a friend at Hi-Tech search through the employee database for me. None of the names turned up. Martin wouldn't say anything else about it. I think he's scared."

A class of law students approached, talking in hushed whispers about a trial they'd just watched. Katy put a finger to her lips, silencing her client, until they were out of earshot.

"Scared of what?"

"Scared of the company, but mostly of Mr. Steele." She squeezed Katy's hand. "You did great in there. Mr. Steele is the most intimidating person I've ever met. Usually when I'm near him, my heart pounds."

Mark stepped out into the hallway and caught Katy's gaze. Her heart skipped a beat and she drew in a ragged breath.

"I know what you mean."

"Objection."

Katy gave an exasperated sigh. She had long passed the point of hiding her frustration. Mark seemed determined to stop her from getting any evidence from Steele, no matter how trivial. As a result, she had been unable to confirm Martha's story and the day was almost over.

"What is it this time?" She let sarcasm drip from every word, enjoying the small pleasure of hearing his slight grunt of irritation.

"Your question isn't relevant to the pleaded case. You know better."

Katy raised her eyebrows. "I know better?"

Steele smirked. She hadn't realized his lips could do anything but frown.

Knowing she was about to lose her cool, she turned to Tim. "Off the record please if Mr. Richards doesn't object to *that*."

She folded her arms and glared at her adversary across the table. She had conducted hundreds of examinations for discovery and dozens of trials. She had dealt with difficult counsel and stubborn witnesses. But Mark wound her up more than anyone ever had and damned if she could figure out why. He seemed to have a sixth sense about which objections would irritate her the most.

"No objection." His cool tone added fuel to her fire and her body heated in anger. Or was it something else?

Tim turned off the recorder and sat back to watch the show.

"You were saying, Ms. Sinclair?" Mark raised a questioning eyebrow.

Katy gritted her teeth at his apparent indifference. She would get a response out of his client if it killed her. But first she had to deal with his disrespectful behavior.

"We need a word in private."

Mark pushed back his chair. "Good idea. I don't think our clients are interested in the legal posturing that threatens to overshadow the real reason we're here."

Katy's mouth dropped open at his clipped tone. Aha. She had ruffled his feathers. Maybe he was not as imperturbable as she had thought.

He stood and walked over to the door. "Twenty-minute break?"

"Agreed." Katy dropped her file down on the table and waited until Martha and Tim left before following Mark into the hallway.

"I think we should go somewhere we can't be overheard. There's an alcove down this way." He didn't wait for her to answer but disappeared around the corner.

Arrogant. Intractable. Condescending.

She considered a few less flattering words to use in the tongue-lashing she intended to give him. He had no reason for making the discovery such a total nightmare unless he was hiding something. But that would be against the rules, and it wouldn't work with her.

Katy followed him to a small alcove hidden at the end of the unused hallway and peered inside. Big, dark and dusty. She wrinkled her nose at the smell of old books. "I'm not going in there," she snapped. "The hallway is fine."

"Then you might want to lower your voice."

Katy snorted. "As I'm sure you've picked up today, I don't like being told what to do."

He took a step forward, closing the distance between them. His broad shoulders and imposing height almost entirely blocked her view of the hallway beyond. "Actually, I picked that up on Friday night." His lips curved into a suggestive smile.

Desire spiked through her body with such intensity she forgot to breathe.

Totally inappropriate.

Inappropriately thrilling.

Her face flushed and she looked away. She had thought, even hoped, he wouldn't bring up her indiscretion at the club. But, after spending a day with him in the discovery, she should have known he would give her no quarter, personally or professionally.

"Not here," she muttered.

He ran the back of his finger lightly over her cheek. "I couldn't believe it when I first saw you this morning. I thought I'd never see you again."

Hot, searing flames of need licked over her body. The world narrowed to the secluded alcove, the scent of sandalwood, and the dark, sensual male towering over her.

Fiercely arousing.

Strictly forbidden.

She drew in a ragged breath. "Well, now you'll get your fill. We'll be stuck in this case for at least two years and I'm sure we'll see each other every few weeks in court."

He shook his head and took a step closer. "It won't be enough."

His scent, spicy, exotic and achingly familiar, engulfed her, teasing her with memories of the wine cellar and the sensual caress of his hands over her body.

"What do you mean?" The inane question squeaked through her lips. There could be nothing between them while they opposed each other on the same case. She pressed her hands against his crisp, white shirt, intending to push him away.

Mistake. Her fingers instinctively fanned out over the cool, smooth cotton covering the rock-hard expanse of his chest. Mark hissed in a breath. She fought the fierce urge to slide her hands around his body and pull him close.

His lips quirked into a smile. "I won't let you run away again."

"I didn't run away. I made a reasoned decision to leave and I'm about to do it again." Her hands tingled as she forced her fingers to lift away, one by painful one.

Once she had detached herself, she stepped back and took a deep breath. "Didn't we come out here to discuss something? I believe it had to do with your lack of respect. I suppose we'd also better address the potential conflict."

Even to her ears it sounded ridiculous. How could she expect respect after their encounter in the wine cellar? And yet, she did. The courtroom and the club were totally different worlds.

He studied her for a long moment. "You play it very close to the line with my client, and you make it extremely difficult to concentrate. But I may have overcompensated and been a tad harsh."

Katy's eyes widened. "A tad harsh? You toss out objections like sweets in a parade."

"If I had known you thought they were sweet, I'd have thrown out a few more."

A small smile curved her mouth. "I don't like sweets."

"Such a shame." He tucked an errant strand of hair behind her ear. "I'm particularly fond of sugar."

Liquid fire shot to her core. She forced herself backward, step by step, until she reached the brightly lit corridor. "What about the potential conflict?"

"We've only had one encounter, and a brief one at that. I doubt the Law Society would consider that worthy of sanction."

"But...you...touched me." The words came out in a harsh whisper.

"Yes. And you touched me."

His words charged the already electric air between them. Desire, barely controlled, burned in his eyes. For a long moment neither of them moved.

Finally Mark drew in a ragged breath and broke the connection. "Do you think it will impair your ability to run the case?"

Katy narrowed her eyes. "Of course not. But, obviously, I can't see you again outside the courthouse."

A smile ghosted his lips and she caught the hint of a challenge in his deep, brown eyes. "What if you have to come back to the club?"

"I don't."

"What if Valerie didn't sign the statement and you had to ask for an adjournment of the hearing to find her?"

Katy narrowed her eyes. "How do you know about that?"

"Wild guess."

"Trixie told you." She had called the club on Monday and talked to the helpful receptionist after Valerie failed to show up at her office.

"I never divulge my sources," he rumbled.

"Why would I come back to the club? I'll just have her come to my office."

Mark shook his head. "She won't go to your office. She's afraid of anything to do with the law—including lawyers. She had a rough start in life. That's why she didn't show up. If you want your statement signed, you'll have to go to her. She's working on Friday. Seven to two."

A shot of adrenaline streamed into Katy's veins, and for a moment she forgot to breathe.

"Will you be there?" Her heart thudded in her chest.

He gave her a slow, sensual smile. "Do you want me to be there, sugar?"

She put her hands on her hips to hide her trembling fingers. "If you are there, you have to promise to behave."

"Do you promise to sheathe those claws, little wildcat? Will you stop provoking my client?"

"Never." Her temper flared, warming her blood.

"I didn't think so," he chuckled. "And I don't make promises I can't keep."

He brushed past her and stepped into the hallway. Katy spun around, reeling at the electric jolt his brief touch had sent through her body.

"Looks like we're in for a fun afternoon." He looked back over his shoulder and winked.

"You're a dangerous man," she muttered, never thinking he would hear.

His eyes darkened, almost to black. "Sugar, you have no idea."

Chapter Five

The doorbell rang.

The jarring cacophony of discordant chimes reminded Katy she had neglected to erase every trace of Steven from the house. The doorbell had been one of the worst presents she had ever received from him.

She opened the door and a uniformed courier thrust a large, white box tied with a purple ribbon into her hands. "Katy Sinclair?"

"Yes."

"What is it, Mom?" Melissa appeared behind her as she closed the door.

"It's just a dress. I'm going out tonight and needed something new to wear. They had to alter it so I couldn't take it home right away." Also, she hadn't wanted anyone in the firm to know she had used up two billable hours of her day to shop in the boutique shops of Yaletown.

They took the box into the kitchen and Melissa perched on one of the bar stools while Katy pulled on the ends of the huge bow. The fabric parted with a soft hiss and she dropped the purple satin into Melissa's waiting hands before pulling off the lid.

A froth of pink tissue paper exploded upward.

Melissa leaned over the box and they pulled the tissue apart.

"Mom, it's so pretty!"

Katy's eyes widened and she smashed down the paper to hide the contents of the box from Melissa's innocent seven-year-old eyes. In the store, the helpful, young shop attendant had assured her the dress was edgy but appropriate for someone her age to wear to a club like Carpe Noctem. But here at home, in front of her daughter, it seemed too risqué.

What on earth was I thinking?

"Mom, take it out."

"Your dad will be here soon, darling. Go and get ready."

"But..."

"Go, please, Melissa. It's just a dress."

Melissa reluctantly left the kitchen and Katy took another peek into the box. Black lace, pink satin ribbons and a brush of pink frills over a very short, black skirt. A corset dress. Her corset dress.

The kitchen door burst open. Katy slammed the lid back on the box and turned to see Steven heading for the fridge.

"Everyone ready to go?"

"Steven, I told you to knock or ring the bell. Close the fridge. I'm sure you have food at your house."

Steven ignored her and took a sandwich from Justin's lunch bag. "What's in the box?"

Melissa joined them in the kitchen. "It's a dress. Mom's going out tonight."

"Don't you have work to do?" Steven frowned. "Where are you going? Do you have a date? Why are you getting all dressed up?"

Katy tuned out the barrage of questions and tucked the box under her arm. Why did he care? Ah yes, she had almost forgotten, Sally dumped him. The pretty blonde intern had probably found herself a nice younger man. Steven favored impressionable young girls who never stuck around for long. Katy had been the one unlucky enough to marry him.

She kissed the kids goodbye and headed upstairs with the box. When she saw Steven's Volvo heading down the street, she stripped off her clothes and slipped on the dress. The cool, silk inner lining caressed her skin, and the corset top hugged every contour of her body. She struggled with the laces at the back, and then twirled slowly in front of the mirror. The dress smoothed out her jiggles, highlighted her narrow waist, and pushed her breasts dangerously high above the half cups. The pink frills gave it a modicum of decency, but only just.

She twirled again and frowned. The skirt could have been longer. She wasn't quite ready for public exposure of her thighs. And yet, compared to the other women in the club, she would still be overdressed. She slipped on a pair of black stilettos and smiled at the vixen in the mirror.

"What the hell are you wearing?" Steven appeared in her mirror as a reflection in the doorway, his face a mixture of shock and disgust.

How had he managed to get upstairs without her hearing him?

Her cheeks blazed. "It's for a...costume party. What are you doing back here?"

"Melissa forgot her inhaler." He stepped into the room and raked his gaze over her body. "A costume party? You're supposed to actually wear a costume. You can't go out dressed like that. It's indecent. You're a lawyer. You have children, for goodness sake. You aren't young any more. What would people think?"

"Get out, Steven." She trembled with the force of her anger. "The inhaler is on her bedside table."

He took a step toward her. "What kind of mother are you? Is this how you're spending your free time? Parading yourself around the city in your underwear?"

His all too familiar sneer sent chills down her spine.

"Go. Now." She stomped across the room and slammed the bedroom door closed, clenching her teeth to stop from saying anything she might regret at a custody hearing.

Minutes later his Volvo disappeared down the road and she collapsed on the bed. Although she hated to admit it, he was right. She no longer had the body for a dress like this or the confidence to wear it. With a sigh, she undid the laces and laid it gently back in the box.

"Katy! Nice to see you back." Trixie greeted Katy at the door with a quick hug and then stepped away and frowned. "Sorry, babe. No suits allowed."

Katy pulled her eyes away from Trixie's strategically sequined, red spandex dress. Maybe it was actually a tube top, which would explain why it only just reached the top of her thighs. And where did Trixie go to buy four-inch, fire-red stilettos with sparkly heels? Definitely not the department store where Katy usually shopped.

"I'm not staying," she said. "I just need to see Valerie for a minute."

Trixie shook her head. "Tony would kill me if I let you in dressed like that. We have a dress code. He made an exception for you last time, but he won't do it again."

Katy sighed. "Could you take a quick look around for me and ask her to come out if you see her?"

"Sure thing." Trixie disappeared through the red door and returned five minutes later. "She hasn't shown up for work. Tony has been trying to get in touch with her. He said you can go in and wait, but you'll need to change. Do you have anything else to wear?"

Katy swallowed. "I have a dress in the car, but I don't know what I was thinking. It's not really appropriate. I was going to return it tomorrow."

"Go." Trixie spun her around and nudged her toward the door. "Bring it in and let me decide. I promise to be totally honest."

Fifteen minutes later, Katy stood in the club change room, wincing under Trixie's intense scrutiny of her new dress.

"Corset virgin," Trixie muttered. "I see it all the time."

"What's wrong?" Katy's voice rose as her anxiety level climbed. "I shouldn't be wearing it, should I? It's not really... I'm too...my thighs." She stammered over all the reasons a mom of two shouldn't be seen in public in a corset dress.

"Are you kidding me?" Trixie grabbed Katy by the shoulders and pretended to shake her. "Have you looked at yourself in a mirror recently? What I wouldn't give to have a body like yours."

"But you look amazing. Really, I shouldn't be wearing it while I'm here on business." She turned away and her shoulders slumped. "I'll change and wait for her outside."

"You will not." Trixie patted her arm. "Let me fix you up and see what you think."

After ten minutes of being subjected to Trixie's tugging and pulling, Katy's respect for her great, great grandmother had increased tenfold.

"Trixie, I can't breathe. It's way too tight." Her breasts seemed to have doubled in size and now threatened to explode from the top of the corset. She stared in amazement at the cleavage she had only ever dreamed of having.

"Just pant. Short, quick breaths. Panting is good. Men love it. Makes them think you're desperate for them. And, wow, babe, if your waist gets any smaller you might topple over."

"If you tie it any tighter, I might pass out."

"Men love that too. The old swooning at their feet routine. Gets them every time. Brings out the protective instinct and they go crazy."

Katy laughed. "Sounds like you have a lot of experience."

Trixie winked at her in the mirror and tied the ends of the corset ribbons into a bow. "I can modestly say I have sampled a moderate selection of the opposite sex."

She ushered Katy out of the change room and then led her through the red door and into the club.

"Do you have a boyfriend?" Katy gasped after each word as she struggled to walk, talk and breathe at the same time.

"I've got my eye on someone but he's got some serious issues," Trixie said, looking back over her shoulder. "Lost his wife a few years ago in a skiing accident and just plays by the night now in the back room."

Before Katy could ask about the object of Trixie's affections, she caught sight of Mark stalking toward them.

God, what a sight.

His black leather trousers and tight, black T-shirt highlighted every muscle and plane on his sculpted body. Could he look any more breathtaking or...dangerous?

"Would you look at that," Trixie whispered. "Someone has eyes only for you. Good thing my heart is already taken."

"That's some dress, Trixie." Mark stopped in front of them and gave Trixie a wink.

Trixie giggled. "I like to keep my boys happy."

"I've been waiting for you, sugar." Mark's gaze swept over Katy's body, blazing a heated trail along her skin. When his eyes fixed on her breasts, Katy flushed, embarrassed at the volume Trixie had magically created.

"Very nice," he rumbled.

Very nice? Curtains were very nice. Hats were very nice. If she had to endure being tarted up to get into the club, albeit in very expensive and beautiful tart wear, he could at least think of a better adverb. She narrowed her eyes, but a subtle shake of Trixie's head stopped her from letting him know exactly what she thought of "very nice".

"I need to talk to Valerie, and apparently I wasn't allowed into the club wearing a suit. Isn't that right, Trixie?" She looked to Trixie for confirmation only to see Trixie's departing back.

"I'll tell Tony to give her a raise," Mark murmured. His eyes, dark with desire, sent shivers dancing up her spine.

"Do you know when Valerie's coming in?"

He caressed her cheek, scorching her skin with his touch.

"Not until very late, I hope."

Katy's throat tightened. "You promised to behave."

He leaned down and whispered against her neck, "I promised nothing."

Heart thundering against her ribs, she cupped his cheek with her hand and brushed her thumb over his prickly five o'clock shadow. The sharp, fresh scent of his cologne mixed with his familiar scent of sandalwood scent tingles through her veins. Boldly, she followed the line of his jaw to his ear and then traced gently along the shell. Anticipation ratcheted through her. How far would he let her go?

Mark hissed in a breath and covered her hand with his own, drawing it away. "You also must behave, Ms. Sinclair. You may look, but don't touch."

"You touched me. It's only fair."

"There's nothing fair about you in that dress."

He likes my dress. Katy tried to suppress a smile.

"Well, look who is back." Tony's voice sliced through the heat sizzling between them.

They exchanged greetings. Like Mark, Tony made no effort to hide his blatant appraisal of her attire. He motioned to her dress with a wicked grin. "This is why I have a dress code. Much better than the suit. Much."

"Did you want something or did you just come to ogle?" Mark narrowed his eyes and took a step closer to Katy.

"I can't get Valerie on the phone," Tony said, his brow creasing in a frown. "I'm worried. I talked to her earlier today and she said she was coming in. She's never missed a shift. Can you drive by her place and make sure she's okay? We're already short-staffed tonight and I can't spare anyone to go and check on her."

Mark glanced over at Katy. "Do you want to come with me? If she's there, you can get her to sign your statement."

Katy nodded. If she didn't get the statement signed by Monday, she would have a hard time convincing a judge to reduce Jimmy's bail and he would be stuck in jail until his trial.

"I'll have to change first."

"I like you the way you are." Mark slid his hand around her waist and pulled her toward him. "Delectable."

He nuzzled her neck and fire leaped deep inside her. She barely registered Tony's departure as she melted against Mark's broad chest.

"What happened to look but don't touch?" Her voice caught in her throat when Mark nipped her earlobe.

"That only applies to you," he whispered. "I am totally unable to resist a beautiful lawyer in a corset."

"Well, then I'd better take it off, or we'll be heading down to the Law Society office for a friendly fireside chat in no time." Katy tried to step away, but Mark held her firm.

"Mmm. Dress off. That would be better. Well worth the risk."

Katy closed her eyes, struggling for calm as fire swept through her body incinerating everything in its path. Clenching her teeth, she took a deep breath and pushed him back. "Changing. Now. Do not follow me."

She shuddered when he released her and then beat a hasty retreat to the change room. Either he was a master player and an expert manipulator, or they were one heck of a volatile combination.

And right now, she didn't need any complications in her life.

To Katy's surprise, it was very easy to break into an apartment, even on Vancouver's busy Beach Avenue. When Valerie didn't answer her buzzer, they waited until one of the tenants came home and followed him inside. Easier still, was their entry into Valerie's apartment, assisted by the broken lock on the door.

Valerie wasn't in the living area or the kitchen. They walked down a narrow hallway and into a very pink, very feminine bedroom. Fluffy toys filled the shelves along with photographs in decorative, heart-shaped frames. Lingerie and clothing covered the white wooden furniture and littered the pink plush carpet underfoot. A huge four-poster bed dominated the room.

An occupied bed.

Katy's hand flew to her mouth as she struggled to process the sight in front of her.

Recognizable only by her short, black bob, Valerie lay curled in a fetal position in the midst of a pink froth of linen.

Hideously swollen. Horrendously disfigured.

Dead.

Katy gasped and buried her face in Mark's chest. "Oh God. What happened to her?"

"I don't know," Mark said, his voice tight. "I'll call nine-one-one and then I'll call my friend, James. He's a homicide cop."

Katy remembered the man with the ice blue eyes from her last visit to the club. She wouldn't want to be a criminal with James on her tail. Based on looks alone, she suspected he would be relentless in his pursuit of any wrongdoer—and merciless when he caught his prey.

Her thoughts of criminals led to thoughts of her client and she excused herself to call Jimmy. She stepped out into the hallway. Calling someone in prison was never an easy task, but she managed to get through and break the bad news.

If Jimmy was distraught, she couldn't tell through the shouting and yelling on the other end of the phone.

"I told her not to touch them, but she obviously didn't listen." Jimmy swore and cursed Valerie for her stupidity and then his voice became urgent. "There should be a plastic bag with some pills in her bedroom. You need to get it before the police get there."

Katy stiffened. "I can't take anything from a crime scene."

"What kind of lawyer are you?" Jimmy growled. "You're supposed to protect me and keep me outta jail. It's not a crime scene until the police get there. Go get the bag. Now."

"I'm sorry. I can't," Katy whispered, worried Mark might overhear. But it was too late. Jimmy was gone.

James's protective suit crinkled when he bent down to examine the body. He didn't know Valerie well, but they had spoken at the club several times and he had bought her the occasional drink when Jimmy was late picking her up. Pretty girl. Such a waste.

The cloying smell of heavy perfume permeated his protective mask. He righted the spilled bottle on the night table beside the bed with a gloved hand.

"Bag." Someone from the forensics squad placed an evidence bag in his outstretched fingers, and he dropped the perfume bottle inside and sealed it. The scent remained strong. James bent down for a closer look. The perfume had dripped down the nightstand and had been caught by a plastic bag lying on the carpet.

"Bag." He put the perfumed bag in the evidence bag and frowned. Another plastic bag. Another swollen body. There had to be a connection. He had been around too long to believe in coincidence.

"Anyone talk to her boyfriend, Jimmy Rider?"

"We checked him out," Mike said, squatting down beside him. "He's currently in jail for assault, possession and dealing. Apparently, he tried to sell unlicensed pharmaceuticals to an undercover operative and then got away. A beat cop picked him up a few blocks later and he resisted arrest. He said the police had the wrong guy."

James snorted. "They all say that."

He pushed himself to his feet. "I want a sniffer dog up here and over at Garcia's place. Check Garcia's cab as well for any drug residue. I'm going down to the station to interview the two lawyers who found her."

Outside the apartment complex, he shed his protective suit and headed for his vehicle.

"Hunter."

James recognized the voice and kept walking. Footsteps rang out behind him. He reached his Crown Victoria and pulled out his keys.

"Hunter, if you don't talk to me, I'll print based on rumors."

He spun around and glared at Phillip Keegan, Vancouver's most irritating crime reporter. Keegan flashed a set of perfect pearly whites and James wondered for the umpteenth time why a guy who looked like a damn blond Adonis had chosen the underpaid life of a journalist.

"No comment."

"I'm hearing rumors about elephant people in our midst. Care to comment?" Keegan held up a small recorder.

James pulled open the car door and stepped inside. "Maybe there's a circus in town."

"Funny. You're a funny a cop, Hunter." Keegan stepped in front of the door, preventing James from slamming it closed.

"You wouldn't think so if I held a gun to your head," James growled.

"I hope you aren't threatening me. Someone needs to find out where the elephant people are coming from before they hurt someone. I wouldn't want one of Vancouver's finest detectives languishing in jail when the city is overrun."

"At least I wouldn't have to see you."

Keegan put his hand on the roof of the vehicle and leaned toward James. "How about I smooth things over with a joke? You used to like jokes when we started our little arrangement."

James looked up at Keegan's hand and then locked his gaze on the reporter until Keegan removed his hand and backed away.

Unperturbed, Keegan tucked away his recorder and pulled out his notebook. "What do you get when you cross an elephant with a skin doctor?" He flipped through the pages and looked down at James. "You'll like this joke because it's relevant to the case. My sources tell me the victim's skin was grotesquely stretched all over her body."

James reached for the interior door handle.

"A pachydermatologist." Keegan laughed. "Reporters can be funny too."

"You've missed your calling." James leaned back in his seat and sighed. Years of experience trying to dodge the persistent reporter told him he would have to throw Keegan a few crumbs to make him go away. "I have work to do. You can quote this. Accidental death. Possibly an allergic reaction. Times two."

Keegan snorted. "I'm not buying it. And if I don't buy it, my discerning readers won't either. People have allergic reactions every day. They don't swell up twice the size and die grossly disfigured. They also don't all have a common friend."

James hissed in a breath. Damn Keegan. Where did he get his information? "You have a loose-lipped friend, likely in the coroner's office, who is about to lose his job. But, you have my attention."

"Tell me an elephant joke and I'll give you a name."

James growled. "How about I tell you the joke about the reporter who got his head shoved up an elephant's ass? Give me the name."

"Jimmy Rider."

James froze and steeled himself to hide his surprise. "Her boyfriend. Currently in jail. Tell me something I don't know."

"He's connected to Garcia."

"How? You're dying to tell me. Go ahead."

"You haven't given me anything worth printing." Keegan tapped his notepad. "I have a deadline. This is going to be in tomorrow's paper with or without your comments."

James racked his brain to think of a way to satisfy Keegan without compromising the case. "There may be third party interest in this one."

"A bit obscure."

"I have every confidence you'll figure it out. Come by the station and let me know when you do." James swung the door closed forcing Keegan to jump out of the way. He pulled away from the curb and rolled down the window. "Hey, Keegan. Don't forget to bring the popcorn."

"Is that your idea of a first date?"

Mark looked up, bleary-eyed, as James appeared in front of him and gestured toward Katy asleep in the crook of Mark's arm. Two o'clock in the morning and the Vancouver Main Street police station was buzzing with activity. He hadn't even heard James approach.

"Where have you been?" he snapped. "We've been waiting here for hours. Your colleagues wouldn't let us leave until we gave you a statement. Friendly types. They haven't said a word to us since we got here. Didn't even offer us a cup of coffee."

James chuckled. "You probably scared them off. Your scowl would unnerve even the hardest of men."

Katy stirred in her sleep and Mark tightened his arm around her, pressing her soft, warm body closer to his side.

"I thought you told me at the bar the other night you had a conflict." James raised a questioning eyebrow. "You don't look too conflicted to me."

Mark sighed. "I feel conflicted. I would drop the damn case in a second but the client's work is the only thing keeping the firm afloat."

Shouts echoed down the corridor. An intoxicated teenager stumbled toward them seemingly oblivious to the commotion behind him. Seconds later he lay face down on the floor, his hands cuffed behind his back by two angry policemen.

"What about her?" James didn't even look over when the teenager threw up in a wastepaper basket. "Can she drop the case?"

Mark shrugged. "I think her firm gave it to her as a partnership test case. If it was me in this economic climate, I wouldn't drop it, and I don't think she will either."

"Conflict."

"Exactly."

James gave him a sympathetic look. "Why did you take her to the apartment?"

"She's acting for Val's boyfriend in a criminal case. I think Val was his alibi, but she didn't turn up at Katy's office to sign her statement.

Katy came with me in case Val was at home."

"I didn't like that guy," James said. "I met him a few times when he came to pick up Val. There was something off about him. I never understood why she didn't throw him out when she found out he was screwing around on her."

Mark stroked his fingers along the curve of Katy's waist. "She lost perspective after he dragged her into the drug scene. Tony was helping her clean up her act. I haven't told him yet, but he's going to take it hard."

James scrubbed his hand over his face and looked down at Katy. "I'm surprised her firm would give her the case. He's got some pretty serious charges against him. Apparently he has a reputation for charming women into his bed, roughing them up and then stealing from them. Not someone I would trust around a young, pretty female lawyer."

Mark agreed, and he wanted to know which of her partners had given her the case. She deserved to know that her supervising partner wasn't looking out for her best interests. Plus, he had a few things to say to the bastard after the case was done.

James's phone buzzed and he checked the message. "I've got to make a quick call. Bring her down to my office in five minutes and we can get those statements out of the way."

Mark looked down at Katy's silken hair spread out over his chest and tightened his arm around her. "I'll be there in half an hour."

"You're making it worse every minute you sit there with her in your arms."

"I can handle it."

"Like you handled Claire?" James lowered his voice. "You've spent ten years on your own because you couldn't deal with your guilt and you weren't to blame for her death. This time, if you're both sanctioned by the Law Society, the guilt will be real."

"Back off," Mark growled. He didn't want to be reminded of the conflict, or the repercussions. He definitely didn't want to be reminded about Claire. He just wanted to sit and think. He wanted to mourn the loss of his friend. And he wanted to hold Katy in his arms as long as he possibly could.

James took one last look at them and shrugged his shoulders. "Don't say I didn't warn you."

Chapter Six

"What are you doing here?" Katy froze, her hand on the door to Courtroom Five. She had almost missed Mark standing in the shadow of the nearby greenery, but when he detached himself from the wall, there was no mistaking the broad shoulders and the tailored, wool suit draped over taut muscles and skirting his trim waist.

"I believe the customary greeting for opposing counsel is hello." His dark eyes crinkled and he walked toward her.

Ambush.

Infuriated, she folded her arms and glared.

Mark stopped a foot away, his lips curling into a smile. "Something wrong, sugar?"

Not trusting herself to speak, Katy pulled open the heavy oak door and stormed into the courtroom.

"You're looking a little flushed," Mark murmured, following close behind her.

Katy gritted her teeth and dropped her briefcase on the counsel table at the front of the courtroom. While Mark unpacked his briefcase, she emptied her supplies pencil by pencil, paper by paper, until she had her betraying body under control.

"You still haven't answered my question." She turned to glare at him. "What are you doing here?"

"You still haven't said hello." He perched on the edge of her table and examined the spread before him. "That's a lot of stationery for a five-minute hearing."

Katy slammed the last pencil on the table and tried not to think about waking up in his arms in the police station or the gentle brush of his lips on her forehead when he told her James had finally arrived.

Enemy. Enemy. Enemy.

"I'm assuming this is an ambush, in which case you do not deserve a greeting of any kind." She had hoped for a few minutes alone to prepare for the hearing. Now it seemed unlikely she would even have a minute of peace.

"Clever girl. Yes, it's an ambush but it doesn't mean you can't observe the usual social niceties."

She straightened the pencils into a neat line, ensuring they all faced the same direction. "Don't be condescending. You said you weren't going to oppose the motion. I just want to interview a few people from Hi-Tech. It's a simple request. You don't need to be here."

He shrugged. "I changed my mind."

"You changed your mind? At the last minute? I'm not prepared to argue the motion. I don't have any cases with me, and no evidence. I thought it was going by consent."

"That is the point of an ambush." He chuckled. "Are you afraid of me, sugar? Don't think you can handle me? Maybe we should call in the partner on the file. Your office isn't far away."

Katy closed her eyes and took a deep breath. No one, not even Steven, had ever riled her up as fast as Mark did in court. "Here we go again. Do I threaten you? You seem to have great difficulty believing I am capable of running the case."

"If I had any doubt about your ability to run the case, I wouldn't have bothered to come. I would have sent an associate. You should be flattered I'm here." The teasing note in his voice did little to placate her.

"Do I look flattered?" She pressed her lips together and glared.

"You look hot," he murmured. "Like you did when we spent the night together."

Katy sucked in a sharp breath. "We were in a police station. I fell asleep on a bench. You can't read anything into that."

His eyes softened. "Speak for yourself."

Katy drew in a ragged breath. Although she would never tell him, she hadn't wanted those precious moments in the police station to end. For the first time in as long as she could remember, she had felt safe, content. She would have been happy to stay in his arms all night long. Unfortunately, James had had other ideas.

"We can't do this. You said it yourself." She gave him a questioning look. "Unless your client wants to settle? I'm sure my client would consider a fair offer."

Mark closed the distance between them. "As he said in the discovery, he thinks your client is a spy. He won't settle."

"So we're back where we started." Her heart drummed erratically in her chest as his scent, spicy and masculine, surrounded her.

He looked behind him at the empty courtroom and then cupped her cheek in his warm palm, drawing her close. "No, sugar. The more I get to know you, the harder you are to resist."

Katy shivered, confused by his brutal honesty and her own heated response to him. Who was this sinfully sensual man? All she knew for certain was a desire so sharp it hurt. She covered his hand with her own, lacing her fingers between his, intending to pull his hand away. But the fierce hunger in his eyes drew her in. She turned her face into his palm and pressed her lips to his heated skin.

"God, Katy." His voice broke and his fingers curled around her jaw.

The door opened and he released her, pushing her away with a sudden thrust. Katy staggered back and gasped at the sudden loss of contact. She gripped the thick oak table to steady herself and took in a ragged breath.

Maybe his advances were simply a ploy to throw her off balance. Maybe he played young, female associates every day, winning case after case as women toppled like dominos in a lust-induced haze. After all, who could resist a man who smoldered like a glowing coal?

"I guess I'll just have to teach you how to respect me in court," she muttered as he walked across the aisle to his seat. "So lace up those gloves and get ready for a fight."

"Mark. Please. Wait."

Katy hurried down the corridor and slipped into the elevator before the doors slammed shut. Mark had left the courtroom so quickly after their hearing she had almost lost him in the hallway. The elevator began its slow ascent to the top level of the courthouse, and Katy swallowed hard.

"I want to apologize. I didn't know you'd just come from Valerie's funeral until you told the judge. Why didn't you ask for an adjournment? I would have agreed. I'm not without compassion."

Mark looked down at her, a curious mix of sadness and amusement in his eyes. "I'm not so sure about that after your performance in court this afternoon. I'm heading over to the hospital after my next hearing to get all the bruises treated."

Katy blushed. "It wasn't personal."

"Really?" Mark rubbed his knuckles over her cheek. "You went out of your way to slice and dice me. Although I deserved it. I would have done the same if you had ambushed me."

"Are you okay? After the funeral, I mean? I know Valerie was a friend."

Mark shrugged. "Death is never easy, but it was especially hard because she was young and she had turned her life around. And Tony...he and Valerie..." Katy wrapped her arms around him and gave him a hug. "I'm so sorry."

He drew her into his embrace and rested his cheek on her head. For a long moment, they didn't move. She breathed in the spicy scent of his cologne and for a few glorious seconds, she knew nothing but him and the quiet *ting* of the elevator counting floors.

With a gentle touch, he loosened her grip and dropped his hands. "I'd better go before I take advantage of your compassion and destroy both our careers."

"Drop the case," she pleaded.

His face tightened. "I can't, sugar."

The elevator doors slid open and three lawyers entered, gowned and ready for court. One of them greeted Mark and when he turned to shake hands, Katy slipped out of the elevator.

What the hell was she doing? She didn't need another man in her life. In fact, she had promised herself after the divorce she would enjoy her freedom. Her visits to the club had been part of that promise. She wanted a life unencumbered by the give and take of a relationship. She wanted to find the real Katy, repressed after so many years.

A man would just get in her way.

Or would he?

"How did the hearing go?"

Mark flinched when Steele dropped his briefcase on the boardroom table of the firm's largest meeting room with a loud bang. Always one for a dramatic entrance, Steele didn't care if his audience consisted of one person or one hundred.

"I'd call it a draw. The judge agreed to let Ms. Sinclair interview two people from Hi-Tech's senior management because they could speak directly to her client's job performance, but I was able to convince him not to accede to her request to interview all the lab staff at Hi-Tech."

Steele narrowed his eyes. "Why did she make she make such a broad request?"

"I'm not sure. As colleagues, they aren't in a position to assess her work. If it wasn't such a simple case, I would suspect her of fishing for something."

Steele popped open his briefcase and dragged it across the mahogany table, leaving a large scratch in its wake. "How was our little kitty?"

Mark stiffened and then forced his body to relax to hide his anxiety from his sharp-eyed client. "Wild. I tried to ambush her to get a feel for what we can expect at trial, but it didn't slow her down for a minute. She's quick on her feet, fiercely intelligent and a highly effective speaker with a firm grasp of the law."

Steele laughed. "I think I'll attend the next hearing. I want to see her in action. Maybe I'll be so impressed, I'll want to hire a new lawyer. A wild one."

Mark gave him a cold smile and gritted his teeth. "What can I do for you today?"

Steele pulled a sheaf of papers from his briefcase and pushed them toward Mark. "There was a disturbing article in the newspaper this morning. I won't go into the details—Gordon is handling the fallout for us—but it's clear we've had a security breach at Hi-Tech. As a result, we've had to bring our new product launch forward. I have a couple of loose ends I need you to tie up before that happens."

Mark flipped through the papers. "What needs to be done?"

"Those settlement agreements you're looking at relate to a laboratory accident that occurred over a year ago. I had Gordon prepare them. We wanted to keep the matter strictly internal."

Mark raised his eyebrows. Gordon was barely competent as a lawyer and Steele only asked him to deal with legal matters he knew Mark would refuse to handle. He pushed the papers back across the table. "If it was a matter for Gordon, then it isn't a matter for me. You know my limits."

Steele pushed the papers back. "The settlement is legitimate."

"So, what's the problem?"

"Drafting issues. I asked Gordon to draft a very tight non-disclosure clause. The Board of Directors didn't want any rumors getting out about an unsafe work environment. But now that we're expecting to be a media fixation with the product launch, I'm concerned the clause isn't tight enough. All I need is for the Work Safety regulators to be stomping around my labs, checking for pencils that are too sharp."

Mark skimmed through the documents. "You're right about the contract. The agreement doesn't cover the knock-on effects of the injuries."

"It also doesn't cover the wives," Steele grumbled. "I had Gordon pay them a visit—"

Mark held up a hand. "Don't tell me anything else. I don't want to know what Gordon gets up to. I can fix the agreements for you and draft new ones to cover the wives on the basis they suffered as well, although you might have to throw in something by way of compensation."

Steele waved his hand in a dismissive gesture. "Whatever you think is reasonable. A few hundred thousand is nothing in the grand scheme of things. This new product is going to make billions for the company."

Mark stacked the documents in front of him. "Anything else?"

"I want you to handle it personally. I don't want anyone else to see the file. No partners, no associates, not even administrative staff. When you take the documents for signature, I want you to make it very clear there will be severe consequences if anyone discloses the settlement or any details about the accident."

Mark stiffened. "I'm not Gordon. I won't do what he does. I'll explain but I won't threaten."

"If I wanted Gordon to handle it, I would send Gordon," Steele snapped. "You have your own way of getting a message across. Just make sure it's understood."

"Don't work too late."

Katy smiled as Ted waved goodbye. He didn't mean it, of course. He wanted her to work late. Bill more hours. Make more money. Prove she had what it took to become a partner. The fringe benefits for her would be freedom from Steven's financial noose and the achievement of a lifelong goal. Definitely worth the long hours.

She sipped her latte and licked the creamy foam off her lips. The caffeine boost would keep her going for a few more hours.

She licked again, imagining Mark's lips on hers. How would he taste this time? Would his lips be soft and warm or firm and cool?

Back to work. No kisses for you.

With a sigh, she opened her file and read her notes about Martha's friend, Martin Kowalski, Chief Scientific Officer and one of Hi-Tech's longest-serving employees. Although Martin had made it clear to Martha he didn't want to be involved, he would be an important witness in Martha's case. She took a deep breath and dialed the number Martha had given her.

"Kowalski residence."

Katy introduced herself as Martha's lawyer. She had just started a brief explanation of the dismissal case when Martin interrupted her.

"Where are you calling from? Is your line secure?"

Katy raised her eyebrows. "I'm in my office, and yes, the firm lines are secure. Are you concerned your phone is being monitored?"

"With Hi-Tech, you never know. We have only three minutes to speak before my line will be traced. You've used up thirty-five seconds already."

Katy's eyes widened. Either Martin suffered from extreme paranoia or genuine fear. Regardless, she wouldn't waste any more time. "Why did you give Martha the list of names?"

To her relief, he didn't deny he had authored the note. "To help."

"Help Martha?"

"And people whose lives may be at risk."

Katy sighed. "Could you give me a bit more detail?"

"If I wanted to do that, I would have gone to the regulatory agencies myself or even the police. But whistle-blowers in the pharmaceutical industry have a tendency to meet with terrible accidents. Altruistic as I am, the simple fact is, I want to live."

Katy's heart pounded. *Backtrack. Tease it out of him like a hostile witness.*

"You knew the men on the list, didn't you?"

His voice tightened. "I did."

"When you gave her the list, you told her it would help prove her allegations about falsifying data and reports?"

"Yes."

Katy sighed into the phone. "Martin, I understand you're afraid to speak directly, but you can trust that I will not betray you in any way, or compromise your safety. I just want to help Martha. Would it be easier if you talked directly to her? I understand sometimes people are reluctant to speak to lawyers."

"Martha's a sweet girl," Martin said. "She's already endangered herself. I don't want to make it worse. You have certain protections as a lawyer, and you also have the resources to blow this case out of the water."

Protection? Not with Ted as a boss. He would send her straight into the lion's den if he thought it would help turn a profit.

"I'm only working on her dismissal case," she explained. "A full investigation into all Martha's allegations is beyond my mandate."

"You don't want to investigate because it's not worth your time."

Katy cringed at the bitterness in his voice. "Martin, please."

"You're just like all the other lawyers." Martin's voice dripped with disdain. "You don't give a damn about justice. For you, it's all about the money."

"That's not true." Katy's heart sank. She hadn't expected the call to go this badly. "I want to help Martha. Following up on your note is only indirectly related to the case. It isn't something I had to do."

Silence.

"Martin?"

"It seems we have nothing left to discuss. I put myself at risk by giving Martha the list and talking to you. This is as far as I go."

Katy swallowed and tried a more aggressive tactic. "If you do have relevant information, I could subpoena you and force you to testify at trial. Please don't put me in the position of having to do that."

Martin laughed bitterly. "You'll have a hard time finding me. I'm leaving the country before the whole thing blows up and I'll never come back."

Damn. Subpoenaing a witness from a foreign country was next to impossible.

"Please just take my name and number in case you change your mind," she said. "If you want to say something but have concerns about your safety, I can always arrange a deposition before you leave. Your evidence would be recorded and entered at trial but I would stall disclosure until you were safely away."

"I'll think about it." He took down her name and number. "I'm sorry I can't be more help, but we're out of time. Don't call me again."

"Wait. Who are the men on the list? Where are they? Did something happen to them?" But she had waited too long to ask the crucial questions.

Mark's Audi TT purred down the TransCanada Highway. Although an associate should have handled the trip to Langley, he welcomed the opportunity for a rare drive in his only extravagance, and the time to think. One thought dominated his mind.

Katy.

Battling the little wildcat in the courtroom had been an exquisite torture. Part of him thrilled at the challenge of a worthy opponent and delighted in their verbal sparring, while the other part wanted to protect her from every harsh word and legal trick he threw her way.

He racked his brain trying to think of a way around the professional conflict. But if he removed the barrier between them, then what? Did he want her in his bed for a night, or did he want something more? He still knew so little about her. But what he had seen had awakened a hunger so fierce he was already veering down the path toward professional ruin.

Before he knew it, almost an hour had passed by and he was no closer to an answer than he had been when he started the drive. He pulled off the highway and took the exit into the heart of the sleepy suburb. A few turns later, he pulled up in front of a tidy, two-story, white stucco house. Planters filled with flowers dotted the well-kept lawn and marked a path up to the covered wooden porch. He had once dreamed of having a house like this and a wife and children to welcome him home. But that dream had died long ago.

Julia Davidson welcomed him into her home and brought him a cup of coffee. Although well into her fifties, her trim body moved with quick efficiency. But her face, lined with stress and exhaustion, aged her beyond her years.

She listened attentively while he outlined Steele's offer and explained the inconsistencies in the existing contract, but when he finished, she frowned.

"I'm not sure I completely understand, Mr. Richards. Why does Hi-Tech want to give me $100,000?" Julia settled herself on a well-worn, brown velveteen couch across from him.

"The company wants to compensate you for the suffering you've endured as a result of the accident." He still didn't know the details of the accident and Steele had not been forthcoming when he had asked. "It would be helpful if I could talk to both you and your husband at the same time."

Julia hesitated for a moment, and then led him to a dimly lit bedroom. Although the file put Peter Davidson at fifty-five years old, the man on the bed looked well over eighty.

If he was a man.

Mark struggled to stem his horror as he looked at the twisted face in front of him. Large swellings protruded from Peter's forehead and lower jaw. Dark, empty eyes peered out from beneath a heavy brow.

"What's wrong with him?" he blurted out.

"He has aggressive lymphatic cancer. The doctors have given him only a few months to live."

"And his face?"

Julia walked over to the bed and helped her husband turn his head in Mark's direction. "That's from the accident. He was with his cleaning team in a lab and they spilled some kind of chemical."

"I'm sorry." The words seemed inadequate for Peter's suffering, but he could offer nothing better.

"Thank you." She gave him a sad smile. "You're the first person from Hi-Tech to apologize."

Mark drew in a ragged breath and explained the amended agreement and proposed payment for Julia as well as the non-disclosure provisions preventing the Davidsons from discussing the accident or the settlements. "You should get independent legal advice so you can be certain you've been treated fairly."

Julia looked up in surprise. "The last lawyer Hi-Tech sent told Peter not to take his agreement to another lawyer. He said the offer would be withdrawn if anyone saw it."

"You may have misunderstood." Mark's jaw clenched. He had no doubt Gordon had obtained the signatures under duress.

Julia shook her head. "We don't need another lawyer involved and we don't have the time to find someone. Peter doesn't have long to live. We'll sign the agreements."

It took Mark only a few minutes to deal with the formalities and bid farewell to the Davidsons. When the door closed behind him, anxiety flooded through his veins. The entire meeting had left him uneasy. He had always known Gordon played fast and loose with the law, but this time innocent people had suffered and they deserved proper compensation.

Even more unsettling had been the subtle shake of Peter's head when Julia had mentioned the accident.

No, no, no.

Chapter Seven

What am I missing?

Katy flipped through Martha's file for the third time in an hour and then stared out the glass walls of her office. Why would Hi-Tech continue to defend the case in the face of the overwhelming evidence against it? She had interviewed two senior Hi-Tech employees and both had confirmed Martha's exemplary performance. Neither of them had been aware of any policy about after-hours' access. She suspected it didn't exist. Despite her repeated requests, Mark had yet to produce the policy or any other relevant document.

Totally unacceptable.

Too bad she couldn't see his face when he received her application requesting access to all Hi-Tech's documents, and not just those relevant to the case. A blatant fishing expedition. She could hardly wait for the fireworks. The buzz of yesterday's courtroom battle still hadn't worn off. Nor had her embarrassment at her inappropriate behavior. But the minute he had touched her, rational thought had fled. She wouldn't make the same mistake again.

She placed the document in the file and Martha's note fell to the floor. She hadn't followed up on the list of names since her dismal call with Martin. Had he really taken a risk by giving Martha the names and numbers? Was the lead worth pursuing? Even if she uncovered some hidden agenda at Hi-Tech, it wouldn't help Martha's case unless she could tie it directly to the dismissal.

Still, the call with Martin had roused her curiosity. Lives at risk. A mystery to unravel. She tapped her pen on her desk. She didn't have to bill every second of the time she spent on the file. She could pursue the investigation on her own and if it came to nothing, Martha wouldn't have to bear the cost.

Decision made, she lifted the phone and dialed the number for the first name on the list, Robert Cunningham. She introduced herself as a lawyer working against Hi-Tech, and explained the case to the woman on the phone who identified herself as his wife, Patricia.

"He's very ill. He can't come to the phone." Patricia's flat, monotone voice said more than a dozen tears.

Katy sucked in a breath. "I'm so sorry. I didn't know. What's wrong?"

"Cancer. It came on very suddenly. We were adjusting to his other injuries when we got this diagnosis." Her voice dropped to a suspicious whisper. "What do you have against Hi-Tech?"

No harm in telling her. The case is on the public record. "We're alleging Hi-Tech wrongfully dismissed my client from her position as a lab tech at the company. I'm investigating the reasons behind her dismissal. She gave me Robert's name and said she thought he might be able to help."

"How can Robert help?" Patricia's voice tightened. "He was a night contractor. He wouldn't have known any of the permanent employees."

"Did he ever mention hearing or seeing anything unusual?"

Patricia's icy silence told her she had hit a sensitive spot.

"I'm sorry." Katy softened her voice. "I didn't mean to bring up bad memories."

"I would like to help you but I'm not allowed to talk about it," Patricia whispered. "Their lawyer had Robert sign something saying we couldn't discuss what happened the night of the accident."

Mark?

Something clicked in her brain. "Did you sign it too?"

"No, just Robert. Why?"

Katy struggled to keep the emotion out of her voice. "You aren't bound by an agreement you didn't sign. Robert may not be allowed to talk about it, but you are."

Patricia's breath hitched. "I am? Nothing will happen to me? They can't take back the money?"

"Legally, no."

Patricia let loose a ragged sob. "It would be such a relief to talk to someone. Robert doesn't have long to live, and I've been so afraid."

Katy's heart pounded. She forced herself to remain calm and not let her excitement seep into her voice. "I'll come to you, Patricia. Tell me when and where."

"Could I take your number? We have so many hospital appointments. I need to figure out the best time."

Katy gave her contact details and hung up the phone. Buoyed by her success, she dialed the second number, belonging to Peter Davidson. She didn't get past her introduction. His wife, Julia, refused in no uncertain terms to speak to her and hung up without a goodbye.

Katy checked the clock. Too late for any more calls. She closed the file, packed her briefcase and tidied up her desk.

The Crazy Frog ring tone blared in the quiet of her office. Katy fished around in her purse and pulled out her phone as the irritating tune played again. She should never have let Justin near her cell.

"Hello?"

"Katy."

She trembled and warmed at the sound of Mark's deep-timbered voice.

"How did you get this number?" She spoke quietly for no reason other than the fact that he had called on her personal line.

"You gave it to James at the police station. I have an excellent memory."

"And you're exceedingly modest." She walked across the room to close her office door. Even if he had called about business, she didn't want to share him with anyone.

"I had an incentive," he said. "If I didn't remember your number, I would have had to ask James for it and that might be considered a privacy breach and worthy of sanction by the Law Society."

Katy laughed. "I'm glad to know professional responsibility was foremost in your mind when you considered engaging your friend in the unethical disclosure of personal information."

"I won't offend your delicate sensibilities by telling you exactly what is foremost in my mind when it comes to you," he murmured.

Katy choked back a gasp as need shot straight to her core. She closed her eyes and tried to bring her racing pulse under control. "So what can I do for you this evening?"

"Mmmmm." His voice rumbled over the phone.

"Mark?"

"Shhh. I'm thinking about your question and I've come up with several suggestions."

Katy snorted a laugh. "Behave."

"Unfortunately, none of my suggestions involve me behaving. Or you, for that matter."

"Then this is going to be a very short conversation." If he wasn't calling about business, she should hang up although it was the last thing she wanted to do. "I'm still waiting to hear why you called."

"I'm still trying to remember," he murmured. "Whenever I hear your voice, I get distracted."

Her pulse pounded in her throat, beating in time to the throbbing in her core. "Excellent. I'll make sure I do a lot of talking in court, and we'll be able to pound out a settlement in no time."

Mark chuckled. "I like it when you talk dirty, sugar."

"Mark...please." Her voice dropped from low to husky.

"If you're going to speak to me like that, you'll have to come to my office to find out why I called." His velvet smooth voice sent warm tingles down her spine.

"Are you crazy? Why don't we just march down to the Law Society, hand over our practicing certificates and let them know what's going on?"

"What is going on? I'm interested to know."

Katy picked up her pen and tapped it on the desk. "Absolutely nothing. And I have to go. It's late."

"Maybe we should discuss absolutely nothing on Wednesday night," he said. "Steele and I are going to Seattle and I might have an answer on the settlement proposal you sent over this afternoon. If you're interested, you can call my cell. You have my number now."

Interested? An evening listening to his dark, sensual voice? Not really a decision, but a foregone conclusion. "Um. Okay."

"Not very eloquent for a lawyer who just sent me a twenty-page document request and a stern letter reminding of my legal duty regarding disclosure."

Katy blushed, glad he couldn't see her face. "That's different. One is business and the other is pleasure." She whipped her hand over her mouth as soon as she realized her error.

"Is pleasure what you want from me, sugar?"

Her breath quickened. "Yes. No. Stop it. I'm in the office."

"The office? It's very late. You should be in bed."

With you. "Look who's talking. I asked around about you. Everyone says you're a workaholic. Case in point, you're in your office right now."

"True," he said. "But now I'm curious. What else did you hear about me?"

Katy leaned back in her chair and kicked off her shoes. Might as well make herself comfortable. "Well, apparently, you're devastatingly handsome and—"

"Apparently?"

She imagined him raising an eyebrow and tried not to laugh. "I'm not feeding your overblown ego. I've also heard you're an incorrigible bachelor who has never been seen with a woman for more than one night." She sat forward, breathless, waiting for his response.

"True again."

She froze. "Which part?"

"Which part is the least incriminating?"

Katy snorted. Typical lawyer, answering a question with another question. Either way, he was unavailable...and she wasn't looking for a man.

"It doesn't matter."

"It matters to me."

She bit her lip as the weight of his words sank in. Too heavy. A little flirting she could handle, but nothing more. "I've got to go."

"I'm not letting you run away yet." His tone lightened. "What are you working on?"

Katy looked at the stacks of files on her desk. What wasn't she working on? "You know I can't tell you."

"You can be generic. I enjoy listening to the sound of your voice."

Her lips curled into a wicked smile. "I've got this big case that could make or break my career, and defense counsel is being a real jerk about document disclosure, so I'm going to drag his sorry ass into court and make him explain himself."

His laughter surprised her, especially since she had just insulted him. "I'm sure he would be delighted with anything you might do to his sorry ass, as you so eloquently put it. When are you going to serve your application on this hypothetical defense counsel, just out of curiosity?"

"Tomorrow. I've just finished it."

"Now." His voice dropped and his low growl reverberated in her belly. God, he could probably make her come without even laying a finger on her.

"What?"

"He's at his office. You could serve him personally. Save on postage."

Sweat trickled down her back as his words translated into raw heat. "I can't. I have...other responsibilities." A babysitter who had to get home. Children. She didn't want him to know about her kids. Not yet.

"What are you afraid of, sugar?"

Not what but whom. I'm afraid of me.

Tap, tap, tap.

Mark pulled the microphone out of its stand and walked to the front of the stage in the Fairmont Hotel's palatial meeting room. "Thank you for joining us for our seminar, Pharmaceutical Regulation in North America. Our guest speaker tonight is Darkon Steele, CEO of Hi-Tech Pharmaceuticals." He rattled off Steele's impressive bio and then took a seat near the back of the stage.

Richards & Moretti's annual pharmaceutical industry lecture always attracted an equal number of lawyers and pharma execs, easily distinguishable by their choice of attire. The pharma crowd favored chinos and button-down shirts, and the lawyers, who had come for the client development opportunity, were all wearing dark suits.

All but one.

Mark sucked in a breath when he saw Katy standing in the doorway, wearing a sinfully tight gray suit and black stilettos. With her long hair fanned out over her shoulders and her pink lips plump and glistening, she was almost too alluring to be real. Every muscle in his body tightened with desire.

She caught his gaze but didn't smile. Instead, she folded her arms under her full breasts, pushing them up and out as if for his appraisal as one trim ankle crossed over the other.

Effortlessly sexy.

Achingly beautiful.

For a moment he indulged in his favorite fantasy: trapping Katy in a courtroom, stripping off her clothing, restraining her with his tie and taking her hard on the judge's desk. His cock stiffened and pressed painfully against his fly.

Damn.

With a shake of his head, he snapped his attention back to the lecture. He wouldn't be able to answer questions if he didn't even know what Steele had said. Worse, he would have to stand up.

"It can take ten to fifteen years to research and develop a drug before it gets to market," Steele explained to the audience. "Usually only one potential drug out of one thousand will make it past the developmental stage, and it can take eight to ten years of further research before it receives approval from regulatory agencies for public sale. However, a successful drug can be worth billions of dollars and the time investment will pay off in the long run." Steele paused to change his slide and then launched into an explanation of the testing procedures.

Mark glanced up at the doorway and frowned. Where was she? Had she come to see him or listen to Steele? He relaxed slightly when she returned and tensed when she left the doorway again.

After a painful hour of watching Katy appear and reappear, Mark joined Steele at the front of the stage. He hadn't expected such a large turnout, but the legal complexities of pharmaceutical regulation apparently held wide appeal. Or maybe their guests had come for the open bar. He kept one eye on the doorway during the panel discussion and the subsequent Q&A session, waiting for her to reappear.

Aha. Back again. But not smiling. He desperately wanted to get away, but the questions kept coming. A victim of his own success. After half an hour of torture, he wrapped up the Q&A and invited the crowd to join them at the bar. He headed for the door, only to be accosted by Phillip Keegan, just a few feet short of his goal.

"Nice to see you again. Interesting lecture."

"Keegan. What are you doing here? I can't imagine pharma regulation will make a good crime story." He had known Keegan in first year law school. After a brief stint reporting for the law school newspaper, Keegan realized he had found his true calling. He had dropped out and never looked back.

"I never know where I'll find a story. Plus, I like to learn new things. Makes me a better reporter."

"You never liked to learn. I don't think I ever saw you in class." Mark tried to focus on the conversation, but his gaze drifted to the doorway.

Keegan affected a desolate expression. "What is it with law types and reporters? We're on the same side, fighting for justice. We should all be friends."

Damn. Where was she? "You don't care about justice. You care about the story."

"And you care about the money."

Mark laughed. "I'll never tell you what I care about."

"The girl in the doorway."

Mark froze. "What?"

"Reporter trick. It's called being observant. You didn't take your eyes off her during the entire lecture. And now, even while you're talking to me, you're looking for her. You're wondering how long I'll keep you here and how you can politely escape before she disappears again."

So true.

Mark folded his arms and gave Keegan his full, undivided attention. "How did you get in here? The seminar is by invitation only. I didn't put your name on the list."

Keegan winked. "Probably the same way she did. I walked. Although I'm sure I didn't look quite as hot. Damn, that girl can wiggle."

Mark growled at the spark of interest in Keegan's eyes.

"Down, boy." Keegan laughed. "I'd better let you go before you drool all over my new shoes. I have some questions for Mr. Steele and I want to look my best." He glanced behind him at the doorway and raised an eyebrow. "Oops. I must have delayed you too long. The mysterious lady has disappeared again."

Katy paced up and down the hallway outside the Fairmont's conference room. Where could he be? The lecture had finished twenty minutes ago. The wait had done nothing to cool her temper. Poor Martha had called, wanting to drop the case. Someone had threatened her. Katy damn well knew who it was. Good thing Steven had the kids on Tuesday nights. Blood boiling after the call, she had wanted to confront Mark right away, and his secretary had sent her here. She hadn't expected to see Steele at the lecture, but she wasn't complaining. After she gave Mark a piece of her mind, Steele would be next.

She chanced another glance at the doorway and almost wished she hadn't. Dressed in yet another beautifully tailored suit, Mark leaned against the doorframe, the faintest smile softening the planes of his face. Katy experienced a flare of annoyance as her heart slammed against her ribs, her body yet again defying the rational side of her brain. She folded her arms and glared.

His eyes narrowed as he got the message. *Shame.* She loved the way they crinkled when he smiled.

"I was hoping this was a social call." He crossed the hallway, his muscular legs eating up the distance between them in a heartbeat.

"Business," she snapped. "Your client threatened my client. I want you to deal with him or we'll involve the police." She realized almost

95

immediately she had been too abrupt when his mouth tightened.

"As always, no hello."

"This is serious, Mark. She's terrified." She wanted to stop herself. Wind the clock back. Say hello. But she had jumped on this rollercoaster ride and she couldn't get off.

Mark knitted his brows. "Who exactly threatened whom?"

Who exactly? Martha didn't know. She had assumed the caller was from Hi-Tech, although she couldn't say with certainty it was Steele.

"Someone called my client and told her to drop the case. He also told her to rein me in and stop meddling in things she didn't understand." She lowered her voice as uncertainty crept through her. What if Martha had lied?

Mark steered her away from the main hallway, his hand pressed firmly on her back. "What was the threat?"

Katy looked over at him and frowned. "What do you mean?"

"Have you been threatened before?"

Katy nodded. "Sure. Lots of times. Usually irate husbands who blame me when their wives ask for their fair share in a divorce."

They stopped at a secluded seating area and Mark motioned for her to sit, but Katy shook her head. She needed to move. Being near Mark only heightened her agitation, and she needed some way to release the energy.

"So you know there is always an *if* and a *then*. For example, if you don't smile, then I will throw you over my knee and spank you."

Katy froze when a sliver of need, unexpected and unwanted, shot straight to her core. *Dammit.* He had to know what his words did to her. Heat bloomed in her cheeks, and she looked down at the plush, patterned carpet.

He continued in the same calm, cool tone. "So what did the caller say would happen to Martha if she didn't drop the case?"

With a shuddering exhalation, she forced herself to focus. "He didn't say anything else. The threat was implied."

Mark shook his head and his sable hair gleamed in the soft lighting overhead. "You know as well as I do his statement would not likely meet the legal test for a threat. Maybe someone was just worried about her."

"Well then, he had a funny way of showing it." They stood not more than a foot apart. Her hands itched to touch him—to run up the broad expanse of his chest and around his neck. She wanted to pull him close and inhale the scent of soap and sandalwood, of him. God, even after their heated exchange in the courtroom the other day, she wanted to kiss him. She licked her lips, imagining his taste.

"What are you thinking, Katy Sinclair?" His voice dropped to a low growl. "If you keep looking at me like that, I might have to make good my threat."

Her heart pounded against her ribcage. Afraid she would betray herself, she pressed her lips together and looked away.

"If we were alone..." he whispered.

"What do we have here? If I didn't know you better, Mark, I'd be worried you were fraternizing with opposing counsel." Steele's voice echoed down the hallway, attracting the attention of the last of the seminar attendees making their way to the bar.

Damn. Mark ripped his gaze away from Katy and spun around as Steele approached the lounge area, his eyes rife with speculation.

"Ms. Sinclair came to see me tonight because someone threatened her client, Ms. Saunders." Mark didn't want to put her on the spot, but he needed a moment to collect himself. Far too perceptive, Steele would pick up on even the slightest glance. He needed to stay sharp.

Katy narrowed her eyes and stared at Steele. "I assume it was you."

Steele laughed. "I wish I had the time to call every one of the hundreds of litigants our company deals with on a daily basis and threaten them. It would save us time and money. But unfortunately, I have a company to run and calling up former employees does not rank high on my list of priorities."

"I'm not buying it," she persisted. "No one else benefits from her dropping the case but Hi-Tech. You might not have handled it yourself, but I'm sure you're involved."

Steele's eyes glittered. "Sheathe your claws, kitty, or I'll do it for

Sarah Castille

you." He reached out and stroked a long, thick finger along Katy's cheek. "Or is that why you are provoking me? Are you begging to be tamed?"

Adrenaline swept through Mark's body, snapping the threads of his control one by one. His hand shot out, but before he could grab Steele's arm, Katy slapped Steele's errant finger away.

"You've crossed the line, Steele. Even if my client decides to drop the case, I'm going to pursue you. You've shown your hand by threatening her. Now I know there is something behind her dismissal and I won't stop until I find out what it is." The ice in her tone froze the air around them.

Steele's eyes hardened. "Don't threaten me, little kitty. You have no idea who you're dealing with."

Moments passed. Steele and Katy locked gazes, the tension thick between them. Mark's body thrummed with pent up anger. If Steele touched her again...

"Hey, guys, why so serious?" Keegan's voice broke the spell, and Mark turned in relief when the reporter approached them, a beer in one hand and a giggling waitress in the other.

"Are the legal intricacies of pharma regulation really that intense?" He cocked an eyebrow and flicked his gaze to Mark with an unspoken query.

Recovering first, Katy held out her hand. "We haven't met. I'm Katherine Sinclair, a lawyer with Knight and Frank."

Keegan winked at Mark. "I see you found her."

He raised Katy's hand to his lips in a mock Victorian gesture. "Phillip Keegan. Always a pleasure to meet a beautiful lady."

Mark and Steele scowled, united for a moment in their disapproval of the smooth reporter's intrusion on their territory.

"Hey, what about me?" The waitress tugged on Keegan's arm.

He kissed her on the cheek. "You know you're beautiful, darling. How about you run off to the bar and get us a round of drinks? I've been trying to corner Mr. Steele all evening. I have a sudden interest in drug development and I don't want him to disappear again."

Katy pulled her hand away. "I have to go. Nice to meet you, Mr.

Keegan. Mr. Steele, I look forward to seeing you in court."

Mark gave Keegan and Steele a farewell nod before following Katy down the hallway. "It's late. I'll walk you to your car."

"No, it's okay. I'm fine. I parked at the office so it's a bit of a hike."

They rounded the corner and out of view of the seminar attendees.

Mark put a hand on her waist and steered her toward the door. "I'm not asking, sugar."

Lana snapped a picture of the subject walking down Burrard Street beside a tall man in a tailored suit. She logged the time in her notebook, eight twenty-seven p.m. She wished she had someone to call. Someone who could share the excitement of her very first case.

She followed close behind the couple, but dodging the crowds meant she couldn't overhear their conversation. A group of rowdy sports fans approached them and the man deftly switched sides, putting himself between the group and the woman. How gallant. Lana didn't know any men who would do something like that. In fact, she didn't know many men. Period. She had only just moved to Vancouver to take the private investigator course and hadn't had time to make friends. Maybe someday.

The subject leaned toward the mystery man, an almost imperceptible movement, but as a highly trained professional, Lana knew to look for subtle gestures. How sweet. She paused to snap a few pictures and then raced after them.

When they reached Nelson Street, they turned and stopped in the shadow of a tall office building. Lana checked her notebook. The subject worked in the building at Knight & Frank. Twelfth floor. She found a secure position and pulled out her camera to take a few pictures of them staring at each other.

The man stroked a finger along the subject's jaw, and Lana sighed at the tender gesture. Her first assignment and already she loved her job. If she could live vicariously through other people's relationships, she wouldn't long so much for her own.

They exchanged a few words and the subject entered the building and disappeared from view. Hopefully she would go home, and Lana could finish off her report.

She turned to leave and realized the mystery man hadn't moved. She snapped a few pictures of him, lost in thought, before he finally turned and walked down the street.

Was he a friend? A colleague? A lover? As a PI she had to avoid making assumptions and consider all possibilities. Still, she liked the look of him. Brooding, intense, confident. But a little too clean cut for her taste. She liked her men rough...with an aura of danger. Kinda like the cop who had chased her and then called her up to chastise her over the phone.

Her lips curled in a smile. Damn sexy voice. All rough and gravelly. Turned out he wasn't immune to her charms. By the end of the call, she'd pulled a chuckle out of him. And he'd pulled one out of her.

She wandered back to the hotel, mentally planning her report. Hopefully, her new employer, Mr. S, would be impressed with her efficiency and give her a bonus. Then she could fix the Jetta. Maybe buy some food and new clothes. An investigator had to blend in with her surroundings, although no one had blinked an eye when she'd wandered around the fancy hotel this evening in her yoga pants and T-shirt. She had some great pictures of the subject with the mystery man, although not once had she been able to capture his face.

She finally reached the Jetta and jumped inside, giving it a pat of encouragement when it wheezed to life. If Mr. S didn't pay bi-weekly as agreed, she would have a hard time seeing the case through. Her poor Jetta needed a major overhaul.

She pulled out onto the road and headed for home. She had been ecstatic when Mr. S had agreed to pay in cash. Cash meant no tax. No tax meant more cash. In return she had agreed to his terms of strict anonymity. He had sent her a postal box key and a box number. She had to deposit her reports and photos on Mondays and Thursdays, and he had agreed to leave the cash after pickup. No real name. No contact details except a cell number. The warning bells had gone off right away, but she wasn't about to turn away a paying client. She had a Jetta needing brakes and a belly needing donuts. Mr. S was her ticket to paradise.

Chapter Eight

"I won't consider settlement." Steele thumped his briefcase on the coffee table in Seattle's Four Seasons Hotel lounge and snapped open the clasps.

Mark leaned back in his dark leather chair and folded his arms. A group of tourists filed into the lobby, complaining about the rain in Seattle. *They should visit Vancouver.*

"We're on the back foot in this case," Mark said. "Saunders's exemplary work record, together with the timing of the dismissal following right on the heels of her failed attempt at whistle-blowing, will do you in even if they can't establish a solid connection."

"I said no settlement." Steele removed a bundle of files from his briefcase and handed them to Mark. "I thought after years of working with me, you would understand the politics of the pharmaceutical industry. We routinely ferret out each other's spies and use the legal system to make an example of them as a deterrent to other competitors. Although we never caught her with her hand in the proverbial cookie jar, I know she was up to something that went beyond the whistle-blowing. Call it gut instinct. I want to see her squirm. I want the competitor who dared send her into my company to be unmasked."

Mark sighed and flipped through the files. Steele's hard-nosed attitude had just cost Hi-Tech a valuable settlement with an American pharmaceutical company this morning and landed Mark with yet another lucrative piece of litigation. He should be thanking Steele, but he knew, at some point, Steele's intractable nature would be his downfall. And when Steele went down, Richards & Moretti would fall too.

"What are you saying?" Mark raised his voice to be heard above the excited chatter of the tourists. "You want to come down heavy on

Saunders? David and Goliath? You'll be slaughtered in the press."

Steele laughed. "I have friends in the press. I have friends in the regulator's office. I golf with most of the judges. I'm not worried about bad publicity, or adverse judgments. I am worried about unpredictable, secretly funded spies. I've read the memo you prepared on Saunders and the investigator's report you obtained. Her sketchy background makes it clear she isn't who she claims to be. What can we do to get the upper hand?"

Mark gritted his teeth. The last thing he wanted was to complicate the legal proceedings and drag the case out for years in court, but he had a professional responsibility to give Steele the best advice he could. "We could counter-claim. I believe you said she took samples of the drug and gave them to the regulators. We could also claim for libel and for possible disruption to your business."

Steele grinned. "That's what I want to hear. Make it happen and do it quickly. I don't want this case affecting our new product launch. I've got enough on my plate trying to contain the security breach."

"What about the current state of affairs?" Mark was loath to mention Katy given Steele's determination to bring her down to assuage his wounded pride, but he could not ignore his legal obligation. "Ms. Sinclair filed a motion for production of documents far exceeding the scope of the dismissal case. I wouldn't be surprised if she has something up her sleeve."

"Nor would I." Steele narrowed his eyes. "She's already sticking her nose where it doesn't belong, but I'm taking care of it."

Mark froze. "What does that mean?"

"It means, I asked you to deal with her and you refused, so I'm handling it myself." He turned away and stared into the crowd of excited tourists.

Mark followed Steele's gaze to a pretty young woman with big blue eyes, long chestnut hair and a very tight T-shirt. He stifled a growl. "You know you can't speak to her directly about the case unless I'm present."

"I don't need to speak to her...now." Steele leaned back and folded his hands behind his head. "But after she drops the case, all bets are off."

Mark clenched his teeth. "Do you mind telling me how you know she's going to drop the case?"

Steele looked at Mark, his piercing gaze missing nothing. "Do you really want to know?"

"Yes."

"If I tell you, I'll put you in a compromising position and I don't want to do that. I need you doing what you do best, and doing it for me."

Sweat trickled down Mark's back. He should have seen this coming. If he had agreed to investigate Katy, he would have been in control of the flow of information to Steele. But now Steele knew something he didn't, and he couldn't ignore the threat.

"You understand if you harm her in any way, I will be legally bound to disclose this conversation." He tried to keep his voice steady.

Steele laughed. "I want to bend her, not break her." His smile disappeared. "And I want her curious kitty nose out of my business."

He nodded to the documents in Mark's hand. "Speaking of business, I have another agreement for you to draft. Same as the last one. Same accident. Same circumstances. Last name of Cunningham."

Mark frowned. "What kind of accident was it? The guy I saw is totally disfigured. The wife said it had to do with some chemical spill."

"I told you before, it's better if you don't know all the details. Is that going to be a problem?"

"You've given me enough to satisfy my duty as an officer of the court but if you're trying to involve me in something illegal..."

Steele snorted a laugh. "I wouldn't dream of it."

"I'm starved. What's for dinner?"

Steven sat down at the kitchen table and Katy sighed. Wednesday. Double-shift night. Every week Steven showed up for dinner between shifts with a few hours to kill. He claimed it was for the children, but it totally disrupted their weekly routine. Instead of doing their homework, the kids played video games with him, watched movies and ate popcorn. Then he sauntered out of the house, leaving her with the mess and meltdowns, overdue projects and tests. She hated Wednesdays but the kids always had fun, and if she couldn't give them a two-parent family, at least she could ensure they had a solid relationship with their father.

"Isn't this great? It's like old times, and look how happy the kids are."

Melissa and Justin grinned on cue and disappeared from the table to set up the Wii.

Steven leaned over and grabbed her hand. The overpowering sickly sweet scent of Drakkar Noir laced with antiseptic assaulted her nose and she stifled a sneeze.

"I miss you, Kate. I want you back. It would be the best thing for the kids. They need both their parents...together." He squeezed her hand hard. Too hard. Katy winced and tried to pull away.

"Steven, let go."

"You suffered as a child without a father," he continued. "Don't put your kids through that." He punctuated his obviously rehearsed speech with a sad, unconvincing smile.

She tugged again. "You're hurting me."

His face flushed and his eyes glittered fever bright. He squeezed harder and her bones grated painfully over each other. Heart pounding, she stared at him in horror. What was wrong him? His callous, demeaning, manipulative behavior during their marriage had bordered on emotional abuse, but he had never once been physical.

She grabbed a dinner knife and held it above his hand. "Last time, Steven."

With a soft sigh, he released his grip. Katy wrenched her hand away. "What the hell was that?"

"I'm willing to forgive you," Steven said quietly. "For tearing the family apart."

"Forgive me? We're divorced for a reason. In fact, many reasons. Should I list all their names?"

Steven didn't even flinch. She knew he felt no guilt about his affairs.

"Think about it, Kate. Try to put the happiness of your children before your own. You need a stable influence in your life. After I saw you in that trashy outfit, I realized you need me back. God knows what people thought, seeing you parading around like a—"

"Don't you dare!" She shoved her chair back and forced herself to walk across the room, away from him. One more word and she would slap him, and not just once. "Did Sally leave too fast for you to find a replacement? Is that why you're trying to get back together?"

He stood up and walked toward the living room, dismissing her with an absent wave of his hand. "We'll talk later. I promised Justin another game of Wii bowling."

Katy threw her napkin at his departing back and stifled her scream.

She tidied the kitchen then headed to her office for a moment of calm before the storm of hyperactive, overtired children descended on her. After the divorce, she had replaced Steven's dark, oppressive furniture with a glass desk, cream leather chairs and open steel-framed bookshelves, transforming the dark, stuffy space into a light and airy oasis. A sanctuary of sorts.

She pulled out the Saunders file and found the list of names. Despite the threat, Martha had decided to continue with the case.

Katy sighed and called the number for the third man on Martha's list, Terry Silver. If Martha had the courage to keep going, she would be with her client every step of the way.

After setting up an appointment to see Silver the following week, Katy closed the file and buried her head in her hands. She couldn't stop thinking about Mark. If she didn't find a way to deal with her fierce attraction to him, she might as well kiss her career goodbye. She knew, without a doubt, one day, in the haze of lust that invariably descended on her the moment he drew near, she would go too far.

If she hadn't already.

At exactly ten o'clock, Mark's cell rang. He settled himself on the tired hotel bed. Well-worn springs creaked under his weight. He hadn't expected her to call. Hoped, yes. Expected, no.

Sarah Castille

He grabbed the phone off the night table and double-checked the caller ID. Why had he even suggested this? He could have just called her office in the morning. But the combination of sexual allure and fierce intelligence turned him on like nothing else. Throw in those luscious curves, the wide, blue eyes and the long, silken hair and she was a recipe for disaster. A recipe he couldn't wait to taste again.

The phone rang a second time.

His body tensed in delicious anticipation. Who was he kidding? The call had nothing to do with the case, and everything to do with hearing the exotic purr of her throaty voice.

He answered on the third ring.

"Mark?"

His body tensed at the low, sultry, breathless whisper on the other end of the phone.

"Katy." He stared at the ceiling and breathed slow and deep. *Slow and deep.* God, that's exactly how he wanted her.

"You said this might be a good time to talk about the case?"

"I'm afraid I have bad news." Mark rushed his words wanting to get the professional part of the call out of the way. "I didn't make any progress with your settlement proposal." He couldn't tell her the situation had gone from bad to worse, and in the next few days she would discover her client was on the other end of a vicious lawsuit.

"Ah, well. That's a shame, but not entirely unexpected. I sent the proposal to your client so we could show the judge we made the effort. I guess I'll see you in court then for the disclosure hearing."

A tiny fissure of fear opened in his chest. He had expected her to be more...disappointed. At least as disappointed as he had been. The settlement would have been an easy way to resolve the potential conflict.

Scrambling for a hook to keep her on the line, he said, "About your disclosure application...you know I won't let you get away with such a blatant fishing expedition."

"How are you going to stop me?" He caught a hint of laughter in her voice.

"Maybe I'll throw something unexpected your way—tie you up so

106

you can't attend the hearing."

"Tie me up?"

Mark closed his eyes as images of Katy, bound and spread out before him like a banquet, flickered through his mind. He imagined licking his way down her body, feasting on the soft bounty of her breasts, sucking her cherry nipples and tasting the nectar between her thighs.

"God, yes," he rasped.

His shaft rose painfully against his zipper. Damn. He was already losing it. He had better control than this. He took a deep breath and stared at the bland, two-toned painting on the wall in front of him. Typical hotel décor. Mind numbing. Just what he needed.

"How would you tie me up?" Her throaty voice made his balls tighten in an instant.

"Emergency injunction? Surprise witness? Last minute amendment?"

"Rope," he blurted out. "Silk is best."

Her gasp, soft and low, sent his arousal soaring. He tensed his body to stave off the urge to rip open his jeans and deal with his burning need for release.

"How would I get to court if I was...tied up?"

"I'd leave you some wiggle room."

"Mmm. What would you be doing while I was wiggling? Grab the opportunity to...handle things...on your own?"

A smile curled his lips when he realized she was playing the game. God, he wanted this woman. Badly. If he hadn't been in Seattle, he would have been hard pressed to stop himself from seeking her out. Ropes in hand.

"I'd stay and watch you wiggle."

"And if I escaped?" Her voice dropped to a low, sultry purr.

"You'd be a very sorry girl," he growled. He squeezed his eyes shut and clenched his jaw. They were right on the line they shouldn't cross, but it was a just a phone call, nothing more.

"The way you say it..."she breathed, "...makes me want to be sorry."

He wanted to be sorry too. Sorry he had started this. Sorry he had no control when it came to her. But he wasn't. Not a bit.

Dropping the phone, he buried his face in his hands and dragged his fingers over his coarse stubble seeking a familiar sensation to distract himself. He'd had dozens of one-night stands over the years. Detachment had never been a problem for him. Until now. Katy got to him on a level he didn't understand. He undid his belt and shoved his jeans down over his hips before picking up the phone.

"So I guess after that we would go to court," Katy said softly.

"Court?" Mark tore himself out of his self-reflection and tried to catch up with the game.

Katy giggled. "I'd have lost all restraint by then."

Restraint. Probably a good idea.

A shiver raced up the length of his spine. "I would like to see you totally unrestrained, sugar."

"If I turned on my webcam, you would." Her throaty whisper held a teasing note.

"Turn it on." His shaft ached and every nerve ending sizzled with need. He shoved the wretched, restricting underwear down to his knees and grabbed his erection as it sprang free of its prison. Big mistake. He clenched his teeth and challenged himself to make it through the call without getting off.

"I can't," she whispered. "But talking like this...it makes me hot."

Mark let his head fall back against the wall with a thud. *Damn it.* He grasped his cock firmly and began to stroke. "Talk to me, sugar. If you won't let me see you, then you'll have to paint me a picture. Tell me what you're wearing."

Her sharp intake of breath kicked his arousal up another notch.

"We're pushing the limits, Mark. Maybe we should—"

"No." He cut her off with a bark that betrayed his need. "It's just a phone call and I have a passing interest in your...sartorial choices, particularly if they involve lingerie or garter belts."

Soft laughter. A rustle. Footsteps. The slide of a drawer opening. A soft thud. Squeaking springs. Panting.

Anticipation ratcheted through him and his fingers curled tight around the phone.

"Red," she whispered. He heard more rustling. The snap of elastic. The hiss of nylon.

He froze. His entire being focused on the sensual sounds filling his ear.

"Silk slip. Lacey garter belt. Suspenders. Thigh highs. Panties and—"

"Stop." Mark hissed out a breath. "It's probably better if you don't say anything else. As you said, there is a line we don't want to cross."

Her soft whimper of disappointment gave him an idea—a way to keep them technically on the right side of that line.

"I'm going to say a few things, sugar. You don't have to answer me. In fact, it's better if you don't. I'll just be musing to myself while you're on the phone, but if you feel the need to interrupt me with those sexy little sighs and whimpers, I won't complain."

"Mark, I—"

He chuckled. "Ah ah ah. You're not supposed to say anything. But I'm thinking about you. I imagine you're lying on your bed in your sexy outfit but it's too hot in your bedroom. Your slip is clinging to your body. You want it off so you slide your hands up and over the silk to your breasts. They're tender, swollen. You cup them, squeeze them gently, relieve the ache. And then you can't resist. You circle your thumbs around your nipples until they peak under the silk. So hot. So hard."

Katy moaned.

"Good girl." He cut himself off and fought for control. His hand tightened around his cock and he stroked once, twice, enough take off the edge, but not enough to send him over.

"If you were going to imagine me, you would probably imagine I ditched my shirt before we even started this call and when we started talking about ropes, I had to ditch everything else. And I'm hard. So goddamn hard for you."

She sucked in a sharp breath and then murmured her approval.

Mark smiled. "I imagine you've got the slip off, but now your panties are wet, too wet. You slide your hands down those luscious curves and unhook the garter straps one by one, then slide off the stockings."

He heard the soft snap of elastic. Once, twice, three times and then four. His cock thickened and he pumped slowly into his hand.

Katy groaned and he heard the faint hiss of her stockings sliding down her legs.

"Now the panties, sugar. Slip your fingers into the elastic and ease them over your hips."

The squeak of springs. A soft whine. He increased the pressure around his cock and began to stroke faster. At this rate, he wasn't going to last very long.

"Are you wet and ready for me, sugar?" His voice caught in his throat and he increased his rhythm. "I am so ready for you."

"God, yes," Katy moaned.

"I'm here for you," he murmured. "Let your hand slide down over your mound to cup your hot little pussy. That's it, sugar. Spread your wetness up and around your clit. But don't touch. Just a tease. A taste. And back down to your folds. Around again. Move your other hand to tweak your nipples, one at a time, rolling them between your thumb and forefinger until they're hard, as hard as my cock."

Her rapid, panting breaths fired his need. He was rough with himself now, quickening his strokes as his hips jerked, desperate to find release. He forced his words through gritted teeth. "I'm stroking myself like there's no tomorrow, sugar. I'm rock hard and ready to come for you."

Katy groaned, a low, guttural, sensual sound that took him right to the edge.

"You're close, aren't you? Slide one finger inside your pussy. So hot and wet. In and out and then add a second finger. Fill yourself like I would fill you if I was there."

Her soft, strangled cry took his breath away. He squeezed his eyes shut and pictured her touching herself on her bed, her eyes half-lidded, lips plump and wet. "Lift your hips and ride those fingers. You want to come for me, sugar?"

"Now," she breathed.

Fuck. Red sheeted his vision. Every muscle in his body tensed. He had never needed release as badly as he did this very moment. He tightened his hand in a vicious grip and thrust hard into his palm.

Katy's voice rose to a thin whine. "Maaark."

"Now, sugar. Flick your thumb over your clit and come with me." He grabbed his underwear and slid the soft cotton over this throbbing shaft.

"Oh, oh, oh. I..." Her muffled scream sent him over the edge. His body went rigid and pressure exploded from the base of his spine, jetting out his cock in wave after wave of mind-numbing pleasure. He groaned; the sound drowning out the last sweet sighs of her release.

For a long while he heard nothing but the sound of her ragged breathing.

"Oh God." The regret in Katy's voice sent a chill through his veins.

"Don't worry." He tried to keep his voice calm and relaxed although he felt anything but. "It's just a phone call—a bit of fun. Nothing serious enough to raise any professional concerns." Mark clenched his teeth as soon as the lie left his lips. But maybe it was better this way. He couldn't hold back around her, but if he pushed her away, it wouldn't be an issue.

Who was he kidding?

Still, her silence rocked him to the core. "Sugar?"

"Sure," she mumbled. "Just a bit of fun. We wouldn't want anything more than that."

Chapter Nine

"I don't want to go to Dad's place." Justin pushed his chair away from the table and Katy sighed.

"I'm afraid you don't have a choice, darling. Ted asked me to take his place at the legal awards dinner tonight. He's the one who put me up for partnership. I can't refuse. It's work and it's important. Plus, this is your Dad's weekend with you. I'm sure you'll have a good time."

But I won't. No club. No Mark. She had messed everything up on the phone. She shouldn't have agreed to the call. In the back of her mind, she had known it wasn't really about work. Maybe she had unwittingly formed some kind of emotional attachment to him. Or maybe she was just confused. Either way, it had to end.

"We won't have a good time," Melissa groaned. "Sally dumped him so we'll have to eat sandwiches all weekend and he'll be in a bad mood."

"Don't be silly, Mel. Justin packed the Wii. Once that's hooked up, you'll forget you even need to eat."

The front door creaked open. Steven's running shoes squeaked across the floor. Of course he wouldn't think to use the doorbell.

"Hey, kids, ready to go?" He walked into the kitchen and his smile faded. "What the hell are you wearing this time?"

Katy looked down at her new dress and smiled, perversely pleased at Steven's reaction. For the first time in years she had wanted to dress in something other than the conservative black wool sheath she usually wore to formal dinners. Something sexy. A few discreet inquiries around the office had sent her to the exclusive boutiques in West Vancouver, and the minute she saw the elegant, mock corset dress she knew she had to have it.

"Don't you like it?" She ran her fingers down the strapless black silk dress, tracing the Asian-inspired brocade of red flowers, white birds and branches with her fingertip. She checked the back laces and tightened the red silk drawstring, letting the loops fall onto the tight pencil skirt that hugged her hips and ended just above her knees. The dress fit so snugly she could barely move, and it pushed her breasts up just enough to be noticed but not so much as to be unprofessional.

"It's indecent," Steven spluttered. "And when you wear it with those fucking bondage boots...Geez, Kate, what's gotten into you? You look like a sl—"

"Watch your language in front of the children," she snapped.

Melissa and Justin shared a glance. "Dad said the f-word," Melissa breathed in awe.

Steven grimaced. "Those boots were a mistake. I should never have let you buy them."

"You would have had a long way to fly." With a few hours to kill between witness interviews in London one winter, she'd wandered around Covent Garden, getting lost in the narrow, twisted little alleyways until she had seen the boots in the window of a fetish store. The soft, knee-hugging black leather and the shiny, silver stiletto heels had called to her, but not as much as the laces. They started at the toe and worked their way to the top, then around and down the back. Just like a corset. Steven hated them. With a passion.

"I can't believe you're going to a legal awards dinner wearing lingerie and bondage boots. Do you not care about your career? I'm sure the judge at the custody review will be interested to know how you conduct yourself in your spare time."

"I think Mom looks beautiful," Melissa said softly.

"Sluts don't dress like that," Justin added, revealing a maturity beyond his years.

Katy and Steven looked at him in horror.

"How do you know how sluts dress?" Melissa voiced the question on everyone's mind.

Justin shrugged. "I'm nine. I know a lot of things."

"This is your fault." Steven pointed his finger at Katy. "He used to be an innocent boy."

Katy fisted her hands by her sides. *Say nothing in front of the children.* "Mummy has to go, darlings. Go get your things. I'll see you on Sunday."

She kissed them and waited until she heard them on the stairs before turning to Steven. "I'm decently covered, just not in the uptight, conservative clothes you encouraged me to wear. And if you ever speak like that in front of the children again or threaten me in any way—"

He cut her off with a bark of laughter. "What? What are you going to do? Sue me? Kill me? The father of your children?"

Her nostrils flared. "Death would be too good for you."

Mark tapped his fork on the white linen tablecloth. An endless parade of penguins marched up to the podium to accept their statues and waddled back again. His firm, Richards & Moretti, hadn't won anything, but then he hadn't expected they would. Litigation work had dried up with the recession, making the Saunders v. Hi-Tech case one of the few pieces of high-profile litigation the firm had secured during the last year.

He sighed when the announcer moved on to another category. Such a bloody waste of time. He should have pulled rank on Tony and backed out of the dinner. As senior partner, he could veto the managing partner's decisions. But Tony could be very persuasive, and one look at the firm's accounts had him lacing up his own penguin suit. The firm needed work and the partners needed to see and be seen. All of them.

"Mark should get an award for the fiercest scowl." Curtis leaned over and grabbed Mark's fork away. The most reserved of Mark's partners, Curtis was well known for his short fuse.

Tony laughed. "The firm should get an award for surviving the recession. I've heard three more city firms have gone under."

"That award would have to go to Mark too." Curtis patted Mark's shoulder. "His client is keeping us afloat."

Mark smiled. He had been lucky to find a small group of friends he admired and respected. Together, they had weathered the rigors of law school and articling, and then started their own law firm. They were brothers in all but name.

The conversation turned to shared acquaintances and the usual salacious gossip. Mark let his mind wander. What was Katy doing now? Probably at work, drafting another motion to drag his "sorry ass" into court and rake him over the coals for his callous behavior. He coughed and choked on his wine.

"You okay?" Tony thumped him on the back.

Mark nodded. "Where did they get this stuff?"

"Who knows? Everyone has been affected by the recession so they probably tried to cut costs by going local. I'm not wasting my time with it. Our new wine shipment arrived at the club this afternoon. Curtis and I are heading over there later to sample the 2006 Cornas Domaine Clape. Probably one of the best Syrahs in the world. You want to join us? Maybe your pretty little lawyer will stop by again."

"She's not mine," Mark mumbled. He hadn't told Tony about Katy and he wasn't ready to explain the situation to everyone just yet.

The lights came on signaling the end of the awards and the beginning of the evening entertainment. Mark pushed back his chair. Time to go.

"Not so fast." Tony grabbed the wine bottle and refilled Mark's glass. "What happened? I thought sparks were flying when she showed up last time at the club."

Mark took another sip of the sharp, bitter wine. "I'm not looking for anything serious."

"I don't believe it. You two had a connection. Is there something you're not telling me?"

Mark looked away to avoid Tony's all too intuitive question. The dance floor was already full—mostly young associates, court staff and...Katy. His heart skidded to a stop.

Vivacious. Breathtaking. Beautiful. He couldn't decide whether it was the boots or the dress, but within seconds his cock stiffened. Rock hard.

Tony followed his gaze and snorted a sarcastic laugh. "Oh yeah. Nothing serious."

Mark barely heard him. He couldn't tear his eyes away. The dress fit her like a glove, highlighting her narrow waist and accentuating her soft, full breasts. God, those breasts. They swelled enticingly over the top of the corset, hidden only by a filmy strip of red lace. She swayed on the dance floor, perfectly in time to the music, never faltering despite the thin, metal heels of the damned sexiest boots he had ever seen. Up and up they climbed, ending only inches below her tight skirt, binding her legs in a sensual feast of lacing.

"Nothing is going on," Mark growled. "She's on the other side of the Hi-Tech dismissal case."

"There had better be nothing going on," Tony muttered, shaking a finger. "Talk about one big, fat conflict."

"Don't worry about it."

"Are you kidding? I saw you with her in the club. I only have to look at you now to know you need to distance yourself totally, either from her or the case, or this is going to end badly for everyone, especially you."

Mark sighed. "I'll be fine, Tony."

Tony drained his glass. "I'm not worried about you. I'm worried about Steele. I'm worried about the firm and I'm worried about the Law Society. I'm also worried about her. I like her. I don't want to see her career destroyed, and I don't want to see her get hurt."

"I have it under control." Mark emphasized each word. Why wouldn't Tony leave it alone? When had he ever given his friend cause to doubt him?

"I'll believe it when you can look at her without drooling." Tony gave him a warning clap on the back.

The band launched into an eighties rock song and the old timers headed for the bar. Katy remained on the dance floor and Tim, the red-haired court reporter, joined her. They exchanged a few words and then Tim closed the distance between them, his eyes fixed on Katy's breasts. He grabbed her hand and spun her around. Katy twirled, laughing as she neared Mark's table. And then she stopped.

"Oh. My. God."

Katy froze. Why hadn't she even considered he might be here?

And Tony. Was he a lawyer too?

She flushed as she caught Mark's gaze and her heart seized. Damn he filled out a tux like no one else.

"Why did you stop, Katy? Do you need a breather?" Tim put his arms around her waist, hugging her from behind, totally oblivious to Mark and Tony watching them with fascination and the faintest glimmer of disapproval.

"Tim, stop. You're drunk." She pulled his hands away and tried, unsuccessfully, to step out of his embrace. For someone thin and gangly, he had surprisingly strong arms.

"Come on, Katy. We were having such a good time." He pulled her closer and palmed her breast with a clammy hand.

"Get off." She tried to wriggle free, but after four shots of tequila, her strength and coordination were not up to par and she couldn't escape without making a scene.

Tim pawed at her breast again. Two chairs slid away from the table in front of them.

"I believe Ms. Sinclair wishes to be left alone." Mark stalked over to them, eyes flashing, Tony on his heels.

"What's it to you?" Tim snapped.

Katy shot a glance over her shoulder at Tim. Why was he still here? Any sane man would've been out the door by now. Could he not see the anger simmering beneath Mark's taut face?

Tony saw it. He edged closer to Mark, his hand outstretched as if ready to grab him and pull him away.

"Take your hands off her now," Mark growled. What a voice. Hard, low, powerful and dripping with menace. Did he use that voice in the courtroom to intimidate witnesses, or was it just for overly friendly court reporters?

A thrill of fear shot through her veins. Although she liked Tim, a part of her almost hoped he would be stupid enough to stand his ground. What would Mark do then?

Disappointment coursed through her when Tim stiffened and loosened his grip. "I'll go and get us a cab," he mumbled.

"She's not going anywhere with you." Mark took Katy's hand and pulled her behind him. "I'll see her home."

"Katy."

She clenched her teeth at Tim's unappealing whine. "It's fine, Tim. I'll see you on Monday."

Tim scowled and trudged away. Katy suffered a moment of regret. She had never seen him anything but cheerful. She made a mental note to call him and take him out for coffee. She enjoyed his company and didn't want to lose a friend.

"Let's go." Mark pulled her in the direction of the exit.

"Wait a minute. I'm not going anywhere. I'm here for work. I'm supposed to be mingling." She pulled her hand out of his grasp and instantly felt the loss.

"You've done enough mingling for tonight. What were you thinking coming here dressed like that?"

The edge in his voice surprised her and she took a full step back. "Are you kidding me? I cannot believe you would say that considering you spend your weekends in a club where women wear leather and chains. And if you are even suggesting the way I'm dressed makes me in some way responsible for someone else's behavior..."

Mark shrugged off his jacket and wrapped it around her, pulling her close. "The women at the club aren't mine," he whispered, so low only she could hear.

Mine. Katy shivered. How deliciously primitive to be thought of as a possession. Too bad she happened to be a legal professional in the middle of a networking event. She flung off the jacket and handed it back. "I'm not yours. You said so yourself. We just had a bit of fun."

He wrapped the jacket around her again. "Perhaps you misunderstood."

Tony took a step toward them and held out his hand, breaking the tension. "Perhaps Katy would like to meet the other partners. I think it would count as networking. We've never been professionally introduced. I'm Tony Moretti, managing partner of Richards and Moretti."

He pressed a cool, callused palm against her hand and slid his thumb around her wrist in a surreptitious caress. Her smile faded and it took all her effort not to jerk her hand away.

"Tony." Mark thundered a warning. Tony let her go and gave her a wink.

By the time she had been introduced to all the partners, her tequila buzz had started to wear off and her dress had become unbearably restricting. She panted against the lacings and excused herself to get a breath of fresh air.

"You're hyperventilating, sugar." Mark caught up to her as she skirted the dance floor. "We need to get you out of that dress."

Mmmm. Yes.

No.

"I'll be fine. I just need a few minutes outside."

His face softened for the first time since she'd seen him that evening. "Good idea. We need to talk. I'll walk you to your car." He put an arm around her shoulders. "Come."

Katy almost sobbed with the desire to go with him, but she couldn't. Not tonight. Ted had given her this chance to prove herself. She took the deepest breath the corset would allow. "The partners of my firm are here and we have a photo shoot for the awards in an hour. I can't leave until they do."

She chanced a glance at his face but couldn't read anything in his neutral expression.

"We'll step outside and I'll loosen the corset for you," he said. "Then I'll leave you to your mingling."

Without waiting for her agreement, he led her across the ballroom and out through a set of glass doors to a small terrace overlooking Coal Harbor. Potted trees dotted the flagstone patio, and a wrought iron table and two chairs huddled against the wall.

Mark steered her to a dark corner between two fragrant potted cedars and turned her to face the railing. The lights of Vancouver's North Shore twinkled in the distance, and she could see the SeaBus, ferrying people across Burrard Inlet.

His fingers slid down her back and tugged at the ribbons holding her corset closed. "Are you and Tim...?" His voice tightened. "I never thought to ask."

"We're just friends."

Katy held onto the cool metal and looked down into the water. Fish streaked past like bolts of silver lightening, daring her to catch them. The last time she had gone fishing, she had been with her father, and blissfully unaware he was saying goodbye. The next week he had driven away and never looked back.

"How did you tie this knot?" Mark pulled the ribbons free. Air filled her lungs as the corset loosened around her.

"It's a trick I taught to—" She cut herself off, not wanting to let him know about the kids. "Never mind."

He turned her around and cupped her face in his warm hands. "Finish what you were saying."

"No."

He leaned down and feathered kisses over her eyelids. "Tell me."

She shook her head.

The look he gave her was speculative, thoughtful. Determined. He brushed his lips along the sensitive curve of her ear, trailing them down her neck to the dip in her collarbone.

"Last chance to bare your secrets, Ms. Sinclair, or I will tease them out of you."

Her breath caught in her throat. She ached with a need only he could fill, but what if the truth sent him running? Should she take the risk? Maybe she should. The truth might be an easy way out for both of them.

"Um…" She couldn't get the words out. She didn't want to know the most precious part of her life had driven him away.

He blazed a trail of fiery kisses along her jaw and then pulled back. "I already know, and I'm still here."

"You couldn't possibly know." She leaned toward him, desperate for his touch, and hating herself for her desire. He had made his position clear after the phone call. Fun. Nothing more.

"Trust me," he whispered.

Katy's stomach clenched. She wasn't good at trust. Not after Steven. But she wasn't good at deception either. Or uncertainty. She wanted the measure of the man who made her melt inside.

She swallowed hard. "Melissa. My daughter. She's seven. I taught her some tricks when she was learning to tie a bow." Her stomach knotted but she forged ahead. "I have a son too. Justin. He's nine."

She reached around her back and secured the laces of her dress. "No husband, though. Not anymore. I was married for ten years to Steven and we divorced last year. He's a heart surgeon at Vancouver General Hospital. We married when I was young—only eighteen. He was older, worldly, and sophisticated. He swept me off my feet. My dad left when I was young and I think I saw Steven as some kind replacement and a way to ensure I didn't wind up alone and depressed like my mom."

Tears welled up in her eyes. She hated talking about Steven. She didn't want to think of the ten years she had wasted in a loveless marriage—the pain, the heartache, or the loneliness—especially the loneliness.

"Is that all, sugar?"

Is that all? Hadn't he been listening? Married too young. Divorced too late. Kids. Baggage of the worst emotional kind.

"I know it's a lot to deal with." She stumbled over her words as she tried to slip around him and out of his life. "Thanks for helping me with this. I'd better go."

"Not so fast." He pulled her close, and his warm hands circled her waist. "You don't get to run away until after cross-examination."

Katy gave him a tentative smile. "Do your worst, counsel. You won't break me."

Mark nuzzled her ear and then licked his way down her neck. "Do you still see him?"

"The kids live with me but we have joint custody so he comes to the house a few times a week. It's...difficult."

Mark pulled away. "Not a friendly divorce, I take it?"

Katy shook her head. "Pretty bad. He had so many affairs I lost count and then he left me for an intern, but when I served the divorce papers he went crazy. He thought he would have his fun and come back like every other time. But I'd finally had enough and I was making enough money by then I thought I would be able to manage on

121

Sarah Castille

my own if he made things difficult."

He cupped her cheek in his hand and tilted her head up. "I'm sorry, sugar."

Katy leaned in to the warmth of his touch. "The kids make it worth the heartache."

"I thought you might have children," he said softly. "Your body tells its own stories." His arms tightened around her and he brushed his lips over her forehead.

Katy pulled away. "That doesn't actually make me feel any better." She didn't like to think about how her body had changed after having the kids.

"It should." He gently tugged the ribbons at the top of her corset, loosening them inch by inch until she could feel a rush of cool air over her breasts.

"What are you doing?" She froze, her moment of relief at not being rejected shattered by the fear of discovery.

"Well, first, I'm not running away. Second, I'm showing you just how much I like your body." He trailed a warm finger over the crescents of her breasts, sending shivers of lightening straight to her core.

"Third, I'm reliving our phone conversation. Except this time, I don't have to use my imagination."

Her heart drummed against her ribcage in time to the waves crashing below them. But the salty ocean spray did nothing to cool her heated skin.

She wrapped her arms around her chest, hiding herself from his heated gaze. "Are you crazy? We were on the line with that phone call. We are definitely crossing it now."

"I'll deal with it." He eased her hands away and placed them around his waist. Katy's breasts brushed against the soft cotton of his shirt and she shivered at the erotic sensation.

"How?"

"I'll ask another partner to handle the file. I'll tell Steele I have a conflict of interest, which I do."

Katy swallowed hard. "You would do that? Drop the case?"

122

"You are tempting beyond belief," he growled. "I can't think clearly when I'm with you." He trailed soft butterfly kisses along her jaw, down her throat and over the curve of her shoulder.

Every nerve in her body thrummed but she was part of this too. His assurance that he would deal with it wasn't good enough. "Mark? Are you really going to drop the case?"

"Mmmm."

"Answer me." Her voice wavered. Was this just a game to him?

"Trust me, Katy. I would never let anything happen to you. I won't endanger your career. I've thought it through and handing over the file is the best solution. He'll have the best litigator in the firm and my promise I'll be available to handle his other work." His hands roamed her body as his lips dusted their way down to the hollow between her breasts.

Her legs trembled. Hundreds of lawyers danced and drank just behind the door. His assurances could not take away all the risk. But she could not pull herself away from the deliciously dangerous man who saw something appealing in her—something she didn't see.

Craving took hold of her, deep and dark. She stretched up and hesitantly brushed her lips over his.

The violence and speed of his reaction shocked her. One minute she was pressed against him. The next, he had her against the wall, her wrists pinned over her head, his thigh between her legs, forcing them apart.

Moisture flooded her sex. She tilted her head back, seeking the warmth of his lips as she rocked her hips against his leg, her courage fueled by the potent mix of alcohol, need and the scent of the untamed sea. "Kiss me," she whispered.

"You didn't have to ask, sugar." He leaned down and captured her mouth in the kiss she had dreamed about since the first day they met.

Stop. Stop. Stop.

But it was already too late. The decision had been made when he had seen her on the dance floor. He kissed her lightly at first, teasing and tasting, savoring the rich tang of wine on her soft, plump lips. Then he gave into passion, diving in deep, claiming her mouth, hot and wet. A sensual feast long denied.

Katy moaned and arched her back, pressing her breasts against his chest. For the briefest moment he considered releasing her to attend to the enticing mounds, now freed of their constraint, but he couldn't pull himself away.

He sucked her bottom lip between his teeth, nipping gently, until a low, rich groan tore from her throat and her head dropped back against the wall. She tugged against his hands, trying to free her arms. But he couldn't let her touch him. Already they had gone too far. One caress and he would lose that single strand of control keeping him sane. Tightening his grip, he deepened the kiss, taking more of her mouth, feeding his hunger. Feeding hers.

Finally he pulled away and captured both her wrists with one hand, freeing the other to shove her corset down further. He cupped her breast, squeezing lightly as he teased the dusky tip with his thumb.

"Oh God. Don't stop."

"I have no intention of stopping, sugar." He turned his attention to her other breast, laving her nipple until she moaned. His cock stiffened and throbbed under the constricting barrier of his clothes.

Waves crashed against the concrete walls below, enveloping them in a cool, fine mist. He brushed water droplets off the velvet softness of her exposed breasts and then trailed his fingers down over the smooth satin of her dress to the concave dip of her belly. When he reached her mound, he tugged at the skirt bunched around his thigh.

Stop. Not here.

But he couldn't stop. He wanted her with a fierce ache, so shocking in its intensity, it almost took his breath away. And yet, he wanted something more.

The glass door rattled and flew open. Mark froze then dropped Katy's hands and forced himself back. A couple joined them on the balcony, so intent on their conversation they did not realize they were not alone.

Heart pounding, Mark pushed Katy behind him. He hid her from view while she straightened her clothing and laced herself up. When the couple turned toward the water, Katy slipped past him and out the door.

He caught up to her in the hallway, his pulse still hammering in his ears. Her cheeks were flushed, her lips swollen from his kisses, her hair in disarray. Sexy as hell. He wanted her even more. "Come to the club, sugar. We're heading over there now."

The look she gave him made his heart stammer in his chest. Regret? Uncertainty? Fear? He couldn't tell. They needed time alone. Time to talk. Time to finish what they started.

"I have work to do. Pictures. Mingling." She blushed and bit her lip. "We shouldn't have..."

Mark smiled. "Maybe not, but I wouldn't trade that moment for anything. Don't tell me you have regrets."

She looked up at him and her bottom lip quivered, still plump and swollen from his kiss. "I do," she whispered. "And I don't."

Katy shifted her weight from one foot to the other. After two long hours of shaking hands and posing for pictures at the banquet, her stiletto boots had finally lost their appeal. She desperately wanted to go home and get the damn boots off. But first she needed a cab. And for some reason, there were none to be found.

The last few partygoers exited the hotel and she watched with longing when they walked down the street to a waiting car. Next time she would forgo the tequila in favor of driving herself home.

She walked to the corner and turned down a side street beside the hotel, hoping to catch a cab before it hit the main road. She had only taken a few steps when a hand grabbed her shoulder and pushed her against the wall with a violent shove.

"Katherine." Jimmy's eyes gleamed fever bright, sending a surge of adrenaline through her veins.

"Jimmy. You're out of jail." She kept her tone low and even, calm, despite her thundering heart. He looked more gaunt than usual, and his dark eyes had sunk farther into their sockets. Still there was no mistaking the menace in his voice or the grim set to his mouth. She slid her hand into her purse and fumbled around for something to use as a weapon.

He nodded. "Thanks to you, the judge reduced bail. I had a friend spring me this morning."

"Great."

Katy's fingers closed over the cold steel of her nail file and she slid it into the sleeve of her coat before drawing her hand out of her purse.

Suddenly, Jimmy's hand shot out and circled her neck. "Not great," he snarled. "I hadn't even gotten a block from the jail when some psycho cop dragged me into his vehicle and drove me down to the police station for questioning. Apparently the cops found a plastic bag at Val's place with my prints on it, and they wanted to know what might have been inside."

"You should have called me." Katy choked on her words as his fingers closed around her neck. "You had the right to have a lawyer present when they questioned you."

"I should have called you and asked you for my fucking pills," Jimmy shouted. "But I thought it would be better if I came in person. Your secretary told me where you were. I've been waiting all night out here."

"I don't have your pills." Her heart pounded against her ribcage, and she slid the nail file into her palm.

"Don't lie to me!" Jimmy yelled. Drops of his saliva flecked her face, and her head jerked back, hitting the wall. He increased the pressure on her throat, cutting off her air. She made a feeble attempt to stab him with the nail file but her arms were suddenly too heavy to lift.

"Val took one of the pills, so they had to be in the apartment. You were the one who found her. I told you about them. The police didn't have them. I'm not stupid. I can do the math. I want them back."

Jimmy faded into a gray haze and Katy sagged against the wall.

"Fuck. Wake the fuck up." He released her and the sharp sting of his slap on her cheek cleared the fog from her brain.

She gasped and drew a breath of sweet, cool air into her lungs as she considered her options. She wouldn't get far running in her damn boots, and he was twice her size, so attacking him didn't have a high likelihood of success. She could scream, but at this late hour and on a side street, she doubted anyone would come to her rescue. She would have to talk her way out. It was, after all, what lawyers did best.

"I told you, I couldn't take anything from a crime scene. I didn't take the pills. And if you touch me again, I'm going to scream. Since you're on probation, one strike will land you back in jail." Her words came out in a rush but with a conviction that surprised her.

"You don't understand," he growled "You don't know who you're dealing with. They are serious players. They know I had the pills and they want them. Just hand them over to me and I won't tell them you're involved."

Katy began a slow backward walk toward the main street. "For the last time. I didn't take them. Someone else must have been in the apartment after Val died." She stopped. Mark. He had been in the apartment too. They had split up to make their phone calls.

Her face must have revealed her thoughts because Jimmy narrowed his eyes. "Tell me," he growled. "Who else was there?"

Katy shook her head. "No one." She reached the safety of the main road and looked for help. In the distance she could see headlights, and a couple walking toward her.

"Get the fuck back here," Jimmy spat. "We're not done. You're my fucking lawyer. You're supposed to help me." He took two steps toward her and then spotted the couple, now only half a block away.

"Fuck." He retreated into the alley and Katy raced down the road toward her unwitting rescuers.

"I don't believe you," Jimmy called after her. "When they come for me, I'm going to give them your name."

Chapter Ten

"Ohmigod, lookit the boots! Not really what I pictured you in, but damn, girl, you look hot." Trixie gave Katy a friendly hug. "But what are you doing here? With Val gone, I didn't think we'd see you again."

Katy bit her lip, hoping Trixie wouldn't see it tremble. "I bumped into Mark earlier this evening at a legal function and he said he was coming here. I need to talk to him." Actually, she needed to go home, calm down and think through what to do about Jimmy. But instead, like an idiot, she had asked the cab driver to bring her here.

Trixie studied Katy intently and her forehead creased into a frown.

Katy's pulse kicked up a notch. Was it Mark? Was he here with someone else? "What's wrong?"

"You'd better come into my office." Trixie led Katy into a spacious room, decorated in warm, earthy colors. Filing cabinets lined the far wall and a glass desk took up most of the center space.

She dropped into a huge, overstuffed, beige chair, motioning for Katy to sit on the chair beside her. "You don't look so good. In fact, I would go so far as to say you're in shock."

"Don't be silly."

"I'm sure it will surprise you to know that I don't work here all the time." Trixie leaned over to pat Katy's arm. "I'm a registered nurse, and I know when someone is in shock. Even if you didn't have the pale and clammy skin, huge pupils, dazed look and trembling hands, I would be concerned about the bruises around your neck."

Katy's hand flew to her throat. She'd been so glad to get away from Jimmy, she hadn't even thought about her injuries. "It's nothing."

"Ha. I've seen marks like that before on...someone else. It isn't nothing. Who hurt you, babe?"

Katy shook her head. Much as she wanted to tell Trixie, she couldn't breach an ethical duty to her client, no matter how evil he was. And that meant she couldn't talk to Mark either. What had she been thinking?

"I shouldn't have come." She stood up but Trixie grabbed her hand.

"No, stay. I'll look after you. Also Mark would kill me if he found out you were here and I let you go. Why don't I bring James in for a chat while I get the first aid kit? He's here tonight."

Katy shook her head. "I don't want to talk to the police. Not yet. I have a few things I have to do first. Plus, I'm sure he's here to relax, not work."

Trixie drew Katy back down into the chair. "James is always working. I can't tell you how many times he's arrested people at the club when he's supposed to be here having fun. Actually I think it is fun for him, wandering around, drink in hand, pouncing on the assorted criminals who make it through the door. He needs to find himself a girlfriend. Someone who'll lighten him up and show him there is more to life than catching criminals." She cocked her head. "You sure you don't want me to get him?"

"I'm fine, Trixie. If you could call me a cab, I'll get out of your hair."

Trixie tucked a blanket around her and put a hand to Katy's forehead. "How about you wait for Mark and let him take you home?"

"I don't need him," Katy said. "Actually, I really don't want to see him. This evening...we went too far. I can't face him. I don't even know why I came here."

Trixie gave her a soft smile. "Because part of you knows he would care. I've known him for a long time. I know what kind of man he is. He would want to know, and he would keep you safe."

"That's just the problem." Katy sighed. "He's the one person who can't keep me safe."

"Well, look who's in trouble again."

Lana sucked in a breath as the cop from the alley walked into the tiny, windowless room at Carpe Noctem. The same cop who had scolded her over the phone for daring to put a brochure on his vehicle. Too bad he hadn't told her his name. Up close, she could see he wasn't as old as she had first thought. He probably had eight to ten years on her at the most. A strong jaw complemented the chiseled planes of his face, and his offset nose, obviously broken many times, only added to his appeal.

Dangerous. Exciting.

A woman followed him in and closed the door. Short and curvy with a shock of platinum hair, she had a pleasant face and a warm smile.

"Where's the camera?" The cop leaned against the wall and folded his arms, studying her with sharp, steel blue eyes. She suspected those eyes didn't miss much.

She shrugged. "What camera?"

"I'm not in the mood for games. Three different people saw you taking pictures, including the owner of the club."

Years of experience in the principal's office had given her the ability to remain cool under pressure, but this cop unnerved her. She hadn't expected hugs or kisses but she had thought he would at least acknowledge their phone conversation.

She steeled herself to continue the lies. "Maybe they confused me with someone else."

"Not in that outfit." He lifted his chin, motioning toward her.

Lana smiled and looked down at her electric-blue, fringed bra and matching spandex mini skirt. Okay, so maybe she shouldn't have squeezed her generous ass and boobs into the unforgiving fabric, but damn did it highlight her curves. Plus, she couldn't resist the color. Hell, why wear black when you were showing off the assets?

She winked. "You like what you see?"

He raised a warning eyebrow. Lana slammed her mouth shut. *Dammit, Lana. This is serious.* But he was so gorgeous; she couldn't resist a little tease.

The woman with the platinum hair giggled and the tassels on her outrageous gold and green outfit shook with the slight movement. Lana liked her right away.

"Your lack of respect is going to get you in trouble."

Lana didn't take her eyes off him. "I'm thinking it already has."

He leaned across the table, grabbed her purse and dumped the contents in front of her.

"Hey!" Lana frowned. "That's an illegal search."

He pawed through the pile of make-up, gum wrappers, condoms and parking tickets. "You waived your rights when you snuck into the club."

"It was an honest mistake. I was dancing at the bar next door. I came out for a breath of fresh air. I saw the unmarked red door. I thought it was another entrance and followed someone in. Imagine my surprise when I found myself in a kinky sex club. My innocence has been corrupted. I'm the one who should be upset."

He pulled a few condoms from the pile on the table and waved them at her. "Innocent girls don't dress like that and walk around with a bag full of condoms."

Lana winked. "That's the second time you've mentioned my outfit. I'm flattered. And the bag isn't *full* of condoms. There are only about ten. This is a sex club, isn't it? Doesn't everyone carry condoms here?"

The platinum blonde snorted a laugh.

Damn. Get the mouth under control. But something about him fired off all her cylinders.

His jaw twitched. Did she see the ghost of a smile? If so, it disappeared in an instant.

Lana pushed back her chair. "Okay. You've had your fun. You can see I have no camera so I'll just collect my bag of condoms and get going. You can keep one as a souvenir. Or did you want to frisk me first?" She gave him a little wiggle and finished with a theatrical pose.

Hysterical laughter filled the room. The blonde dabbed at her eyes and gasped in a breath.

"Trixie."

The blonde froze at the cop's sharp reprimand. "Sorry."

She had a soft, musical voice. The kind of voice Lana had always wanted. But no, not for her. At best her voice could be described as husky.

131

He ignored Trixie and glared at Lana. "Who are you following and who are you working for?"

Lana folded her arms. "A little professional respect here. I have to maintain client confidentiality."

"Maybe we should take her to the back. I've always wanted to watch a good spanking." Trixie's voice took on a sharp, discordant edge.

Lana scowled at her new friend. *Platinum is just so out.*

The cop rubbed his hand over his chin. The five o'clock shadow looked good on him. Roughened him up just the way she liked 'em.

"Maybe..."

Lana jumped up. "You are not seriously considering spanking me. I'd have the police down here so fast your head would spin. Then I'd hire the best lawyer in the city to sue you until you didn't have a dime. That's after I take that paddle and stick it where the sun don't shine."

Trixie slapped a hand over her mouth to stifle a laugh.

The cop raised an eyebrow. "The police?"

Ooops. "I mean the other police."

"Sit," he commanded.

She sat. *How did he do that?*

He took the chair across from her. "I want the camera. I know it's here."

His eyes glittered as if he was a snake charmer trying to hypnotize her. Maybe he was hypnotizing her. Damned if she could look away. Liquid arousal shot through her veins, startling her with its intensity. Wow. When had she ever responded to a man that way?

Don't look at the lipstick. Don't look at the lipstick.

She dragged her eyes away and looked at the lipstick.

"Thank you," he murmured. His soft rumble made her cheeks flame. She imagined hearing that sensual voice in her ear at night, telling her exactly what he planned to do with her body.

Holy cow. Get a grip. Danger situation here.

He picked up the lipstick and pulled it open. The tiny camera lens glinted in the overhead lights.

"Nice piece of equipment. Whose pictures am I going to find on here?"

Her bottom lip quivered. Her best surveillance equipment and her best photos gone in a flash. Mr. S wasn't going to be pleased. Poor old Jetta. It would have to wheeze along for another few months.

"No comment."

He picked up her wallet and pulled out her ID. "Private Investigator Lana Parker, your license states you've been an investigator for all of one month."

She blushed. "We all have to start somewhere."

"Not in this club, you don't." He put the lipstick in his pocket and stood up. "Trixie, get Rick to escort her out. Tell him to make sure she doesn't hang around outside."

"Aren't you going to give her your card, James? Just in case she needs to get in touch?" Trixie caught Lana's gaze and gave her a wink.

Lana's lips quivered with a repressed smile. "James is a good name for a cop." She took the card from his outstretched hand. "Strong. Steady. Sensitive. James is a powerful name but soft on the tongue."

He stared at her, his face impassive, his body still. But for the twitch of his jaw and a slight flare of his nostrils, she would never have guessed her words had affected him at all.

"My God," Trixie muttered under her breath. "You shocked him."

"You can go now, Lana." The sensual rumble of his voice as he said her name grabbed hold and buried deep. Desire rushed up inside her, nearly overwhelming her with the need to touch him.

Distance. She needed distance.

Trixie's eyes widened. "Um. Maybe you should get her contact information...you know...in case you need to...contact her."

"Not necessary," James said, his eyes lingering on Lana's lips. "I already have it."

"Hell."

Mark slammed the door to Tony's club office and threw himself

133

into Tony's worn, leather desk chair. He scrubbed his hands over his face and tried to get a grip on the extent of his stupidity.

What the hell had happened? If they hadn't been interrupted on the terrace, he would have compromised both their careers. When exactly had he lost control? When he'd first seen her dancing with Tim? Or when Tim had crossed the line? No. He'd kept his cool. Tim was still alive.

The door creaked open.

"Here, Tony said you might need this. He's tied up with a staff matter and won't be in for a while." James handed him a glass of whiskey and dropped into the chair across from Tony's steel-framed desk. The décor in the office reflected the design of the club. Ultra modern, light and functional.

"Where were you all night?" Mark swirled the amber liquid in his glass.

"We caught a private investigator sneaking around the club. Cheeky little thing. I didn't get much out of her, but I have her camera. I'll take it to the lab and find out who she was following."

Mark raised his eyebrows. "I didn't realize you even knew the word cheeky and I find it hard to believe you weren't able to get any information out of her. You. The esteemed and seasoned detective who has extracted confessions from dozens of hardened criminals." His glass clinked when he put it on the table. "Something tells me you didn't try very hard."

"Don't go there."

Mark tried not to smile. He couldn't remember the last time James had evinced even the slightest interest in a woman except for the odd fling. When he had his own problems sorted, he would have to look her up. He couldn't imagine a woman strong enough to capture the interest of his oldest friend.

"You want to be left alone?"

Mark shook his head. He needed to talk and James knew him better than anyone. Even when Mark had pushed him away, James had never given up on him. He traced the scar across his neck. If James hadn't come looking for him that day...

"I heard Katy came in." James stretched out his legs.

Mark choked on his whiskey. "Katy came here? Tonight?"

James nodded. "Apparently she was looking for you."

"Fuck." Mark slammed his glass on the desk and threw himself back in his chair. "I told her I would be here, but Tony kept me at the damn banquet chatting up some mid-level firm looking for a merger."

James sipped his whiskey, his blue eyes cool and calm. "Probably a good thing since you have a conflict and all." He paused and lowered his glass. "Trixie said she was pretty upset."

Mark took a sip of his whiskey. The bitter liquid suffused his taste buds before it burned its way down to his stomach. "Things got...complicated."

"Complicated?" James leaned forward. "I'm hoping complicated isn't the reason for the bruises Trixie saw around her neck."

"Bruises?" Mark pushed back his chair. "Where is she? What happened?"

James held up a hand. "Calm down. Trixie looked after her. Any idea who might have hurt her?"

"Why are you asking me?"

James shrugged. "I thought she might have confided in you. I checked the system and she hasn't filed a police report. If someone is assaulting women, he needs to be caught."

Mark rubbed his hand over his head and took his seat. "She has an acrimonious relationship with her ex-husband and there was a guy at the banquet, a court reporter, who wasn't too happy when I stopped him from pawing her on the dance floor. When I find out who hurt her—"

"Don't even think about it." James cut him off. "If she reports it, the police will handle it. If she doesn't, she'll have a reason. You know you can't get involved."

Mark shot back the last sip of whiskey. "I am involved."

"So what are you going to do?"

Mark shrugged. "I've got a plan to resolve the conflict. But even then...I keep thinking about Claire. I pushed too hard, and look what happened."

"You know what I think about Claire," James grumbled. "Yes, you pushed her. You made her look at herself and realize what she needed. And what she needed you couldn't give. You didn't love her. She got that. She moved on. What happened afterward was the result of her choices. It had nothing to do with you. I have never understood why you can't let her go."

"She reminds me of who I am and why I can't get seriously involved with anyone ever again." A life on the streets with a drug addict for a mother had not prepared him for the give and take needed to sustain a relationship. How could someone who had never known love have anything to offer? He hadn't been enough for Claire. He wouldn't be enough for Katy.

"If you really believe that, then you'll back off before it's too late."

Mark gave a bitter laugh. "It's already too late."

Dear Mark

Dear Mr. Richards

Mark

Katy deleted the email and checked her watch. Fifteen minutes until her next court hearing. With Mark. No time to run out for a coffee. She put her laptop on the seat beside her and leaned against the wall. A flurry of lawyers raced down the corridor, their robes fluttering behind them. Late for court. She knew the signs.

Palm fronds rustled in their wake and leafy shadows danced across the carpet. A beam of sunshine flooded through the atrium, catching the tips of her shiny, black Manolo Blahniks. She didn't bother much about her suits, but she always bought nice shoes.

She flipped again through the document list Mark had sent over and snorted. Ten documents. What a joke. Hi-Tech had to have more than ten documents relating to Martha's dismissal. Her performance reviews should have filled a file folder. What about board minutes, HR files, internal emails? Where were the security tapes? Even if they'd been erased, they should have been listed. He wasn't even claiming the missing documents were privileged. Apparently they just didn't exist.

She should call him and demand further disclosure. If he had been any other lawyer on any other case, she wouldn't have hesitated to pick up the phone. But how could she call him after the banquet? What would she say? Would she tell him she regretted the risk they had taken or that she regretted they had not taken things further? Email would have to do.

She flipped through the amended pleadings he had sent over this morning, and her eyes narrowed. What the hell? She read quickly through the outrageous counterclaim and her mind clouded with anger. How could he do this to Martha? Why now?

"Am I interrupting something?"

Katy's head jerked up at the familiar sound of her managing partner's voice. "Ted! What are you doing here?"

As always, Ted was impeccably dressed in a starched white shirt, pressed black wool suit and a crisp red tie. He was rail thin, with sharp, hard features and silver-gray hair that matched his eyes. He had earned his court nickname, the Silver Fox, not because of his looks—he had been young and dark-haired when he was awarded the moniker—but because he was sly, cunning and an unabashed opportunist.

"I just wanted to check in and see how my favorite associate is handling her seminal case. I have to report back to the partnership committee on your courtroom performance, so I thought I'd sit in on today's hearing." He squeezed Katy's shoulder. "I'm also worried about you after that incident with Jimmy Rider. I want to make sure you're still able to do your job."

Katy swallowed hard. No way would she tell Ted just how much Jimmy had shaken her. She hadn't slept in two days nor had she been able to focus on preparing for today's hearing. She had even contemplated asking Steven to sleep over after he brought the kids home on Sunday. Ted couldn't have picked a worse time to assess her.

She heard voices in the corridor and recognized the timbre of Mark's deep voice. She spotted him outside one of the nearby courtrooms, talking to a client. His perfectly tailored gray suit highlighted his broad shoulders and slim waist. She couldn't decide if he looked better in a suit or in his tux. Or maybe he would look best without any clothing at all...

No. Look away. But the warning came too late. When she glanced up again, dark eyes drew her in. Katy flushed under Mark's scrutiny and managed a faint smile when he walked toward them.

"Ms. Sinclair. A pleasure to see you again." The formality in his tone gave her the strength she needed to reach out and shake his hand.

"Mr. Richards." She couldn't think of anything else to say. Not about the weekend. Not about the case. Not even about the weather. The memory of their kiss lingered on her lips even as her blood boiled.

He shifted his gaze to Ted who stood fuming beside her, unused to being ignored. "Knight."

Ted nodded. "Richards. Haven't seen you for ages." The two men shook hands but their movements were stiff and forced. Katy frowned. They clearly knew each other, but what was the reason for their animosity? A heated case? Professional discourtesy? Or was it personal?

"I hope you're not being too hard on my associate." Ted's smile didn't reach his eyes.

"She's definitely giving me a run for my money."

"I'm looking forward to seeing that." Ted winked at Katy. "I'll see you inside."

They watched him pull open the heavy oak door and disappear into the courtroom.

"Very nice shoes, but I think I preferred the boots," Mark murmured. He stood so close, she could feel the heat radiating off his body and smell the familiar, spicy tang of his cologne. She gripped her bag so her hands wouldn't be tempted to wind their way around his neck and pull him toward her.

Two men in gray suits walked past them and a group of court watchers stopped beside the courtroom door to check the court schedule. Katy waited until the hallway cleared before thrusting the amended pleadings at Mark's chest.

"How could you do this? Your client is suing Martha for theft, libel and interference with contract? She has no job thanks to Steele. She's mortgaged her house to pay my fees. If she loses, she'll be totally destroyed."

Mark shrugged. "I'm sure you advised her about the risks of suing a company with unlimited financial resources, especially after the regulators dismissed her allegations. Hi-Tech only wants to protect its reputation and to send a message to other wannabe whistle-blowers."

"Maybe Hi-Tech isn't the shining beacon of corporate responsibility you make them out to be," she snapped.

"Maybe your client isn't as innocent as you would like to believe."

Katy sucked in a sharp breath and tightened her jaw. "She has nothing to hide. She was trying to do the right thing."

"It's not personal, sugar. It's business." He ran his fingers along the edge of the silk scarf Katy had tied around her neck to hide the bruises Jimmy had left behind.

"It's bad business," she mumbled, pulling away. She didn't want him to see the state of her neck. Even Steven had been shocked.

"Why the scarf, sugar? It isn't something you normally wear." The steel threading his voice sent a chill up her spine.

Katy batted his hand away. "I wanted to try something different."

"You wanted to hide something." He yanked on the scarf and it slid off her neck with a violent hiss.

"No." Katy grabbed hold too late.

Mark studied her neck and his voice dropped to a low growl. "Was it Steven? Tim? I promise you, whoever did this will never touch you again."

Katy grabbed her scarf and wound it back around her neck. "It's a law firm matter. Ted is handling it. There's no reason to get involved."

"Ted?" Mark barked out a laugh. "He doesn't give a damn about your safety. All he cares about are his fees and his reputation. Did he tell you not to report it? I'll bet he did. That means whoever did it is still out on the street. Give me a name, sugar."

Katy blushed and looked away. Ted had been adamant she keep the incident quiet. Not only that, he had been reluctant to take her off Jimmy's case. Only her threat to talk to one of the other partners had finally changed his mind.

"I can't," she whispered.

Mark's lips thinned into a tight line. "Then, I'll guess. Firm matter, which means he's a client. Violent, which suggests criminal tendencies. I know one of your criminal clients. I also know he likes to throttle women who don't give him what he wants. I saw the same bruises on Valerie's neck. Tony and I had several discussions with him."

Katy swallowed hard and gave him a worried glance. "Please, don't do anything. He's dangerous."

Mark clenched his jaw. "So am I."

Chapter Eleven

"So what do you think of the Forensics Lab?" Trixie waved her arm in a sweeping gesture meant to encompass the entire restaurant and narrowly missed a potted plant on the ledge behind her.

"I keep expecting someone to give us a box with evidence samples or ask us to solve a murder." Katy swirled the last of the Caymus Conundrum around her glass. Mark would have appreciated the slightly sweet wine she had chosen to complement their Asian meal.

Stop it. But she couldn't get him out of her mind.

"To be honest, I didn't even know this restaurant existed," she said. "I don't really get out much." And after tonight, she wouldn't be going out any time soon. Hi-Tech's application to amend the pleadings had been approved. She and Mark were in for one hell of a long, drawn out fight.

But more than that, she and Mark were done. After the hearing, he had apologized for what happened on the terrace and assured her it wouldn't happen again. *Keep it professional,* he had said. *Steer clear of conflict.* She couldn't understand why he had backtracked after he had been so adamant he was going to turn the case over to another partner in the firm. But of course she had agreed. Although his rejection had stung, it was best to end it before anyone got hurt.

Too bad her heart didn't agree.

Trixie laughed. "I know every restaurant and bar in town. Gotta keep up with the competition. Tony lets me expense everything if I bring him back new ideas for the club."

"I'm not letting you pay tonight," Katy warned. "It was nice of you to call and invite me out. I've neglected my friends for so long; no one even bothers with me anymore."

Trixie laughed. "You'll never get rid of me. When I meet someone I like, I stick like glue. Plus I wanted to check up on you in case you'd been hit with post-traumatic stress disorder. You were pretty shaken when you came into the club the other night."

"It wasn't traumatic. Just...unsettling," Katy lied. She leaned back in her chair and looked out at the boats in Coal Harbor. Situated beside Stanley Park and overlooking the water, the cozy restaurant with its dark wood tables and richly hued walls couldn't help but do well. "I'm fine, really. I'm just worried about Mark. He figured out who it was and he said he was going to deal with him. I don't want him to get hurt."

Katy took a quick look around the restaurant to make sure no one could overhear their conversation. A few couples, a group of men in suits and a woman dining alone. No one she knew, but busy for a Monday night.

She looked at the woman again. *Brave.* Had she ever dined alone? The woman scribbled in a notebook, engrossed in her writing. Her food sat untouched on the table in front of her. She reached up to tuck her hair behind her ear. Beautiful, flame red hair. Was she waiting for someone? Women that beautiful didn't need to eat alone.

"I wouldn't worry about him," Trixie said. "Have you taken a good look at the guy? He'll wipe the floor with Jimmy."

"You knew who it was too?"

"The thumb marks on the collarbone and fingerprints along the neck are his trade mark." Trixie waved a hand toward Katy's scarf. "I also knew he was your client so it wasn't hard to put two and two together."

"Who else knows?"

Trixie grimaced. "I might have mentioned it to James, and he might have organized a patrol car to check your place periodically at night."

"Trixie!"

She shrugged. "I'm not bound by any confidentiality rules, and it was just a guess. But a good one. Jimmy's a bad customer. I just wanted you to be safe."

"That's what Mark said." Katy glanced over at the red-haired woman. She was eating now so obviously not waiting for anyone. Or maybe someone had stood her up. Was she a writer or a reporter? Maybe in Vancouver on business? She looked up and Katy quickly turned away.

Trixie reached across the table and grabbed Katy's hand. "He means it."

"I believe you, but it can't work between us and not just because of the legal conflict I told you about. I've only started getting back on my feet. I don't want someone interfering in my life and messing things up. I don't want another Steven."

"He doesn't want another Claire," Trixie murmured.

"Who's Claire?"

Trixie's eyes widened and she slapped a hand over her mouth. "Pretend I didn't say that."

"Tell me," Katy demanded. "Does he have a girlfriend? A wife? I never thought to ask. It's been so long since I..."

"Dated?" Trixie offered.

The red-haired woman looked over and arched an eyebrow with obvious interest.

"We're not dating. We can't be dating. We've never had a date and never will."

Unabashed, Trixie smiled. "Stop beating yourself up. Claire was in the distant past. So the answer is no, he doesn't have anyone. But he needs someone. You."

Katy slumped in her seat. "Not me. He made that clear today."

The red-haired woman waved down the waiter and asked him for the bill. Katy caught him on his way to the cash register and asked for their bill as well. She had to pay time and a half for her babysitter's overtime and if she wasn't careful now, she'd be in trouble when trial season was in full swing.

They collected their coats and headed outside to hail a taxi. Trixie leaned against a lamp post and chewed on a long red nail. "Was your solution to the professional conflict working before last Saturday?"

Katy shrugged. "You mean stopping myself from jumping all over him whenever he walked into a room? I suppose it worked until I drank too much tequila." She shivered, remembering their risky behavior on the terrace. "There's no way to resolve the conflict unless one of us drops the case. He offered to do it and then changed his mind. I can't make the same offer."

Trixie gave her a wicked grin. "Maybe he needs more of an incentive."

"Trixie!" Katy laughed. "This isn't high school. I'm not chasing after him, and I'm not going to interfere with his legal practice. It didn't work out. I'm okay with that. Sometimes life gets in the way." She had always thought herself a good liar but Trixie's snort of disbelief said otherwise.

"When are you seeing him next?"

"Wednesday morning. We have a court hearing. It's going to be one hell of a fight."

A taxi pulled up at the curb and Trixie waved Katy toward it. "Ooooh delicious. It's perfect." She put her hand on the door. "Call me tomorrow. I know exactly where you need to shop."

Katy opened her mouth to protest but Trixie cut her off.

"I know. It can't work. But he was clearly willing to try until something changed his mind. Why not test his resolve? Besides you could really use a new suit."

"Storm? Who wrote 'storm' on my whiteboard? This isn't a weather report."

James looked over at his team. No one liked the daily seven a.m. meetings, but the only signs of protest were the increasingly large cups of coffee scenting the air.

"I did, sir." Mike walked up to the white board and began to draw. James took a seat beside Joanna, the newest addition to his team. She smiled and took a deep breath, her breasts rising and falling under her tight, red sweater.

But not as tight as Lana's mouth-watering, electric-fucking-blue, barely-an-excuse-for-a-top. And that goddammed skirt. Where the hell did she get off dressing like that? Her outfit was outrageous even for a fetish club. Well, maybe not outrageous, but definitely not something to be shared around. After catching her snooping around Carpe Noctem, he had hustled her to his club office as much to get her away from the lascivious stares of the patrons as to interrogate her.

And what an interrogation. James bit back a laugh. Lana was all confidence and a whole lot of sass. He had never been sassed like that in his entire life. Usually his harsh manner cowed people into submission. Maybe she had no sense of self-preservation. She should have been running in terror instead of teasing him with her lush body and then giving him a glimpse of her soft side with her little speech about his name.

Mike finished his drawing and pointed to the pattern of small circles resembling a military plan of attack. "The pathologist now believes Garcia died of multiple organ failure caused by something called a cytokine storm. It's an overactive response of the immune system that's often fatal. When there is a pathogen present, the body produces cytokines that signal immune cells to travel to the site of the infection. The immune cells attack the pathogen and make more cytokines. Usually the body keeps it all in check, but sometimes the reaction becomes uncontrolled and healthy cells and tissues are attacked too. The cause isn't clearly understood but the pathologist said it can happen if there is a new and highly pathogenic invader."

James raised his eyebrows. "Such as?"

"A number of infectious and non-infectious diseases have been identified as causing cytokine storms. Things like SARS, smallpox, bird flu and sepsis. The pathologist has ordered tests to try and identify the cause in this case."

"So you're saying Garcia might have had a fatal reaction to some kind of illness?"

"Yes, sir."

"Any luck getting his medical records?"

Mike shook his head. "No medical records. He's never been to a doctor, at least one who keeps records."

"What about Valerie Wood?" James frowned. They were getting nowhere fast with the evidence, and the clock was ticking.

"We don't have the toxicology results yet, but the preliminaries suggest the same thing. The pathologist found the same evidence of multiple organ failure, but more acute."

James raked his hand through his hair. "So where are we? Our victims share the same symptoms, so they might have caught a new disease. If that's the case, the coroner will have to be notified. But if it is a disease, why do we have only two victims? My gut tells me we're on the wrong track."

"What about the baggies, sir?"

James nodded. "Two baggies, both fingerprint-linked to a known drug dealer, Jimmy Rider. Unfortunately, Mr. Rider disappeared shortly after I hauled him in for questioning. But first he managed to find time to assault his lawyer. I think we have enough to get a warrant to search Rider's premises. I also want his picture in every police station and community police center in the city. If he's in Vancouver, we'll find him."

James dismissed the team and then leaned back in his chair and sighed. They were underfunded and undermanned. Too bad he couldn't hire an investigator to help them. A red-headed one with the sweetest ass he had ever seen. Maybe after he pulled up the pictures of her target, he would give her a call. He would need a name to attach to the pictures. After what he'd seen in the club, he doubted she would give it to him. Another interrogation might be necessary.

He could hardly wait.

"Martha?"

Katy raised her voice, hoping her client wouldn't hear Steven and the kids fighting over the Wii. Steven had switched his double shift and now she had to endure his presence for an extra night this week. The things she did for her children.

Martha didn't seem to mind the background noise, and Katy briefed her on the counterclaim, the document request hearing scheduled for the next day and her planned meeting with Terry Silver on Thursday. "I also heard from Martin. He's leaving the country on Friday and has agreed to a deposition on Friday morning. I'm going to spring it on opposing counsel in the hearing tomorrow so he won't have time to interfere. I'm pretty sure the judge will allow it."

"I can't believe it." Martha said. "Martin refused to get involved before. How did you change his mind?"

"I would love to take credit for his decision, but he contacted me and made the offer. He said he'd read something in the newspaper that made him realize he could save lives by giving evidence."

She quizzed Martha about what she expected Martin to say and took copious notes until Martha had exhausted her knowledge about Martin's time at the company.

"I'm afraid my other news isn't so good." Katy sighed and leaned back in her chair. "I can't get in touch with one of the men on the list, Andrew McIntyre. The Davidsons refuse to speak to me, and I haven't heard back from Patricia Cunningham. If it's okay with you, I have another meeting in Burnaby tomorrow afternoon just a few blocks away from the Cunninghams' house and I might just stop by on my way home to see if she'll talk to me."

"Sounds good," Martha said. "I really want you to get to the bottom of this. And don't worry about the fees. Do whatever you have to do."

Don't worry about the fees? She had never had a client who didn't worry about fees.

"I've done some digging into the men on Martin's list," Katy said. "They were all employed by Cleenaway, a cleaning contractor. I called the manager, but he wouldn't give me any details except to confirm they no longer worked for his company. Does the name ring any bells?"

"Sorry. I didn't pay much attention to the cleaners. They always came in as I was leaving."

Steven's shadow loomed large in Katy's office and she waved him away. When he didn't leave, she got up, slammed the door in his face and returned to her desk to continue the call.

"You should be aware that opposing counsel will be present at the deposition and he'll report the substance of the evidence to Steele. We'll lose the advantage of surprise by bringing the evidence out now, but I don't see we have a choice given Martin's imminent departure."

Steven knocked on the door. The constant *tap, tap, tap* set her nerves on edge. She pressed the phone closer to her ear. "I'll try to work it in. Other than that, things are progressing as they should be.

147

We expect to have a trial date for spring or summer next year."

Martha gasped. "That's almost a year from now. I didn't realize I would have to wait so long."

"We're lucky," Katy assured her. "Some of my clients have to wait two or three years before they get to court."

The door burst open and Steven stormed in, fuming. Katy frowned and pointed to the phone and mouthed the word *client*. Steven didn't take the hint. He leaned against the bookshelves and folded his arms.

Katy wrapped up the call with a few housekeeping matters and then turned to glare at the man she had once thought was the center of her world. "What the hell is wrong with you? I was on a call with a client. You know perfectly well I can't conduct confidential business with you in the room."

"You're seeing someone."

Katy froze. "What? Don't be ridiculous."

"I bumped into Sonia Rutledge on my way in. She said you didn't get home until two o'clock on Saturday morning."

Katy rolled her eyes. Eighty-two year old Sonia spent her days and most of her nights collecting gossip to share at her weekly tea party. "Well there's a good source of information," she snapped.

"Don't be unkind, Kate. It's not like you. In fact, you've changed over the last few weeks and I don't like it. Is it him? Your new boyfriend? Is he the reason you're running around in the middle of the night and snapping at me when I just want to share some family time together?"

Katy toyed with the letter opener on her desk. Long, sleek and very sharp. Almost like a knife. With his formidable medical skills, would Steven be able to save himself if she stabbed him?

Get a grip, Sinclair. She put the opener in the desk drawer and slammed it shut.

"Not that it's any of your business, but I am not seeing anyone. And if I was, you would be the last person I would ever tell."

"Come play on the Wii with us." He held out his hand, expecting her to take it.

"I'm in court tomorrow. I have to prepare."

"Just one game. You never play."

Katy didn't like his accusatory tone nor did she like his competitive streak. Usually family games ended with Steven punching the air in victory and one of the kids crying.

"I have an idea, Steven. How about you clean the kitchen, help the kids with their homework, get their things ready for school tomorrow, do the laundry, sew Melissa's ballet suit, make the lunches and put the kids to bed? Once that's done and my work is finished, then I'll play."

Steven narrowed his eyes. "Don't pull that crap with me. I know what you're up to on the weekends and it isn't work. Maybe you should stop pretending you're eighteen and start acting like a mother again." He stormed out of her office, slamming the door behind him.

Mark drummed his fingers on the counsel table at the front of the courtroom.

He had exhausted every avenue at his disposal, pulled in favors, even visited some very old and unsavory friends, but he couldn't find Jimmy Rider. James had refused to help him. Apparently Jimmy was a person of interest in an open case and James had warned Mark away. But Mark couldn't let it go. He couldn't sleep knowing Jimmy was still walking the streets. If James hadn't arranged for the police check at Katy's house, he would have been outside her home every night.

He looked down the center aisle but the heavy doors were still shut. A few lawyers and court watchers chatted at the back of the courtroom. He tried to focus on the papers in front of him but his mind kept drifting to Katy. Breaking it off had been the right decision. The surge of protective anger that had almost overwhelmed him when he had seen the bruises on her neck had been the wake-up call he needed. He had fallen too hard, too fast. It had to end before someone got hurt.

A rush of cold air hit his neck as the door opened behind him. He turned to look. No posturing today. He needed to see her. Make sure she was okay.

His eyes widened. *What the hell is she wearing?*

Mark leaped from his chair and left the counsel table, moving to intercept Katy before she made it to the front of the room. Every male in the courtroom had to be ogling her as she sauntered down the aisle. The judge would sanction her for...what? Being so damned sexy he could barely breathe?

Katy didn't spare him a glance as she walked toward him, her hips swaying in her too-short, too-tight pencil skirt and stiletto heels. Her fitted jacket hugged every curve of her lush body and the plunging neckline of her white shirt highlighted the full, round breasts he couldn't get out of his mind. Her hair fanned out in a silken sheet across her back. No ponytail today. Totally indecent. He wanted to grab her and hustle her outside, or better yet, throw his jacket over her and cover her up.

"Katy. Stop. You can't go..."

She stared through him and sidestepped his outstretched arm. After dropping her books on her counsel table, she walked up to the bench to give her details to the court reporter.

How had he missed Tim at the front of the courtroom? He should have been blinded by the shock of red hair.

Mark sat down and watched Tim's shifty eyes slide down Katy's chest as she leaned over to sign her name. If Tim so much as laid a finger on her, he was going to grab him and shove him through the nearest wall. Katy leaned forward to whisper in Tim's ear and her skirt hiked up high enough for Mark to catch the flash of a red garter strap.

Hell. Why couldn't she have just worn pantyhose? Was she deliberately trying to distract him? He shifted uncomfortably in his seat.

"All rise."

Katy returned to her table and they stood when the judge entered the courtroom. The proceedings commenced and Mark dropped into his seat, grateful for the cover the table provided.

Katy remained standing and outlined her application for Hi-Tech to produce all relevant documents. She railed at Mark and Hi-Tech for ignoring or rejecting her previous requests and was warned by the judge to tone down her remarks.

Confident, articulate and damn sexy, she talked the judge

through the documents and cases with dizzying speed. Impressive. Especially for an associate. If she hadn't been arguing against him, Mark would have hired her on the spot.

While the judge sifted through the file, Mark's mind drifted into his favorite fantasy. He imagined her on the judge's desk, her skirt hiked up, her lacy garter belt exposed, her shirt unbuttoned, bra off, soft creamy breasts awaiting his pleasure. This time he took the fantasy a step further, laying her back on the judge's desk and running his tongue...

"Mr. Richards, do you have a response?"

You bet I do.

Mark jerked back to reality and shifted his trousers to hide his *response.* The judge waited. Katy waited. Everyone in the courtroom waited for his answer. He recovered his composure, grabbed his file and spent fifteen minutes in arguments, ensuring Steele's money was well spent. By the time he reached the end of his submission, Katy was visibly fuming.

"They are hiding documents," she spluttered.

Mark ground his teeth. "My client's representative assures me Hi-Tech has no relevant documents that have not already been disclosed."

The judge shuffled through the papers. "If there were relevant documents, Mr. Richards, where would they be located?"

Mark grimaced. The judge had clearly decided against him. "I believe all Hi-Tech's documents are at the head office on Broadway Street."

The judge smiled at Katy. "I agree with Ms. Sinclair. I find it difficult to believe there are no other documents pertaining to the plaintiff's dismissal. I'm going to rule that all the documents requested by Ms. Sinclair be produced within seven days of today. If that does not happen, then Ms. Sinclair may apply to attend at Hi-Tech's premises for a document inspection."

Mark slammed his file closed. The judge had been way too lenient with her. Anyone else would have seen right through her fishing expedition.

"Anything else, Ms. Sinclair?"

Katy shot Mark a sideways glance and for the barest second he caught the hint of a wicked smile. "Your Honor, the defendant's amended pleadings are high-handed and the allegations are outrageous. Libel? Theft? Interference? It is a waste of the court's time and our clients' money to bring a case against the plaintiff. Defense counsel knows perfectly well my client does not have five million dollars to satisfy the damage claim, especially since his client is the one who fired her. I move to strike the amendment."

Adrenaline rushed through Mark's veins. Nothing fired his blood as much as a good courtroom scrap.

In response to Katy's motion, he argued that his client had a reputation to protect, no matter how impoverished the perpetrator of the alleged libel. Further, Hi-Tech could lose billions of dollars if a competitor got access to the highly confidential information Saunders had allegedly stolen from the company.

The judge agreed.

Mark glanced over at Katy. He expected disappointment, maybe anger or resentment. She had just lost a major point in the hearing. Instead, she tossed her hair and gave him a wink. She clearly wasn't done with him yet.

"Anything else, Ms. Sinclair?"

"Yes, Your Honor. An application to depose a witness."

Mark frowned and sucked in his lips. An ambush.

Katy smiled. "Gotcha," she mouthed at him.

Mark shot out of his seat. "I wasn't given any notice of this application."

"I apologize, Your Honor," Katy said. "I only just found out the witness intends to leave the country on Saturday and, as a result, it is a matter of some urgency. His name is Martin Kowalski. He is a former employee of the defendant." She outlined the importance of the witness's evidence and handed Mark a bundle of papers.

"Mr. Richards, have you any objection?"

Mark tapped his foot. He would have to be on guard not to underestimate his little wildcat in the future. "I'm not in a position to take instructions from my client. I respectfully request an adjournment to consider the application further."

The judge huffed. "I'm going to make the order. I don't see how justice would be served by taking the risk that the witness leaves before an order can be made."

Katy beamed. Mark tightened his lips and drummed his fingers on the desk. Steele would be less than pleased, but there was nothing he could have done to prevent the ambush.

The judge rushed out of the courtroom, no doubt annoyed his afternoon hearings had all overrun and it was now well into dinner time. Mark followed Tim and the court officials out the main door. The court watchers had been ushered out an hour earlier when the courthouse officially closed for the evening. He waited for Katy to join him, but when she didn't appear he headed down the hallway to the security desk.

Time to call in a favor.

Chapter Twelve

Katy froze when the courtroom door cracked open and a rush of cool air sailed down the aisle and up to the judge's desk where she sat in guilty splendor.

"I see someone has delusions of grandeur after her impressive performance this afternoon," Mark said from the back of the courtroom.

Katy sagged back in the huge, red leather judge's chair. "Oh God. I thought you were security or one of the sheriffs." She took a deep breath to try to slow her racing heart. "I heard a rumor that someone was caught sitting at a judge's desk and the judge sent him to jail for contempt of court."

"Then you'd better hope I don't report you." Mark walked down the aisle toward her. His Italian leather shoes thudded softly on the plush red carpet. He stopped at the counsel desk at the end of the aisle, loosened his tie and rolled up his sleeves. Was he looking for another fight?

For a long moment they simply stared at each other.

"I was drafting the order for you to sign, and when I realized I was alone, I thought I'd try it out." She waved her hand over the judge's desk and gave Mark a guilty smile.

"We've all been up there at some point, although most of us do it when we're junior associates." Mark's eyes crinkled with amusement. "But unlike the rest of us, you've been caught."

Katy's lips quirked into a smile. "What do you think the judge will do with me?"

Mark approached the bench with slow, deliberate steps. "Well, for starters, he wants you out of his chair."

Katy's stomach flipped and tension curled around her, stealing her breath.

Mark held out his hand and when she took it, he pulled her out of her seat and took her place.

"I suppose you'll need to question me to ensure I have a fair trial. Do you want me in the witness box?" Katy motioned toward the padded seat in the wooden box beside the judge's desk.

Mark curled his hands around her hips and motioned to the desk in front of him with a nod of his chin. "I want you right here where I can see you."

"I thought you said this wasn't a good idea."

"I changed my mind."

She shook her head. "You can't have it both ways. You're going to get us both in trouble."

He lifted her easily and seated her on the desk facing him. "I'll prepare the papers to withdraw as counsel as soon as we leave."

She bit her lip and gave him a pained look. "You said something similar last time and then you didn't follow through. I can't—"

"Shhh. Let me explain." He traced lazy circles up her inner thighs, sending shivers of need straight to her core.

"The minute you walked into the courtroom, I knew I had made a mistake. I shouldn't have second guessed myself. I want you, Katy. I want to get to know you. Now. Two years is too long to wait." He nipped her earlobe and feathered kisses down her neck. "Tell me you'll give me another chance."

"I don't think this is appropriate behavior for a courtroom," she whispered, knowing that despite the risk, she wasn't about to jump down and walk away. Unlike Steven, who had made it clear she wasn't enough for him, Mark made her feel wanted. Desired. And in that moment she wanted nothing more than to let herself go. She had never known a rush like the heady sensations he coaxed from her body. And damned if she wasn't going to seize this chance to do something to fill the ache in her soul.

"Definitely not." His voice was thick with desire. "You're wearing far too many clothes."

Katy shrugged off her jacket. "What if someone comes in?"

"No one is coming in. I have a friend in security who owed me a

Sarah Castille

favor. He's got his eye on the door until his next shift. We have about forty-five minutes."

"I hope he's a good friend. You're putting both our careers in his hands."

He rested his hands on her knees. "I wouldn't take a risk with you."

Katy laughed softly. "What's this if not a risk?"

"This is you opening for me, sugar." He gently pressed her knees apart.

Lust, raw and ragged, tore through her body, burning away her inhibitions. She braced her hands behind her and parted her legs as far as her skirt would allow.

"That's my girl," he growled deep and low.

Katy sucked in her breath. She had never imagined such condescending words could be so fiercely arousing.

He traced his finger down her throat to the cleft between her breasts. "There are special rules in my courtroom," he murmured. "First, there is to be no touching the judge. Your hands will stay on the desk at all times. Is that clear?"

Katy gave him a wicked grin. She sat up and pressed her hands against the cool, smooth cotton of his shirt, then slid them up and over his rock-hard pecs to encircle his neck. "So I can't do this?"

He pulled her hands away. "No."

"And I can't do this?" She circled his narrow waist and pulled him between her legs, pressing her breasts against his taut chest.

Mark disengaged her hands. "Definitely not."

Her gaze drifted down below his belt and she stroked a finger along the erection clearly outlined beneath the thin wool of his trousers. "What about this?"

Mark gently slapped her hand away. "Don't even think about it."

"It's all I'm thinking about," she murmured.

"The second rule is, you follow my directions, no questions asked." He lowered his mouth to the heated skin revealed as he slowly unbuttoned her shirt.

"I'm not very good at following directions." Katy ran a finger along

156

the square line of his jaw, enjoying the feel of his scratchy stubble over her skin.

"Ah ah." Mark pulled away from her touch. "You, Ms. Sinclair, are now in contempt of court." He trailed his hand down her thigh, flipping open her suspender clips one by one before sliding her stocking down her leg in a silken caress. He repeated the process with her other stocking and then stood back and studied his work. Katy tried not to smile under his intense scrutiny. Trixie had been right after all.

Mark held her chin between his thumb and index finger and tilted her head back. "Smiling is also not acceptable in my courtroom. We'd better remedy the situation immediately."

Before she had time to even take a breath, he meshed their lips together. His tongue stroked hers and she melted with the passion of his kiss. Her lips parted to taste him, her hands slid around his chest to pull him closer, and her back arched, pressing her aching breasts against the cool, soothing cotton of his shirt.

Katy was on fire.

Mark slid his arms around her, pulling her close. Too close. Even through his clothing, he could feel the heat between her thighs and his shaft pulsed with need.

He deepened the kiss, drowning in the sweet sensation of her honeyed mouth. He wanted her with a desperate ache that reached into his heart. He wanted to possess her fully. Body and soul.

He reached for his blue silk tie and slowly, deliberately, undid the Windsor knot and tugged. The tie slid from his neck with a soft hiss. He wound the ends in his hands leaving a two-foot length between them and then he pulled it taut with a loud snap.

Katy jumped.

"The penalty for contempt is a fine or imprisonment. Choose."

A thrill shot through his body when she offered her delicate wrists with only the barest hesitation. "I choose imprisonment," she whispered.

Mark bound her wrists together and eased her back until she lay across the smooth, hard surface of the judge's desk. "Hands over your head. Feet on the edge of the desk." She lifted her arms, kicked off her shoes and placed her heels on the smooth oak surface without a word.

"Well done."

Mark settled himself in the judge's chair, barely able to believe he was about to live out his ultimate fantasy. He traced circles up the insides of her silky soft thighs, and tugged at the edges of her lace panties. "These have to go."

She trembled as he slowly slid her panties over her hips.

"Relax, sugar." He pressed her legs gently apart. "You're going to be here for a very long time."

Katy closed her eyes when Mark pressed a soft kiss to her belly button. His cool lips slid over her heated skin sending tiny shivers down her spine. He continued his gentle assault, moving down her body to feather kisses over her belly and then along the sensitive skin of her inner thighs, but never touching the one place she wanted him to go. His hair brushed lightly over her sex and she moaned at the sweet torment.

"So soft," he murmured. Katy moaned and struggled to free her hands, desperate to thread her fingers through his hair and guide him to her throbbing center.

"Mark. Untie me. I want to touch you."

"I've waited so long to taste you, sugar. Let me enjoy the pleasure." He gave her only those few words of warning before he slid his tongue up through her folds and around her swollen nub.

Katy gasped and jerked her hips at the delicious sensation. Her eyes slitted closed and she arched up, determined to take all she could get before reality came knocking.

"Don't move," he warned. The relentless stroke of his warm tongue sent fiery flames licking over her skin. He seemed to know exactly how far he could go to keep her on edge. Exquisite torture.

"Mark. Please."

He slid a finger through her wetness and circled her entrance until she quivered. When she thought she couldn't take any more, he slipped two fingers inside her stretching and filling her until violent trembles shook her body.

Mark pulled away and chuckled. "Lawyers are so impatient. They never take the time to savor an experience. Always wanting it now."

He smoothed his hands up her body, flicked open the front clasp of her bra and pushed it aside, cupping her breasts with warm hands as he freed them from their containment.

"You have beautiful breasts, sugar." He bent down to suckle a tight nipple between his lips, then laved gently over the tip. Katy writhed on the cold, hard table, as her insides tightened. He turned his attention to the other breast, suckling and laving until every nerve was on fire and her body screamed for release.

"No more," she gasped. "Let me go."

He pulled away and frowned. "Are you presuming to tell the judge how to run his case?"

"What if someone comes in? It's not like we have lots of time."

Mark chuckled. "Trust me, sugar. We won't be disturbed." He laved her aching nipple again, and plunged his fingers inside her throbbing sex. Katy arched her back at the unexpected and intimate intrusion. Her hips bucked, following the rhythm of his fingers as they stroked her closer and closer to her peak. Rational thought, fear and anxiety gave way to the naughty thrill of being tied up on the judge's desk and subject to Mark's pleasure. She closed her eyes and let herself drown in the erotic sensation of his hands and mouth, touching, kissing and tasting every part of her body until she knew nothing but him.

Mark dropped back down into his chair and flicked his tongue over her clit before he sucked it gently into his mouth. His breath, hot and heavy, fanned over her swollen center. "Tell me what you need, sugar," he rasped.

Tell me what you need. Words she had longed to hear during her marriage. Not once had Steven ever made her feel this way, or brought her even close to her peak, now only a heartbeat away.

"I need you. I need...to...come."

"Let go for me." His lips surrounded her clit and he nipped gently, pumping his fingers deeper inside her sex. Everything inside her shattered and she cried out as waves of pleasure crashed through her body, rolling outward to her fingers and toes.

Mark drew out her orgasm, stroking his fingers along her sensitive inner core until he brought her to the crest of another climax. She convulsed around him unable to believe she was physically capable of such intense pleasure. Finally, he withdrew his fingers and she trembled as her orgasm subsided. She barely registered the slide of silk when he released her hands.

Mark pulled Katy into his lap and wrapped his arms around her. She closed her eyes and let his warmth envelop her, breathing in his scent now mixed with her own. Sex and sandalwood and lilies. His erection pressed against her hip as he pulled her closer.

"What about you?" She ran her finger along his hardened length. "It seems you weren't satisfied with the outcome of the case."

Mark hissed in a breath and pulled her hand away. "You can't imagine how I get off watching you, but we've run out of time."

Katy leaned into his chest and squeezed her eyes shut. What would it be like to have someone like Mark to hold her at night, or when times were tough? "Are you sure?"

He laughed. "We've used up my favor and then some."

"What happens now?" Katy mumbled into his shirt.

"I'll speak to my partners and to Steele about transferring the case. The conflict will be resolved by the end of the day tomorrow. I promise you that."

Katy stiffened. "It's my problem too. Maybe I'll talk to Ted—"

"I said I would deal with it."

"I can't let you do that," she said, her voice wavering. "It's not right."

"You can and you will."

She shivered at his sharp tone and buttoned up her shirt. She couldn't let him carry the burden of their indiscretion. It simply wasn't fair.

"Mark..."

"I want to see you tomorrow after I have everything settled."

Katy shook her head. "I'm interviewing a witness in Vancouver in the morning and another in Burnaby in the afternoon. Then I'll need to prepare the statements while the evidence is fresh in my mind." She took a deep breath. "Maybe you should wait before you speak to them. Just in case either of us..."

Mark cupped her face between his palms. "I've made up my mind, sugar. There is no turning back."

"Keegan."

"Hunter." Keegan pulled a packet of cigarettes out of his pocket and offered one to James.

"Filthy habit." James waved the pack away.

Keegan laughed as he lit up. "Filthy habit for a filthy boy." He looked around for an ashtray, and then tapped his ash onto the ground.

James rolled his eyes. He didn't smoke. Had never smoked and didn't have any friends who smoked. Except Keegan. But he wasn't really a friend.

Keegan looked around at the busy street and the busier courthouse behind them. "I like these covert meetings in broad daylight and full public view of the courthouse. Very cloak and dagger." He blew smoke rings toward the crowded sidewalk. "So what can I do for you?"

"I want Jimmy Rider."

Keegan took another drag. "Do I look like your fairy godmother? It doesn't work that way in the real world, Cinderfella."

Damn Keegan. Always playing games. He didn't have time for games. The trail had gone cold and Keegan knew where to find his only lead. "It does if I decide you've interfered with a police investigation."

Keegan turned his back to James and then looked over his shoulder. "Hey, Hunter. I've got an itch. Gimme a scratch."

"Fuck you."

Keegan turned back and tapped more ash onto the sidewalk.

"That's not the way to get your glass slipper. I didn't come here to be abused. In fact, it's a terrible inconvenience. I'm supposed to be having lunch with the mayor up in the Harbor Centre tower. You should go there sometime. Amazing view. Or maybe cops aren't paid enough for fancy lunches."

James sighed. "What do you want, Keegan?"

"What I always want. Throw me some crumbs and I'll give you a pumpkin."

After a quick look around to ensure they couldn't be overhead, James capitulated. "Rider is connected to both Garcia and Wood. We have his prints on baggies found at each scene."

Keegan finished his cigarette and dropped the butt on the ground. "Tell me something I don't know. I gave you that lead."

James shrugged. "We might be dealing with a new type of illness. Something like SARS. I don't have anything conclusive from the pathologist yet, but the coroner is concerned. He's put a team on it as well."

Keegan pulled out another cigarette. "I can't write that story. It will cause widespread public panic and heads will roll. Mine included."

"I held up my end of the bargain and you're walking a thin line. Someone must have tipped off Rider because he has mysteriously disappeared."

"Are you suggesting I'm playing both sides?" Keegan raised his eyebrows in mock surprise. "Although you may be disappointed to hear it, I don't have a death wish."

"Where is he?"

Keegan blew a wisp of smoke. "All I've turned up is a dead end."

"Dammit, Keegan. If I have to drag you kicking and screaming into the station to make you talk, I will."

Keegan narrowed his eyes. "You won't have to, my friend. I'll be on television giving a press conference in which I tearfully name all my confidential sources." He locked gazes with James. "Are we done with the posturing?"

James sighed. He and Keegan had played this game for years. Although he hated to admit it, Keegan had his ear to the ground and was as comfortable with the underworld as he was with the police. Their arrangement had brought many criminals to justice and raised Keegan's profile as a star reporter. Everyone was happy.

"Could be a new street drug."

Keegan's eyes snapped to his. "Now you have my attention. That makes more sense if Rider was involved."

James shrugged. "It's all I have."

Keegan leaned in close and lowered his voice. "I've heard he likes swimming."

"More."

"With the fishes."

Damn. His key witness was dead.

Keegan glanced over James's shoulder and smiled. "Look, there's your brother."

James turned to see Mark entering the courthouse. "He's my friend, not my brother."

"That's not what I heard. Beat cop and single dad saves a bad-ass kid from the drugged out pimp dealer who killed his crack-head mother. Gets him off the streets. Raises him alongside his son as his own."

"He wasn't a bad ass kid," James snapped. "He had principles. He went looking for the dealer to avenge his mother's death, but he was only twelve years old. The dealer tried to force him to be a drug mule to pay off his mother's debt. He refused. Dealer slit his throat and left him to die."

Keegan continued to watch Mark until the courthouse door slammed behind him. "You might want to remind him of those principles. Sometimes they get lost when temptation comes calling. I met his little temptation last week. Big blue eyes, long, silky chestnut hair. I would have asked her out, but I don't like swimming."

"Leave them alone, Keegan."

Keegan laughed. "I leave everyone alone unless there's a story to be told. I love a good story."

Chapter Thirteen

Katy cringed when yet another tree branch scraped along the side of her SUV. Did she have the right address? It was hard to imagine anyone used the narrow, overgrown driveway with any frequency—unless Terry Silver didn't care about the paint on his vehicles. Or his shocks. The repairs to her vehicle from this little venture were going to eat up most of her monthly slush fund.

Damn Steven. His child support payments were always late, making it difficult for her to manage the monthly finances. But that was Steven. Totally unreliable. He didn't even need the money. He had rented a small two-bedroom apartment in South Granville near the hospital. He drove an old Volvo. He didn't own any man toys and he bought nothing for the kids. Her salary paid the bills, but with the sizeable mortgage on the house, she wasn't left with much at the end of the month. Once she made partner, though, her salary would triple. She could hardly wait to be free of Steven's financial noose.

She parked in front of a small, run-down house with an incredible view of English Bay and the North Shore. Siding lay in broken pieces on the ground and exposed wooden patches dotted the walls and roof like open wounds. What did he do when it rained?

Properties here in Kitsilano were exorbitantly priced, and often homes were passed down through families reluctant to sell their little piece of paradise. Silver's home must be one of those. Too expensive to maintain, but too precious to sell.

At least he had agreed to see her. Through the coughing and wheezing on the phone, she understood Terry had been told he only had a few weeks left to live, and he had something to get off his chest. Something he said would help Martha and maybe others as well. But he had refused to talk over the phone. What was it with people and phones these days?

Katy picked her way over the muddied drive and headed up a stone path to the wooden porch. A rusted lawnmower, broken flower pots and an old swing set were scattered over the grass. Did he have children? If so, they must be grown and gone.

She knocked on the screen door, startling when it swung open of its own accord. Taking a deep breath, she stepped inside and called for Terry. No answer. She took a moment to adjust to the gloom. The smell of rotten food and stale air, sickly sweet and pungent, turned her stomach. She gave one last, lingering glance at the door behind her before walking down the hallway. Such a tiny little house. The kitchen might have been cozy with its glassed-in breakfast nook and spectacular view, but the piles of dirty dishes, spilled food and ecstatic cockroaches took away from the ambiance.

No Silver. She looked in the living room and peeked into the bathroom with its old-fashioned, chain-pull toilet and rusted sink, then she headed for the bedroom.

Light flooded into the tiny wood-paneled room. She turned and saw a man asleep on the bed, his covers pulled up to his chin.

"Mr. Silver?" Katy placed a hand on his shoulder and gave him a gentle shake. A moment later, her brain registered the cold skin, the brown stain across the pillow and the small black hole in his forehead.

Dead. Shot. Gun.

Katy screamed and ran for the door, fumbling in her purse for her phone. Once outside she called nine-one-one and then locked herself in her car while she waited for the police to arrive. Her heart pounded furiously and her hands shook.

Who would shoot a dying man?

Ten minutes later the police arrived in a cacophony of sirens, shouts and banging doors. A police officer knocked on her window.

"You the lady who called this in?" he shouted through the glass.

Teeth chattering, Katy nodded at the young, blond police officer and lowered the window.

He patted her hand. "You just wait right here. One of the homicide detectives will be here in a minute to talk to you."

She rested her head on the steering wheel as she listened to the hustle and bustle outside. Shouts about contaminating the scene and securing the area filtered through her window, but her mind remained numb to everything but the cold press of wood veneer on her forehead.

"Katherine Sinclair...Katy?"

Katy took a deep breath and looked up at the face in the window. A familiar face—rough, dangerous. Her tension eased the tiniest bit. He hadn't been overly friendly at the police station but at least she knew him.

"Detective Hunter."

He nodded. "Why don't you step out of the car and we can find somewhere to talk? For an officer of the court, you seem to attract an inordinate amount of trouble."

She stepped out of her car and followed him to a broken-down picnic table outside the police-taped area.

"Are you okay?"

"A bit shaken, but I'll be fine."

He pulled a notebook from his pocket and unclipped his pen. "I'm interested to know how a young lawyer manages to stumble across two dead bodies in only a few weeks. What are you doing here?"

"I came to interview Mr. Silver." Her voice wavered and she took a deep breath. "I set up the appointment last week. He said he had only a few weeks to live, and he had something he wanted to tell me before he died."

A crash from the house startled her and she turned to see two people in white crime suits carrying large metal boxes into the house.

"Someone shot him." Her voice rose as panic replaced shock.

He squeezed her hand. "The police and the coroner are inside looking after him, but I need your help. Now, tell me about the case you're working on."

Her brain finally clicked into gear. "I...uh...don't think I can breach client confidentiality."

James frowned. "A man is dead. Shot in the head. The killer is loose. There's a potential threat to public safety. I don't believe the Law Society will have a problem with the disclosure."

Katy cringed at his cold, brief assessment. "I've actually...never dealt with this situation before. I would really feel more comfortable if I could run it by a partner first."

A smile ghosted his lips. "I know a partner who might be able to help."

Blood rushed to Katy's cheeks. "Of all people, he can't know. He's on the other side of the case."

James studied her intently. "That case seems to be causing you two a lot of problems."

"I'm not having problems," she snapped. "It's fine." She turned away to watch the people in their white crime suits gathering evidence. They reminded her of Justin's Lego astronauts.

"Look at me." He tilted her chin up with a gentle touch. His piercing blue eyes held her still. "Do you know what your problem is?"

"I'm sure you're about to tell me," she muttered.

He raised an eyebrow. "You don't know what you want."

"Thanks for the psychoanalysis, but for your information, the issue is not me. We have a professional conflict."

He smiled, an uneasy gesture on his fierce face. "Any conflict can be overcome. You just have to want it enough."

Katy grimaced. Mark had wanted it enough to give up the case. But what about her? Would she do the same for him?

"I don't remember asking for your advice."

James snorted a laugh. "Still feeling panicked?"

"No." She made the admission with reluctance, knowing she had let herself be manipulated.

"Anger does it every time."

Katy studied his face, softened by the sunlight. Not as scary as she had first thought when she'd seen him in the club, or even under the florescent lights at the police station. His was a face to be trusted.

"Now, about those questions..." He tapped his notebook with his pen.

Back to business. As if their entire conversation hadn't happened.

"Can I talk to you after I've spoken to my partners?"

"Go ahead. Give them a call. I'll wait." He gestured to her purse.

"I mean maybe this evening. I have another witness to see at lunch, and one after that. I can tell you now about the scene I walked into this morning and about my phone call with Mr. Silver, but the case details I need to run by them."

James gave her a reluctant nod and she filled him in on her visit from the moment she had turned up the driveway. When she finished, he handed her his card. "Call me if the next one turns up dead too."

"What do you mean get rid of her? This isn't the mob."

Mark pushed his chair back and stalked over to the boardroom window to watch the endless sprawl of rush hour traffic below. Why did Steele want Katy off the case? Was it something other than the simple dismissal it appeared to be? Or was it personal? He should have talked to Steele earlier about withdrawing from the case. Now it would have to wait until he knew what Steele was really after.

Steele sighed. "You know what I mean."

"Only Saunders, Katy's managing partner or a judge can remove her from the case if she doesn't want to withdraw," he said.

Steele steepled his fingers and rested his chin against his hands. "Corporate spies are not easily scared away. But if Saunders loses a second lawyer and has to start over, she might be deterred. There has to be something you can do."

Alarm bells rang in Mark's head. Had Steele tried to scare Martha away? Had he been behind the telephone threat?

"You could settle."

"Never."

Mark snorted. The understatement of the year. Steele never settled. Even when the odds were against him. His willingness to take risks had helped him turn a small biotech start-up into one of the biggest pharmaceutical companies in Canada.

"Well, she's upped the stakes so you might want to reconsider. She's been granted an order to depose a witness tomorrow on an emergency basis. She caught me by surprise at the hearing, but I'll be there to cross-examine him."

168

"What witness?"

"Martin Kowalski, your former Chief Scientific Officer. Apparently he's leaving the country. He agreed to be questioned under oath so his evidence can be entered at trial."

"Goddammit." Steele pounded the table with his fist. "He thinks he can drop a bomb and run away. I told Gordon that Kowalski was going to cause trouble. Can you stop the deposition?"

"I tried this morning and my appeal was unsuccessful. Ms. Sinclair must have been confident about the outcome. She didn't even bother to show up. She sent an articling student in her place." Mark paced the room, straightening the red leather chairs around the giant mahogany table as he walked. "I haven't received a witness statement so I can't even speculate about the evidence she hopes to get."

"I know what she's after," Steele growled. "And if she keeps digging, she's going to get more than she bargained for."

"Care to share that information with me? I can't represent you properly unless you keep me informed."

Steele shook his head. "Not this time."

"That's what you said about the Cunninghams." Mark shoved two documents across the table, trying not to let his agitation show. "I went to see them this morning after the appeal. Robert signed his amended agreement but his wife, Patricia, refused to sign hers."

Steele balled the unsigned agreement in his fist. "I should have sent Gordon. This would have been signed if he had been there. You're letting me down, Mark. Your dogged insistence on adhering to every rule in the law book is becoming wearisome. The world doesn't work that way. Billion dollar pharmaceutical companies are not run that way. You have to be prepared to bend the rules."

Ah, the irony.

Mark turned and leaned his back against the glass. A sliver of doubt worried its way through his mind. "You're responsible for the other lawyer dropping the case, aren't you?"

Steele's eyes never left his. "Do you really want me to answer that?"

"Probably best if you don't. Why do you want her off the case?" He tried to keep his voice calm and neutral as if they were talking about any other lawyer on any other case, while inside he fought the overwhelming urge to smash something. Like Steele's nose.

"Curiosity is taking that little kitty to dark and dangerous places." Steele joined Mark by the window. "You need to have a talk with her. I'm not the only one with something to lose if she continues to interfere."

Mark's throat tightened. "I can't do that. She would see it for what it really is...a threat. Aside from that, it would be unethical."

"Spin it." Steele patted him on the back. "Make it into a friendly warning. You have a law firm depending on my good will."

Mark rubbed his hand along his jaw. If he hadn't already decided to withdraw from the case, he would have had to do it now. Running a simple case against Katy was one thing, but threatening her was entirely out of the question. Steele had unwittingly just given Mark an easy way out of the conflict.

He grabbed at it with both hands.

"I'm going to have to hand the case over to someone else. I won't even consider crossing that line. If you've been honest with me, it's a simple case, and Gordon can handle it for you, but if you want it to stay in the firm, Tony—"

Steele cut him off. "Unacceptable."

Mark shrugged. "Your only other option is to let me run the case in the normal way. No threats. No warnings."

"Also unacceptable. She seems to have forgotten what kind of case she's supposed to be running. And you seem to have forgotten just how reliant your firm is on Hi-Tech's legal work. I have the means to save your firm from becoming another casualty of the recession. All I ask is that you get the little kitty off the case. I don't care how."

Mark folded his arms. "I won't do it. I'm sorry. I'm afraid I have to step down."

Steele studied him for a long moment. "What about the deposition tomorrow?"

"I won't prejudice your case. I'll lodge my withdrawal documents with the court this afternoon, but if you can't find new counsel, or Ms.

Sinclair refuses an adjournment, then I'll attend at court tomorrow morning to make an emergency application to have the deposition delayed." He stiffened and prepared himself for Steele's explosive temper.

But Steele didn't react as he expected.

"I'm disappointed but not surprised," Steele said bitterly. "I always knew it would come to this. You've never had the balls to take the risks that separate the men from the boys. I won't forget your betrayal." His low voice sent chills down Mark's spine. He had never seen this side of Steele. His quiet menace had every hair on Mark's neck standing on end and his fists clenched and ready to strike.

Steele slammed his briefcase closed and pulled open the door. "I'll have to handle Kowalski and that naughty kitty myself."

"You need to calm down."

Katy paced up and down the small meeting room at Richards & Moretti. "Don't tell me what I need, Tony. If I was calm, I would already have called the Law Society." She glared. "Where is he? If he isn't here in the next five minutes..."

The door opened and Mark stepped inside, his face grim. "What's going on? I could hear you from my office, as could our staff and clients. Steele was here. You're lucky he didn't recognize your voice."

"What's going on?" she shrieked. "You tampered with my witness."

"I did no such thing." Mark walked around the table to stand beside Tony.

"You did Patricia Cunningham was willing to talk to me, but when I stopped by her house this afternoon, she sent me away. She said you'd been to see her this morning. I don't think there could be any clearer case of tampering."

She felt no relief once the words were out. Her anger had been building since Patricia had suddenly gone tight lipped and sent her home. Fuming in rush hour traffic hadn't helped. She hadn't even gone back to her office. She had come straight to see Mark. She wanted answers. She wanted to know how she had been so naïve as to trust him.

"I didn't know you had planned to interview her. It was a coincidence." He spoke with a calm even rhythm as if he was explaining something complicated to a child. "You know there is no property in a witness."

"Bullshit. I don't believe it. I told you about the interview. I trusted you and you turned around and stabbed me in the back." She clenched her fists by her sides. "We can both interview the witness, but one of us can't coerce the witness into refusing to talk."

"Stop right there." Mark's rejoinder echoed in the small space. "You told me you were going to interview a witness in Burnaby. You didn't say who it was."

Tony held up his hands. "I've known Mark a long time. I've worked with him in two businesses. I trust him implicitly. If he says he didn't know, then he didn't know. He doesn't play games in his practice. He is always totally above board. Sometimes too much."

Katy clenched her teeth and focused on taking deep breaths. Of course Tony would back him up. He stood to benefit from any profit Mark made in the case. "I don't believe you either. You're probably in this together."

Mark's face tightened. "You're overreacting. Why don't you sit down and we can discuss this without all the hysterics?"

If she'd been angry before, his condescending tone tipped her over the edge. "Don't you dare patronize me," she yelled. She yanked out the heavy tortoiseshell clip holding back her hair. "You push and you push and when finally I give in and trust you, you betray me. Just. Like. Steven."

Mark ducked as the clip skimmed past his head and smacked against the glass window behind him. Katy's hair spilled out across her shoulders in a glorious chestnut wave. The fire of her fury drew him like nothing else. Her eyes glittered, her cheeks flushed and her breasts heaved under her tight shirt. She looked as delectable as she had on the judge's desk in the courtroom. Maybe more.

But first, he had to sort out this mess. What the hell had she been doing at the Cunninghams' house? Even he had trouble believing his own explanation about a coincidence, but he still didn't know why she needed to speak with Patricia.

With a quick nod, he sent Tony away and walked around the boardroom table, stopping just inches away from her. She trembled but didn't back down. Instead, she held his gaze, her anger clear in the taut lines of her face.

He cupped her cheek and stared into the raging blue sea. "I didn't betray your trust and I did not purposely tamper with the witness."

Purposely. He had to say it because if Patricia Cunningham had truly changed her mind about talking to Katy, then in some way he had influenced her. Maybe he should have said knowingly.

Her breath hitched and she pulled away. "I'm done here. We're done. I'm going to speak to Ted about getting removed from the case so I never have to see you again."

She turned to go but Mark snaked an arm around her waist and pulled her toward him. "I won't let you leave until we clear this up."

"You can't keep me here." Her voice rose to a high pitch. She twisted around and tried to push him away, but she was no match for his strength.

He locked his arm and pulled her tightly against him. "Calm down, sugar. You're overreacting."

Wrong thing to say. She shrieked and wiggled as she tried to escape. The soft, sweet curve of her breasts rubbed against his chest, her pelvis ground into his shaft, and when he slid his hand over the curve of her ass to hold her still, he realized she was wearing that damn garter belt.

"Be still." His heart raced and blood roared through his veins, fuzzing his brain with carnal passion until there was nothing but the scent of her arousal, the heat of her anger and the tormenting rub of her body against his. His control began to slip, disappearing too fast for him to catch it, until he had nothing to go on but primal instinct.

"Fuck." He grabbed her, shoved up her skirt and slammed her against the wall, cupping her sweet ass in his hands. She moaned and wrapped her legs around him, pressing her mound firmly against his erection, barely restrained by the thin layers of clothing between them.

"Even when I hate you I want you," she spat out.

"Listen to me." He raised his voice above the rasp of her labored breathing. "I didn't tamper with your witness, and as of this afternoon, I'm off the case. As promised. No more conflict."

He slanted his head and pressed his mouth firmly against hers, forcing her lips open. His tongue invaded her, thrusting and demanding until she shuddered and met him stroke for stroke. Her legs tightened around him as he plundered her mouth, taking what she gave, demanding more.

"You're off the case?" she murmured against his lips.

"Yes."

"Nothing to come between us?"

"Nothing." He choked out the word barely able to speak with the effort of containing weeks of pent up sexual frustration.

She licked his bottom lip. "You didn't tamper with my witness?"

"No."

"Kiss me again." Her throaty demand was all the encouragement he needed.

With a low groan, he dove back into the sweet honey of her mouth and their lips fused in a kiss that sent a wave of heat scorching through him. Her teeth slid across his lip and the metallic tang of blood rolled over his tongue. The primal taste stripped away the last thread of his control. He pulled away and yanked her head back, exposing her throat to his lips, his tongue and the sharp nip of his teeth. He breathed in her scent, sultry and sensual, and his cock throbbed in response.

"I want you, sugar." He nipped the delicate skin at the base of her throat and laved his way down to the cleft of her breasts. He wanted to live out every fantasy of her he had ever had.

Here.

Now.

Without waiting for her answer, he tore open her shirt. Buttons pattered across the carpet like raindrops. She moaned and kissed him harder, a clashing of lips and teeth, stoking the fire of his hunger for her.

"More." Her moan vibrated against his chest, inflaming him.

He shoved the fabric aside and flicked the front closure of her bra, freeing her soft mounds for his pleasure. He took one rosy nipple between his teeth and bit and suckled until she whimpered and writhed against him, grinding her pussy against his throbbing shaft. The barrier between them became unbearable. He wanted to feel her. Everywhere.

"I need you," she groaned. "Can't wait."

Spurred by the ferocity of his need and her arousal, he pinned her to the wall with his hip and pulled a condom from his wallet, tearing the packet open with his teeth. "I'm going to take you, sugar. Hard and fast. If you want me to stop, tell me now." He barely recognized his own voice, dark and husky with need. He ripped her panties away with a quick jerk then undid his belt and slid his clothing down his thighs.

She placed a hand on his chest and lifted her eyes, half lidded with desire. *So beautiful.* He could feel the warmth of her palm through his shirt. For a long second, anxiety ratcheted through him. Would she push him away? If she did, would he be able to go?

With a sudden jerk, she tore open his shirt and raked her nails down his chest. Buttons shot across the room like bullets. Blood beaded on his skin.

"Christ." The need to possess her obliterated his rational mind. In one swift motion, he sheathed his cock and then plunged into her hot, slick entrance. *So fucking wet.* The urge to drive further into her became unbearable. He wrapped his arms around her waist and pulled her down until he was buried deep. Her sex closed around him like a hot velvet sheath and he set up a steady rhythm, one he knew he couldn't keep up for long.

"Don't stop." She rocked her hips against him seeking the friction of his body against her clit. He slid one hand between them and rubbed her moisture up and around her swollen nub until her groans became whimpers and his fingers were slick with her wetness.

"God, I love the sounds you make," he rasped.

He rubbed one finger over her clit and changed to a hammering pace. Her body tightened and she arched her back, digging her nails into his shoulders. When she stiffened and gasped, he covered her mouth with his own, swallowing her scream as her pussy convulsed around him in heated waves.

Exquisitely tight. Unbearably wet.

His cock, denied for so long, pulsed inside her throbbing sex. He pulled almost all the way out, and then slammed into her, yanking her against him. Two strokes were all it took before he came in a violent rush. A groan ripped out of his throat, drowning the hammering of blood in his ears.

When her tremors had finally slowed, he pulled back and studied her for a long moment, drinking in her dazed eyes and swollen lips. "You're beautiful when you come, sugar," he whispered.

He withdrew, smiling at her unhappy moan after he let her down to dispose of the condom and adjust his clothing. But when she reached to pull down her skirt, he grabbed her hand.

"I'm not done with you yet."

She gave him a wicked grin. "Good. Because I'm not done with you."

He lifted her and placed her on the table in front of him, positioning her near the edge, legs bent, and heels planted. "Lie back," he commanded.

She bit her lip but did as he asked. "What about my plans for you?" she whispered as he gently pressed her thighs apart and settled down between her legs.

A smile curled his lips. "Don't worry, sugar. The night is still young."

Katy wiggled off Mark's lap and straightened her clothes. She wasn't in the mood to be cuddled. Despite the mind-blowing orgasm on his boardroom table, the beat of desire still pulsed through her veins. Unleashed. Out of control.

She didn't know this Katy Sinclair—half undressed, lips swollen, hair tangled, nipples aching, core throbbing—the woman who had just fucked opposing counsel in his boardroom.

Fucked. A harsh word. A forbidden word. A word that had earned Justin a week long electronics ban.

But apt. The last hour had been nothing but hard, dirty, desperate fucking.

It was what she had dreamed of in her bed at night and imagined during their phone call. It was what she thought about every time she saw him. So why wasn't it enough? Why did she hunger for more? What if this was all he wanted—the thrill of the chase, the satisfaction of conquest, and no strings when he walked away?

She wandered over to the window and stared down at the street below. Although small on the world-scale, Vancouver was always busy. Traffic jams. Crowds of tourists. But no one complained. It was all worth it for the view—mountains sweeping their way down to the ocean, the inky blue water of Burrard Inlet. Spectacular.

She felt Mark before she heard him. His body heat warmed her back through the thin cotton of her shirt when he came up behind her.

"What are you thinking, sugar?" His cheek brushed against her temple, his breath hot and moist in her ear.

"Just admiring the view."

He smoothed his hand down her back and kneaded her bottom, squeezing gently. "So was I."

A tremor ran down her spine. He was insatiable. How could he want her again? Didn't he need time to recharge? Steven had never managed to stay awake for more than thirty seconds after their seven minutes of "fun time" and then he wouldn't bother again her for at least two weeks.

Mark's powerful arm circled slid around her waist, pulling her against his long frame. His erection pressed firmly against the cleft of her buttocks. Rock hard and ready to go for the third time in under two hours. Apparently he didn't suffer the same limited endurance or lack of enthusiasm as Steven.

"Mark, I think we should—"

"Shhh. The office is closed. The cleaners are gone. No one is going to disturb us. I've been waiting far too long to let it end now." His hand drifted over the front of her shirt and eased under her bra to capture her breast. She gasped at the intensity of the sensation and arched into his heated touch.

"No clothes this time," he said, his voice husky and low. "I want to see all of you."

He didn't wait for an answer. His hands swept down her body stripping her of her shirt, bra and skirt without a wasted movement. He spun her around to face him then raked his hungry gaze over her body.

A blush crept down from her face to her breasts and her nipples tightened under his scrutiny.

"You're beautiful, sugar."

Flustered, disbelieving, she had no idea what to say. Her mouth opened and closed but no words came out.

"You don't believe me?"

"No."

He cupped her hand with his own and placed it on his chest. Then he dragged it down over the hard planes of his pecs and his rigid stomach muscles to the arousal clearly defined beneath his trousers. He pressed her hand over his engorged length.

"Do you believe this?" he murmured.

Katy stroked his arousal and squeezed gently. She believed he wanted her. Enjoyed her. But the question was, for how long?

Mark hissed in a breath. "Take it out. I want you to see what you do to me."

His words awakened something primal in her, carnal. A fevered desire rushed through her, filling her core with liquid heat. She tugged open his fly, and slid his clothing over his hips.

His erection sprang free—long, thick, and threaded with pulsing veins.

She couldn't tear her eyes away.

Mark stepped out of his clothes and kicked them to the side. For a long moment, she indulged herself, drinking him in. She hadn't realized how much she had craved this view of him. Mark in clothing was mind-numbingly gorgeous but without clothing...his body was nothing short of divine. She was not only aroused, but entranced. Need shot deep to her darkest, most secret core and she murmured her approval.

Mark crossed his arms over his chest. "Are you going to keep staring at me, sugar?"

Her cheeks flamed and she bit her lip. "Yes," she breathed. "Oh, yes."

She let her gaze play all over him, moving along muscular thighs, taut abs and a well-defined chest. Finally, her gaze drifted down the soft, dusky trail of hair to his shaft, engorged and straining toward her.

What would it be like to feel the swollen head in her mouth, smooth and glistening, or lick the teardrop of moisture at the tip? How would he taste? Salty? Sweet?

"If you keep looking at me like that, I'm going to come for you," he rasped. "Do you want that, sugar? Is it what you were imagining when your nipples peaked?"

She dragged her gaze up to his eyes and then back down to his throbbing shaft. "I was imagining...how you would taste."

His heavy sac tightened before her eyes. His crown engorged, becoming a deep pink, almost purple.

"Come and find out."

She sank to her knees in front of him, her mouth watering in anticipation.

"Suck me, sugar."

She took him in her hand and dusted the swollen head with her breath, marveling at the contrast of silky skin over rock hard flesh. His hips bucked and her touch grew bolder, following the veins from tip to base. She breathed in his scent—musk and soap and the essence of male.

"I'm not going to last if you keep playing." He clasped his hand around the base of his heavy shaft, and brushed the swollen tip over her lips. "Open for me."

She parted her lips and his cock slid into her mouth. As she closed her lips around him, her fingers curled into his buttocks, drawing him closer so she could take him deeper.

Too deep.

She choked. Gagging and coughing, she pulled back and then dipped her head, letting her hair sheet over her flaming cheeks.

Mark threaded his fingers through her hair, tugging her head back until she was looking up at him.

Katy's eyes watered. "Sorry. I'm not...very experienced."

"There's not much you can do wrong. Relax, sugar. Slow down. I like everything about your hot, wet little mouth."

He reached for her hand and placed it around the base of his shaft. Palming her head, he drew her forward. This time she couldn't resist circling all around the pearly tip with her tongue. He tasted salty and sweet, decadent. Her belly clenched and her own need rose. She moaned, her lips vibrating against his head.

"God, Katy, you're killing me." He tightened his grip on her hair. "Open wider."

His guttural demand sent shivers down her spine. Fingers splayed around the base of his shaft, she relaxed her throat and tried to take him deeper than she had before.

His groan of pleasure delighted her. Steven had rarely been interested in oral sex. She had always thought the problem had been her lack of skill, but maybe the problem lay with him.

She ran her tongue across the underside of his shaft and then set up a steady rhythm with her mouth. He grunted and stiffened. The muscles of his thighs grew rigid and his back arched.

The taste of him made her hot, wet and hungry. She snaked her free hand down between her legs, spreading her moisture around the swollen tissue. Her juices flowed between her thighs and she struggled to hold on. She wanted to give him the pleasure he had given her. But she knew she couldn't take much more.

"Condom," she rasped, pulling away.

Mark froze. "I'm all out."

"Lucky for you, Trixie stuffed a handful of samples in my purse. She said Carpe Noctem had a storeroom full of freebies." She retrieved a condom and rolled it gently over Mark's hardened length.

This time she didn't tease. She took him in as far as she could in one long, hard slide while her hand drifted down between her legs to deal with her own need for release.

"Christ," he muttered, as he watched her fingers glide through her folds. "That's it, sugar. Touch yourself. Come with me."

His fist closed on her hair and he pumped into her mouth with rapid, deep strokes. She moaned in delight and dragged her fingers over her swollen clit.

He pulled back and then thrust forward, tightening his fingers in her hair. "Fuck." The word came out in a roar as his cock became impossibly firm. He came fast and hard with a sharp jerk of his hips and a deep, low groan of pleasure.

Pleasure she had given him. Satisfaction and a last flick over her clit sent her over the edge. A shower of stars tingled through her veins and she moaned her release around his shaft.

He slowly withdrew and looked down at her, his eyes warm with a hint of humor. "That was damned amazing, but you're a very naughty girl."

"Did I do something wrong?" The question trembled from her lips.

He cupped her cheek and his face softened. "The pleasure of touching you is mine, sugar, and I'll be wanting that pleasure again before the night is out."

"Is that Tony sleeping in there?" Katy buttoned up her suit jacket to hide her torn shirt.

Mark snorted at the sight of his friend asleep on the couch in the hallway. "I can't believe we put him to sleep."

"He was here? Listening? The entire time?" Katy grabbed his sleeve and worry creased her forehead.

Mark put his arm around her. "He was worried about you. He thought I'd lost control."

"Did you?"

He didn't answer right away. He didn't want her to know the lawyer famous for his control had lost it in his own boardroom. And he didn't want her to know he regretted the loss.

What the fuck had he done? How had he let it go so far, so fast?

Why hadn't he stopped after the first time? He should have moved slowly, taken the time to get to know her, decide if he could risk exposing himself to the pleasure and pain of loving and losing all over again.

Instead, he had succumbed to raw need and the overpowering desire to possess his beautiful, fiery opponent, body and soul.

Now in the dim light of the empty hallway, he knew he'd made a terrible mistake. He was back on the road he had resolved never to go down again. He wasn't ready. Not by a long shot. He couldn't take what he couldn't give.

What a fucking disaster.

Katy followed him into the elevator. The doors slammed closed and they hurtled down to the main floor.

"Mark?"

His heart stuttered when he looked down at her worried face. Lips, swollen from his kisses. Hair, a sexy tumbled disarray. He could drown in the depths of her azure blue eyes and die a happy man. But what about her? She deserved more than he had to offer. She deserved better than him. She deserved to find someone who knew how to love.

He pulled her into his arms and brushed his lips softly over the lines creasing her forehead. *Now is not the time for admissions.* "Shhh," he whispered.

Katy drew in a ragged breath but mercifully didn't press him for an explanation for his silence.

He walked her out to the street and they waited for the cab he had called before they left. At this late hour, few people were around, but he didn't want to take the risk of pulling her close, although he ached to feel her body snuggled against him. Not now.

"Since you're off the case, the next time I visit your office, I'll come prepared and forgo the panties." She gave him a half smile, but she couldn't hide her anxiety. She knew something was wrong.

He sucked in a breath, knowing he had to tread carefully. "There won't be a next time."

Confusion flashed in her eyes and she brushed imaginary fluff from her jacket. "You're right," she said cautiously. "It was inappropriate. Maybe somewhere less risky?"

His pulse raced as if he were trying to pick his way through a mine field...blindfolded. Images of Claire flitted through his mind. Claire laughing in her kitchen. Claire crying as she walked away. Claire dead in an alley. Because of him. Because he hadn't loved her enough.

"Katy. I—" He choked on the words he knew he should say.

"I don't understand." She bit her bottom lip and her face grew taut and still.

Tension grew thick between them. He still had a chance to diffuse the situation. But maybe this was better. End it before she got hurt. Before he led her down the same path that had led Claire to her own destruction.

The cab approached, and Katy whirled around to flag it down. She opened the door and turned back to face him. The devastation in her eyes sliced through him, piercing his heart more surely than any words could have done.

And then she was gone.

Chapter Fourteen

"Surprise!"

Katy dropped her briefcase on the floor with a thud and stared in horror at the balloons and streamers decorating her kitchen. Steven and the kids sat around the table, wearing purple party hats decorated with sparkly pompoms. On a Friday morning. At seven-thirty.

She clenched her fists. "What is this, Steven? The kids are going to be late for school."

"It's our anniversary today. You didn't forget, did you?"

Melissa pointed to a giant, pink monstrosity of a cake in the center of the table. "Dad took us after school yesterday to buy a cake. Justin wanted lemon but Dad let me choose and I picked chocolate because that's your favorite and pink icing because that's Dad's favorite. They even wrote *Happy Anniversary* in purple icing." Melissa twirled around the kitchen in a pink party dress two sizes too small and totally inappropriate for school.

Katy's anger over Mark's rejection last night was nothing compared with the rage that now coursed through her veins. "Steven, may I speak to you alone, please?"

He didn't move. "Come on, Kate. It means so much to the kids."

She gritted her teeth. She couldn't deal with this right now. Her head throbbed. Her heart ached. She had been up all night, berating herself for making the mistake of becoming emotionally involved with someone who was interested in her only for a bit of fun. And she was emotionally involved. No doubt about that. But Steven, smirking in her kitchen, reminded her exactly why she did not need a man in her life. She should thank him for bringing her to her senses.

"Melissa, go change your dress and then get in the car. Justin get in the car now."

She ignored their glum faces and waited until the children were gone before rounding on Steven. "What is the meaning of this?" She waved her arm around the room at the decorations. "Why would I want to celebrate our anniversary when we're divorced? How dare you involve the children? Did you think you could guilt me into pretending we were a happy family again?"

"Come on, Kate. I just wanted to show you how much I missed you." His eyes hardened, and he switched tones as quickly as he had switched beds. "I won't say anything about your twisted lifestyle to the court or the concern it gives me about how you are raising the children if you'll just reconsider..."

A red haze filled her vision. Blood hammered in her ears. She picked up the cake and hoisted it into the air. "Steven. Go."

His lips curled into a snarl. "I'm getting tired of this. I don't know what's going on with you but I don't like it. The slutty clothes, strange parties, the defiant attitude. It's not you. Not the sweet, innocent, gentle girl I married. You're my wife. Mine. I was your first and I'll be your last. We're a family. A piece of paper isn't going to change that. I'm not giving up. We'll be together again. I promise."

He pushed open the door and looked back over his shoulder at the cake. "Don't do something you're going to regret. The Kate I know doesn't give herself over to rash behavior."

She heard a scream and was surprised to discover it was her own.

Lana lifted her camera when the front door opened. How did the subject manage her life on so little sleep? Lana had almost given up last night, worn out from following the subject around, when she had emerged just after midnight from the office building on Burrard Street. Disheveled and with the mystery man. All smiles and heated looks until something sparked an altercation and the lovey-dovey scene had ended with a cab door slamming and the mystery man alone on the street. Poor guy. She'd have given up on the subject by now. Or maybe not. Lana pinched one of the rolls on her stomach. Maybe if she lost a few pounds, she could have tall, dark handsome men chasing after her.

She checked her appearance in the rearview mirror. Nice green eyes, although a little big, creamy skin, pale complexion marred only by a smattering of freckles. And lots of men liked red hair. She should grow it out. Give them something to hold. Still the subject sure led an interesting life. What she wouldn't give to have a man look at her like there was no one else in the world.

A strand of hair fell in front of the camera lens and she brushed it away in irritation. What if she dyed it auburn? Would the contrast with her light features be too much? She stared at her reflection, trying to imagine herself as a brunette.

A movement in the car behind her caught her attention. The man in the black Chrysler 300C had been sitting in his vehicle for over an hour. Had Mr. S been unhappy with her last drop? Had he hired someone else?

She slunk lower down in her seat and pulled out a tiny mirror with a long handle. Handy for watching without being seen. Yup. There he was. Blue button-down shirt, buzz cut. Average looking except for the eyes. Black eyes. Sinister eyes. Even from a distance they scared her. No point confronting him. She didn't even know who he was watching. Maybe he was on a different case altogether.

She still couldn't figure out why her employer wanted the subject followed. It couldn't be a marital dispute. The subject was divorced, although the ex spent a lot of time at her house. Must have been an amicable split. She'd heard about amicable divorces, although she had never seen one. Maybe the mystery man had a wife or a jealous girlfriend and had enlisted a male friend to hire Lana. It wasn't unusual. Or so she'd heard.

A scream pulled her into the present. The ex raced out of the house just as a huge pink cake flew out the door, landing only a foot behind him. Pink icing spattered all over the back of his scrubs. She couldn't press the button fast enough on her camera.

The ex turned and raised his fist, shouting something about a custody hearing. The door slammed. She expected him to stalk away fuming. Instead he bent down and scooped some icing off the sidewalk. With a smile, he sauntered across the street to his car, licking the icing off his finger.

Friggin' psycho. Why didn't he go for the cake?

Katy paced in front of the Vancouver Law Courts. If Martin didn't show up soon, she would forfeit her deposition slot. She didn't want to lose her only chance to validate Martha's story or to dig behind Hi-Tech's corporate veil.

She looked up and down the street for the hundredth time. Maybe Martin couldn't see her under the dark awning shadowing the entrance to the courthouse. She walked over to a stone bench and sat down amidst a collection of planters filled with bright flowers.

Mark wasn't here yet. No doubt he was scrambling to prepare an application to have her deposition adjourned. Well this time she was prepared. She had her cases and evidence ready and the determination to push the deposition through.

And yet, a part of her didn't want to win. How would she get through an entire day, hating him and wanting him at the same time? Did the intense night of sex in his boardroom mean nothing to him? Why, even after the conflict was resolved, had he pulled away? Had he been interested in her only for the element of danger and the thrill of the chase? She couldn't take the emotional uncertainty. She needed him out of her life and out of her mind.

"Katherine Sinclair?"

A slight, middle-aged man wearing a faded gray, button-down shirt and oversized chinos approached her. She stood to greet him. "Martin?"

He nodded and ran his hand through his thick, silver hair. "I hope I'm not too late." His eyes darted back and forth across the street, lingering on the courthouse entrance to their left and the sheriffs posted near the door. Finally his shoulders relaxed and he held out his hand.

She shook the limp, sweaty palm then picked up her briefcase. "Not at all. I'm glad you changed your mind about giving evidence, and I know Martha is too."

"I wanted to get my involvement in the whole thing straightened out before I leave and I need my conscience to be clear. Hopefully I can save some lives and help Martha out."

Katy swallowed. "Why are you doing a deposition instead of going

187

to the police, or even the press or the regulatory authorities?"

"If I involve the police, they won't let me out of the country. I don't trust the press. The story would disappear and so would I. As for the regulators, Hi-Tech is a powerful company. They have the money to bribe anyone and top-notch lawyers to deal with those who stand in their way. You know what happened to Martha."

Top-notch lawyers? Ha. "You're very cynical."

Martin shrugged. "Realistic. I've been in the business a long time. Too long. I'm looking forward to my retirement. I leave the country this afternoon and I'll never come back."

Katy shivered at his ominous tone. "Did you bring any documents? I'll need to make copies before the deposition."

Martin sighed. "Unfortunately, no. After I gave my notice the security guards wouldn't let me back in the lab—not even to pick up my personal items. I wish I'd been able to take my personal journals. I made a duplicate handwritten copy of everything—every experiment, every trial, every result. When I first started out as a scientist, the journals were protocol. Now everything is on the computer. But old habits die hard."

"We might be able to get them through the discovery process, if we can establish relevance," Katy offered. "After the trial, you could have them back."

Martin shuffled his feet and made yet another visual sweep of the street. "I know it's just going to be us and no one from Hi-Tech knows we're here, but I would feel safer if we went inside."

Katy frowned. "Hi-Tech's lawyer knows you're here. I thought you understood. A deposition is like a mini trial. I go through your direct evidence and then he will cross examine you."

Martin froze and his eyes widened. "Hi-Tech knows I'm here?"

"I'm sure Mr. Richards, their defense counsel, would have told them about the deposition. He might not be the one appearing today, but someone will be here to represent Hi-Tech." The skin on her neck prickled, whether in response to Martin's sudden agitation or something else, she didn't know.

Martin grabbed her hand and squeezed it until the bones moved over each other. "Oh God. What have I done? I thought it was just you. I've kept quiet for so long and they've left me alone. But now...." His head jerked and he looked from side to side. "Quickly! We need to get inside."

"What is it? What are you afraid of?"

Martin tugged on her hand. "They'll come after me. I know too much. It's all a big cover-up. There never was a chemical spill. No lab accident. Those men on the list were—"

A loud crack startled her. Martin's eyes widened and he looked down. A red stain appeared on his shirt, flowering quickly across the cotton expanse. He grunted and lunged toward her.

Katy stepped back, trying to get away. Her heel hit something heavy, and she fell backward, pulling Martin on top of her. Another shot sounded. And then pain carried her away.

"Ohgodohgodohgod."

Lana spun around, snapping pictures wildly, then dropped her camera on the ground and fumbled for her phone. *911911911911*. The numbers raced through her head, but before she could make the call she heard sirens. Sheriffs and police swarmed around the bodies lying in front of the courthouse and pressed the crowds back.

She held her breath. *Getupgetupgetup. Please get up. You have children, a happy divorce, a great job and a man who looks at you like nothing else exists in the world. Pleasepleaseplease get up.*

But she didn't get up. Ambulances arrived. Two. She heard the shouts of the officers calling to the attendants. *Two victims. Both unconscious. Serious. Very serious.*

The police pushed the crowds back and she watched them lift her onto the stretcher. Blood. So much blood. Her head, her clothes, her face. Even her beautiful shoes.

She heard his hoarse cry before she saw him. The mystery man. Running toward the ambulance. His black coat flying behind him. God, he ran fast. Calling for her. Pushing and shouting at the ambulance attendants to let him through.

And they did. Something in his face backed them down.

He saw her and staggered back. But he recovered quickly. He stepped closer and stroked her hair and her cheek and then he leaned over and whispered in her ear. Even though she couldn't hear him.

Tears streamed down Lana's face. The sirens wailed and the ambulances drove away. The mystery man stood still as a statue, watching them go. She ached to go to him. Wrap her arms around him, comfort him and take comfort herself. She felt as though she knew the subject as well as any friend. Maybe better.

No, not the subject. Katherine. Katherine Sinclair.

Or, as the mystery man had shouted, his voice breaking as he ran...Katy.

Chapter Fifteen

Katy opened her eyes to a sea of white.

Didn't I just paint the bedroom mauve?

She looked around and tried to turn her head. *Pain.* Her neck ached, her shoulder throbbed and fatigue weighed her body down. She couldn't move. Not even a finger.

Beep. Beep. Beep.

She frowned at the noise intruding on her quiet until she realized it had always been there. That and the cloying smell of...antiseptic.

Steven? Working late again?

Beep. Beep. Beep.

No. Not Steven.

She tried to lift her hand and a sharp pain shot up her arm. A cold, plastic tube rubbed over her skin. It led to a plastic bag hanging on a pole beside her.

IV. Hospital. What am I doing here?

"Katy." A rich, deep voice startled her. "How are you feeling?" She strained to turn her head. Her heart thudded. The beeping increased. She knew the dark, handsome man beside her. She knew the warmth in his brown eyes, the softness of his sable hair, the contours of his jaw, thick with stubble. But not the exhaustion lining his face. And not his name.

Her heart seized up at a barely remembered pain. She whimpered, a soft sound not meant to be heard by anyone. Especially him.

He stood up immediately and cupped her cheek in his palm. "What's wrong, sugar?"

Sugar. The term of endearment warmed her inside but her mind stayed muddy. Good guy or bad guy? She couldn't remember and the strain of trying to wade out of the confusion made her head ache.

A nurse wearing Mickey Mouse scrubs poked her head in the door. "Ah, you're awake, dear. I'll call Dr. Hughes...I mean Steven. He wanted to be notified as soon as you regained consciousness...and Dr. Watson too." The nurse checked Katy's pulse and then rushed out the door.

"Mark, I brought you some coffee."

Mark. She remembered the name, but not the man.

"She's awake, James. The nurse just went to get her doctor."

A blond-haired man with a rough, angular face came into view. Vaguely familiar.

"Hey, Katy. How are you doing?"

She knew she should answer, but her swollen tongue and parched throat made it impossible to speak. She salivated at the rich, earthy scent of coffee and managed to whisper, "Water."

Mark poured a glass of water from a pitcher and put a straw between her lips. She gulped down the cool liquid. Coffee would have been better.

"Thank you." Her voice came out as a weak croak. "Wh...what happened?"

Mark stroked her hair. "You were outside the courthouse. Someone fired shots. Your witness fell on top of you, and you banged your head on one of the stone planters. Probably saved your life. One shot hit your shoulder as you fell, but if you'd been standing it would have killed you."

"Martin?" She remembered the name. "Is he okay?"

His hand froze mid-stroke. "Don't worry about him. Everything's under control."

"How long?"

"You've been here three days." James had a gruff voice, like fingernails on sandpaper. "Mark has barely left that chair since they brought you in."

She twisted slightly to get a better look at the man who had sat beside her for three days. Not even her mother would have done that. A sharp pain shot through her shoulder and she winced.

He noticed. "Try not to move. I'll get the nurse to bring you some pain killers."

The door opened with a bang, flooding the room with cold air.

"Kate. What the devil were you thinking? What have you gotten yourself involved in? Why would you put yourself at risk? You're a mother for godsakes. I should never have let you go to law school. This is how I'm rewarded. Now I've got the kids and the babysitter to deal with. Not to mention work. It's chaos. I'm stressed out of my mind."

Katy froze. *Steven.* Even in the haze clouding her mind, she knew him. Even in her muddied consciousness she remembered her anger.

His tirade went on and on. *Words, too many words.* She closed her eyes and tears washed down her temples. Too much noise. Too much emotion.

Mark dabbed her tears away with a tissue. "That's enough. You're upsetting her. She's only just woken up. I hardly think shouting at her is going to speed her recovery."

She opened her eyes and stared at him. *Good guy.* But fighting a losing battle. *Don't you know? In the hospital, Steven is God.*

"I'm a doctor, for chrissakes. A surgeon at this hospital. Don't presume to tell me what I can and can't do," Steven shouted.

Shoes squeaked across the floor. "He's right, Steven. She's been unconscious for three days. She needs peace and quiet." Dr. Doug Watson, emergency room physician, and family friend, patted her hand. Their kids went to the same school and played together at the park. Why did she remember him? Why couldn't she remember Mark and James?

"Kids?" she whispered. Where were Melissa and Justin?

"Who the hell are you?" Steven snarled, pointing at Mark.

"Mark Richards. I'm a...friend. You would know me if you'd even once come to see her after they brought her in." He held out his hand but Steven didn't shake it.

"What would have been the point of that?" Steven said in a sharp voice. "She was unconscious."

Mark's brows drew together and his jaw twitched.

James put a cautionary hand on his arm. "Don't bother. He isn't worth the effort."

Oblivious to their exchange, Steven continued his rant. "You can go now, Richards. My wife is fine. Doug is going to discharge her and I'll get my secretary to call a cab to take her home. Her kids need her. The babysitter can't cook for shit and she doesn't make lunches. She says it's not in her job description. The kids have been surviving on peanut butter sandwiches and cereal. Plus I've got back-to-back shifts to make up the time I had to spend looking after them. It's a nightmare."

Two growls. Low. Barely audible. But she heard them. Mark and James weren't pleased.

"I thought she was your *ex*-wife," Mark said.

Steven waved his hand, dismissing the comment. "It's a technicality. We're working through it. She wants our family together again as much as I do."

"No," she whispered.

Mark stroked her cheek and she turned into the comfort of his hand.

Dr. Watson shook his head. "Steven, I can't discharge her if I know she's not going to get twenty-four hour care. She needs to rest and she needs to be watched. She has a concussion and the dressing on her shoulder from the bullet wound will need to be changed. I think it's best if she stays here for the rest of the week."

"No. No hospital." Hot, wet tears slid down her cheeks. She had spent too much time in hospitals when her mother's depression had become unmanageable. But worse, she would be at Steven's mercy. She wouldn't be able to get away.

"For godsakes, Doug," Steven spluttered. "What am I supposed to do with the kids? The babysitter only works three hours a day after school and refuses to do any overtime. I need Kate at home. She'll be fine as long as she doesn't go into the office. A little housework won't kill her. She'll finally have time to do a proper job. And I'll be at home on the nights I'm not on call."

Steven at home? No, no, no. She tried to speak but her throat was too dry. She whined instead and shook her head against Mark's warm palm.

"Shhh. I know," he murmured in a soft voice.

Dr. Watson sighed. "You're putting me in a difficult position. She's my patient. She needs care. You know as well as I do that the concussion may not be symptomatic for another few days. Keeping her here is the best option if she can't get the care she needs outside the hospital."

"Is there somewhere else she can go?" James interjected. "A friend, other family?"

Steven snorted. "Her mother is a crackpot. Spends her day wandering around her garden, talking to herself. Her dad ran out on the family when she was young. She's got no sisters or brothers. All her friends work and have their own families. That's what she needs. Her family. Me and the kids."

"She's coming home with me." Mark's deep voice echoed in the small room.

Katy's heart skipped a beat. Had she been to his home before? She couldn't remember. He reached over to brush a lock of hair from her face and gave her a wink. Katy's lips curled into a weak smile. Safe. Mark was safe.

Steven's mouth tightened in a grim line. "Don't be ridiculous. I don't even know you. I won't agree to that."

Mark rested his hand on her cheek. "She needs to be with someone who can look after her. Clearly, that isn't you."

Definitely one of the good guys. Strong. But Steven didn't like confrontation. There would be hell to pay.

Steven's eyes narrowed. "Are you the twisted fuck who dresses her up and parades her around sick parties?"

Welcome to hell. She hadn't expected Steven to retaliate quite so quickly. Usually he waited and attacked when she was alone.

But now she remembered Mark. Bits and pieces. Hugs and kisses.

"That's enough." James stepped between them. The low, guttural warning in his voice made her shiver.

"Who the hell are you?" Steven's face reddened. His fists clenched by his sides. Not good. Seconds away from exploding. Katy squeezed her eyes shut.

"Detective James Hunter, Homicide. I'm investigating the case."

Startled, she opened her eyes again. Homicide? Didn't someone have to die for the homicide department to be involved?

Steven retreated a step. Even "God" was afraid of the police. "I want her home with me," he snapped.

"Why don't we ask Katy what she wants? She's not incapacitated so I believe it's her decision. Isn't that right, Doc?" Detective Hunter looked over at Dr. Watson.

Dr. Watson cleared his throat. "Er...yes, that's right."

Katy turned to look at Mark. His warm, brown eyes held her gaze, calm and steady. Reassuring. Safe.

"Mark." She pushed the word out through the tightness in her throat despite a niggle in the back of her mind and a sharp stab in her heart.

"Are you sure about this?" Detective Hunter raised his eyebrows and looked at Mark.

Mark nodded and Katy shuddered with relief.

"What about you, Dr. Watson? You have the final say." Somehow Detective Hunter had managed to take control of the room.

The doctor nodded and gave Katy a sympathetic smile. "I'll keep you two more nights and then if everything checks out, I'm happy to release you early, provided you promise you will rest. That means no looking after the children, no housework, no work and no running around."

Mark gave her shoulder a soft squeeze. "I'll make sure of it."

"This is absolutely absurd," Steven fumed. "We have children who need their mother. I won't forget this." He stormed out of the room, his white coat flapping behind him. Detective Hunter and Dr. Watson followed, leaving Mark alone beside her bed.

Katy sank into the pillow. She had no energy left. Not to think. Not to fight. Not to be alone.

"Don't leave me," she pleaded as the whiteness rushed to greet her.

"I'm here, sugar. I won't leave you again."

"More coffee?"

196

Mark took the paper cup from James, grateful for the caffeine fix. He had grown used to the taste of the vending machine coffee—liked it even. He turned off his laptop while James searched around for a chair. In the absence of meetings, phone calls and distractions, he had managed to stay on top of his work during his five days with Katy in the hospital.

But even if he hadn't been able to work, he would never have left her alone. Not with her ex in the hospital. Self-centered bastard. If James hadn't been there the afternoon she first woke up, he would have shoved the idiot out the nearest window. Over the last two days Steven had come by only to drop the kids off to visit with their mother. He never stayed. Never spoke to Katy. Never even bothered to ask how she was.

"So what did Dr. Watson say?" James pulled up his chair and settled down beside Mark.

"He's releasing her this afternoon."

"Good news. Did she say anything about the shooting?"

Mark took a sip of the aromatic black liquid, enjoying the bitterness on his tongue. "She still doesn't remember much and I haven't told her the truth about Martin." He knew it was wrong, but he was grateful for her temporary memory loss. It gave him a chance to make everything right. Undo his mistake.

"I'm surprised you offered to take her home. What about the conflict?"

"I dealt with it before the shooting, and yesterday I spoke to her managing partner. He's pulling her off the case."

James widened his eyes. "I hope it was on his initiative and not yours. From what I know of her, she won't take that lightly."

"He's going to take over the file as soon as Katy has recovered enough to tie up some loose ends." Mark quickly looked away. James didn't need to know the details of the deal he had worked out with Ted.

"Ahem." James raised an eyebrow. Mark laughed. He should have known James would see right through him.

"Okay. I admit it. I might have contacted him and made a suggestion. But it wasn't because I wanted the conflict resolved. That was done. It was for her safety. Her managing partner only cares about the bottom line. He would have put her back on the case the minute she was out of bed."

But more than that, he suspected Steele might have been behind the shooting and he wanted Katy as far away from him as possible.

"Shouldn't that have been her choice?"

Mark gritted his teeth and struggled to keep his voice low. "Fuck, James. Just leave it alone. I know I shouldn't have called him. But I almost lost her. When I saw her at the courthouse..." His voice broke. "I'll do what it takes to keep her safe. I can deal with the fallout."

James sipped his coffee, seemingly unperturbed by Mark's uncharacteristic outburst. "I stopped by your firm looking for her the night before the shooting. She had stumbled on a murder scene when she went to interview a witness earlier in the day. Your case, apparently."

"My case?" His hand shook and coffee splashed over the side of his cup.

"Guy named Terry Silver. She didn't want you to know about him, but now he's dead and she's off the case, so it doesn't matter. Ring any bells?"

Mark shook his head. What was she up to? First Silver, then Cunningham. How were they related to the dismissal?

"Strong woman," James continued. "She was really shaken but she recovered quickly and blew out of there to interview another witness in Burnaby."

Cunningham. Of course. Did Steele know she had been in touch with the Cunninghams too?

James checked his watch and headed for the door. "I don't know what's going on in this city. Nothing unusual for six months and suddenly I have bodies all over the place."

"What about Katy and Kowalski? Any leads?"

James shook his head. "She may have been in the wrong place at the wrong time, but I have my doubts. The suspect got Kowalski on the first shot. He was dead before he hit the ground. The witnesses said a second shot was fired as Katy fell. Why did he shoot again unless she was a target?"

"Maybe he wasn't sure he had hit Kowalski the first time."

James dropped his coffee cup in the garbage can and pushed open the door. "We've put a team on her kids twenty-four seven and when she leaves the hospital, she'll have protection until we have someone in custody."

Emotion welled up in Mark's throat and he gave James a tight nod.

"There's something else," James said. "The private investigator we caught in the club last week had pictures of Katy on her camera. Any ideas?"

Mark's stomach clenched. It had to be Steele. First an investigator and now a murder attempt. Steele hadn't just crossed the line; he was half way into the end zone. He desperately wanted to tell James his suspicions, but his ethical duty of confidentiality protected Steele unless he had hard evidence. Steele's comments in the boardroom could just have been idle threats.

"Mark?"

He shook his head. "I have a faint suspicion, but it's nothing I can discuss."

James sighed. "Even a clue? Katy's life may be in danger. The PI might be connected to the shooter."

"I'll follow up on it as soon as I can, but I don't want to risk implicating an innocent man and find myself at the mercy of the Law Society."

James looked over at Katy, asleep in bed. "She's one in a million. Don't fuck it up."

"Thanks for the advice."

"It wasn't advice. It was an order."

Chapter Sixteen

"You didn't have to carry me. I can walk perfectly well."

Katy clung to Mark's neck as he carried her into his apartment. Over the threshold. Like newlyweds.

"You're supposed to rest." He locked the door with her still in his arms.

Katy looked around the bright, spacious penthouse. The minimalist décor didn't suit him. Stiff brown and tan leather sectionals, wooden cube tables and geometric prints. A few artfully arranged sculptures dotted the shelves and a massive brown granite island gleamed in the kitchen. Cold and impersonal. Unlived in and unloved. Still the view took her breath away. His penthouse took up the entire top level of the building. Floor to ceiling windows showcased Coal Harbor and Stanley Park only a stone's throw away. "It's...nice."

Mark huffed a laugh. "It was a show suite. I didn't have time to buy furniture and decorate it myself, and I'm rarely here except to sleep." He jerked his thumb toward a massive wooden double door at the far end of the open-plan living space. "The bedroom is down that way, which is where you're going to be spending the next few days. I called your babysitter and she'll bring Melissa and Justin whenever you feel up to seeing them."

Katy swallowed past the lump in her throat. "You didn't have to do this. I have friends who could have helped out." His care and compassion, and his easy acceptance of her children touched her deeply.

"People work." He settled her on a carved wooden bench in the hallway and removed her shoes.

"So do you." She had recovered all her memories, save for the day before the shooting. But Dr. Watson had been optimistic it wouldn't take long.

"You'll discover one of the benefits of partnership is not having to answer to anyone for your time. I don't have anything pressing this week...unless you sent over another court application behind my back."

Katy blushed and shook her head. She didn't want to think about work, or the case. She felt safe here. Hidden away from the world.

A wave of fatigue hit her. Maybe she wouldn't fuss about lying down after all. But she would have to borrow a shirt from Mark. All she had to wear were her clothes from the hospital. Steven had refused to pack her a bag and had forbidden the children from bringing her clothes.

She looked down at the faded cotton shirt the nurse had given her from the charity box to replace the shirt and jacket the paramedics had cut off in the ambulance. Not a very good match for her suit skirt. If she hadn't been so desperate to get out of the hospital, she might have taken Mark up on his offer to buy her something to wear.

"What's this?" She brushed at a flaking, dark brown stain on her skirt. Where had it come from? She hadn't noticed it at the hospital, but then she had dressed as quickly as she could in case Steven found out she was leaving.

"Blood."

Katy startled at Mark's gruff tone, and a shiver crept up her spine.

"Blood?" She didn't deal well with the sight of blood. Steven had always been the one to fix up major cuts and scrapes.

"The gash on your head bled a lot. Martin bled on you. Your shoulder..." His voice cracked. "There was so much blood...I thought you were dead."

Her gasp echoed in the quiet apartment. "Martin?"

"He didn't make it." Somehow she had known the answer, but hearing it brought a wave of emotion to the surface.

Oh God. I'm covered in a dead man's blood.

"Get it off! Get it off!" she shrieked, pushing herself off the bench. She struggled with button in the back. "Mark, please, get it off me," she begged.

He crossed the hallway in a heartbeat, ripped the button open and

Sarah Castille

slid the skirt over her hips. Then he scooped her up and carried her into a huge marble bathroom, cradling her in his arms while he turned on the water.

Less than a minute later, stripped bare, she stood under the warm, soothing spray of his enormous shower. Mark undressed and slid in behind her, pulling her down onto his lap as he settled himself on the marble bench. Under the soothing cascade of warm water, he wrapped his arms around her and buried his face in her hair.

For the longest time, they didn't move.

Katy closed her eyes and felt her tension ease under the pulsing beat of the shower and the steady beat of Mark's heart against her back.

She shifted on the bench, wiggling to find a more comfortable position. Mark gave a sharp groan and pulled her closer, his erection pressing firmly against her bottom.

Raw need replaced fear. Dr. Watson hadn't said anything about avoiding sex. She wiggled again, slowly this time, grinding herself against his shaft.

Mark unlocked his arms and slid her forward, away from him. "This wasn't such a good idea," he rasped.

He trickled soap down her back and massaged gently, taking care to avoid her shoulder. Katy breathed in the familiar sandalwood scent and looked back at him over her shoulder. "Were you at the courthouse when it happened?"

"Up." He helped her stand and placed her hands against the glass wall of the shower. All business, he rubbed shampoo into her hair and massaged her scalp until her eyelids briefly slid closed.

"I got there just after you were shot." He rinsed her hair and then ran his hand down her back to cup her bottom.

"And James? Is he involved because of Martin?"

He bent down and lathered her legs with long, firm strokes. "He asked his sergeant to take on the case as a favor to me." He rubbed toward her inner thighs, and her insides tightened. She must be well on her way to recovery if all she could think about was sex.

"Mark?" Her voice was soft, questioning.

202

"No." With a gruff bark, he shoved her legs together and pulled her back against his chest. Soapy hands smoothed over her stomach, around her ribs and across her hips. She lifted her arm, drawing his attention to her breasts.

A sharp pain quelled her arousal.

"My shoulder." She pointed to the huge wad of bandages covering her left shoulder and upper arm. "Should I be in the shower?"

"Probably not, but Trixie is coming over later to change the dressing. Just keep it still." He cupped her breasts, sliding his slippery fingers around them in a satin caress. How could anything feel so good? Her head dropped back against his shoulder and his fingers teased her nipples into hard buds. Katy groaned in frustration.

"You can't say no and then touch me like that."

"I can do anything I want. You're too weak to fight me."

She couldn't help but smile at the teasing note in his voice. "I'm not that weak. I'm pretty sure I could—"

"And I like the little sounds you make." He nuzzled her neck and pinched her nipples again. Desire sizzled through her and she moaned.

"God. Just like that," he whispered in her ear. He rubbed her breasts again, but without the soap the friction aroused her even more.

Her eyelids slid closed. "I need..."

"You need to be thoroughly washed. They only sponged you down at the hospital and they didn't get off all the blood."

He lifted her knee and placed it on the bench. "Open for me, sugar."

Katy parted her legs and his fingers slid through her wet folds, with a teasing, feather-light touch.

"Stop. Mark. You're torturing me. Haven't I been through enough?"

"So hot and wet." His words, and the rough edge to his voice, sent her arousal soaring out of control.

Using her own moisture, he stroked his finger over her swollen clit. Katy struggled to stay still but her hips tilted, straining to his touch. She yearned for release and the mind-numbing pleasure of climax under his sensual fingers.

Sarah Castille

"Mark..." She leaned back and pressed herself against his hot, hard shaft.

"Okay, we're done." He turned off the shower and stepped outside.

"We're done?" Water beaded off her heated skin and she shuddered with the ache of unfulfilled need. "I don't want to be done."

"Out." He held up a fluffy towel and she stepped onto the bathmat—beige, like everything else.

"But...I need you," she groaned.

He dried her completely and with a brusque efficiency that made her head spin. "You're just out of the hospital. You need rest."

"What was that in the shower?"

"Me being stupid."

She huffed out a frustrated breath when he lifted her in his arms and carried her toward the bedroom. "I'm not broken."

"You will be if I don't put you to bed." He pushed open the double doors to reveal a modern, low-rise bed with a massive padded leather headboard. Very masculine. Very bachelor. Very big for one person.

He threw back the blankets and settled her in the bed. Katy moaned with disappointment when he drew the sheet over her, covering her with excruciating gentleness.

If he noticed, he didn't say. Instead he tucked the blankets around her, adding a thick feather comforter so heavy and warm her body melted into the mattress. The silk sheets slid decadently around her, and the slick touch on her sensitive flesh almost sent her over the edge.

"Don't go," she whispered as sleep overcame desire.

"I'm not going anywhere, sugar." He climbed on the bed and put his arm around her, holding her tight as she drifted away.

Mark paced up and down the hallway outside his bedroom. Trixie had come and gone and Katy had fallen asleep after her dressing had been changed. He had managed to distract himself with work for a few hours, but he could no longer resist the pull of the beauty in his bed.

An unfamiliar peace had settled over him when he realized he

204

would have her all to himself. Here nothing could come between them. He could indulge his desire to look after her. Protect her. Hold her.

He pushed open the door, stripped down to his underwear, and lay down on the bed beside her. He had done her no favors by allowing his needs to spill out of the courtroom and into their personal lives. But after almost losing her, he was glad he had taken the risk.

He drew back the covers and trailed his fingers between her breasts and over her stomach to her bare mound with only the lightest of touches. So beautiful. Her skin glowed in the moonlight streaming through the window. He circled each nipple, delighted when they pebbled beneath his touch. So responsive. Even in her sleep.

He should leave her alone. Let her rest. But his body refused to move.

She whimpered and he realized his fingers had been rolling and pinching her nipples of their own accord. He slid his hand between her legs and ran a finger along her folds. So wet. For him.

Trixie, with her usual lack of inhibition, had informed him he wouldn't hurt Katy if he wanted to take advantage of having her captive in his apartment. But he had to be gentle.

Gentle.

It had been a long time, but he could do gentle.

Katy stirred and he leaned over and ran his tongue in light circles around her nipples before taking one in his mouth and sucking it into a hard peak.

She awakened with a gasp. "Oh God."

"No, sugar, just me."

Her eyes, when they focused on him, were half lidded with sleep and the stirring of arousal. "What are you doing?"

He leaned over to kiss away the little worry lines creasing her forehead. "Looking after you." He sucked her nipple and then nipped gently. Katy arched her back and moaned.

"I thought you were going to let me rest."

Mark turned her on her side and pulled her back into his chest, cupping her soft, warm breast and squeezing lightly. "I changed my mind."

Sarah Castille

She winced and gave a soft cry.

Damn. He had forgotten about her shoulder. "Sugar, I'm sorry." He helped her roll back and pushed himself off the bed. "I'll get you some pain killers."

"No." Her voice rose. "Please don't leave. We just need to be careful."

"I don't want to hurt you."

"You won't hurt me if you misbehave properly. No teasing and leaving. And no rolling."

He chuckled and lay down beside her again. "Well then I want you to lie still and let me give you what you need, and I'll take my pleasure in giving it to you."

She huffed her disapproval. "I want to touch you."

"Hard to do when you can't move your arm or your shoulder." He propped himself up on his elbow, tracing circles over the smooth, taut skin of her belly. "But if you have a problem with the other hand, I can restrain that one too."

He shook his head and mentally chastised himself.

Gentle does not involve tying her up.

Mark's deep, velvety kisses branded Katy's lips, filling her senses. Pleasure washed over her in languid waves, chasing away the last remnants of sleep.

His mouth moved lower, painting from her throat to the crease of her breasts with soft, brushed kisses. His hands replaced his lips, cupping and squeezing until she ached under his touch.

"I like my scent on you," he murmured. "It tells me you're mine."

She shuddered and gave in to the deep hunger unraveling inside her, the need to be possessed utterly and completely by the man who had not left her side for five days. For this moment in time, there was nothing but him, his warm breath on her skin, his gentle caress and the tortuous exploration of his wet, silken tongue.

His hot kisses moved lower, down her sternum to her belly button. He teased and tortured the neglected area before grazing his

206

chin over her mound.

Katy panted in anticipation as he blew a hot breath over her folds. She threaded her fingers through his thick hair, guiding him to where she wanted him to go.

How many nights had she lain beside Steven imagining a lover like this? A lover who wanted to touch her. Tease her. Drive her insane with pleasure.

"Hands off, sugar."

He abandoned her aching sex and continued his exploration of her body, as if she were a new land to be discovered. He licked and kissed every finger and every toe and the hollows of her ankles, wrists, elbows and neck. He nuzzled the sensitive skin of her inner thighs, whispered in her ear and sifted his fingers through her hair.

Her world narrowed to each heated touch and lingering caress. The scent of sandalwood enveloped her as she writhed on the cool, silk sheets and licked his minty taste off her lips. Sensation piled on sensation until need filled her with such an ache; a carnal groan escaped her lips.

"I need you inside me. Now."

"Not yet." His fingers dipped into her body, spreading her moisture along her folds and up around her sensitive clit, stroking until it throbbed.

"Please." Katy jerked her hips in a silent plea for more as his agonizingly delicious touch sent flames of need licking through her body, burning the last clouds from her mind.

"Trust me."

She barely heard him as images tumbled into her mind. The missing pieces. The day before the shooting. Silver, James, the end of the conflict, the boardroom and the silence.

She stiffened and edged away.

Mark froze. "What's wrong? Did I hurt you?"

Katy shook her head and swallowed hard. "I remember. That night in your boardroom. I trusted you and you turned your back on me."

He pushed himself up beside her. "Katy...I made—"

She cut him off with a finger over his lips. "I don't know much about guys. My Dad left when I was young. I had a few boyfriends in high school, and then I met Steven. But I suspect there aren't many men who would spend five days and give up a week's worth of billable hours to sit beside an injured...friend. Or who would take her into his home to care for her, just to save her from the clutches of her irritating ex-husband." She threaded her fingers through his thick, sable hair. "Tell me it wasn't just for fun," she whispered. "Tell me it was something more. Tell me you don't regret it."

Mark shuddered and slanted his mouth over hers. The now familiar taste of him spiked through her, sending quivers of need down her spine.

"It was something more," he murmured against her lips. "So much more that I was afraid of hurting you. And yet, that's exactly what I did. I regret that more than you could know. I'm sorry, sugar."

"How sorry?" Her bottom lip trembled.

He gave her a cheeky grin and pushed himself down her body, settling himself between her legs. "Very, very sorry," he rasped. He peppered little kisses along her inner thighs until he reached her aching center, and then he licked down through her folds with one long, luscious stroke.

Katy gasped and her hips jerked off the bed. Mark's firm hands held her down and he licked again, this time flicking his tongue over her clit.

The muscles of her thighs tightened as she tried to angle herself to where she wanted his mouth to be. But when his tongue pushed inside her swollen tissues, a long desperate wail left her lips.

"Does that feel good, sugar?"

Clit throbbing for attention, she nodded and arched her back, seeking out the delicious torment even as it pushed her to the edge of her control.

"I want to hear you say it." He sank a finger all the way inside her. "Tell me."

"Yesssss. It feels good. So good. Don't stop."

He stopped and pulled away.

Katy sucked in a sharp breath. "Nooooo. I said don't stop."

His voice dropped, cracked. "I need to be inside you, sugar. I need to feel you everywhere. I need to know I haven 't lost you."

She heard the crinkle of a condom wrapper and then his warm body lowered over hers. His heart drummed wildly beneath her palms and she arched into him, seeking the fulfilling sensation of having him buried inside her. The tip of his erection teased against her swollen entrance and she moaned.

"Maybe that's enough. I think I've paid the penalty for hurting you."

Katy glared. "Are you kidding? You'll have to try harder than that." Anything to get him inside her. She had forgiven him, but he didn't need to know it. Not yet.

He grunted with satisfaction and plunged into her, hard and deep, sending shock waves of unbelievable pleasure through her body. Her hips wiggled uncontrollably, her sex clenched and her body coiled tighter and tighter. He slid in and out, increasing his rhythm, building her tension.

Katy dug her nails into the tense, hard muscles of his back. His hand slid between them and he pinched her nub firmly, changing his thrusts to a hammering pace. The room became a red haze as hot, blinding shards of pleasure consumed her. Sensation swept everything from its path, filling her with ecstasy as her sex clenched over and over again in a firestorm so intense, she barely registered when he gripped her hips and came with a low guttural groan.

When Katy's body finally softened beneath him, Mark kissed her softly, tasting her sweetness. Her long, silky lashes drifted down over her eyes, showing only a glimmer of her dark blue gaze.

He slid out of her warmth and quickly disposed of the condom. Then he lay on the bed and pulled her into his arms, wrapping the coverlet around them.

He could do gentle. Maybe he could do more. He knew, even after they left the sanctuary of his apartment, he could never give her up. He felt a connection to Katy. Maybe even the connection he had longed to have with Claire.

She gave a contented sigh as she lay on his chest. Her chestnut hair spilled across his body, as soft and silky as he had always imagined it would be.

"I never knew it could be like this."

Neither did he. After years of casual affairs, he thought he had done it all. But Katy had opened him up. She had shown him a level of intimacy that transcended sex and moved into his heart.

"What are you thinking, sugar?"

"I was wondering how many women you've brought here and what sorts of things you did with them in this bed."

"You're the first." The one. The only. He could not imagine sharing his inner sanctum with anyone else. "I bought this place after..." He stopped. Did he want to tell her about Claire? Could he?

"After what?" She pressed soft kisses along his jaw.

His arms tightened around her. "Claire. We were together for almost three years. She...died."

Katy's eyes filled with tears. "I'm so sorry." She slid one hand around his neck and hugged him tight.

"Let's talk about something else." His gruff voice betrayed his emotion, and his arms instinctively sought the comfort of her sweet, warm body.

"Am I allowed to ask you more questions?"

He tangled his fingers through her hair, tilting her head back for a lazy kiss. "Feel free to ask, but I may not answer."

"Do you have any kids?"

He frowned. Not the question he had expected. "No." He ran his hand up and down her back, marveling at the silky softness of her skin.

"Do you want kids?"

"I did, but I think it's a bit late now."

She cocked her head to the side. "How old are you?"

"Thirty-five."

Katy snorted a laugh. "Definitely not too late. That's when most guys get started. I think you'd be a good dad."

His head jerked up. "How could you possibly know that?" Except for James's dad, he had had no role model. Dads rarely stuck around in the world of his youth, abandoning mothers and children in search of their next fix.

She reached up to caress his cheek. "Just a feeling. Sorry if I hit a nerve."

He clenched his teeth, annoyed at his loss of control. She had an innate ability to see into his soul, unearth his deepest desires and bare them for the world to see.

"What about your parents? Do they live nearby?"

"My mother died when I was twelve. I didn't know my dad."

"I'm sorry again," she murmured. "I seem to be asking all the wrong questions. Sounds like you had a hard time growing up."

Hard did not even begin to describe the nightmare of his lost childhood.

"James's dad saved me from a life of foster care. To this day, he won't tell me how he managed to adopt me. He was a single parent, a cop, living on the East Side. He must have pulled every string and called in every favor. He treated me like his own son. He turned my life around."

Emotion welled in his chest and he scrambled to change the topic of conversation. "What about your parents?"

"My dad left when I was nine," she said in a quiet voice. "He met someone new, packed his bags and just disappeared one day. We never heard from him again. My mother spiraled into a depression. She was never the same after he left."

No wonder trust was an issue for her. First her dad, then her husband. The men closest to her had betrayed and abandoned her.

And he had almost done the same.

He pulled her on top of him, easing her head into the hollow of his shoulder, a perfect fit.

"I loved him," she continued. "I loved spending time with him. We had fun together. He's the only person who ever really understood me."

"It's hard to lose someone you love no matter what the circumstances." He smoothed the hair away from her face and rubbed his knuckle over her soft cheek. "Any more questions?"

"Favorite hockey team?"

He chuckled. "Some questions are too personal to answer."

"Do you have any hobbies?"

"The club. Running. No time really for anything else." How sad was that?

She traced her finger gently over the scar across his throat. Mark stiffened and then forced himself to relax. No one had ever touched his scar before. No one had ever wanted to.

"How did you get this?" She leaned up and pressed a gentle kiss to his neck. He couldn't feel anything on the scar itself, but he could feel her hot breath and her tender lips on either side. The promise of acceptance.

"You don't want to know."

"I want to know everything about you."

He drew in a ragged breath. "After my mother died, I evaded the authorities by living on the streets. More than anything I wanted to avenge her death. I hunted down the dealer responsible but I was too cocky for my own good and too stupid to play by the rules. His guys caught me. He told me I was responsible for my mother's debt. I refused to be a drug mule and he taught me a lesson I'll never forget." He tensed, expecting shock or horror. But instead, she snuggled closer and caressed the scar again.

"Then what happened?"

Mark took a deep breath. "James and I had been friends before my mother died. After I hit the streets, he didn't give up on me. Every day he hunted me down and tried to get me to go home with him. I told him I was just another bad kid destined for a life of crime. But he wouldn't take no for an answer. He came looking for me that day, same as every day...found me bleeding in an alley...called his Dad. They saved my life in more ways than one."

Katy pulled herself up, sliding her body along his. His shaft stirred to life as her mound brushed over his sensitive flesh.

"I'm glad they did." She pressed her lips against his in a slow, sweet kiss that took his breath away. He palmed her head and pulled her closer.

"So am I."

"Sounds like you have at least one friend." Her voice took on a teasing note and she pulled away. Mark grabbed her hips to stop her sliding back down and setting him off.

"Any others?"

"The partners," he rasped. *Fucking hard to concentrate.* "A few guys from the club."

"And me?" she whispered. "Am I your friend?" She pushed herself all the way down until her lips hovered over his shaft.

Mark groaned as she circled her tongue over the tip. "Sugar, you're a whole lot more than that."

Tap, tap, tap.

Lana froze when a hand knocked on her driver's side window. A face peered in. A familiar face. Devilishly handsome.

What the hell is he doing here?

She rolled down the window and sighed loudly for effect. "Yes?"

"Well, look who it is. My favorite PI."

Lana glared into amused blue eyes. "James."

"Detective Hunter to you."

She raised her eyebrows in mock surprise. "So formal. I thought we were friends since we know each other from the sex club. What can I do for you, Detective Hunter?"

"I suppose it depends on what kind of trouble you're in today."

"No trouble. Just sitting here, minding my own business. What about you? What are you doing here? Just walking down the street at seven in the morning, looking for litter? Or maybe you haven't shouted at any PIs today and needed your fix."

His jaw twitched and he flashed his badge in her face. "Patrolling a police restricted area."

Lana waved the badge away. "You don't need to show me your badge. I know you're a cop. Or are you trying to turn me on? I have to admit I have a thing for detectives in tight jeans and kick ass biker T-shirts."

He chuckled. "And I have a thing for sassy PIs who keep turning up where they aren't supposed to be. Step out of the car please."

She left the safety of her Jetta, and he motioned for her to put her hands on the hood.

Lana sighed and took the required position. "Is this really necessary? I'm just doing my job."

"Feet apart."

She widened her legs. A sudden wave of heat crashed through her. Sweat trickled between her breasts. What the hell? She should be afraid. She had just been caught by a cop with one hell of an attitude. Yet her body had other ideas.

"James? Are you going to frisk me or what?"

Silence.

She peered over her shoulder. He stood directly behind her, his eyes fixed on... "Hey, are you staring at my ass?"

"Did you just call me James?"

She swallowed dryly. "A slip of the tongue. But since you have me in this position, and you've been staring at my ass, we might as well drop the formalities."

His gaze lifted to her own, his face expressionless. Well, not quite. His lips quivered. "I should have spanked you at the club. Might have taught you to hold that tongue. They have a special room in the back for lessons in discipline and restraint."

Phwoar. Lana bit through her lip. After following Katy to the club, she knew all about the back room. Fantasized about it constantly. James had been part of those fantasies. Every. Damn. One. And now was he saying...?

Don't go there.

"You even think about laying a finger on this ass and I'll have you on the ground so fast you won't know what hit you." Lana swayed, glad she'd decided to wear her most flattering yoga pants for the morning stakeout. "This ass is by invitation only."

She gave herself a mental kick and lifted her hands off the vehicle.

Stop sassing the cop.

"Stay where you are," he barked. He leaned into her car and fished around the front seat, finally pulling out her camera and notebook. "We're going to have a more serious conversation today, by which I mean you're going to answer my questions."

"I don't have to."

"Don't push me, Lana."

Did he just use my name?

He grabbed her hair and pulled her head back. Firm but not hard. A tingle ran down her spine. A nice tingle.

"Hey, police brutality," she joked.

He yanked harder and her neck cracked. "*That* is police brutality, sweetheart."

"Okay, okay. Just let me go." She strained to look around. So far, the street had been surprisingly empty for the morning rush hour. No one to save her from the dangerously handsome cop with a penchant for pain.

He released her hair and her head flopped forward, almost hitting the Jetta's rusted hood.

"I'm not a criminal, you know. You don't need to get rough with me." She paused and wiggled her ass. "Unless you want to."

"Christ, Lana. Don't push me. Turn around." He had such a sexy voice. Low and husky with a hint of a rasp. The kind of voice she imagined whispering sensual promises in her ear at night.

Lana spun to face him. He was wearing a pair of worn, low-slung jeans that hugged his muscular thighs and a black T-shirt with a Harley Davidson logo on the front. His face, his clothes and his stance all screamed danger. Her mouth watered.

Don't look at the package. Don't look at the package.

Oh my!

"You've now become embroiled in a police investigation," he said. "You have a professional responsibility to assist. If you don't want to talk to me, you can go down to the station and give your statement to one of my colleagues."

She lifted her eyes from his package, hoping he hadn't noticed.

215

"No station. Ask away. How do you want me? Sitting? Standing? Or do you want me to assume the position again so you can question me and stare at my ass?"

Watch the mouth, Lana.

But she couldn't. Something about this cop drew out the worst of her sass. And he liked it. She could see it in the quiver of his lips, the warmth in his eyes, and the quickened beat of the pulse in his neck.

"Just so you understand. I ask the questions. You answer. And you'll keep that mouth of yours under control."

Her heart sank. Maybe she had pushed too far. "Sure thing."

Lana leaned against her Jetta and rubbed her head while he pulled out his notebook and clicked his pen.

"What's wrong?" His eyes focused like laser beams on the gentle movement of her hand.

"Your demonstration of police brutality was very effective."

Regret flared in his eyes. "Had to get your attention."

"It's okay. I've suffered worse and enjoyed better."

He studied her intently and his lips parted. For a second she thought he might ask her what she meant, and she silently berated herself for the slip. She had buried her past years ago. Why her subconscious had dredged it up now, she didn't know.

He shook his head, an almost imperceptible gesture, as if he was annoyed at himself. "I have your pictures. I know you've been following Katy Sinclair. Who are you working for?"

"I don't actually know. He calls himself Mr. S. We did the transaction over the phone. He sent a key to my office. I drop my reports in a post box and he picks them up and leaves cash."

"Risky, not knowing your client."

She shrugged. "Some of us don't have the luxury of a steady income. When was the last time you had cereal for dinner?"

A smile ghosted his lips. *Ha.* She could get under anybody's skin.

"How long have you been following her?" James tapped his pen on his pad.

"About two weeks."

"I'll need the key, address of the postal unit and the box number."

"In my bag in the car. Do I get compensated for premature termination of my contract?"

He reached into the vehicle, retrieved her backpack and dropped it on the hood of the Jetta. Lana winced when he pulled out her spare panties along with her iPod, a box of cookies, a toothbrush and a box of condoms.

"You always come prepared?" His mouth twitched as he held up the condoms.

Lana smiled and winked, determined to get him to crack a smile. "Just a box this time, not a full bag."

He snorted and looked away. "You won't be terminating the contract with your Mr. S. You'll continue doing your job until we've identified him. I'll make a copy of the key and have it returned to you."

Lana grinned. "So I'm like a double agent?"

"You're like a very green PI who is in a lot of trouble and should be grateful to have been caught by a cop with better things to do."

Her gut twisted. Better things to do must mean hunting for the shooter. Lana twirled her hair around her finger. "Is she okay?"

His eyes bored into her skull. "Were you there when she was shot?"

"I was across the street."

"Did you see the shooter?" His eyes sparked with interest.

"I didn't see his face. I saw where he was standing, and I took some pictures of him running away."

A frown creased his brow. "Did you give a statement to the attending police?"

Lana shook her head. "I was too upset at the time. Plus, Mr. S gave me special instructions not to let her out of my sight. I had to find out where they were taking her. When I went home and downloaded the pictures I didn't think anyone would want them. They weren't very good. My hands were shaking so bad at the time they were all blurry...and I dropped the camera. "

He scrawled something on his notepad, ripped off the paper and handed it to her along with his card. "Looks like you get a trip to the

Sarah Castille

station after all. Ask for Joanna Smith. You'll need to bring your camera and memory card. She'll also need your key and the details of the postal outfit. Oh, and your phone. We'll try to trace the calls you had with your Mr. S."

He rounded her vehicle and copied her license plate number into his notebook. "If you're not there in an hour, I'll obtain a warrant for your arrest. Are we clear?"

Lana sighed. "Sure."

His eyes softened. "I know it must have been hard to watch. If you need to talk to someone, there are victim support counselors—"

She held up her hand and cut him off. "I'm good. I don't need to talk to anyone. I've dealt with some pretty heavy stuff. I haven't led what you would call a sheltered life."

He ran his hand through his hair. "You know...if you change your mind, you can call me. I've been through...heavy stuff too."

"Okay," she murmured. "Thanks, Detective Hunter."

He finally cracked a smile. "You can call me James."

Chapter Seventeen

Katy awoke with a start.

Light filtered through the window blinds, illuminating the sleeping form beside her.

Mark.

Mark's apartment. Mark's bed.

She desperately needed to pee. Moving quietly so she didn't wake him, she slipped out of the covers and left the room. Traffic crawled through the streets below. She checked the giant clock over the fireplace. Eight a.m. She should be at work.

After attending to her needs, she found her purse and pulled out her Blackberry. Six days and 800 messages worth of work awaited her at the office. She scanned quickly through her emails and found a message from her secretary about a phone call from Julia Davidson. Julia had changed her mind and would speak to Katy but only at eleven this morning.

Damn. Mark would never let her go. He had woken her half a dozen times to make sure she was okay. Exhaustion had finally dragged him into a deep sleep in the early hours of the morning. Maybe she could go and come back before he woke up.

She gave herself a physical check. Shoulder still throbbing, body still aching, head still pounding. Dizzy. Good enough for work.

She stuffed the Blackberry in her purse and found her clothes neatly folded on the hall bench. Shirt from the hospital, now missing several buttons. Blood-stained skirt, missing one button. No bra or panties. Blood-stained heels. Very professional. All set for a witness interview.

She rubbed down the shoes and secured her clothing with a few safety pins from her briefcase. Then she tiptoed toward the door.

"Going somewhere?"

Startled, Katy gasped and spun around. Mark leaned against the wall, arms folded, biceps bulging, six-pack rippling. Thank God he'd put on a pair of gym pants. Her brain ceased functioning the minute he stripped off his clothes.

"I have to interview a witness at eleven. I didn't want to wake you. I would have called you from the cab."

He looked her up and down, taking in her shabby ensemble. "Like that?"

Katy grimaced. "I was going to stop at home and change first." Her knees wobbled, and a wave of dizziness hit her. She rested her hand on a nearby chair to steady herself, hoping he wouldn't notice.

He studied her, his face impassive. "You aren't going anywhere except back to bed."

She closed her eyes for a second and took a deep breath. "This is work. It's important. The witness initially refused to talk to me and she has only given me this one window. I have to go."

"I'm sure she'll understand if you tell her what happened."

A dull ache began to pound in her chest. She didn't want a fight. Not after last night. "I can't take the risk. I appreciate your concern, but I'm fine."

His eyes wandered over her trembling body. "No, you're not. Even if you make it downstairs, James is outside. He won't let you go anywhere. In fact, he'll probably throw you over his shoulder, carry you up the stairs and handcuff you to the bed."

Having seen James in action at the hospital, Katy had no doubt he would do exactly as Mark said.

He took a step toward her. "Bed. Now."

Katy didn't move. Couldn't move. Her body and mind at war.

"I'm not asking, sugar," he said softly. "I promised to look after you, and I don't break my promises."

"If I want to go, you can't stop me." She willed her legs to stop shaking, her head to stop pounding and her body to stop shivering.

He walked over to her and unclasped her hand from the chair. "I won't have to."

Without the chair for support, her body gave up the fight.

Dizziness blackened her vision and she reached blindly for support.

"I've got you." He caught her and pulled her down onto his lap as he settled on the chair.

She leaned against the broad expanse of solid muscle and breathed in his scent of sleep and sex and sandalwood. "Fuck."

He ran a warm finger over her lips. "That's not a nice word for a lady to use," he whispered in her ear. "My lady—who shouldn't be hiding things from me."

"I couldn't tell you. First, I knew what you'd say. Second, it's for our case and I don't want you to know who my witness is."

He leaned his forehead against her cheek. "There's no property in a witness. You know that. Our duty is bring the best evidence to court. Plus I've withdrawn as counsel." He circled his fingers along her inner thigh, so close to her sex she could feel the heat from his hand.

"Does Steele have a new lawyer? If not, I may still be at risk of losing my tactical advantage." Her voice caught as his finger flicked along her folds.

"With a body like this, you don't need any tactical advantages."

Katy pushed his hand away. "Stop it. We're having a serious legal discussion."

He peppered little kisses along her jaw line and pushed up her skirt. "I think this is seriously legal in almost every country." His hand dove between her thighs again.

Katy drew in a ragged breath. "How about a deal? You take me to the witness and I will agree to return to bed."

His hand froze and his eyes glittered. "Considering the fact you are still recovering and likely unaware of exactly what you're offering, I would be taking unfair advantage if I agreed to your terms." He wrapped one arm around her and cupped her breast. "Also you cannot offer me something I intend to enforce anyway." He pinched her nipple and her belly tightened with desire.

Katy glanced down at her watch. If she didn't hurry this up, she'd run out of time. What did he want? The fact he hadn't dismissed her offer told her he would take her, but what was the price?

She cupped his face between her hands, running her fingers over the rough stubble on his strong jaw. "Please come with me?" She brushed her lips over his, softly, gently.

With a grunt of satisfaction, he palmed the back of her head, pulling her closer to him. He teased her mouth open and then plunged inside, sweeping every inch, until she forgot everything but his taste, his touch and her overwhelming need to crawl back into bed with him and drown herself in the sensuous feast of his body.

Finally he pulled away, leaving her breathless and flustered. "You just had to ask."

Fifteen minutes later, dressed and shaved, he escorted her out of the elevator and into the main lobby. "Look lively," he said, tightening his arm around her waist. "You have one more obstacle to overcome."

"Where the hell do you think you're going?" James stood in the foyer, his feet braced and his arms crossed.

"I'm taking her to interview a witness. I assume you'll have someone following us." Mark edged them toward the door.

"You're not going anywhere. Look at her. She's in no condition to be running around. I was there when the doctor said she was to stay in bed. Plus, we don't have an ID on the shooter yet. It's not safe to leave."

Katy crossed her arms. "I have a job to do, just like you. Mark is coming with me and you can have someone follow us, but I'm not going back upstairs."

James stared at her and then glanced at Mark, his clear, blue eyes missing nothing. "Guess I'm joining the party."

"Please let me go by myself."

"No." Mark trailed Katy through the crowded Metrotown shopping mall in Burnaby with James following close behind them. When had he last been in a mall? He eyed the brightly lit stores filled with shoppers and grimaced. Definitely not something he missed.

"I thought you were going to sit in your car," she said, sidestepping a man weighed down with shopping bags.

Mark sighed. "I can't watch you from the parking lot, and neither can James. Why couldn't you meet with the witness at your office or at her home?" He dodged two women with baby carriages, so engrossed in their conversation, they didn't realize they had narrowly missed running him over.

"Her husband is very ill and she doesn't want to upset him by having people in the house. Apparently, he became very distressed last week when they had a visitor. She also can't leave him alone too long so the drive to my office is out." She smiled up at him. "Probably a good thing. Ted wouldn't have let you into the interview room, no matter how much you growled."

"I don't growl." His voice rumbled deep in his chest.

Katy laughed. "Of course you don't."

Did she know how much pleasure her laughter gave him—especially when he had thought he would never hear it again? Would she still be laughing when she found out Ted was going to pull her from the case because of him? Would she believe he had been motivated solely by his desire to protect her?

After seeing her at the courthouse, covered in blood, only the stronger need to stay by her side had kept him from seeking Ted out right then. He knew Ted well enough to genuinely fear for Katy's safety when she returned to work. The bastard wouldn't hesitate to throw her back into the fray. If she uncovered something at Hi-Tech, the publicity would be even greater than the shooting itself, and Ted never turned his back on free publicity.

Katy led him into a coffee shop. "I'm meeting her in the café opposite this one. You'll have to content yourselves with spying on me from here, but I'll buy you both a coffee first." She reached for her purse, but Mark grabbed her wrist.

"No."

Katy rolled her eyes. "It's the twenty-first century. It's okay if I buy you a coffee. No one will think you're any less of a man."

"I don't care what anyone thinks."

"Fine," she said.

Mark's surprise at her capitulation gave way to concern when she looked around and pointed to a nearby chair. "I just need to sit for a minute."

"We shouldn't have let her come," James said, echoing Mark's thoughts.

"Damned if I could stop her."

He watched Katy weave her way through the tables and chairs, her hips swaying gently as she walked. What it would be like to see her every day? To make her laugh, share her stories and play with her kids? To know she would be in his bed every night?

"Mr. Richards?"

Mark spun around, recognizing the woman in the blue coat at once. Julia Davidson.

She gasped and stepped back, her hand flying to her mouth.

Suddenly Katy was beside her. "Julia Davidson? I'm Katherine Sinclair. Is something wrong?"

Julia's eyes narrowed. "What's he doing here? I thought you said it was just you?"

"You know him?"

"Hi-Tech's lawyer? Yes, I know him. He came to our house last week. He's the reason Peter became so agitated." Julia shuddered and glared at Mark. "I don't know what kind of game you're playing, Mr. Richards, but I didn't say anything to anyone and you won't trick me into saying anything now." She whirled around and ran out of the café.

"Julia, wait." Katy took a step and staggered. Mark grabbed her around the waist to steady her.

"I thought I could trust you." Katy's accusing glare shriveled his heart.

"You can," he said. "I don't know what the hell is going on, but I'm going to find out and we aren't leaving you until I do."

"I take it that was the witness." James motioned them over to a free table and Mark helped Katy to her chair.

"Mark got to her," Katy said. "He told her not to talk to me. Just like last time."

James raised an eyebrow and settled himself at the table. "Doesn't sound like Mark. Sit. We'll sort it out."

Mark raised his eyebrows at the tone in his friend's voice. A tone he hadn't heard in a long time. Although he was older than James by two years, his friend had always managed to gain the upper hand with the force of his will, the strength of his conviction, and that tone his voice.

Mark joined Katy and James at the table. Katy rested her head in her hands but wouldn't look his way. Her body trembled as she struggled to stay upright, and Mark had to fight the urge to put his arm around her, knowing she would just shrug him off.

James fixed them both with a cold, hard stare. For a moment Mark felt as if he was back in the principal's office after a schoolyard fight.

James sighed. "Right. I understand you have restrictions on what you can disclose but the coincidence seems hard to believe. You said it happened twice, Katy?"

She nodded.

"Same case?"

"No." Mark shook his head. "I went to see the other witness on a matter unconnected with the case we're working on together."

Katy looked over at him and her eyes widened. "How can it not be connected? Two random people, two random cases? I don't buy it."

"Neither do I." James pulled out his notebook. "Usually when trouble comes calling there's no such thing as coincidence. How did you find the witnesses?"

Katy drew in a ragged breath and glanced over at Mark. "I can't tell you with him here."

"I'm off the case," Mark said. "The papers were filed with the court the day before your...accident. If you want me to whip up a non-disclosure statement on one of the napkins and sign it, I will."

Katy frowned. "Maybe I should call Ted first."

"No." Mark's voice rose almost to a shout. The last thing he needed was for Ted to tell her over the phone she was off the case. "If you don't trust me or you're uncomfortable with a name or detail, then write it down on a napkin and give it to James."

"Good idea." James pushed a few napkins in Katy's direction and handed her a second pen. "Okay. Shoot."

"The two witnesses were on a list my client got from..." She wrote a name on the napkin and handed it to James.

"Fuck," James muttered as he stared at the napkin. "It's all connected. This is why I needed to speak to witnesses right away. Now I have a possible motivation for the killing."

"I thought the motive was pretty clear." Katy cut herself off when two women walked past their table.

Mark's mind raced. That one wasn't hard to figure out. Martin. Was this what Steele had been referring to when he had complained about Katy poking her nose into his business? Did he know about the list?

James scribbled furiously in his notebook. "Who else is on the damn list?"

Heat flushed Katy's cheeks and she wrote on another napkin and slid it across the table.

"Christ." James slammed his fist on the table. Coffee sloshed out of the cups, spilling across the worn surface. "Did you not think that was information I needed to know?"

"James." Mark growled a warning, his frustration and anger boiling over.

Katy mopped up the spilled coffee with a napkin. "Sorry I didn't tell you at the hospital. Things have been a bit overwhelming."

Reeling at the possibility she might be even more involved than he had thought, Mark grabbed the remaining napkins and crushed them in his fist. "We're done here."

"I want that list," James said to Katy. "I don't give a fuck what the partners in your firm think. If I don't have it today, I'll get a warrant to search your damn office."

"She'll get it for you," Mark said. "Calm down. We're all doing our best to sort this out."

James stared pointedly at the crush of napkins in Mark's fist. "I'm not the one who needs to calm down."

"I remember another name," Katy interjected. With slow, gentle strokes, she traced along each of Mark's tightly clenched fingers, lifting them one at a time until his hand opened, allowing the white blossom of compressed tissue to spring free.

Mark held his breath, eyes riveted on her delicate fingers, as she carefully drew a napkin from his palm. For a moment everything fell away. His world narrowed to the brush of the napkin over his skin, the slide of Katy's fingers over his wrist, and the heat of her breath on his cheek.

"I see you've soothed the savage beast," James chortled, breaking the spell.

Katy scrawled on the napkin and handed it to James. "He never returned my calls. I tracked him down to an apartment building on the corner of 13th and Hemlock. I was going to pay him a visit before..." She choked off her words. *Before she was shot.*

Mark couldn't sit by any longer and watch her fade. He dragged her chair over to his and pulled her against him. She didn't protest, but leaned into his chest with a soft sigh. He looked at James and narrowed his eyes. "She's done here. I'm taking her home."

James nodded and snapped his notebook closed. "I need to get my team on these leads. I'll meet you both at the station at four o'clock. Get whatever clearance you need from your firms and the Law Society and be prepared to give me all the facts."

Mark frowned. "She shouldn't—"

"I'll be fine," Katy murmured.

"You won't."

"She'll have to be," James said, his face grim. "There's a killer on loose. Maybe more than one."

"I'm pulling you off the case." Ted folded his arms and leaned back in his chair. Katy had rarely seen him so still. Usually he was in motion: foot rocking, pen tapping and body swaying. But today, except for the rise and fall of his chest, his body was frozen with disapproval and his eyes glittered with anger.

Katy sucked in a breath, shock and horror giving way to crushing disappointment in a heartbeat. She should have taken Mark up on his offer to take her home and saved herself from this unwanted surprise.

"Why, Ted? I'm okay. I'm fit to work." Did he know she was lying? Or that the doctor at the hospital had told her to take at least another week off work? No way could she do it. In the "up or out" culture of a big city firm, another week of sick leave would not only destroy her chances of partnership, it would kill her career.

"Where should I start?" Ted's voice was uncharacteristically cold and hard. "Someone killed your witness and tried to shoot you. Another one of your witnesses is dead. You are running around when you clearly should be in bed. And you are compromising the reputation of the firm by engaging in a relationship with opposing counsel."

She closed her eyes for a second and tilted her head up to the ceiling. She had known in her heart they would never get away with it. They had danced on the edge of the abyss and now they would have to pay the price.

Still she couldn't stop her emotions from flooding her face. "Ted—"

"Don't look so surprised," he said abruptly. "The legal community is a small one and you already had a reputation for causing trouble. I bent over backwards to get you into this firm. You let me down."

"It's not what you think."

"Bullshit. Don't lie to me, Katherine." He pushed back his chair and rounded the desk. "When I called Steven to find out where you were, he said you'd gone to Richards's place, and you've just finished telling me you went with him to see a witness. How is that going to look to the client, or to the Law Society? You're lucky no one else has found out."

"But he had withdrawn as counsel before I went to his place."

"I should have known something was up when he called," he muttered to himself.

"When who called?"

If he heard her question, he chose not to answer. "It's not just that. I like you, Katherine. You're a nice person and one hell of a lawyer. Steven was a bad choice. But someone like Richards would be far worse. You have no idea what he's really like. He runs a sex club in his spare time for chrissakes. He'll corrupt you, use you and throw you away."

"But he was off the case," she said again.

"Was he?" Ted arched an eyebrow. "We haven't received any documents from the court or from his office to that effect. He lied to you and I think it's obvious why. I never thought you'd be so gullible."

Katy sucked in a breath. No documents? There had to be a mistake. Why would he deceive her?

For a bit of fun.

She shook her head. She didn't believe it. Not after everything he had done for her. Even now her gut told her he wasn't lying—not about the withdrawal and not about the witnesses.

"It's not just that," Ted continued. "Jimmy Rider is dead. Someone beat him to a pulp and left him in an East Side alley. I spoke to the detective in charge of the case. Witnesses saw a tall, broad-shouldered man in a black suit fleeing the scene. The police believe it was personal and not drug-related, but they haven't said why. I don't suppose you know someone with a questionable past who might fit that description and who might be upset to find out his girl had been roughed up?"

"Oh God." She wanted Ted to stop talking. Stop filling her with head with doubts. Mark had threatened to make sure Jimmy would never hurt her again. Would he have used the experience he had gained on the streets as a youth to make good that threat? Had she misjudged him as badly as she had misjudged Steven?

No. She couldn't reconcile the gentle lover from last night with the portrait Ted was trying to paint of a violent and dishonest man. She wasn't ready to give up. Not on Mark and not on the case.

"Martin told me lives are at stake," she said, her voice steady and clear. "Martha is relying on us. It's not fair to her or to Martin's memory if we just let this go. No one knows the case as well as I do. I'm on to something and I've got the police protecting me now. Let me see it through."

Ted shook his head. "I don't want you involved in this case. Someone shot at you. Two men are dead. I'll take it over myself and settle with Steele. I've already drafted the press release."

"Justice won't be served that way," Katy said. "I know Martha. She's a good person. Steele will offer next to nothing and she'll take it so no one gets hurt. Just give me some time. A few more days. I have a document review scheduled at Hi-Tech on Friday and I might be able to find the evidence we need to expose them. Think about the publicity for the firm if I do uncover something. It will eclipse the publicity of a settlement."

Ted exhaled a long breath. "I know I'm going to regret this, but I'll give you two days. The file is yours until after the document review...then I'm calling Steele."

Mark rolled his eyes when he walked into the boardroom. The long, serious faces of his fellow partners told him this "impromptu" partners' meeting had been planned well in advance. Could his day get any worse? Exhausted and emotionally drained, he didn't know if he could take what he knew they were about to give.

"An ambush?" He sat down and waited for the circus to begin.

Tony took a deep breath. "I'll get right to the point. You have to break it off with her. We've all agreed you've crossed the line into conflict territory. If you're caught, it could damage the reputation of the firm."

"And we don't want to lose the client who is single-handedly keeping the firm afloat." Curtis didn't meet his gaze. A contracts solicitor to the core he abhorred confrontation.

Mark tightened his lips. "After all these years, do you not trust me?"

"When it comes to her, no." Tony didn't mince his words.

Mark spun his chair around and stared out over the water, bitterly disappointed at his fellow partners. "Over the last few years, Steele has been pushing me close to the ethical line. When he finally he asked me to cross it by scaring Katy off the case, I decided Hi-Tech was not the kind of client we wanted to represent. No client is worth compromising our reputation. I withdrew as counsel before she was shot. What happened after that is of no concern to the firm or to Steele."

No one moved. No one spoke. The loss of Hi-Tech's work could ruin the firm, and they all knew it.

"Fuck." Curtis ran his fingers through his hair. "Why didn't you do what he wanted, but in a roundabout way?"

Mark shook his head. "You know Steele. If I crossed the line once, he would expect me to do it again and again. Before you know it, I would be destroying documents and forging signatures. I wasn't prepared to step onto that slippery slope."

"You should have come to us before you so blithely dumped the firm's major client." Tony rested his forehead in his hands and stared down at the table.

Mark gritted his teeth. "I'll admit I was already looking for a way out of the case. And maybe I didn't try as hard as I could have to salvage the client relationship, but Steele has gone down a road we can't follow without giving up our principles. He gave me an opportunity to bow out and I took it."

"We can probably make up the shortfall with the Translife Electric litigation." Always the optimist, Tony broke the silence with a way forward.

Mark shook his head. "I've withdrawn my bid. I asked Ted to pull her off the case, and he wanted something in return. The tender was his price. We were his only real competition. To be honest, after the publicity surrounding the shooting, I think he had planned to take it from her anyway and steal the limelight. I just gave him a reason to do what he wanted to do."

"Have you gone fucking crazy?" Curtis growled. "That was the biggest piece of litigation we've seen all year. You're going to destroy the firm over a woman."

Mark swiveled his chair. "We were never guaranteed to get the tender, so I'm not affecting our bottom line, and it seemed a small price to pay to keep a fellow lawyer safe. Everyone in the legal community knows what Ted's like. He doesn't give a damn about the welfare of his associates, so long as they fill his pockets or get him in front of a camera. She was assaulted by her client, Rider, and Ted didn't want to pull her off the case until he collected his fee. Now she's been shot at, the killer is still on the loose, and yet he told me he planned to send her back out on the street, chasing down witnesses."

"I don't think any of us have an issue with saving a fellow lawyer from Ted," Tony said. "But there is more to it than that."

Mark nodded. "You're right. This isn't about profits or even looking out for a fellow lawyer. It's about principle."

"At this stage, with our books in the red, I'd give up principles for profit," Curtis muttered. "If you had just kept yourself under control, you wouldn't be in the position of having to pay any price."

"But then I wouldn't be able to protect Katy from Steele," Mark countered. "I don't think we could have continued to represent him in any event." He folded his arms and paused for effect. "I think he arranged the shooting."

The partners inhaled a collective breath.

"Go on," Tony said.

"I don't have anything concrete. Steele made veiled threats during several of our meetings and in the last one he said he would deal with the witness and Katy himself."

"Why?" Tony scratched his head. "It doesn't make sense. You said it was a dismissal case."

Mark shrugged. "Steele hinted she had uncovered something he wants to keep hidden. He has a big product launch coming up. Something revolutionary. Worth billions. If the two cases are connected, she might have found something worth killing for."

Tony pressed his lips together. "I think we all understand the motivation behind your actions, but the bottom line is you put the firm at risk and you didn't consult us. We'll have to discuss everything that happened and then form a view as to whether or not we ask you to step down from the partnership or impose some form of sanction."

He sighed and looked away, unable to hold Mark's gaze. "I'm sorry. We all are. But you're the one who wrote the rules."

Mark swallowed and forced himself up, despite the overwhelming sense of betrayal crushing his chest. These were the men he had thought would stand behind him no matter what. Men he had trusted.

Unable to speak, he gave them a curt nod and left the room. He didn't regret his actions. He had always stood by his principles. But more than that, he would do what it took to keep Katy safe. He hadn't been there for Claire. But he would damn well be there for Katy.

"So where are we with our mountain of cases? Surprise me."

James looked around the war room at his exhausted investigation team. They were working round the clock and their weariness showed. The cups of coffee were larger, the jokes lamer and the smiles less frequent.

Mike took a deep breath. "Forensics analyzed the residue of the contents of the two baggies. It's not a known substance, although the components are readily identifiable. Whatever it is, Wood and Garcia both ingested it and both died as a result."

"I think we can tell the coroner's office we've ruled out the possibility of a communicable disease," Joanna said.

James nodded for Mike to continue.

"Our street team has confirmed that Rider was the go to guy for black market pharmaceuticals, and he was pedaling some new product before he was arrested." Mike twisted his lips and looked away. "We...um...have no leads on who killed him."

"Are we still thinking this is a new kind of street drug?" Joanna flipped through her file and pulled out a sheaf of papers.

James shook his head. "Not if we only have two bodies. A street drug would be widely disbursed. There would be other players involved and likely more deaths." He wrote a few notes on the whiteboard and turned back to the group. Although Joanna and Mike did all the talking, their report was the result of a group effort. A group that was growing by the body.

"Anything else on Rider?"

"We've talked to people at the club where he used to hang out." Mike flipped through his notebook. "He was cheating on Valerie Wood with a woman we haven't been able to identify. Apparently he told his friends she was too classy for them. The only lead we have is a description from the landlord at his apartment building of a woman who didn't fit the usual profile for his evening entertainment. Early thirties, short blonde bob, gold-rimmed glasses. Always wore a black suit. We'll keep on it."

James nodded. "Joanna, how are you doing on the Kowalski

murder?"

"We haven't been able to get an ID on the shooter yet. The best we've come up with is a tall man, over six feet, with broad shoulders, average build, wearing black and driving some kind of black sedan. Forensics still can't determine if Sinclair was a target."

James scrubbed his hand over his face. "Let's keep a team on her and her kids. Apparently she's ruffled a few feathers. She's also connected to Silver through the same case. I think there has to be a connection between Silver, Garcia and Wood through the facial swelling. Do we have a toxicology report for Silver yet?"

Joanna shook her head. "The pathologist said he died from the gunshot wound but he was also suffering from aggressive lymphatic cancer. He also had suffered damage to most of the major organs in his body from...get this...a cytokine storm."

James smiled. "I don't suppose forensics found any plastic bags at Silver's place?"

"No, sir." Mike gave him a weary smile.

"Well good work everyone. I've got Sinclair and another lawyer coming in this afternoon. I'm hoping they'll have some of the missing pieces to the puzzle... if they can stay out of trouble for the next few hours."

Chapter Eighteen

"Perhaps I didn't make myself clear." Looking as though he would happily throttle her, Mark leaned against the door to Andrew McIntyre's apartment building, arms folded, white shirt stretched tight over his broad chest. "You were to see Ted and then go straight home to rest before our meeting with James."

Katy's lips thinned. She didn't have time for this. She wanted to make the most of her two days, and already her injuries were slowing her down. Three cups of coffee, two cans of Red Bull, a handful of painkillers and she still longed for her bed.

"What are you doing here? How did you find me? I wrote the name on a napkin so you wouldn't see." She took a step back, suddenly worried he would scoop her up and carry her away.

He huffed with annoyance. "You seem to have a nose for trouble. I called your cell. No answer. I called your home. No answer. I called your office. No one could tell me where you were. Right away, I knew you were up to something. So I called James and asked him to track down your fan club." He pointed to the surveillance team in the police car across the road. "And here I am." He puffed out his chest with arrogant pride.

"And here you will stay." She brushed past him and pulled out the piece of paper with McIntyre's apartment number. "You are not coming in with me."

A guttural sound escaped Mark's lips, primal and protective. He closed the distance between them and backed Katy up to the wall. "That's because you aren't going in. You're going home."

Her mouth went so dry she couldn't swallow. "I'm going in."

"Christ." He balled his hands into fists. "You're the most stubborn woman I've ever met. I knew you just couldn't let this go. You're supposed to be off the case."

She frowned. Something he said niggled at her brain. *Later.* Right now, she had a witness to see. "I don't want you to interfere."

"We're on the same side now, sugar. I want to find out what's happening just as much as you. But more than that, I want you to be safe."

"Are we on the same side?" Katy folded her arms. "Or are you still acting for Hi-Tech? Ted told me you didn't make the application to withdraw as Steele's solicitor for the case."

Mark gave an exasperated sigh. "The documents were filed over a week ago. You know these things take time."

"All I know is I wouldn't have gone as far with you as I did if I had thought you were still on the case. Maybe you lied to me so you could have your bit of fun."

A shadow of hurt crossed his face, but in a second it was gone, replaced by a mask of cold indifference. "If that's really what you believe, then I'll leave you alone, but not before I make sure you're safe inside the apartment."

Her gut clenched. He didn't deserve to be on the receiving end of her anger with Ted, or her stress at having only two days to solve the mystery. But his threat to stop her from going in had unsettled her. McIntyre was her last lead. Unless she found something in Hi-Tech's documents on Friday, she would have nothing to show for the two days Ted had given her to finish the case.

The door swung open. A pretty young woman with long, curly brown hair struggled out, her arms laden with boxes.

"Here I'll give you a hand." Mark took the boxes and Katy held the door while he carried them to the woman's vehicle parked down the street. For a split second she considered running inside and leaving him to figure his own way in, but knowing Mark, it wouldn't take long and she would have to deal with an angry...what? Boyfriend? Lover? Friend? Colleague? What was he to her? *Don't go there. Not now.*

Mark returned and followed her into the foyer. "I didn't think you'd wait," he murmured.

Katy looked over her shoulder. "Neither did I."

The building contained only twelve apartments and it didn't take them long to find number two. Katy reached up to pull the old-fashioned doorknocker on the sickly pink door, but Mark stayed her hand.

"Look," he mouthed. She followed his gaze to the partially open door.

"Come." He grabbed her elbow and tugged her down the hallway.

Katy shook him off. "What if something is wrong? What if he's ill or hurt?" She pushed the door and it opened with a soft creak. Fingers of light poked through small windows facing the back alley. The main room had been decorated in a Southwestern style, with a colorful Mexican rug, soft orange furniture and a shelf full of tequila bottles. A large, framed picture of a cactus hung over a flat-screen TV. They walked across the tiny living space to check the kitchen, more an alcove than a room, and then the small adjacent bedroom.

"Looks like no one's here."

A soft groan sent her flying into Mark's arms. Her heart pounded frantically against her ribs. "What was that?"

Mark pushed her behind him and they followed the sound to a small bathroom decorated with black and white tiles. The edge of the door had been splintered. A man lay on the floor, clutching his stomach. Blood smears covered the tiles, the toilet and the rim of the tub.

Katy pushed past Mark and grabbed a towel. "He needs an ambulance. The police should still be outside." Mark rushed out the door and Katy pressed the towel over the man's wound.

"Are you Andrew?"

He nodded and licked his lips, then coughed a bubble of blood. "Someone broke in. I tried to hide, but he was after me, not my stuff."

Katy squeezed his hand. "An ambulance will be here any minute. Just hang in there." She pressed harder, applying pressure to his wound. The front door creaked and footsteps thudded across the floor behind her.

"Mark, I need another towel." She looked over her shoulder and froze.

Not Mark. Black clothes. Ski mask. Gun.

Her heart thundered in her chest. She had always imagined what she would do in a life-threatening situation, and in every imaginary instance, she screamed and assaulted her attacker before running away. She had never had any doubt she would rise to the occasion if her life was ever in danger.

She didn't rise.

She didn't even scream.

Instead she crouched on the floor, frozen in place, eyes wide, pulse racing, as she desperately tried to staunch the bleeding from Andrew's stomach.

She shifted her gaze away from the shiny black gun, the first real one she had ever seen, and into the eyes of a killer. No doubt about it. His cold, black eyes held no emotion. No fear. No anger. No joy.

"You always seem to get in my way." Ordinary voice. Calm. Smooth. The gun clicked when he cocked the trigger. She drew in a ragged breath and prepared to die.

I didn't hug Mel and Justin goodbye. I didn't tell Mark...I believe him. I trust him.

I love him. She knew that now. Too late.

He motioned her away from Andrew with the gun. "I have a job to finish. You interrupted me."

Stunned, she looked down at the semi-conscious man on the floor, white from shock and loss of blood.

"Please don't do this." She would beg for his life because he could not.

"No body, no pay."

Her teeth chattered although the room was stifling hot. "What about me?"

"No pay, no body."

She saw the shadow only seconds before he did. Before he could turn to meet the threat, Mark grabbed him and threw him backwards across the hallway and into the television. He landed with a heavy thud. The gun clattered to the floor.

"I can't leave you, even for a minute." Mark pulled her up and out of the bathroom.

A soft grunt startled her. Footsteps. The man in black pushed his way past them and disappeared into the hallway.

"First, I have to say, going into McIntyre's house alone was beyond stupid." James glared at the two lawyers sitting on the other side of his desk. Exhaustion lined Katy's face. Blood seeped through her bandages, staining her shirt. He figured he had maybe twenty minutes before she collapsed. Mark should have left her in the hospital instead of letting her run around the city. If she'd been his girl, he would have handcuffed her to the hospital bed until she had fully recovered.

"Where's my list?"

Katy pushed a piece of notepaper across the table. Within minutes James had arranged a police detail at both the Cunningham and Davidson households.

"Now." He looked at Mark and Katy. "From the beginning. I don't want to hear about conflicts or Law Society rules. I want the facts, all of them. Mark, why did you go to see the two witnesses?"

Mark put a protective arm around Katy. "Apparently there was a lab accident. Steele didn't give me details and I don't know how many people were involved. Hi-Tech kept it quiet and settled with the victims. Their in-house lawyer handled the legalities. Steele asked me to renegotiate the agreements."

He stopped and rubbed his hand through his hair. James had never seen him so wound up, emotionally or physically. A man on the edge.

Mark cleared his throat and picked up where he had left off. "Davidson's wife said the accident involved a spilled chemical in the lab. Neither of the witnesses could confirm anything. They're both dying of the same rare aggressive lymphatic cancer and are beyond the point where they can speak. I found the coincidence strange in itself."

Aggressive lymphatic cancer. Like Silver. How rare can it be?

James knew Mark well enough to see something wasn't sitting right. "What's bothering you?"

"I might have imagined it, but I thought Davidson shook his head

239

when his wife told me about the accident. Also, his injuries didn't seem consistent with a chemical spill. The men were grotesquely swollen but their skin wasn't affected."

Katy shook her head. "Martin said it wasn't a chemical spill. He said it was a set up...just before he died."

"Wait a minute." James jumped out of his seat, his pulse racing. "Did you say both men were swollen? Like Valerie?"

"Not as bad, but yes."

"What about these two?" James pulled the post-mortem photos of Silver and Garcia from a file on his desk and thrust them under Mark's nose.

Katy gasped and turned away. Mark nodded. "Again, not quite as bad as this one..." he pointed to Garcia, "...but very similar to this one." He tapped Silver's photo.

James grabbed the phone and called Joanna. "I need you and Mike to go and interview the wives of two contract cleaners when you're done in the lab. You'll find their details on my desk. I want to know everything about a lab accident at Hi-Tech. I also want you to prepare a warrant application to search Hi-Tech's head office on Broadway."

He covered the receiver and nodded at Katy. "Would your client know anything about the accident?"

Katy shrugged. "I can call her and ask."

"I'll send someone to her house. I need a name and address."

"Martha Saunders. I think she lives at—"

James cut her off. "Your client is Martha Saunders?"

Katy frowned and nodded. "Do you know her?"

With a heavy sigh, James leaned back in his chair and stared at the report Joanna had just prepared. She had just identified Jimmy Rider's new girlfriend—a laboratory technician named Martha Saunders.

Chapter Nineteen

"This is it." Katy's heart sank when Mark pulled up in front of her house. Steven's Volvo sat in the driveway and music blared through the windows. Nine o'clock and the kids were still awake...and at the wrong house.

Katy sighed. Another confrontation with Steven. For a split second she thought about asking Mark to take her to his apartment. But Melissa and Justin were inside and except for their brief visits to the hospital, she had hardly seen them in the last six days.

"Thanks for taking me to the hospital to get the dressing checked, although I didn't appreciate it when you tried to convince them I needed to stay overnight. Maybe I'll see you—"

"Now." Mark turned off his vehicle. "I'm not leaving until I know you're safely tucked up in bed."

Katy pushed open the car door. "Please, Mark. I have family issues to deal with and I just want to be alone."

"Not this time." He stepped out of the vehicle and made his way around to help her out. "You aren't getting rid of me that easily."

She hesitated only for second and decided not to press the issue. She needed to save her energy for the imminent fight with Steven. She stalked up the path and threw open the door. "Steven!"

Moments later, Steven appeared, wearing only a pair of pajama pants. "Hi, babe—" He cut himself off when he caught sight of Mark in the doorway and his lips pulled back in a snarl. "What's he doing here?"

She steeled herself to stay on the offensive. "What are *you* doing here? You're supposed to have the kids at your place."

His face softened. "I've moved back in to look after you. I called Ted and he said you'd been at the office, so we've been waiting for you to come home and make dinner. We're starved. All we've had to eat is popcorn." He looked back over his shoulder and yelled down the hallway, "Kids, your mom is home. Finally."

Justin and Melissa came barreling into the hallway and threw themselves at her with such force she staggered backward and into Mark, standing directly behind her. He put his hands on her shoulders to steady her while she hugged her children and blinked back the tears. God, she'd missed them.

"Get your hands off my wife," Steven bellowed.

Everyone froze. The kids clutched her clothes and looked wide-eyed at their father, his face taut and his eyes narrowed in anger. Pushed past the limit. She knew the signs. She shouldn't have let Mark come in.

"Melissa. Justin. Go upstairs." For the first time ever, they obeyed her at once.

Not wanting to agitate Steven any further, she stepped away from Mark. "I am not your wife. Not anymore. Why can't you understand that?"

Steven glared. "I'm not having a discussion about our relationship with him in my house. He's the one who turned my sweet, innocent Kate into some kind of whore."

She didn't even see Mark move.

One second Steven snarled in front of her. The next, he staggered back, his head snapping to the side as Mark's fist connected with his jaw.

"Steven! Mark!"

Is that what he did to Jimmy? She pushed the betraying thought out of her mind.

"My God, Kate. He's crazy. I think he's broken my jaw." Steven rubbed his face and righted himself.

"If I broke your jaw, you wouldn't be able to speak. Maybe I should give it another try. It would be a definite improvement."

Katy shivered at the icy menace in Mark's voice.

Although shaken, Steven appeared to be fine. She suspected Mark had held back. With the power she sensed coiled in his tight, muscular body, she had no doubt he could have broken more than Steven's jaw

242

if he had wanted.

Kill him, even.

No. She had made her decision. She would not doubt him again.

"You've just asked for a whole lot of trouble." Steven shook his fist in Mark's direction. "I'm calling the police."

Mark snorted a laugh. "Ask for Detective Hunter. You met him before at the hospital. I'm sure he'll be more than pleased to help you out. He can explain the defense of provocation to you."

Steven stormed past them toward the door. "You've gone off the deep end, Kate. Look who you're associating with. You need stability in your life. You've become a bad influence on the kids. A bad mother." He threw on his jacket and stomped out the door, oblivious to his state of semi-undress. "I'm not giving up on you, even though you gave up on me. You're mine, Kate. Mine."

"Kids in bed?"

Katy nodded. "They liked you. You impressed them with your ability to play video games and make sandwiches at the same time."

A shadow of longing crossed his face, but in an instant it was gone. "They're good kids."

Katy leaned up and kissed him on the cheek. "Thanks for making dinner and helping out this evening. I've never been so exhausted in my life."

Mark wrapped his arms around her waist. "You should be in bed. I'll tuck you in before I leave."

Katy stiffened and pulled away.

"What's wrong, sugar?"

She worried her bottom lip and looked up at him. "I need to ask you something."

"Go ahead."

Katy took a deep breath. "Jimmy Rider. Ted told me someone...beat him to death."

He studied her for a long moment before dropping his arms. "You think it was me," he said quietly. Disappointment creased his face.

Katy's heart pounded but she pressed on. "No. But after you told me about your past..." She choked on her words. "I had to ask."

Mark tightened his jaw. "You think I'm still that person?" The pain in his voice sliced through her like a knife. She took a step toward him, but this time he stepped away. "I shouldn't have told you, but I didn't want there to be any secrets between us. Looks like even that wasn't enough to earn your trust."

Katy's stomach clenched. "Mark...I—"

"I didn't touch Jimmy. I couldn't find him. Even if I had, he might have suffered a few broken bones at the most." He grabbed his coat from the kitchen chair. Katy stepped in front of him, blocking his path to the door.

"I didn't believe Ted," she said in a firm voice. "If I did, I would never have let you spend time with my children. And I'm glad you told me about your past. My relationship with Steven was built on a foundation of lies. I appreciate your honesty more than you could know."

"If you didn't believe Ted, why did you ask?"

Katy took a deep breath. "I wanted to hear it from you. I didn't want to have any doubts. I love you, Mark, and I never thought I'd feel this way...ever."

He didn't speak for the longest time. Finally he nodded toward the stairwell. "You should get some rest. I'll see you upstairs and then I'll go."

Nausea gripped Katy so hard she almost couldn't move. She opened her mouth, hoping to resolve the situation, but one look at Mark's taut, impassive face and she knew there was nothing she could say to make it better.

He followed her up the stairs and into her bedroom. As with the home office, she'd redecorated after Steven left. The dark, wooden sleigh bed had been replaced with an airy, wrought iron frame. Freshly painted mauve walls matched the silk bedspread, and a light purple curtain brushed the newly polished wood floors. The scent of lilies from her garden drifted in the open window. Her sanctuary.

"Okay, into bed with you."

"Will you stay?" As hard as it was to ask, it would be harder to let him go.

He shook his head. "The last few days have been rough...for both of us. It's probably best if we get some sleep." The firm rejection stung but the slight note of hesitation in his voice gave her hope.

She reached behind him and locked the door.

"What are you doing?" His low, husky voice told her he had some idea.

She crossed the room and stood beside the bed. Gritting her teeth, she removed her clothing, piece by piece, until she stood naked before him. She pushed away every negative thought she'd ever had about herself, every snide remark Steven had ever made and she lifted her eyes to his.

His eyes raked over her body, returning to her face with a hunger that matched her own. Still he didn't move. If not for the rapid rise and fall of his chest, he could have been one of the beautiful Greek statutes she had seen in the British Museum. But not with those eyes. Dark now, almost black, and carnal.

Go to him. Fight for him.

Trembling, Katy closed the distance between them until she stood only a foot away. "I meant what I said, and if you don't feel the same way, I'll understand. But right now, I want to show you how I feel."

"You don't understand what you're saying." His deep, low voice soothed away her tremors.

Guiding his hands to her hips, she leaned up and brushed her lips over his. "I know exactly what I'm saying."

He tightened his arms and returned the kiss with fervor.

"Please," she whispered. "Please don't leave."

Mark clenched his jaw as he looked down at the beautiful woman trembling in his arms. Her lack of trust had stung, but not enough to turn him away. Instead, the three words she had uttered had almost been his undoing. He had seized on her declaration as an excuse to run away—from the one woman he had been waiting for his entire life. The woman Claire had known she could never be.

Now or never. His future shivered in his arms. She had the courage to bare herself to him. How could he show any less faith in what he knew sparked between them? She had awakened a fierce hunger inside him that only she could satisfy. A yearning like nothing he had ever felt before. Had Claire felt this way about him? Was her descent into addiction truly an attempt to fill the void of unreciprocated love, or was it, as James had always maintained, something else—something that had nothing to do with him?

He rested his chin on Katy's head and looked around the room at the pictures covering the walls. Happy family pictures. Children's artwork. Vacations. Walks in the park. He ached with longing. He had never thought himself capable of the love needed to build a family, but now he wasn't so sure.

"I'm not going anywhere." His voice was rough and hoarse with need. He lifted her and placed her gently on the thick duvet. After stripping off his clothes, he stretched out beside her, propping his head with his elbow and breathing in the comforting scents of lavender and lilies. Of her.

He brushed his fingers down her chest, circling her nipples with his thumbs, delighted when they peaked under his touch. With slow, deliberate strokes, he caressed every part of her body, memorizing every sensitive crease and every inch of her silky skin. When he feathered kisses over her taut abdomen, she moaned softly and ruffled her fingers through his hair.

Mine.

He would never tire of her body or her heated response to his touch.

So beautiful.

He kissed his way up her body and captured her lush lips, drawing them into a soft and gentle kiss.

So sweet.

A cool breeze fluttered the curtains and Katy shivered.

"I'll close the window." Mark pushed himself up, but Katy held him back.

"It's got a tricky catch. I've had years of practice."

She slid off the bed and reached up to release the latch. The window rumbled down with soft thud.

"Stay there." Mark left the bed and closed the distance between them. He wrapped his arm around her waist, drawing her into the warmth of his chest.

"You stood like that in the wine cellar." He nuzzled her neck, and growled in satisfaction when she tilted her head to give him better access. "It's burned into my brain. Your sexy ass, your long legs, your body stretched up..."

She whimpered softly and his voice thickened. "Do you know what I imagined, sugar, when you were reaching for that Meursault? Do you know how close I was to shoving your skirt over your hips and taking you right there?"

A thin whine escaped her lips. She tried to turn in his arms but he held her firm.

"I want you like that," he growled. "Up against the wall. Fully available for my pleasure. Just like I imagined."

Her low throaty groan was all the consent he needed. He snaked his hands along her arms and positioned her palms against the wall, not so high she would lose her balance, but high enough to make her slightly uncomfortable and aware of her vulnerability.

"Good girl," he whispered against her ear. "But I remember your legs were wider." He gently kicked her legs apart and she responded with a soft moan.

"You like that, sugar, don't you? A little rough. I saw that hidden wild side in the cellar when you tried to seduce me."

She stiffened and looked over her shoulder. "Seduce you? You seduced me."

He cupped her breast, and then rolled her nipple between his thumb and forefinger until it stiffened into a tight peak. "Who kissed whom, little minx?"

Katy hissed in a breath. "Who put his hands all over me and whispered naughty things in my ear?"

Mark chuckled. "I was just being friendly."

"So was I." Katy wiggled her ass against him. He licked his lips, considering, then he slapped her right ass cheek—not hard enough to hurt, but with enough force to get his message across.

"Don't move, sugar. I won't last."

Her body went rigid and she sucked in a sharp breath. "Did you just...spank me?"

"It was more of a love tap," he chuckled. "I'll take you to the back of the club one night and you'll see what spanking is all about."

"I don't think I—"

"I think you do," he murmured, cutting her off.

He slipped his hand between her legs and dragged his fingers through her wet folds, spreading her moisture down along her inner thigh.

"I think you really do," he growled. "You're so wet, sugar, it makes me want to do it again."

"Take me. Don't play," she begged.

He cupped her hot sex and then plunged two fingers into her tight, wet sheath. Her body shook as he drew his fingers in and out, angling upward to rub against her most sensitive spot.

Soon he would bury himself in her lush heat just as he had imagined doing in the wine cellar. His cock throbbed with readiness and he brushed the crown over the soft curve of her ass to cool the flame.

Now that was a mistake.

Clenching his teeth to maintain his control, he kept a steady rhythm with his fingers until her wetness dripped down her inner thighs and her body glistened with the effort of holding her position.

"I want to turn around," she moaned. "I want to touch you."

"Not yet, sugar." Unable to resist, he withdrew his hand and slicked his cock between her thighs, reveling in her wetness, before he angled himself to slide over her swollen nub.

"Oh, Mark." The desperate, pleading note to her voice told him she was close. So close. He could bring her over the edge with one more stroke. And himself as well.

He left her wet and trembling to retrieve a condom from his wallet. Katy looked back over her shoulder, her eyes hooded with desire.

"Hurry."

He sheathed himself and gave her a wicked grin. "You know better than that. Now, you'll have to wait."

He covered her with his body, licking his way down her neck and along her spine, savoring her sultry, salty taste. By the time he reached her cleft, her legs were shaking and her skin was slick with heat.

Time for action. He pushed himself to his feet and pressed himself tight against her body.

"I'm going to take you like this, sugar," he rasped. "Bend forward. Palms lower on the wall."

She was whimpering, on the edge, but she did as he demanded.

"That's my girl," he whispered. He gave her only a second to adjust to the position before he drove into her hot, wet channel with one hard thrust. The angle didn't allow for deep penetration, but it gave him better access to her hidden center. When she sucked in a sharp breath, he knew he had hit his mark. He grabbed her ass and pounded into her, his hips falling into a natural rhythm.

"Can't hold on," she gasped.

Neither could he.

"I want to hear you, sugar. Tell me what you want."

"Love me, Mark." Her hoarse, throaty voice was music to his ears. Although it almost killed him to hold back, he slowed his tempo, wanting to give her the ultimate crescendo.

He slid his hand over her hip and down until he found her clit, swollen and erect, begging for his touch. He smoothed her moisture up and around and then pinched gently. Just once. Her body jerked, and she threw her head back and let out a high-pitched whine as she went over the edge. Her sex clenched tight around him, drawing him in.

Not enough. He wanted to bury himself deep inside her. Possess her fully. With an arm tight around her waist, he eased them down to the floor and positioned her on her hands and knees.

"Don't...stop," she panted. "Need more."

He grabbed her hips and thrust fast and deep, his fingers digging into her soft flesh. Heart hammering violently, he picked up the pace. Her pants gave way to a low, long wail and she climaxed again. With one last jerk of his hips, the pressure in his spine exploded in blistering shards and he came in wave after heated wave of pleasure.

As he collapsed beside her, something stirred in his chest. Katy was his. Not just tonight, but forever.

A loud bang wrenched Katy out of a deep sleep. Mark was wrapped around her, his warm, hard body cradling her own.

"Shh. Just a car door. It's still early," he murmured into her hair.

Early. Not late. He had been here all night. She must have drifted off in the middle of their conversation. She had told him things she had never shared with anyone. Baring herself to him, body and soul, had given her a sense a freedom. Or maybe it was the night of wild sex and the multiple orgasms that had left her so deliciously exhausted.

"I should let you go." She pulled away with a sigh. "The kids will be up soon and I don't think I'm ready to explain why you're here."

He pulled her back down for a long, leisurely kiss before he finally answered. "I'm in court this morning and for the next two days. Good thing you're not on the other side. I might suffer for lack of preparation."

"I'm going to be busy too. I've got witnesses to see and the document review to do on the Hi-Tech case."

Mark frowned. "You're supposed to be off the case."

"Ted gave me a few days to wrap things up." She tilted her head. "How did you know he pulled me off the case? You mentioned it yesterday too. I made a point of not telling you because you seemed to have a bad history with Ted." The niggling feeling she had had outside McIntyre's apartment came back with a vengeance.

He hesitated and then shrugged. "Ted and I were on a very long, very bitter case together. He played it too close to the line and made a mockery of the justice system, not to mention the concept of professional courtesy. I reported him to the Law Society. So, yeah, a bad history. As for pulling you off the case, it's what I would have done in his situation."

Katy wrapped the sheet around her and slid off the bed. Something wasn't right. "You didn't ask. You knew. How?"

He drew in a ragged breath. "I spoke to him when you were in the hospital."

"Are you saying he told you what he'd decided before telling me?"

"I asked him to take you off the case."

For a few moments, she forgot to breathe. "You. Asked. Him." She spat out each word. "Ted does not have an altruistic bone in his body. He wouldn't have agreed just because you asked. Especially if there was bad blood between you. There's something more."

He held up his hands in a gesture of mock surrender. "We both just wanted you to be safe."

Katy balled her hands into fists. "Ted cares about profits, not safety. You said so yourself. What did you do?" She hurled the words at him, knowing in the end his answer wouldn't matter. The guilt on his face had already broken her heart.

Mark pushed himself off the bed and quickly dressed. Katy seethed, waiting for an answer. Finally he turned to her and said, "I agreed to withdraw my bid for a tender he was after if he agreed to pull you from the case."

Her entire body shook. "You had no right," she shouted. "It's my case. My career. My decision. You can't even begin to understand what it means to me. I could have made partner. I could have become financially independent from Steven. You just bargained away my career like it was nothing."

She no longer cared if the children woke up. They wouldn't be seeing him again. She had trusted him. Opening herself up to him last night had not been easy. His betrayal stung worse than anything Steven had ever done.

Mark squared his shoulders. "There will be other cases. This isn't the only path to partnership. You're a brilliant lawyer and I have no doubt you'll succeed in whatever you do. I also don't think financial independence will rid you of Steven. You need to set limits for him and stick to them or he'll continue to knock them down. I had no intention of destroying your career. You were in danger. All I wanted was to keep you safe."

"Get out." Rage and anguish crawled under her skin. "Now."

He gazed at her for what seemed to be an eternity and then he turned and disappeared out the door.

Chapter Twenty

James leaned back in his uncomfortable, steel-framed chair and threaded his fingers together behind his head as he studied Martha Saunders. Not the type of woman he would have expected to associate with a low-life scumbag like Jimmy. Her blonde hair was short and neatly cut, and her black suit, although faded, was clean and pressed.

Her eyes, bright behind her elegant, gold-rimmed glasses, darted around the interview room, but there was nothing to see. The stark white walls and glaring florescent light would serve only to remind her that this was no social encounter.

James allowed himself a brief smile when she began to twist her watch around her wrist. Back and forth. Faster and faster. Betraying her anxiety.

Time to begin.

"How long were you and Jimmy together?"

Martha pursed her lips and frowned. "We weren't really together. We met in a bar one night. He was really nice. Charming. Hot. Usually guys like that don't talk to girls like me. He said he was a middle manager for a paper company. I was really drunk and I went home with him. We got together a few times after that, mostly for sex."

James raised an eyebrow when her voice hitched. Clearly there was more to the relationship than she had let on.

"You used to work for Hi-Tech Pharmaceuticals, isn't that right?"

Martha nodded.

"Did you know how Jimmy made a living?"

"Not when I first met him. I found out later...when things went wrong." She held his gaze without flinching. "Do I need my lawyer?"

James kept his face impassive. "I asked you here for an informal chat, but if you would feel more comfortable with a lawyer, feel free to call one."

"It's just...I'm getting the feeling this isn't only about Jimmy." Her voice shook and she threaded her fingers together so hard her knuckles turned white.

"True. I'm also interested in the case you started against Hi-Tech."

Martha shrugged. "The pleadings are public documents. I worked there as a lab tech. I discovered they weren't acting ethically. I reported it to the regulators and then I was fired. So I started a lawsuit."

The overhead light flickered on and off. James frowned. He didn't want anything to disturb the momentum of his questioning. Martha could shed some light on Jimmy and his two swollen bodies, but if he wasn't careful, he would scare her away, or worse, send her running to a lawyer.

"I read the pleadings," he said. "Hi-Tech says they dismissed you because you went into the building after hours."

"I forgot my purse."

"I think you forgot something else." James shifted his weight and leaned toward her. "Drug samples. Jimmy had to get his supply from somewhere."

Her eyes widened and she sucked in a breath. "My purse."

James reached into the box he had strategically placed on the table before the interview. "I have the security tape from the night in question."

Her eyes flicked to the tape and back to him. "My lawyer requested the tape from Hi-Tech and was told it had gone missing."

"I found it." Did he see her tense the tiniest bit? She would be trying to decide if he was bluffing or if he had indeed found the original tape. Which he had. At Kowalski's residence. Kowalski must have been trying to protect her. But did she know it had been partially destroyed?

She swallowed and licked her lips. "Then you'll see I'm telling the truth."

James smiled. She was sticking to her story, which meant she suspected he couldn't view the tape. Damn good liar. But so was he. "You want me to play it for you?"

She shook her head and worried her bottom lip. "No, that's okay."

"You want to tell me about that night?" The effort of keeping his body relaxed and focused began to take its toll. Sweat trickled down his back. Over the years, he had interviewed dozens of criminals, from murderers to arsonists, petty thieves to irate husbands, and he had always been able to see past the masks and bravado to the hidden core of the man. But Martha was an enigma. Either she was totally guileless or the best damn liar he had ever met.

"There's nothing to tell. I forgot my purse. I signed in at security. I got it from my lab. I went home."

James nodded toward her trembling hands. "You afraid of something?"

Martha drew in a ragged breath. "I'm afraid the people who killed Jimmy will be unhappy when they find out you're nosing around. He told me if I ever talked to the police they would find me and kill me."

James folded his arms. "If you're telling me you know who killed Jimmy, I could arrest you right now for obstructing justice, withholding evidence or maybe even conspiracy." He paused, waiting for the threat to sink in, and then raised an eyebrow. "But maybe we can help each other."

Martha stilled and her eyes welled with tears. "I'm tired of trying to help people. I made a mistake with Jimmy. A big one. Then everything spiraled out of control. When I tried to fix it by reporting to the regulators, I lost my job. Now you want my help, but this time I'll pay with my life."

"We can protect you."

"That's it?" She lifted her eyes and peered through her glasses. "I need more than that. I want to walk out of here and know no one will ever come looking for me again, including you."

James shook his head. "I can't do it. I need to know how you're involved before I can decide whether or not to let you walk away. Maybe you killed Jimmy. Maybe you supplied him with illegal and possibly deadly pharmaceuticals. I can't let a killer back on the streets."

She crumpled, sagging in her seat as she buried her face in her hands. "I'm the victim here," she sobbed. "I'm the one who was blackmailed and threatened and...used."

"Talk to me. Let me help," he cajoled.

Martha shook her head. "If I talk to you, I'll be the next one to die."

Katy walked up the steps of the tidy two-story house in Aldergove. The white siding looked new and the lawn had been well kept. Flower boxes decorated the open porch and the two wicker chairs looked inviting after the stuffy car ride.

Her head throbbed from the hour-long trip. She knew she shouldn't be driving yet, but she had only one more day and she didn't want to let Martha down. More than that, she needed to get out of town and away from anything that reminded her of Mark. Every time she thought about him, her heart seized up. How could he accuse her of not trusting him when he had gone behind her back and done the one thing that would hurt her most? His excuse about keeping her safe wasn't enough. She didn't need anyone to keep her safe. She'd been doing just fine on her own.

Well...except for being shot outside the courthouse and then almost shot at McIntyre's apartment. Her stomach clenched. She had called the hospital this morning to check up on McIntyre only to find out he had died during surgery. With the possibility of two murderers on the loose, she would never have considered visiting Patricia Cunningham if she hadn't had the police protection team watching her twenty-four seven.

She glanced over her shoulder and spotted the police car parked across the street. One of the policemen waved. Katy returned the greeting and then rang the bell.

A short, solidly built woman in her mid-fifties answered the door.

"Patricia Cunningham?"

The woman nodded.

"I'm Katherine Sinclair. We spoke about the Hi-Tech case over the phone. I know you don't want to talk to me, but if you could just spare five minutes to hear me out, I would be very grateful."

Patricia studied her closely. "You're the lawyer all over the news.

The one who was shot outside the Vancouver courthouse. I recognize you now. How are you, dear?" Her wariness turned to sympathy.

"Good. Just tired." Katy eyed the couch. "You wouldn't mind if I sat down for a moment, would you?" She hated to use Patricia's sympathy to gain her trust, but at this stage she would try anything.

Patricia ushered her into the small living room and Katy settled herself on a worn leather couch. Patricia shooed her cat off the faded wingback chair and sat uneasily on the cushion.

"I didn't sign it," she blurted out. "I didn't sign the agreement that Hi-Tech's lawyer brought over. You said if I hadn't signed anything I could talk to you." She paused and her voice wavered. "I'm sick of secrets. Sick of Hi-Tech. I want someone to know what happened."

Hope swelled inside her. "You can talk to me."

Patricia clenched and unclenched her fists, clearly struggling over her decision to talk. The cat stretched out on the worn, stained gold carpet and then curled up at Patricia's feet.

By way of distraction, Katy picked up a picture of a balding, heavyset man with a red nose and twinkling blue eyes.

"Is this Robert?" She kept her tone light, hoping to ease Patricia's fears.

Patricia's eyes teared. "Yes, that's him, although he doesn't look like that now, not since the accident."

"I understand his team spilled some kind of chemical."

"That's the story Robert was told to say," Patricia said in a hushed whisper. "They weren't supposed to tell anyone what really happened or Hi-Tech would take back the settlement payment. But Robert told me. We've been together since we were sixteen. We don't keep secrets from each other."

Katy sat still, barely breathing. For a moment she wished Mark was here. She wanted him to hear what Patricia had to say. Not just about keeping secrets, but so he would know she hadn't been chasing ghosts. She wanted him to understand that bribing Ted to pull her off the case had been the wrong thing to do. She pushed Mark from her mind and turned her focus back to Patricia. "Tell me what happened."

"Robert is...was a custodian. He worked for Cleenaway, a

contracting company. His team went out to Hi-Tech on a six-month contract. But one night I got a call to come and pick him up. When I got there, his head was swollen and parts of his body as well. He was very ill. They have some kind of medical facility and he was hooked up to all sorts of machines. I wanted to take him to the hospital, but they said they couldn't move him because of the possibility of contamination. They said there had been a spill in the lab he was cleaning and he had an allergic reaction to the chemicals."

"Had he ever had an allergic reaction before?"

Patricia shook her head. "Never. Healthy as a horse, except a bit overweight, but we were working on that. I didn't want him to have a heart attack and leave me early." Tears welled up in her eyes. Katy offered her a tissue but she shook her head.

"I stayed with him all night and the next day too. They gave him lots of drugs but the swelling didn't go down. He improved, though, and he could talk and make jokes like usual. He wasn't the only one involved. There were three others. One of them had a wife, Julia. I talked to her in the coffee room, but I never saw any of them after we left."

Katy nodded. "Strange they didn't send him to the hospital when he began to recover."

"I thought the same thing but they said, as a private facility, they could provide him with better care and they were concerned about cross-contamination from the chemicals. They did look after him very well. He had his own nurse, three-course gourmet meals, fancy bedding and a big screen TV. When I pushed for him to go to the hospital, he said he was happy in their facility. After a couple of days a man came to see us. Said he was a lawyer for Hi-Tech. Offered Robert two million dollars compensation if he kept quiet."

"That's a lot of money."

"Especially for us. I'm a secretary so we had a steady income, but it wasn't much, and we were worried about retirement. Anyway I wanted to take the document to a lawyer but he said Robert had to sign there and then or not at all."

"Duress."

Patricia frowned. "What's that?"

"An agreement isn't binding if it's signed when you are under pressure or if you are being threatened."

"That's exactly how it was. Anyway, Robert signed it and they sent us home. The money appeared in our account the next day, which was a good thing because Robert couldn't go back to work. He had trouble walking and although the swelling went down, his face was never quite the same. Then we found out he had cancer."

"I'm so sorry." Katy put down her cup. "Why did you change your mind about talking to me?"

"Well I was going to call you and then Hi-Tech sent another lawyer. Nice fellow. Decent. He said the other agreement had problems and explained what they were. Robert didn't care. He just signed the new one. He wants to make sure I'm looked after when he dies. The lawyer had one for me too. But I didn't sign it or accept the money he offered. I didn't want to have anything to do with that company. He said that was fine but he asked us not to speak about the settlement or the accident."

"Did he threaten you or blackmail you to keep quiet?" Katy held her breath. *Please don't tell me Mark crossed the line.*

"No not at all." Patricia smiled. "He was very nice. He was concerned we were treated fairly and didn't lose the money."

Katy let out her breath with a whoosh. *Nice. Honest. Compassionate.* How could she reconcile the different aspects of the man she had thought she loved?

Patricia brushed a few loose, gray strands of hair behind her ears. How old was she? Maybe fifty-five or sixty? Too young to be contemplating a life alone.

"Hi-Tech wants to kill you, don't they?" Patricia asked in a hushed whisper.

Katy startled at the abrupt change of topic. "The police haven't caught the shooter and if they have any theories about who it was, they haven't shared them with me."

"But the newspaper said your witness was going to testify against them and I saw the police are still protecting you."

Katy swallowed. "I think the shooter was just after my witness but the police don't believe me."

"That's why I want nothing to do with Hi-Tech," Patricia said. "I thought after the last lawyer's visit, I'd just keep quiet, but now Robert has taken a turn for the worse and..." her eyes flooded with tears, "...I don't really care what happens to me after he's gone. He's been my whole world since I was a girl."

Sympathetic tears spilled from Katy's eyes. She envied Patricia the deep love she shared with her husband—the kind of love that could have lasted a lifetime. The kind of love Katy had only tasted and lost.

"What really happened?" she asked, after they had both dried their eyes. "You said you told the story you were given. What's the real story?"

Patricia tensed. "It wasn't an accident; it was an experiment. They offered my Robert and three of his co-workers three thousand dollars to try a new drug. They told him it had already been tested and it had only minimal side effects. So he agreed. But right after he took it, he began to swell up and he was in so much pain. When I got there, he was crying in agony. They all were. My poor Robert." Her eyes flooded with tears again. "I hate them. They must have suspected what would happen. They treated Robert like some kind of lab rat."

"Do you know if he signed anything at Hi-Tech? A consent form or something like that?"

Patricia shook her head. "If he did, he didn't tell me."

"Did they tell him what the drug was supposed to do?"

"No," she sniffed. "He was going to use the money to take me on a holiday. We were going to go abroad. He always wanted to see France." Tears rolled down her cheeks. "Now he never will."

"We didn't get the warrant to search Hi-Tech."

James froze. "Say again, Joanna?"

"I'm sorry, sir. The judge denied our application. He said we didn't have enough evidence to tie the bodies or the cleaners to Hi-Tech."

"Is he crazy?" James threw his pen across the room. "I can understand Garcia and Wood alone. That was a shot in the dark. But we have four men, all who work for the same company on the same contract to Hi-Tech. We now have bank records showing they each received a transfer of two million dollars. We have copies of their settlement agreements with the company. We have established they all suffered from similar injuries, and contracted the same rare form of cancer. It doesn't take a genius to do the math. What more does he want?"

Joanna took a step back, her eyes wide. Ah...she had never seen him lose control. Usually he managed to keep the pens on his desk.

"The judge agreed there may be a link between them, but we don't have enough evidence to establish Hi-Tech has done anything wrong." She stared at the pen on the floor and her voice wavered. "He said it is plausible the four men were injured at work and settled out of court. Or that all six people had similar symptoms but different causes. He wants something concrete. He'll reconsider on an expedited basis if we can give him one hard piece of evidence. I have a feeling the judge wouldn't be as cautious if Hi-Tech wasn't such a high-profile company."

"Fuck." James slammed his hand down on his desk. "We need a connection between Garcia, Wood and the four cleaners. Saunders is the key but she's afraid to talk."

"How do you think she's involved?"

James sighed. "I think she took drugs from Hi-Tech and gave them to Jimmy Rider to sell on the street. If she was being honest in the interview, then I suspect the drug was highly successful and Rider started blackmailing her for more. If she had given him even one sample, he would have had something to hold over her head."

"Makes sense." Joanna nodded. "Maybe he sold something to Garcia, who unfortunately had a fatal reaction, but for the most part everyone was fine. But when Martha got caught sneaking into the building to replenish his supply, he would have been cut off."

James picked up her train of thought. "He might have had an extra stash at Wood's place but before he could get to it, he was arrested. Wood might have found it and tried it out."

"And had a fatal reaction as well," Joanna said.

"Yes." James punched the air as more pieces fell into place. "That

261

ties in nicely with the assault on her lawyer. He must have thought she took the drugs when she went to Wood's apartment."

Joanna picked up the phone. "So can we bring Saunders in for theft, dealing and obstruction? We should have enough leverage to get her to talk."

"We're still missing a few pieces of the puzzle." James drummed his fingers on his desk. "Did Wood take all the drugs or did someone get to her apartment first and empty the bag? The break-in suggests she had a visitor before the lawyers found her. Jimmy was in jail, so it wasn't him."

"What about the same people who scared Saunders away?" Joanna's face brightened. "Maybe they're the ones who also shot at Sinclair to scare her, thinking she had the stash."

James sighed. "But that means someone else took it, and I find it hard to believe that we have another player involved in the whole mess. I still think Kowalski was the primary target of the shooting."

Joanna's shoulders slumped. "We still haven't established a connection to the cleaners." Exhaustion lined her face. The team had been working round the clock and the stress and late nights were beginning to take their toll.

Time for a little outside intervention.

James grabbed his leather jacket from the back of his chair. "Bring Saunders back in. Make sure she understands her right to have a lawyer present. But not Katherine Sinclair. I can just see the case being thrown out on the basis of a conflict of interest."

"Where are you going?"

James slung his jacket over his back. "To see my fairy godmother."

Chapter Twenty-One

The door opened. Just a crack at first, and then wider.

Katy looked up.

Impeccably tailored suit, Italian leather shoes and blue silk tie. *Mark.* Carrying a lunch tray.

The scent of soap and sandalwood filled the small storage room, one of many in the basement of the office tower housing Hi-Tech's headquarters. A deliciously familiar scent. Ruined by the smell of chicken broth.

Bastard.

She scowled and flipped through the file she had just pulled from one of the dozens of boxes stacked against the wall. She couldn't believe how many files Steele had suddenly managed to produce. Mark must have had a talk with him before he withdrew as counsel. But of course, no one had warned her about the volume of disclosure. There was no way she could get through all the documents by herself. Even though her meeting with Patricia had helped her focus the search, it would still take weeks. She only had an afternoon.

Mark sat down across from her and placed the tray on the table.

"You are still recovering, sugar. You need to eat. You've been here since seven and I know you didn't have breakfast so I took the liberty of visiting the cafeteria."

"I'm quite capable of feeding myself."

Typical male. No greeting. No apology. Sauntering in here like he owned the place. Like he owned her. He could go to hell.

"If you don't eat this, I'll feed you myself." A hint of warning sharpened the smooth tenor of his voice.

She caught her breath. There was no doubt in her mind he would do exactly that. But she was too angry for caution. Too hurt to care about the consequences.

"I'd like to see you try," she growled. She glanced up to see his reaction.

Damn.

His steady, heated gaze made her shudder. Possessive. Dominant. Unyielding.

"Would you really?" His dark eyes glittered at the challenge.

Katy sighed. "Mark, please just go. Leave me alone. I have work to do." She scribbled on her page. Nonsense words. Pretending to be busy as her heart turned back flips.

Stupid heart. You're supposed to be broken.

"You won't make it through all the documents if you don't have the energy." He pushed the tray towards her.

She jerked back and slid her chair away from the table. "I asked you to leave. For once, try to make an effort to respect what I want."

Whispers in her ear. Soft lips on her neck. Promises. Secrets. The memories hurt.

"You aren't safe. I've been watching the door all morning. There are several businesses in the building with storage rooms down here. A lot of people have access to the basement. Steele should have let you review the documents in his office. I think he put you down here for a reason."

"You're overreacting," she snapped. "The police are watching the elevator and the stairwell."

He rested his elbow on the table, his finger brushing over his bottom lip, drawing her eyes to the mouth that had kissed her with such tenderness and spoken the words that had broken her heart.

"How did I get in then?"

She narrowed her eyes. "I don't care how you got in, but for the record, it was a supremely stupid thing to do. If you're caught down here, Steele will have a hands down case of conflict of interest against you, not to mention all the other ethical breaches involved in breaking into a former client's storage room and talking to former opposing counsel."

His gaze locked on hers. Beautiful eyes. So familiar. She didn't know how long they simply stared at each other. Why was he really here? To torment her further? To distract her? She didn't want to consider the other option.

"I'm willing to take that risk to keep you safe. I care about you, Katy."

She left the table and headed over to the wall of boxes. "If you cared, you wouldn't have interfered." She had opened herself up. Trusted him. Now she knew she'd done it for nothing. In the end, men always betrayed her.

Lesson learned. She wouldn't make the same mistake again.

She stood in front of a precariously stacked pile and searched for the next one in the series. She could feel his eyes on her body, as if he were touching her with his hands.

Well let him look. He would never touch her again.

His chair scraped the floor. Italian leather heels thudded softly towards her.

She froze. Closed her eyes. Breathed in his scent. Steeled herself against him.

"Look at me," he commanded.

A shudder rocked her. Unable to resist, she turned her head, looking back at him over her shoulder. His tie glimmered under the soft florescent lighting. Another memory. Another event she wanted to forget.

Gently, slowly, he turned her around to face him.

"I understand how important your career is to you but I knew, between your stubbornness and Ted's ambition, you would continue to pursue the case. Even after what happened. You just can't let things go. Someone needed to look out for you."

She took a step back and folded her arms. "How unbelievably arrogant." A quiver of anger worked over her body. "How many times have I told you? I don't need you to take care of me."

Her elbow hit one of the boxes and the stack tilted forward. Mark reacted before she even sensed he had moved. One minute, she was standing in front of the avalanche and the next, she was cradled under his arm as his other hand shot forward and slammed the tumbling boxes into place.

She closed her eyes. Every inch of her skin came alive, her temperature soared. Her body leading her mind. Again.

"Stop protecting me," she muttered into his chest.

He laughed with a deep rumble, his breath warm and moist in her ear. "Not a chance."

He crushed her to him and banded his arms around her waist. "I love you, Katy. I don't want to lose you."

Her heart pounded. Her thoughts slowed down. The stacks of boxes receded until there was only Mark.

She missed him.

She hated him.

She loved him.

He kissed the top of her head and leaned forward to nuzzle her neck. "This is when you're supposed to run away."

She moaned. Needing him. Despising him.

"I love that sound," he rasped. He cupped her face with both hands and slanted his mouth over hers.

A creak startled them both.

"I always trust my instincts." Steele's voice, dark and dangerous, echoed through the small room. The door closed behind him with a loud bang.

Mark pushed Katy behind him, an instinctual move and totally ineffective. Katy immediately stepped away and into Steele's line of vision.

"As usual, they never let me down." He leaned against the door, arms folded, blocking their only means of escape. His hooded gaze raked over Katy, and then flicked over to Mark. "I thought something was going on during the discovery. After the seminar at the Fairmont, I was almost convinced. But I knew for certain when I discovered where your little kitty went to recover after her terrible accident."

"I'm not his kitty," Katy snapped.

Steele snorted. "The label doesn't matter. You're his. It's written all over his face. Now I understand why he was so eager to drop my case."

"You asked me to do something unethical," Mark said. "It had nothing to do with her."

"You're a hypocrite as well as a coward." Steele toyed with the Rolex on his wrist. "You've had a conflict, possibly since the day of the discovery. Whether you acted responsibly is neither here nor there. I have to assume you compromised my case. I think the video footage of this afternoon's activities will prove to be quite informative to the Law Society."

"What do you want?" Mark growled. Steele would have reported them already if that had been his intent.

A sensual, carnal smile tipped Steele's lips. "I think that's obvious."

"Humor us," Katy said, her words laced with venom. "Spell it out, or is the word blackmail too hard for you?"

"Katy." Mark cut her off with a bark. Attacking Steele would only lead to disaster. Had she not learned that lesson before?

Steele's lips curved into a smile. "The question is, kitty, will it be too hard for you? Looks to me like you need someone to tell you what hard really means."

Katy wrinkled her nose. "You're disgusting. If you think for even a moment that I would sleep with you—"

"I assure you, in my bed you wouldn't be getting any sleep," Steele chortled.

"Bastard."

"The thought of being with a real man excites you, doesn't it?" Steele smiled at Katy's outburst, his feral gaze blazing a trail across her body. "I can see it in the flush of your cheeks and the rapid beat of the pulse in your neck. We have chemistry, kitty, and I know all about chemistry."

"Enough." Mark crossed the room in three long strides and stood toe to toe with Steele. His body shook with the effort of containing his fury. He drew his arm back, but Steele held his hands up, palm forward and took a step away.

"Are you sure you want to add assault to your growing list of misdeeds?" Amusement laced Steele's tone. "I'm just playing with your little kitty, but you don't seem to have fully grasped your situation. You have a serious problem—an undeclared professional conflict of interest. I should really call the Law Society and file a complaint...unless..." his gaze settled on Katy and he beckoned her forward, "...I get what I've always wanted."

A surge of anger coursed through Mark, electrifying his body. "You can't have her."

Steele snorted a sigh and shook his head. "You're thinking with the wrong part of your body. I don't want her. Well I do, but not at the cost of billions of dollars. What I want is the fucking case off my desk and her nose out of my business. You..." he pointed at Katy, "...are going to bring me a settlement agreement, signed by your client, and we'll finish this case once and for all. Tonight."

Katy shook her head in confusion. "What kind of game are you playing? You know I can't force my client to sign anything."

Steele's eyes hardened. "By the time you've drafted the agreement and made your way to her house, I can assure you she will sign anything you put in front of her."

Son of a bitch. Mark let loose. One fist found Steele's jaw and the other pounded into Steele's gut. *One. Two. Back away.* Just as he had learned on the streets.

But Steele was no lightweight. Although his head snapped to the side and he hissed out a breath, he didn't move. Instead, he put a hand to his jaw and rubbed it over his chin. "Now that was uncalled for. Here I'm trying to save two promising legal careers and I'm assaulted for my efforts. I just hope kitty's client isn't as...recalcitrant."

"Gordon," Mark growled. "You're going to send Gordon after her."

Steele spat blood on the concrete floor and wiped his mouth with the back of his hand. Mark felt a faint twinge of pleasure. His punch had had an effect after all.

"Gordon lacks the finesse for this kind of work. Saunders and I have a few things to discuss. Private things. I'll be paying the little troublemaker a personal visit."

Katy bristled. "You stay away from her."

Mark's fingers twitched at his side, but he leashed his anger. Beating Steele to a pulp would achieve nothing and instead would only prove to Katy that her fears about his past resurfacing were true. He would have to find another way.

Steele fixed his gaze on Katy. "You will bring the signed agreement to my office tonight at eight o'clock. Mark, you will be there to ensure it all checks out and to witness my signature. I want it all legal. No loose ends."

Mark clenched his teeth so hard he was surprised they didn't crack. Legal? Steele didn't know the meaning of the word. But at least Katy wouldn't be alone. He gave Steele a curt nod.

"Excellent," Steele continued. "And just in case our kitty gets any ideas about double crossing me or sticking that little nose into my affairs ever again, I've got these." He held up two photos. Mark recognized them right away and his heart thudded into his stomach.

"Melissa and Justin, I believe." Steele tucked the photos into his breast pocket. "They look like you, kitty, but they both have Steven's nose."

Mark had no idea how Katy crossed the room so quickly but within seconds she had her hands around Steele's thick neck.

"If you ever touch my children..." she shrieked, "...if you ever hurt so much as a hair on the heads—"

Mark grabbed her and pulled her away. "Leave him," he whispered urgently in her ear. "He wants you to make it worse. We'll find another way."

"Let me go." She wriggled in his grasp, frantic to get at Steele. Mark wrapped his arms tightly around her, grimacing when her heels hit his shins.

Steele opened the door, but paused on his way out. "As I said before, that kitty needs to be tamed. It's a shame you're not up to the task."

The door slammed closed. Mark released Katy and thudded the wall with his fist.

All. My. Fault. He had endangered Katy when all he had wanted was to keep her safe.

Katy's sobs wrenched him back to the present. Crimson splotches scored her cheeks. "I hate him. I wish I'd never met him. I wish I'd never taken this case. I wish I hadn't asked Ted keep me on it."

Mark put his hand on her shoulder and tried to draw into his arms. He ached with the need to comfort her. Hold her. Protect her. "We'll sort it out, sugar. Together."

"No." Katy slapped his hand away. "You've done enough. I don't need your kind of help. I'll deal with it on my own."

"You can't take him on by yourself."

She grabbed her briefcase and pulled open the door. "The hell I can't."

"Hunter."

"Keegan."

"Fancy meeting you here in front of the Vancouver Art Gallery. I didn't know cops appreciated art."

"We read it every day in the newspaper."

A group of tourists ambled past, following meekly behind a woman with a collapsible umbrella.

"I hope you're not suggesting my stories are anything less than total fact." Keegan pulled out a cigarette and lit it with the casual grace of someone well practiced in the art of self-destruction.

"I might be able to help you with that problem."

"So you're the fairy godmother now?" Keegan flicked his ash into the air.

James sighed and leaned against the smooth brick wall. "Talk to me, Keegan. Tell me a story. I've got bodies coming out my ears and no way to connect the dots."

Keegan blew three smoke rings in quick succession. "I went to an interesting lecture the other day down at the Fairmont. Darkon Steele spoke about bringing new drugs to market. Apparently it can take up to fifteen years and cost millions of dollars, but a successful drug can net over a billion dollars a year."

"Are we going somewhere with this?" James saw a flash of red and for a split second he thought Lana was at the art gallery too. But no. Just a mother and her two kids, all with shocking red hair.

"Good stories start with a prologue," Keegan said. "If you miss the prologue, you won't understand the story. Where was I? Oh yes, Steele said drugs have to go through lots of testing: lab testing, animal testing and then at least three levels of human testing. All strictly regulated, of course. A company can't progress from one level of testing to another if the drug doesn't meet certain safety thresholds."

"Why don't you go back to school, Keegan? Sounds like you missed your calling. You'd make a good scientist."

Keegan looked up when a helicopter thundered past overhead. "Nah. Too dangerous."

"I'm still waiting for the story."

Keegan dropped his cigarette butt and twisted it into the ground with his toe. "Do you have your blankie, Hunter? It's a scary story. Once upon a time, a company developed a fabulous new drug, but when they tested it on animals, bad things happened. But they were so convinced of its potential they decided it would probably still be okay in humans. They fudged their numbers and got approval to test it on human subjects. The drug did work amazingly well, but in a few people, terrible, terrible things happened. They tried to cover it up. Paid out a lot of money. Signed a lot of agreements. Came down heavy on the victims to keep them quiet. They knew they would never get approval for the next phase of testing, but the drug was just too fabulous to give up on and they still thought they could iron out the kinks."

Keegan paused to light a new cigarette. "If I was illustrating my story, at this point I would draw my characters with dollar signs in their eyes. Billions of them."

James snorted. "They obviously don't work in public service."

"Or for a newspaper." Keegan chuckled and took another drag on his cigarette. "So the company tweaked the drug, fudged some more numbers and drafted some fake authorizations. Then they went to a country where no one would look too hard at their documents as long as they greased a few palms along the way. An impoverished country with many illiterate people who were desperate for money and willing to do anything or sign anything to get it."

"They don't sound like nice guys."

"They're businessmen. They wear fancy suits and drink expensive lattes while they sit in leather-clad comfort in steel and glass towers making decisions that can destroy lives."

"So what happened?"

"I'm glad my story has captured your attention. Sort of like a well-endowed red-headed investigator."

James stiffened. How the fuck did he know about Lana? Where the hell did he get his information?

"Something bothering you?" Keegan brushed imaginary fluff off his sports jacket. "Did I get the color wrong?"

"Get on with it," James growled.

"Well again some people suffered terrible side effects and some people died, but in the grand scheme of things, the testing was a resounding success. The drug worked amazingly well in many people, so the company pretended the bad reactions didn't happen. Documents disappeared. People were paid off. They weren't worried. After all, who would find out? It all happened in a land far, far away."

James raked his fingers through his hair. "Let me guess the rest. They came home with their fake results, bribed a few regulators and put it on the market. Everyone lived happily ever after, except the handful of people who suffered and the relatives of those who died."

"And the employee who got fired when she tried to pre-empt my Pulitzer Prize winning story by going to the regulators. The same guys who had just returned from their all-expenses-paid vacations."

James nodded. "So what's the drug?"

"It isn't on the market yet. Top secret. But maybe you've picked some up on the street?" He raised an eyebrow and gave James a questioning look.

James shook his head. "We only got traces of an unidentified compound."

"Good thing." Keegan blew a smoke ring. "Can you imagine how angry they would be if they discovered someone had misappropriated samples of their secret product and given them to a low-life drug dealer to sell on the black market? The risk of a competitor getting hold of the product and stealing away the billion dollar prize would make anyone—"

"Angry enough to kill." James mentally cleared Jimmy's case file off his desk and made a note to send a patrol car to Saunders's residence. "Unfortunately there doesn't seem to be much substance behind your story, enjoyable as it was."

"The proof's in the pudding, or should I say, the pharma." Keegan raised his eyebrows, a silent request.

Damn. He had hoped Keegan had dug something up. "Judge wouldn't give me the warrant."

Disappointment creased Keegan's face. "Someone needs to get inside."

James scrubbed his hand over his face. It could take weeks to set up an undercover operation. But if he could find someone who already had access to the office, and no love for Steele...

"I have an idea. When is the launch?"

"Three days from now—Monday."

"Fuck."

Keegan grinned. "That, my friend, is what the story is really about."

"Should I ask?" Tony handed Mark a glass of bourbon and poured one for himself before replacing the bottle on the shelf behind the bar. Except for the splash of amber liquid and the clink of glassware, Carpe Noctem was eerily quiet. It wouldn't last. But by the time the crowds started to trickle into the club, he would be long gone.

"No." He wasn't in a mood to talk, and especially not to the man spearheading his removal from the firm. He shot back the bitter whiskey, barely tasting it, and pushed his glass across the counter. Tony filled it up again.

Where was Katy? He had tried her cell, her office, even her home, but she hadn't returned his calls all afternoon.

Damn. If Katy had just trusted him, he could have sorted everything out. But she had made it very clear trusting him was the last thing she would ever do.

He slammed his glass on the table, amazed it didn't break.

"Bad day at the office?"

The low, calm rumble of James's voice in his ear and the steady hand on his shoulder did nothing to soothe the anxiety ratcheting through his veins.

"You could say that."

"I've been looking for you," James said. "Your secretary told me I would find you here." Mark shoved the glass across the counter and pushed himself off the stool. Tony was already at the door greeting the first client of the evening.

"I've got a meeting at eight o'clock. What do you want?"

James frowned. "What the hell is up with you? You look rough and you sound worse."

"Steele found out about Katy, ironically after everything fell apart between us. He used the professional conflict as leverage to orchestrate a settlement of the case."

"Blackmail." James scowled. "Since it's a criminal offence, did it occur to you to contact the police? Maybe you know someone..."

Mark scrubbed his hand over his face. "I thought about it, but it would just bring the professional conflict to light. I wanted to talk it over with Katy, but she disappeared after our altercation with Steele. She's planning something and I'm worried she's going to get hurt. It's fucking killing me. I want to help but she's made it clear she doesn't want me to interfere in her life."

"I might have a solution to your problem." James poured himself a glass of whiskey. "Sit down. I have a story to tell you."

For the next twenty minutes Mark's worries took a backseat to disbelief while James spun his incredible tale of illegal clinical trials and fatal drugs. If James had it right, Steele's concern about Katy's investigation and his insistence on tying up loose ends from the earlier clinical trials made sense. Still he had trouble believing Steele had finally crossed the line from dangerous to deadly.

"What I don't understand is what he's planning to do after people start swelling up and dying after the launch." James drained his whiskey glass and spun it on the counter.

Still reeling from the disclosure of just how far Steele was prepared to go, Mark said, "He'll conduct very controlled secret post-clinical trials to show the drug is safe. He'll explain away any bad reactions as being due to outside factors. So long as the deaths or serious side effects stay below a certain percentage, the regulators will just slap on a warning sticker. If the numbers get too high, he might just send people out with blank checks and settlement agreements to keep it all quiet."

James raked his hand over his head. "I need to get inside. Dig up some proof. I tried for a warrant but the damn judge probably plays golf with Steele. He said I didn't have enough evidence to make a connection."

Mark snorted. "Katy and I are meeting him at his office tonight to finalize the settlement agreement. Maybe you could come disguised as an articling student."

"I have a better idea," James said. "Have you ever worn a wire?"

Chapter Twenty-Two

"Martha?"

Katy rang the doorbell of Martha's False Creek townhouse for the third time. Was Martha inside? Had Steele visited her? Was she hurt?

She contemplated breaking in, but that would just add fuel to the Law Society fire after Steele reported the conflict. She had no doubt he would report it. Once he had the settlement agreement, he would have no reason to hold up his end of the bargain.

"Katherine?"

Katy spun around. Martha had just pulled up in front of the townhouse in a shiny, red Porsche.

Porsche? How could she afford a luxury car without a job?

Katy walked down the sidewalk and peered in the open window. "I need to talk to you and I couldn't get through on any of your numbers."

Martha shrugged. "I had them all cancelled. I'm leaving town."

"What about the case?"

Martha's bitter laughter took Katy by surprise. "The case? Are you serious? You were shot. Martin is dead. I read in the paper that one of the men on the list, McIntyre, was killed. I appreciate your dedication to the case, but come on. It's not worth it. At least not to me."

"But...we're so close to finding out the real reason behind your dismissal and what happened to those men."

With an exasperated sigh, Martha pushed open the door. "Get in. It's dangerous out there, even with your police tail parked a block back."

Katy slid into the black leather seat. "Where are we going?"

Martha peeled the car away from the curb. "Nowhere. You want to talk, then talk. You have ten minutes before I head out of the city. I'll amuse myself by trying to lose your escort."

Katy tightened her grip on her briefcase as Martha shot through a stop sign. "Did Steele visit you today?"

"I haven't been home," Martha said. "I knew Steele would come looking for me. He's not the only one. I've got Jimmy's friends on my tail and I've got a scary psycho cop riding my ass because of my relationship with Jimmy. I just came by to see if it was safe to pick up the last of my stuff."

Katy stifled a gasp. "I didn't know you were with Jimmy. When you said he recommended the firm, I thought he was just a friend or an acquaintance. I heard what happened to him. I'm really sorry. No wonder you want to get away."

Martha's face tightened. She took a sharp corner and headed west on Fourth Avenue. "Yeah, well he knew what he was getting himself into when he started dealing again. He wasn't a...good guy, if you know what I mean. He stole from me, cheated on me and used me. I should have left him at the beginning, but when we were together, it was so good. He told me...he loved me."

Katy gave her a sympathetic smile. "I know what it's like to have your partner cheat on you. My ex had so many affairs I lost count. Each one hurt more than the last. But I didn't leave. We had two children and I didn't want them to grow up in a single-parent family. It wasn't until I finally got the divorce that I realized what a mistake I had made. He never really loved me. You don't hurt the people you love. Like you, I wish I'd left him sooner."

"Maybe you loved him." Tears slid down Martha's plump, rosy cheeks and she dabbed at them with a tissue.

Katy swallowed. "Maybe I thought I did. But now I know what real love is, and that wasn't it. Not even close."

Martha pulled into the parking lot at Jericho Beach. For a few long moments they sat and watched the container ships and freighters sailing into Burrard Inlet.

"You've been really great," Martha said. Her eyes fixed on the beach in front of them and she took a deep breath. "Better than I ever expected a lawyer to be. You went out of your way. You put your life on the line. You're a good person. Maybe the regulators will listen to you."

She pulled a baggie from her purse and handed it to Katy.

"What is it?"

"The key to Martin's desk in the lab. He gave it to me when he gave me the list. His journals are in the bottom drawer. I'm pretty sure no one will have found them because the desk is used for storage. You'll be able to bring Steele down with the information in those journals. Hi-Tech too."

Katy's eyes widened. "Why didn't you tell me before?"

"You would have had to disclose the existence of the key to Hi-Tech. Isn't that how the discovery process works?"

"Yes that's true. But we could have requested copies of the journals."

A bitter laugh escaped Martha's lips. "You have no idea how companies like Hi-Tech work. Those journals would have disappeared the minute they knew they existed."

"Why now? If you're leaving, it doesn't matter if it benefits your case."

Martha's faced tightened. "Martin died for those journals. He was a good friend to me and I betrayed him in the worst way. I want Steele to pay. I want Martin's death to mean something."

Katy offered the baggie back to Martha. "I don't think..."

Martha waved her hand away. "Please. Take it. Bring Steele down before anyone else gets hurt."

Claire.

Mark stared at the photograph on the credenza beside Steele's desk. The eight-by-ten glossy had to have been taken after Claire left. Her long hair had been cut—no, hacked—into a short bob and she was pale and drawn. So unlike the bubbly vivacious girl he had met on the day he and Tony had opened Carpe Noctem.

She was standing at the bow of a motor-yacht, holding up a bottle of champagne. Claire loved champagne, but she wasn't smiling in the picture. Not a real smile. Not a smile from her heart.

She wasn't smiling in any of the pictures. So many pictures. So much unhappiness. No wonder Steele had never invited him to his office. The credenza was like a shrine. To Claire.

His Claire.

How long had she and Steele been together? Had Steele been there when she died, or had she really overdosed alone in the East Side alley where the police had found her body?

"You're an hour early." Steele leaned back in his cream leather chair as Mark made a quick visual sweep of the office for more photos. Three times the size of Mark's corner office, Steele's sanctuary at Hi-Tech's head office on Broadway, was a tribute to corporate minimalism. Big glass desk. Glass credenza. Meeting table with four black chairs. Wall-mounted flat screen television. Cream leather couch. Bar in the corner. No clutter. No books. A few papers on the desk. It could have been a show suite.

"I need to speak to you before Katy gets here with the settlement agreement. I thought we could work something out."

Steele shrugged. "There's nothing to work out, unless of course she didn't get the agreement signed, which may be a possibility because Saunders wasn't home when I called."

Mark gritted his teeth. "If she doesn't get it signed, I want to offer—"

Steele cut him off with a bark of laughter. "There's nothing you have that I want. Nothing you could offer me to change my mind. If she doesn't bring me the signed agreement, let's just say I haven't made up my mind whether reporting the conduct of two scheming, disreputable lawyers to the Law Society is enough to make up for your betrayal."

Mark's heart skipped a beat. "You wouldn't—"

"But if she does get a signature," Steele continued, "then the case settles, everyone goes home happy and we all keep our secrets. I'm good at keeping secrets. From the look on your face when you walked in, I take it you never knew about me and Claire."

Mark gritted his teeth. "What did you do to her?"

Steele gave him an amused glance. "Nothing she didn't want me to do. Everything a man does with his woman." He leaned forward, his eyes glittering. "And all the things you wouldn't do."

With a roar, Mark lunged over the desk and grabbed Steele's shoulders. But Steele's seated position and heavy frame made him awkward to move. He pushed his chair back, forcing Mark to release him.

Mark staggered back. The wire in his ear shifted and he put his hand up to readjust it. Had James heard the conversation?

"I deserved that," Steele said, pulling his chair back to his desk. "I should have told you I was with her, but I knew you wouldn't continue to represent me, and despite all your faults, you're a damn good lawyer."

Mark grunted and tried to clear the red haze from his vision.

"I still miss her," Steele said wistfully. "I cared about her a great deal."

"I find that hard to believe," Mark snarled. "If you cared about her, you would have pulled her out of the drug scene. You must have known she had an addictive personality." Drugs, sex, smoking, coffee. Claire never did anything in half measures.

Steele shrugged. "She made her own choices. They were just the wrong ones. Except, of course, when she came knocking at my door. She knew life was precious. Too precious to be wasted on someone who didn't love her. She was my kind of girl. I told her that the first time you introduced us, and I let her know my door was always open."

Mark clenched his fists. If not for the wire, and the need to get the evidence to implicate Steele, his hands would already be around Steele's throat.

Steele looked over at the credenza and sighed. "But you didn't come here to talk about Claire. You came to save your kitty. Unfortunately I need that agreement signed tonight. The product launch is on Monday and I don't want anything to detract from the revolution I'm about to unleash on the world. Hi-Tech has to be the epitome of a well-run, transparent, charitable company that treats its employees well and its shareholders even better."

Mark swallowed. If he could keep Steele talking, he might be able to uncover the evidence James needed to make an arrest.

"She should be here shortly," he said. "Why don't we have a drink while we wait?"

Steele raised a brow but pushed back his chair and walked over to the bar. "Attack me one minute and drink with me the next. I can't keep up." He poured two shots of bourbon and handed one to Mark.

He took the tumbler Steele offered. "Maybe I know which fights are worth fighting."

"Maybe you do. Maybe that's why you let Claire go."

Mark swallowed his anger and tried to redirect the conversation.

"So what is the revolutionary wonder drug?"

"We're close enough to the launch that I can tell you," Steele said. He perched one hip on the bar and sipped his bourbon. "It's called Libidex and it has made it through all the proper regulatory channels. Everything has been documented, stamped and approved."

"Libidex?"

"Drug of the century. Ostensibly it'll be for erectile dysfunction, but in reality, it increases libido and improves sexual performance ten times better than the leading competitors. Basically it's a sex drug. We expect its recreational use to far outstrip any legitimate medical application. In our trials, men were able to go all night without even the slightest diminishment in performance."

Mark wished James would make a sound. Cough. Hiss. Whisper. Anything to let him know the wire was still working. He tasted his bourbon, waiting for a signal. He had never liked bourbon. The smooth, sweet taste of smoky oak and molasses reminded him of burnt toast and honey, the only breakfast his mother had ever made.

No sound. Not even a crackle. He couldn't wait any longer. He gave Steele an appreciative nod. "Impressive. What about side effects?"

"It has a few kinks," Steele said. "Nothing we can't handle."

Mark looked out over Burrard Inlet. Clouds had gathered over the mountains on the North Shore sending wispy fingers of rain down to the city below. "Did you work them out in clinical trials?" He kept his voice light and casual, although inside his pulse raced.

Steele narrowed his eyes. "When a drug is as important as this one, we pull out all the stops to ensure the clinical trials go smoothly and the regulators get the...assurances they need."

Damn. Not even close.

Steele checked his watch. "Your kitty should be here in about forty-five minutes and I have some business to attend to before she arrives. I'll send Gordon in to keep you company."

Double damn. Steele wasn't taking any chances. He was clearly suspicious of Mark's motives for arriving early. So much for his plan to sneak away and take a quick look around. With Gordon in the room, he wouldn't be going anywhere.

And when Katy arrived, neither would she.

Katy typed her name on her letter of resignation and sent it to the printer. Thank God no one was in the office tonight. She could leave it on Ted's desk and disappear. After all the partners had done for her, she didn't want to damage the reputation of the firm, or drag them into a scandal. Once Steele made his call to the Law Society, all hell would break loose.

But more than that, she didn't want to stay. Ted's bargain with Mark was as much a betrayal by him. Even if he let her stay, she knew she would never forgive him.

She retrieved the letter from the printer and signed her name on the firm letterhead for the last time. *Katherine Sinclair.* Not Hughes. She had never taken Steven's last name, much to his annoyance. Maybe the next time she signed a professional letter her name would be at the top. Wouldn't that be something? Run her own firm. Be her own boss. Answer to no one.

She dropped the letter on Ted's desk and returned to her office to pack up her boxes. Not much personal stuff. Pictures of the kids, law books, the pen Ted had given her when she had won her first trial. Her legal files had all been transferred to colleagues when she had been in the hospital so there was no reason for Ted to hold to her to her notice period. Not that he would. Ted hated notice periods. He had paid off every departing employee to avoid having them linger around the office.

Only one file remained on her desk. Saunders v. Hi-Tech.

She picked up the file and took it down the hall to Ted's office. Just before she reached Ted's door a white card slid out and fell onto the carpet. Her access pass to Hi-Tech. She must have forgotten to return it on her way out of the document review this morning.

She flipped the card over and an idea formed in her mind. Crazy. But what did she have to lose? Steven had the kids for the weekend; she had no job and she was about to be sanctioned by the Law Society. And Mark? She'd lost him too. But maybe she could take down Steele. For Martha and for herself.

She could see justice done after all.

Lana watched Katy load boxes into her car in front of her office building. One hell of a lot of work to be taking home. Was she planning to stay up all night? She turned the key in her Jetta, wincing as it struggled and gasped for air. Finally the engine turned over with a cough.

Poor Jetta. She still didn't have enough money to pay for an overhaul. Double agents didn't get double pay. Instead, they got a double dose of James hollering into the phone that she should be honored to be performing a public service. She had weathered the storm. Tossed out a few jokes. His temper had cooled quickly, as she knew it would. Such a sexy voice. So damned hot. He could yell at her any day, especially if he turned all soft afterwards and mumbled he'd pay her from his own salary.

How sweet was that?

Too bad she had been hit hard with a big dose of conscience and turned down his offer. The Jetta might have been purring like a kitten instead of wheezing like freight train.

She glanced behind her and snorted when she saw Matt slumped against his steering wheel, fast asleep in his patrol car. She had become friendly with the surveillance officer when they discovered they were both watching the same person.

Tsk tsk. Someone was going to get in trouble. Their long phone discussion about her past boyfriends must have put him to sleep.

She grabbed her cell, intending to give him a wake-up call when Katy jumped in her vehicle. Damn. One bar of power left. And she didn't have her charger.

Katy pulled out onto the street and Lana floored the accelerator. She couldn't waste her battery on Matt. She had to report to Mr. S or she wouldn't get paid. He had called her yesterday with a special assignment. He wanted hourly text updates on Katy's location for forty-eight hours. Triple pay. She might be a double agent but she wasn't going to pass up a good opportunity.

She blew Matt a kiss in the rearview mirror and followed Katy down the road and over the Burrard Street Bridge. Rain pattered on the windshield. She turned on the wipers and peered through the smear at the flash of red in front of her. Time to replace the wipers too.

Katy turned onto Broadway and travelled down the street, following the route they had taken this morning. When she finally turned into Hi-Tech's parking lot, Lana frowned. She couldn't possibly be visiting her client this late at night. Maybe she had to drop something off. Katy entered the building. After ten minutes, Lana picked up her phone and sent a text to Mr. S.

Subject has just entered Hi-Tech Pharmaceuticals on Broadway.

She sent the message and the phone beeped twice and shut off. *Damn.* Hopefully Mr. S didn't have any questions. She didn't want to piss him off. He didn't seem like a forgiving kind of guy.

Chapter Twenty-Three

Katy's heart pounded as she crept through Hi-Tech's clinical lab, using the tiny flashlight attached to her keychain to light her way. Any minute now she expected the security guards to rush in and grab her. She had been incredulous when they had let her in after she had shown them her business card and the access pass and spun a story about how she'd left her purse in the document room this morning. Martha's story. Of course it might have helped that they'd been told Steele was expecting her in half an hour.

Determined as she was to bring down Steele, she wasn't prepared to do anything illegal. She would find Martin's journals, smuggle them downstairs to the document room, and then put them into the box of documents she had copied this morning. The box had been too heavy to carry and Steele's secretary had promised to courier it to her office on Monday. She couldn't be accused of theft if the documents were freely given. If anyone caught her in the lab, she could just say she had lost her way going to Steele's office. Dicey, but do-able.

Too bad Ted would have the fun of uncovering the secrets in Martin's journals.

She dragged her fingers through her hair. She was taking a gamble by assuming Steele had not already found Martin's lab books and a bigger gamble trusting a client who had withheld information from her.

Footsteps sounded in the hallway. Katy froze. Blood pounding through her veins, she ducked under a battered wooden desk covered with books, boxes and papers. The door creaked open. The beam of a flashlight shone around the room, and then the door banged shut. A routine check. Relieved she slid out from under the desk. Martin's desk. It had to be. There were no other wooden desks in the lab.

The key Martha had given her fit the lock on the bottom drawer.

She unlocked it and found a stack of notebooks with Martin's name penciled neatly across the front.

Her lucky day. She grabbed the notebooks and stuffed them into her briefcase.

Now to get to the document room.

"What the hell is going on?"

Although he wasn't surprised to see Gordon with a gun, he couldn't help the exclamation escaping from his mouth when Gordon pointed the gun at him.

Heart racing, he looked over at Steele, now perched on the edge of his desk. Until seconds ago, everything had been going as smoothly as things could go for a prisoner in Steele's palatial office. Steele had gone to make his calls. Gordon had joined him in the office. They'd had a drink, shared a few war stories, watched a few minutes of the news on Steele's big screen TV. Steele had reappeared and asked Gordon to step outside. When they returned, Steele had a grimace and Gordon had a gun.

Steele folded his arms and sighed. "Your kitty is here and she's been very naughty. Overly curious. Like you."

Mark's gut twisted and time seemed to slow. What had she done?

"Where is she?" he growled.

Steele smiled but his dark eyes were cold and hard. "So selfless. So caring. Your life is in danger and you're thinking about her. Such a shame you didn't care as much about Claire. Maybe she would be alive today."

Fist raised, Mark took a step toward Steele. Gordon cleared his throat and waved him back with the gun.

"I tried to protect you," Steele said. "I purposely did not give you all the information about the settlements with the cleaners because I knew you would see them for what they really were. And what did I get in return for my efforts? Nothing. You wouldn't follow my directions. You wouldn't hire an investigator. You wouldn't keep your mouth closed or your eyes shut. You wouldn't even warn that kitty away."

Mark swallowed and looked at the door only two quick strides away. He needed to get out. Warn Katy. "There's no need for the gun." He raised his voice on the last word, hoping James would hear through the wire, wherever he was, and come to the rescue.

"We differ again," Steele sighed. "The gun is necessary because you know too much. Not only that, you betrayed me. And all because you couldn't resist a little pussy. Did you think I needed you here tonight *just* to witness a settlement agreement? You're here, Mark, to say your goodbyes. To Claire. To your kitty. To me. I can't have any loose ends or flapping tongues. There is too much at stake."

Where. The. Fuck. Is. James?

The door opened.

Katy's angry shriek rang through the office. An oversized security guard dragged her in front of Steele's desk, pinning her against his chest with a massive arm.

"Here's our curious kitty now," Steele chortled.

Mark's heart pounded and he scanned the room, desperate to find a way out.

Katy squirmed and struggled in the security guard's grasp. "Let me go. Obviously I can't run away so there's no point trying to break my arm."

Mark took a step in her direction. Gordon coughed a warning and he froze.

"I found her outside one of the labs downstairs," the security guard said. "She told me she'd left her purse in the document room this morning. She had a pass and an appointment with you so I let her through. When I caught her, she told me she'd got herself lost on the way."

"I'm surrounded by idiots," Steele muttered. "Did anyone not notice she's carrying her purse?" He walked across the room and grabbed Katy's purse and briefcase out of her hands.

"A girl can have more than one purse," Katy snapped.

Steele slapped her. The crack sliced through Mark's brain unleashing a tidal wave of rage. He lunged for Steele. Gordon stepped between them and shoved the barrel of his gun into Mark's stomach.

287

"Back off," he growled.

Jaw clenched tight, body trembling, Mark raised his hands and took a step away.

"That's how you tame a kitty." Steele stroked a finger over Katy's bright red cheek. "You let her know right away who's in charge."

Katy narrowed her eyes and growled.

"She likes it," Steele chuckled. "Listen to her purr."

"Bastard." Katy hit his hand away.

Steele barked a cold laugh. "You're the one who broke into my office. I'm the victim here."

"I walked in. I showed my ID. The guards consented to my entry. I just got lost on the way to get my purse."

"I think I've heard that one before."

Mark's hands balled into fists. "Let her go, Steele."

"Not until I get what I want." Steele opened Katy's briefcase and pulled out a bundle of notebooks. He flipped through them and his face tightened.

"Kowalski's missing lab books! We thought he'd shredded them. Oh, dear kitty. That curious nose has got you in trouble again. And I don't see a settlement agreement here. Looks like you and Mark will share the same tragic fate. Like Romeo and Juliet."

Katy gasped and staggered back.

"Steele. No." Mark's pulse pounded through his veins. If James didn't get his ass down here quickly, illicit pharmaceuticals would be the least of his worries.

Steele threw the notebooks on this desk and then grabbed Katy's chin between his finger and thumb, forcing her head back. "I don't understand you. It was a simple dismissal case. Why couldn't you leave it at that?"

Katy jerked her head, trying to break Steele's grip. "I'm a sucker for justice and you left too many clues I couldn't ignore."

Steele tightened his grip and Katy hissed in a breath. "Clever kitty. Too clever for your own good. We'll have to think of a clever way for you to die."

Katy's eyes flicked over Mark, her fear clear to see despite her outward show of bravado. He shook his head, warning her to keep quiet.

Steele caught their exchange. "Don't look at him. He would have sold his soul to keep you safe. Unfortunately it wasn't enough."

He released Katy and nodded to the security guard. "Get me some rope and duct tape. We don't want our kitty to escape again."

"Yes, sir." The guard left, closing the door behind him with a dull thud.

Steele sighed and settled himself in his chair. "You disappoint me, Gordon. You should have finished her off when you took care of Kowalski."

"No pay. No body. You said to scare her, not kill her."

"You?" Katy's eyes opened wide and she stared at Gordon. "You were at the apartment? You killed Andrew McIntyre?"

"It was touch and go for a while." Steele shook his head in mock regret. "He did a much better job with Silver. Clean. Quick. Efficient. No evidence. But really, you shouldn't be so horrified. Silver and McIntyre were dying anyway. Aggressive lymphatic cancer—another unfortunate side effect of the drug. They only had a few weeks to live. Gordon did them a favor."

Mark's mind raced. If the wire was working, James would have more than enough evidence to arrest Steele and Gordon. Something must be wrong. He had to act. He just needed a distraction.

The door behind them clicked open.

"Mr. Steele, I've got the rope." The security guard stepped inside. Mark saw his chance. He powered toward the unsuspecting guard, keeping his body low. A bullet whizzed past his shoulder and hit the wall with a loud thud. But Mark kept going. Within seconds he had reached his target. He rammed his shoulder into the guard's sternum, knocking the wind out of him. The guard doubled over and Mark's fist connected with his jaw, sending him reeling back into the wall, stunned. Another blow rendered the guard unconscious, and he slid down the wall to the floor.

A second shot rang out and splinters exploded outward from the door. Mark grabbed Katy and shoved her into the hallway. "Run."

"Not without you."

"Go," he shouted. He pulled the door closed and locked it.

She was safe.

Now it was time to deal with Steele.

The front door of the building opened and Lana jerked to attention. Katy barreled out of the building at full tilt.

What the hell? She fumbled on the seat for her camera as Katy ran to her car. Why the urgency?

Katy pulled on the door handle, and then slammed her hand on the door and screamed. Quite an overreaction for losing her keys. Maybe she was having a bad day.

Lana lifted her camera and peered through the lens. Only then did she see the shadow detach itself from the darkness. Not a shadow. A man. Tall, slightly stooped. Lana snapped a few pictures before she even realized the danger. Woman alone. Dark parking lot. Man behind her. Her eyes widened and she reached for the door handle.

The man must have spoken because Katy turned around. Through the camera lens, she saw him jab a hypodermic needle into Katy's neck. Katy staggered back against her car. He caught her when she collapsed and scooped her up in his arms. He stepped out of the shadows and Lana saw his face. A familiar face. The man who ate icing and not cake. The ex.

Oh God. Oh God. What should she do? She opened the door, but even as her foot hit the pavement, she knew she wouldn't make it. They were too far away. By the time she was out of the car, he had already unlocked Katy's vehicle and put her in the back seat. Bastard must have kept his set of keys.

"Help!" She screamed at the top of her lungs, but who would be hanging around a vacant parking lot at night?

He froze and turned in Lana's direction. Lana threw herself back in the Jetta and lay trembling on the seat. Thank God she had parked in the shadows. She scrambled to find her phone, remembering, as her fingers touched the plastic, the two beeps she had heard earlier. Dead.

With one last look in Lana's direction, the ex jumped in Katy's Acadia and started the engine. Lana turned her key. Nothing.

Please, please, oh please, baby, please.

Tires squealed as the Acadia pulled out of the parking lot and turned onto Broadway Street. Lana tried again.

A cough. A wheeze. Then the Jetta roared to life. She stomped on the accelerator and peeled out of the parking lot. She could just see the Acadia's tail lights in the distance ahead of her. She kept her foot down, praying she wouldn't hit a red light.

Police. Police. Police. Where were the police when she actually needed them?

The Jetta wheezed as it raced down the street and Lana tried to remember if her course had covered high-speed chases. Why hadn't she paid more attention in class? Water dripped onto her arm and she looked up. Leak? No. Tears. She touched her face and realized she was crying.

Dammit. Pull up your big-girl panties, Lana.

The Jetta coughed and she looked at the gas gauge. Almost empty. Could the day get any worse? *Please don't leave the city. Please don't leave the city.* The mantra worked. The ex turned up Main Street and then drove a zigzag course through the streets until he pulled up in front of a derelict apartment building. Pulse racing, Lana parked a few spaces down and watched him carry an unconscious Katy into the building.

When she saw a light on the second floor, she threw herself out of the Jetta and raced down the street to the convenience store they had passed only a block back. Her heart thundered as she pounded the pavement in a performance worthy of an Olympic medal. *Gotta finda phone.* Wheeze. *Gotta finda phone.*

For the first time in his life, Mark felt gratitude for the years he had spent on the streets and the lessons he had learned. He threw himself to the floor just before a bullet embedded itself in the wall above him, then rolled and came up in a crouch. "Steele, call him off," he yelled. "What the hell are you doing?"

"I won't have this launch compromised. It's worth too much. We've invested ten years and millions of dollars to get the drug to market and that damn lab tech almost ruined everything. Gordon has been working day and night trying to clean up the mess. He had to retrieve the samples that deadbeat dealer left with his girlfriend, get rid of the dealer and then contain the damage as your kitty ran amok."

Mark looked around. Nowhere to hide. He could play cat and mouse but inevitably Gordon would win.

Unless he ran out of bullets. Or, by some miracle, the cavalry arrived.

He would have to stall for time, draw Gordon's fire.

Hope.

"What happened to you, Steele? After you saw what the drug did to those four cleaners, how could you try again and put so many lives at risk?"

Steele's face tightened. "I wanted Claire's death to mean something. I shouldn't have given her the drug, but she begged and pleaded and I was curious. We'd already had incredible results in the preliminary tests. I wanted to know if it worked on women. I never thought it would kill her." His voice caught in his throat. "Her drug addiction made it easy to cover up. She trusted me..." His voice trailed off.

"You killed her." The world fell out from under him. It wasn't his fault after all. And the cause of her death was standing in front of him.

Steele sighed. "I loved her. It was the biggest mistake of my life. I have to live with what happened every day. But so many people will benefit from this drug. It will be her legacy. She died to bring happiness and sexual fulfillment to the masses."

Gordon had lowered the gun as he listened to Steele. Mark saw the faintest sliver of hope.

Keep Steele talking.

"What about all the other people who will suffer side effects? You're destroying lives."

Steel shrugged. "It happens all the time. A sacrifice for the greater good."

Gordon's gun dropped lower. Mark saw his chance. He threw himself sideways, hitting Gordon side-on and into the wall. Gordon's head snapped against the plaster. The gun fell to the ground and Gordon slumped to the floor, unconscious.

Steele lunged for the gun and Mark let loose. Only barely aware of the door crashing open, he pummeled Steele until four police officers pulled him away.

"It's over." James's voice was firm and steady in his ear.

"No." He pushed James's arm away. "I need to get Katy."

Chapter Twenty-Four

Katy opened her eyes. White surrounded her. Again.

Hospital? No. Wrong scent. She breathed in deeply. Chinese food? She tried to rub her eyes but her hands didn't move. Fire seared through her shoulder. She looked up.

Her arms were chained above her head.

Fear roared through her like a runaway train and sent her heart into overdrive. She tried to free her hands and the chains rattled loudly with each tug and jerk of her arms. Pain screamed through her injured shoulder.

"You're awake." Steven leaned against the doorframe, holding a take-out carton and a pair of chopsticks, his eyes glittering under the naked bulb overhead.

Katy tilted her head back, taking in the giant eye bolt in the ceiling, the cuffs on her wrists and the chain attaching them. Her toes barely touched the lino floor. Bare toes. Like the rest of her. Completely. Naked.

"What the fuck is this? Let me down, Steven. Have you gone absolutely crazy?" She took a deep breath and screamed as loudly as she could, letting out her anger, fear, rage, and...hope.

"No one will hear you, Kate. This building is vacant. It's being torn down next week. I got a good deal on a two-day rental." He took a bite of his chow mien and stared at her while he chewed.

Sheer terror took her breath away. "What do you want?"

"You." He put down his carton and ran a finger along her jaw and down her neck, stopping at the cleft in her breasts. It was the single most intimate gesture he had ever made since she'd known him.

"But why this?" She struggled to keep calm, focused. Distract him while she figured a way out.

"This is what you want. I know about the fetish club and what you do there. I found the flyer. After I paid them a visit, your new slutty clothing made sense." He paused and then gave her a cold smile. "I can give that to you. In fact, it's what I like best. I never thought I would get to share my kink with you. I thought you were too virtuous. Too conservative. Good for my image, not for my bed."

He cupped her breast gently in his palm, rubbing his thumb over her nipple.

Horror flooded through her. "What are you talking about?"

"I like pain, Kate. *Sadistic Personality Disorder*, I believe it's called. But don't worry; it's not a bona fide mental disorder. There are lots of us out there. Unfortunately, it still isn't acceptable in polite society and especially not with my sweet, lovely wife. So I had to find...alternative sources of enjoyment. Women who shared my kink. Unfortunately none of them shared my intensity and they always ran away. I couldn't go to the club like you. I have a reputation to protect."

She tried to speak, but her throat froze and she could only manage a croak.

"Imagine my delight when I discovered we shared a common interest. No wonder we were so attracted to each other in the beginning. Subconsciously, we knew we could fulfill each other's deepest, most hidden needs."

"No." Bile rose in her throat and she fought to keep it down.

"The children are at Doug's for the weekend. I told him we were taking a break to reconcile. We can indulge ourselves here for two whole days. I've even brought my medical kit. I can patch you up when we're done, and then we'll go home. One big, happy family again. I've drawn up plans to set up our own special room in the basement. Sound-proofed. We wouldn't want the children to hear you scream."

Her body turned to ice. Blackness rushed in at her and her lungs tightened, making it impossible to breathe.

She heard the crack of his palm on her cheek before she felt the pain from his slap. "No panic attacks, please. You'll ruin everything I have planned. I've even taken time off work for this." He cupped her chin and tilted her head back. "Look at me and breathe."

She gasped as air rushed into her lungs followed by a rush of adrenaline that made her heart thunder.

"Good." He rummaged in a bag on the floor, finally pulling out a long, black leather whip.

"Steven, please." Her voice shook as the full horror of the situation finally hit home.

He smiled and cracked the whip. Her body tensed and her toes touched the cold lino floor. *He didn't tie my feet.* She stretched her body further and gained a secure hold on the ground. How could she use the leverage?

Steven turned to look at her and she carefully lifted her feet, not wanting him to know she could touch the floor fully.

"I thought we could start with this." The violent hiss of the whip sent a chill down her spine. "I should really warm you up with a flogger so you can take more and mark less, but I can't wait. I bought this single-tail especially for you."

Katy swallowed past the lump in her throat. "I don't want this, Steven. Why don't we go home? I'll make dinner and we can watch a movie like we used to do."

"What we used to do sucked the life out of both of us," he sneered. "But now we can bring the excitement back into our marriage."

The Crazy Frog ring tone broke the silence. Her heart leaped in her chest. Then she remembered. Melissa had changed her ring tone. It was Steven's phone.

"Dammit. I'm not on call. Why won't they leave me alone? I want this time to be special." He walked behind her and stroked her back. "You're lucky I'm a doctor. I know what areas to avoid." He patted along her sides and lower back. "The kidneys for example, are a definite no-no."

The Crazy Frog ringtone played again.

Steven sighed. "I have to answer or they'll just keep calling and I'll worry it is something important. I don't want any distractions. I need to be focused or I might cause you irreparable harm." He gave her a wink. "I'll only be a minute. Don't run away."

He stomped over to the bag and grabbed the phone.

"No screaming, please," he said, looking back over his shoulder as he left the room. "I have a bull whip in the bag and I won't hesitate to use it for disciplinary purposes."

Katy waited until she heard his hello and then she screamed. *Nothing to lose.*

Steven poked his head around the corner and gave her a cold smile. He stared pointedly at the bag and then stalked into the bathroom and slammed the door.

Violent shudders wracked her body. She breathed slow and deep and tested the restraints. No give. She tightened her stomach and tried to pull up her legs. Her muscles protested fiercely and her legs dropped. *Again.* She pushed off the ground and pulled up her knees. It might be enough. But if it wasn't, she would have hell to pay.

Steven returned with a crooked smile on his face. "They don't think they can manage without me, but I told them I have something important to do this weekend that takes priority over work. You, Kate. Do you see how important you are to me?" He stroked her face with a long, elegant finger. A surgeon's finger.

Katy shuddered and drew back.

Steven frowned. "Is that what you do when he touches you? Richards? I don't think so. I think the only reason you're with him is because you didn't know I can give you what you need. Me. Your husband. But now you know and you won't be seeing him again. Ever."

"You don't understand. I don't want this. I don't...consent."

Steven laughed. "I don't need explicit consent from my wife." He stroked the whip. "But we've delayed too long and I'm dying to have some fun."

"Kiss me." She forced the words out through gritted teeth.

His eyes widened. "What?"

"Kiss me before you start. Aren't we rediscovering our relationship? What is the pain without the pleasure?"

His eyes softened. "Of course. You're right. But that is the last time you will be allowed to speak without my permission. Hereafter, any breach of that rule will be met with swift and severe punishment."

He sighed and walked toward her. "You were so beautiful at eighteen. Young, innocent, desperate to please and so trusting. You looked at me like I was a god. We can have that again. I promise."

"Close your eyes. Pretend I'm eighteen again," she whispered.

"Ah ah. I see our first punishment coming up. Looks like we'll get to use the bullwhip early. But first..." He closed his eyes and leaned toward her, lips puckered in a tight kiss.

In one swift movement, Katy pulled herself up on the chain and pushed off the floor. Her knees shot up and she smashed her feet as hard as she could into Steven's groin.

With a strangled cry he staggered backward, his hands between his thighs, his face a mask of rage and pain. "Oh, Kate. You're going to be sorry. So very, very sorry."

Blood hammered in her ears. She opened her mouth and screamed.

The door burst open.

Mark. James behind him. And Police. Lots of them.

James grabbed Steven mid-stagger and threw him to the ground.

Mark raced to her side. "Easy, sugar," he murmured. He reached up and unclipped the cuffs, catching her when she tumbled, trembling, to the ground.

She buried her head in his chest and sobbed, oblivious to everything but his warm arms, his deep, rich voice, and the scent of soap and sandalwood.

"Keegan."

"Hunter."

"What are you doing here? Don't you have a fancy dinner planned at the Harbor Centre tonight?"

"I had a craving for Chinese food. Nowhere better than here in Mount Pleasant."

James laughed. "What a coincidence. There might be a story here for you."

Keegan pulled out a small plastic tube of toothpicks. "It's a busy night for stories. I've just been over at Hi-Tech's office. Apparently shots were fired, a security guard was injured and the police took the CEO and a lawyer away in handcuffs. Thought I saw your car there. Gray Crown Victoria. So distinctive."

"No comment."

Keegan put a toothpick in his mouth and chewed it with vigor.

"No cigarettes?"

"Decided to quit. Filthy habit. I went to a lecture the other day. I discovered nicotine is a drug. Addictive. Like, say, coke or heroin. Amazing how those drugs are smuggled into the country. Do you want to hear a story about drug smuggling?"

James raised an eyebrow. "Do you want to hear the epilogue to your story about the big bad pharmaceutical company?

Keegan tossed his toothpick on the ground. "Same time. Same place?"

James spotted Lana across the street, giving her statement to a policeman. "Let's try something different. How about science instead of art?"

"Science World it is." Keegan pulled out another toothpick. "I hear they have a good cafeteria. Maybe I'll buy you lunch. It's not the Harbor Centre, but we'll get there one day."

"See you around, old friend." James gave him a wave and crossed the street toward Lana.

"Red is a good color on you," Keegan called out.

James spun around. "Keegan?"

Keegan raised an eyebrow.

"Thanks."

"Anytime you've got an itch."

Lana watched the police haul the ex out of the apartment and into a waiting police van. Mark had already whisked Katy away to his vehicle as if she weighed nothing. Maybe this time they would have their happily ever after.

I wish I weighed nothing. She took a quick glance behind her and caught sight of a familiar, rugged face.

"You checking out your own ass?" James rasped.

Darn. Caught in the act. She wasn't sure whether to smile or pout so she did a bit of both. "I wanted to make sure it was still there after I had to run two blocks looking for a damn phone."

James walked a slow circle around her. "Pretty fine."

Lana put her hands on her hips. "You checking out my ass?"

"You giving me an invitation?" His blue eyes captured hers and she drank him in.

"Hell, yes," she whispered.

Chapter Twenty-Five

"Katy!"

Trixie wrapped her arms around Katy and squeezed her in an enormous bear hug. "I didn't think you'd ever come back. How long has it been?"

"Only about three months, but if feels like forever."

Trixie released her and took a step back, her eyes widening as she took in Katy's outfit. "Holy crap. Where did you find that? I didn't think you would ever wear latex."

Katy ran her hands down the skin-tight, black dress with its death-defying neckline. "Neither did I, but I couldn't resist. Steven transferred his share of the house to me to try and make up for what he had done and I used some of the money to take Mom and the kids on a little holiday to London. Given everything that happened, the school was actually quite supportive. We went to Covent Garden and when I saw this dress, I couldn't resist."

"I wouldn't have been able to resist either." Trixie grinned. "Of course, I would have gone for a brighter color. And tassels. Maybe some sequins. Tony likes sequins. Mark...not so much."

Mark.

It had been three months since they had last spoken. Would he be happy to see her or had she lost him forever?

"Why wouldn't you call him?" Trixie waggled an admonishing finger. "He's been moping around here making everyone's life hell."

Katy shrugged. "I had some things to figure out. Trust issues to deal with." And she had needed some time to understand and forgive.

Trixie patted her arm. "Love isn't an easy road."

"You don't have to tell me." Katy's gaze fixed on the red door in front of them, and she bit her lip. "He might not even want to see me."

Sarah Castille

"Uh...right." Trixie snorted a sarcastic laugh. "So what else have you been up to while you've been tormenting Mark with your silence?"

Katy grinned, unable to hide her excitement. "I'm setting up my own law firm. The Law Society cleared us both of conflicts, although I had to be embarrassingly candid with them. I've even got some new clients—the families of the four men who went through the clinical trials."

"Good for you. That story sure got a lot of press." Trixie gave her a warm smile. "What about your other client, the one who started the case against Hi-Tech? Did she win?"

Katy studied her for a moment, mulling over her words. Should she admit Martha had duped her? She still found it hard to believe the confidences they had shared in her car had been part of a set-up to ensure Hi-Tech's product never made it to market. And it had worked. Once the regulators got their hands on Martin's lab books, Hi-Tech had been shut down indefinitely.

"Steele was right about her. She was a corporate spy. Another pharmaceutical company launched a similar drug shortly after Steele was arrested. Detective Hunter came to my office last week and gave me the whole story. Apparently she goes from company to company, stealing secrets and selling them to the highest bidder. Then she changes her identity and moves on. He hasn't found her yet but I have no doubt he will. She fooled him as well, and from what I've seen of him, he's not the kind of man to let something like that go."

"Understatement of the year." Trixie checked her appearance in the mirror and adjusted the top of her purple and black corset. Katy looked away in case Trixie's vigorous manhandling of her girls resulted in unintentional overexposure.

"So why did your client file a lawsuit?" Trixie fluffed her hair and air kissed the mirror. "Once she was caught, she could have just moved on."

"Detective Hunter thinks she was using the case to get access to Hi-Tech's documents. But I think there is more to it than that. She had a relationship with Jimmy Rider. I think she loved him."

Trixie's eyes widened. "Jimmy? What was it with that guy? He was such a scumbag and yet women were constantly throwing themselves

302

at his feet. I don't get it."

Katy swallowed, remembering his hand around her throat. "Neither do I. James thinks Jimmy found the drugs she had smuggled out of Hi-Tech and then blackmailed her for more. Once the drugs hit the street the bigger, badder drug dealers wanted a piece of the action and when Jimmy lost the stash he left at Valerie's house and couldn't deliver—"

Trixie made a slicing motion across her neck. "Time to pay the piper."

Katy cocked an eyebrow and laughed. She had missed Trixie's sense of humor.

"What about Steele?" Trixie motioned Katy toward the door. "His face was all over the news. Evil bastard."

"He's going to be tried for the murder of Mark's old girlfriend, but the case doesn't look good. She was cremated, so there's no body, and the evidence linking him to her death is circumstantial at best. He hired the best criminal lawyer in the country, and they've already had the wiretap evidence thrown out on a technicality."

Trixie shook her head. "That's just wrong. He can't get off with nothing more than a slap on the wrist."

Katy snorted a laugh. "Don't worry. He also faces conspiracy charges for murder and attempted murder—Martin, the cleaners, Jimmy, me and Martha. Detective Hunter found evidence Steele intended to kill her too. Steele's in-house lawyer, Stanton, might do a deal and testify against him for a reduced sentence, although that seems unlikely since Stanton is facing several life sentences. And after all that, Steele still has to deal with the regulators about the clinical trials, bribing officials, and the stuff he did overseas..."

"I heard Mark really did a number on Steele." Trixie giggled. "I told you he could take care of himself."

Katy gave her a half smile. "Steele was in the hospital for almost two weeks." She hesitated. "Is Mark still with his firm?"

Trixie giggled. "Of course he is. Those guys come as a package. Sure their feathers were ruffled, but in the end, they look after each other. Tony said they never seriously considered throwing him out. Plus they need him. The firm just won a tender for some high-profile electric company case and Mark is running the show. Tony was so happy; he gave me a little bonus." She adjusted the gold ribbons on her corset. "I'm wearing it. He won't be able to help but notice me today."

"You'll have to take me shopping some time." Katy laughed. "I've thrown out everything in my house that reminded me of Steven, and that included most of my suits."

"What happened to him?"

Katy winced. "He's out on bail awaiting his trial. He's only allowed supervised access with the kids and there's a protection order keeping him away from me. He's going to plead temporary insanity on the basis of overwork. I talked to him when he was in jail. He was genuinely contrite. He couldn't believe how far he went. For the sake of the kids, I hope the judge isn't too hard on him."

Trixie pushed open the door. "I hope the judge sends him back to jail for a very long time," she muttered. "People like him give fetish clubs a bad name."

Katy paused in the doorway and her breath hitched. Only four months ago she had stood here, trembling with anxiety and afraid to go inside. This time, her only fear was that Mark wouldn't want to see her.

Her latex dress rustled when she took a step forward, a contrast to the stiff black suit she had worn that first night. She spotted Detective Hunter weaving his way through the crowd, drink in hand. He nodded and smiled.

"He's got a new girlfriend," Trixie whispered. "He never brings her here so he thinks no one knows, but we all do. Mark let it slip on one of the many nights he sat here drowning his sorrows until the wee hours of the morning. Of course it spread through the club like wildfire. No one ever thought he would find someone strong enough to pierce his armor. But he did and you know her."

"Who?" Katy couldn't imagine anyone she knew with James.

"Lana. The private investigator your ex had hired to follow you. The one who saved you. James caught her snooping around the club and hauled her into an empty room for questioning. I knew right then they were meant to be together. You should have seen the sparks fly.

She sassed him like there was no tomorrow and he ate it up like a Thanksgiving dinner."

There's no accounting for taste. Katy bit back the words before they slipped off her tongue. After the way she had treated Mark, she likely wasn't anyone's taste either.

Tony waved to them from across the dance floor and Trixie sighed. "I think he dresses like that to drive me crazy. Look at those tight leather pants. Nothing left to the imagination. Well actually I can imagine a lot. And that vest—it's like a big tease." She stiffened her spine. "I can't help myself. I'm a masochist at heart. I'm going over."

She gave Katy's arm a quick squeeze. "Mark's at the bar. He's waiting for you. He hasn't taken his eyes off you since we walked in."

Katy watched Trixie go and then steeled herself for the meeting she had been both dreading and anticipating for the last three months. Her boots clicked lightly across the tiles as she walked toward the bar. She couldn't help but remember the pain on Mark's face after she had sent him home the morning after her abduction. Although she had been grateful for his comfort, she needed time. To heal. To trust. Asking him to go had been the hardest thing she had ever done.

She kept her eyes down until the bar stools came into view, afraid to find out too early that she was too late. Her stomach fluttered as she lifted her gaze.

"What can I get for you?" He set a wine glass in front of her.

Her heart sank at his formal tone. "White wine, please."

"Anything in particular?"

She was all too aware of the counter separating them. His cool, detached manner. His impassive face. She bit her lip to stop the tears. She shouldn't be surprised. She had hurt him and sent him away after he had opened up his heart.

"I don't suppose you have any Meursault?" Her bottom lip quivered.

A hint of a smile played on his lips. "I might have a bottle down in the wine cellar."

Hope bloomed in her chest. She rounded the counter, stopping only a foot away from him. She looked up, trying to tell him with her eyes the words her constricted throat would not say. For an agonizingly long moment, they just stared at each other, and she saw her own conflicted emotions reflected in his warm, brown eyes. Her heart pounded as she silently pleaded for the tiniest sign that it wasn't all over.

"Mark." Her voice came out in hoarse whisper.

And then he pulled her into his arms, crushing her against his chest in a fierce embrace. "God, I missed you, Katy." He buried his face in her hair and his arms tightened even more around her.

Hot, soft tears spilled over her cheeks, staining his T-shirt. "I'm sorry," she whispered. "I needed time."

"Don't be." He pressed a soft kiss to her forehead. "I love you, Katy. I would have waited forever."

She leaned up to brush her lips over his, but Mark drew back.

"No more conflict?" A smile tugged at the corners of his mouth.

She laughed softly. "No more conflict. Of any kind."

His finger brushed the bloom of her cheek. "No psychotic ex-husbands, calculating managing partners, corporate conspiracies, deceitful clients or armed villains?"

"All gone," she whispered, breathing in his scent of soap and sandalwood. Comforting. Arousing. Achingly familiar.

"Any doubts?" He threaded his hand through her hair and gently tugged her head to the side, exposing her neck to his heated lips. Everything inside her warmed then flamed.

"None. This is where I want to be. With you. Forever."

He kissed her, a long, deep kiss that said more than words.

Katy melted into him, needing him so badly she could barely breathe. She returned the kiss, then pulled away and opened the door to the wine cellar.

"Shall we go and find that Meursault?"

Mark gave her a wicked grin and turned on the light. "I might have put it on the top shelf this time."

"Then you'll have to give me a hand." She took the first few steps down into the cellar.

"That was the idea."

Katy stopped and looked back over her shoulder. "How did you know I would come back?"

"I trusted my heart."

"And I trust mine." She felt the undeniable truth of her feelings deep in her soul.

Mark pulled the door closed and they made their way down the stairs. When they reached the wine cellar, he turned Katy to face him and then cradled her face between his hands. "I imagined this."

Katy laughed softly. "I remember. We lived out this particular fantasy of yours in my bedroom."

A smile curved his lips. "No. This." He leaned down and slanted his mouth over hers, kissing her with a passion that left her breathless.

"Loving you."

About the Author

Award winning author, Sarah Castille, pens steamy contemporary romance and erotic romantic suspense. She has been an established lawyer both on the West Coast and at one of the world's largest law firms in London, England. Her thrilling sensual tales feature red-hot alpha males, kick-ass heroines, dark desires and dangerous passions...all with a legal flavor.

After many years of working and travelling abroad, Sarah traded in her briefcase and stilettos for a handful of magic beans and a home in the shadow of Canada's Rocky Mountains. When she is not glued to her keyboard or e-reader, she can be found playing piano, shuttling munchkins and burning dinners.

Sarah is a firm believer in justice, caffeine and the seductive power of a sexy...smile.

The more she wanted out, the more they dragged her back in.

With A Vengeance
© 2013 Jacqui Jacoby

Daughter to murdered CIA officers, niece to a deputy director, Jaime Walsh has never known life outside the world of espionage. Until a high-action case in Buenos Aires leaves her gutted. Physically, emotionally...and professionally.

She'd planned for her long-overdue vacation to be a time to rest and reassess. With her longtime partner Stephen not far behind, it's a tropical paradise away from work. A paradise where boundaries will be tested.

From their training days, Stephen Reid has watched Jaime kick ass while performing what has become his second job—watching her back. But now his feelings have grown.

As best friends look at each other in a new light, they like what they see. And Jaime dreams of a new life outside "the company".

Except someone from their past won't be satisfied until Jaime and the man she loves are hunted to the brink of death. Now Jaime must find the strength to trust her heart and let go of her fear. Before she loses everything...

Warning: This book contains world travel with stops in exotic locations, a kick-ass heroine who just wants to be left alone and a sexy hero who can't seem to stop himself from watching her back.

Available now in ebook and print from Samhain Publishing.

They've got the sex factor in spades. But can love survive the "ex" factor?

Knowing the Ropes
© 2013 Teresa Noelle Roberts

Selene has harbored kinky, submissive fantasies most of her life, but her experience as a domestic abuse counselor leaves her leery of giving up that much control. Case in point: the ex-fiancé she didn't love quite enough to test the limits of trust.

At a BDSM meet-and-greet, she sets out to learn how far is too far. Nick seems like the ideal dom to show her the ins and outs of ropes, floggers, and paddles—with no commitment clause.

After losing a sub he loved too much, Selene's country girl common sense and smoking sensuality is like a dream that Nick never dared to have—a perfect blend of kink and long-term domestic bliss.

Yet it's tough to figure out just how far they can push their limits when they've both agreed to a no-strings affair. Especially when an ex needs Nick's muscle and Selene's counseling skills to get out of a dangerous situation. By then it may be too late for love to survive all the things they're afraid to say.

Warning: Sexy, kinky, geeky dominant guy. Smart submissive woman. Crazy ex. A little experimentation between girlfriends. And lots and lots of kinky sex.

Available now in ebook and print from Samhain Publishing.

It's all about the story...

Romance

HORROR

www.samhainpublishing.com

CPSIA information can be obtained at www.ICGtesting.com
Printed in the USA
LVOW07s1552290115

424893LV00006B/661/P